WINDFALL: INVITATION

3·7

PHIL FARRAND

[Dedication goes here.]

Greetings!

This is the "beta" release of *Windfall: Invitation (3.7)*. That means there will be typos! Part of your job as a beta reader is to help me find them so that I can fix them in the final release. And yes, I tend to bend the rules with sentence structure when I'm writing, but I try to match tenses correctly.

Also, I would love to hear your thoughts on the book.

As always, while I am delighted to receive any input you may have on the book, I may or may not take it into consideration regarding the production version of the book.

As to *how* to return input to me, you can just mark up the physical book and send it back. I can also send you a PDF of the book's interior, and you can use Adobe Reader (it's free) to highlight the words and leave comments. Or you can type out all your comments in a Word or Excel document. However, that will be more work both for you and for me. That said, I will *gladly* receive it in any form that you choose, **but it really will be easier if you just mark up a PDF... if you don't want to send back the book.**

And now for the legalese: All submissions become the property of Phil Farrand and will not be returned. Submissions may or may not be acknowledged. By submitting material, you grant permission to use your submission and name in any future publication by the author.

Thanks for your help! Everyone who gets back to me with any kind of typo, suggestion, or reaction will be mentioned in the acknowledgments at the end of the production version. And I'm always looking for quotes to put on the back cover! **The submission deadline is November 15, 2025**, but if you could have it back *sooner*, that would be great! Thanks again for your help!

Phil Farrand

417 844 8244

me@philfarrand.com

TABLE OF CONTENTS

The darkness drops again but now I know

That thirty centuries of stony sleep

Were vexed to nightmare by a rocking cradle,

And what rough beast, its hour come round at last

***Slouches towards Bethlehem** to be born?*

THE SECOND COMING

Lines 18-22

By William Butler Yeats

As Published in *The Dial*

November 1920

Author's Note

There are many prophecies about the "end-times" in the Bible. There are even more interpretations of those prophecies. And there are even more books that have been written about the interpretations of those prophecies.

This is not one of those books.

Like the rest of the books in the Windfall series, this book simply uses one of the events foretold in the Bible as part of the end-time events as a backdrop (if you happen to believe in a literal interpretation of Revelation, Chapter 20).

Traditionally, this event has been called the Millennial Reign of Jesus Christ. According to a literal interpretation of the verses in Revelation, Chapter 20, Jesus Christ will return with his followers to the Earth to subjugate Earth's population and rule over it with "a rod of iron" for 1,000 years.

This setting has fascinated me for years: A race of titans appears in the sky. They claim to be Jesus Christ and his followers. They set up a utopia. They rule absolutely.

In another series that I began many years ago called *The Son, the Wind, and the Reign*, I used this same backdrop to explore ideas about belief and how humans use their beliefs to interpret their experiences. After all, if this race of titans did show up—and if they claimed to be Jesus Christ and his followers—how would you *ever* know if they were telling the truth? As the tagline for that series asks, "How would you know the difference between aliens and the divine?"

That question remains unanswered in the *Windfall* series, but it is joined by many others, such as "Can any moral stance survive the fear of annihilation?" In other words, if your very existence was threatened, would you hold to the same principles that you currently claim?

In *Windfall*, the race of titans—known as the Wind—has disappeared after governing an authoritarian utopia for 960 years. Humanity is left with a single guiding principle, "Treat others as you wish to be treated."

Humanity is also left with the extraordinary technology of the Wind, but some of it, like all the formidable energy weapons, no longer functions. There is *still* abundance and plenty. Humans are still free of poverty and sickness, and death is no longer inevitable. But the rule with the rod of iron has disappeared. And it was that rule that ensured the humans living under the authority of the titans acted with kindness and generosity towards one another.

Also, there are other humans who long ago fled the totalitarian rule of the titans. They have far different ideas about what's best for humanity.

Windfall then is a fictional account of the great and final war to determine mankind's future.

Just to be clear, however… aside from using the Millennial Reign as a backdrop, the rest of the *Windfall* series is merely fanciful—and hopefully enjoyable—storytelling. At times, I will quote from the Bible, and those passages will be taken from the New International Version. But the interpretations of the passages by the characters in this series belong to the characters themselves and are not necessarily claimed by me.

THE NIGHTMARE OPUS

PART SEVEN

996 ADR

(ANNO DOMINI REDITUS, "IN THE YEAR OF OUR LORD'S RETURN")

CHARACTERS AND TERMINOLOGY

(Note: The following list is roughly in order of revelation. For an alphabetized list, see the glossary at the end of the book.)

The Wind – a race of titans who invaded Earth in the 21st century of the Common Era. They claimed to be Jesus Christ and his followers—returning to rule the Earth with a rod of iron for a thousand years. The Wind quickly subdued the Earth and instituted two rules: "Submit or die" and "Treat others as you wish to be treated."

Anno Domini Reditus (ADR) – "In the year of Our Lord's Return." ADR represents a new calendar system introduced by the Wind celebrating their conquest of Earth. The arrival of the Wind occurred in 1 ADR.

Pax Christi – "Peace of Christ." An era of peace and prosperity made possible by the technology of the Wind. During the *Pax Christi*, humanity has been freed from hunger, poverty, crime, and disease. There is also an abundant, seemingly-inexhaustible supply of energy.

The Realm – the collection of star systems populated by humanity during the *Pax Christi* that still hold to the authority of Earth and its capital, Jerusalem.

Judicial Center – a local seat of authority for the Realm.

Curled Space Funnels – stable pathways through curled space that allow a spacecraft to traverse the distances between star systems in minutes. All known endpoints terminate above the poles of stars. While the pathways through the curled space funnels are stable, they are not static. For example, a given curled space funnel might have a total of seven pathways and as many as fourteen different endpoints, but those pathways will not all exist at the same time under normal circumstances. Typically, they will alternate over some regular hourly intervals in groups of two or three. Curled space funnels are also known by the nickname "boom tubes."

960 ADR – the year of the disappearance of the Wind. The disappearance was abrupt and without warning. Only the titans themselves disappeared. All structures and technology remained behind, although some of the technology—such as the energy weapons—ceased to function. In some circles, the disappearance of the Wind is called "Windfall." However, that term is considered derogatory and disrespectful since it implies that the Wind's disappearance was beneficial to humanity.

The Leadership Council of the Realm – a hastily formed group of chosen individuals who had previously served the Wind in various capacities. The Leadership Council provides guidance. It also issues proclamations of encouragement to the hundreds of planets and moons in the Realm as it continually attempts to remind the citizens to hold fast to the First Principle of the Realm: "Treat others as you wish to be treated."

Realm Force – a police force commissioned by the Leadership Council to protect the Realm and guard its borders.

Elijah Ton – a member of the Leadership Council and the Leadership Council's special liaison with Realm Force.

Hachmoni Gellemier – a former member of the Leadership Council and the Regent of the School of the Prophets.

The Night – any settlement that exists beyond the Realm. There is no known official record of the number of populated planets and moons in the Night. In fact, until the disappearance of the Wind, few knew of *any* settlements that existed in the Night. It has become apparent in recent years, however, that many of the settlements in the Night have existed for decades—and perhaps even centuries—populated by humans who had quietly slipped away from the Realm to pursue lives outside the authority of the Wind.

Horde – any formalized and organized group in the Night that has denied the authority of the Leadership Council. Hordes are considered the enemies of the Realm.

Marauders – a former Night Horde that specialized in hijacking Realm freighters and trading the goods stolen from those freighters for technology and supplies created by other Hordes.

Night's Keep – the former main Marauder stronghold. It was built into the side of a canyon on a small planet that orbited a red dwarf star.

G'Utz – the founder of the Marauders. Through G'Utz's willingness to sacrifice his pilots, Marauders learned to do "shock-drops" from curled space funnels. Using this technique, Marauders leaped directly into Realm space to highjack Realm freighters, though this fact is not universally known.

Shock-drop – a technique discovered by the Marauder Horde that allows a spacecraft to bypass the normal endpoint of a curled space funnel. When flying inside a curled space funnel, firing at the wall of the funnel with the appropriate amount of force will tear a hole in the side of the funnel, allowing a spaceship to fly through the hole. And if the ship's shield generators are tuned to the correct frequency, the ship will safely traverse the anaphasic boundary between curled and normal space and "shock-drop" back into normal space without passing through an endpoint. The actual final destination depends on the curled space funnel and the impact point.

Mercenaries – one of the most feared Hordes in the Night. Mercenaries offer their skills for hire and are among the most disciplined and well-trained fighters in the Night.

Troyd – an unaligned secretive group believed to inhabit a planet somewhere deep in the Night. Beyond the fact that the Troyd excel at creating and breaking centralized processing systems, little is known of their actual creed or purpose. Many stories are told of their technical wizardry and their preference for data over "organics"—their term for humans.

Mechs – the only known machine-based Horde in the Night. Mechs are typically angry, rude, and easily frustrated. They constantly fight among themselves except when they are on a rampage, pursuing and destroying others. It was thought that Falcon and the crew of the *Dominion* destroyed the Mechs during the mission to the Mech Hive, but they reappeared on the freighters that were used to eliminate "Shadow," a few years later. They have since been seen at the secondary Marauders keep, in a group that attacked Hades, and in a freighter orbiting Rigel Three.

Beast – a small horde in the Night numbering only in the hundreds. However, Beast has an outsized effect because of a network of artificial intelligences that are capable of performing highly accurate assessments of human behavior both at an individual level and at the level of a group of individuals, and under some conditions, even a very large group of individuals. Beast has a stated goal of destroying Realm Force, invading the Realm, and overthrowing the Leadership Council.

Shadow – an area that previously existed along the outer rim of the Realm. Following 960 ADR, many of the settlements on this outer rim began to question the authority of the newly formed Leadership Council of the Realm, and this rift—along with other altercations—led to the eventual closing of the border between Shadow and the Realm. In 978 ADR, the settlements in Shadow were forcibly evacuated by Beast.

Alnitak Five – home to a legendary group of temptresses with a well-known reputation in the Night as purveyors of pleasure. At one time under Rachel Falcon's control, most of the population was slaughtered in a subsequent attack by Beast.

Angel Haze – a psychoactive compound discovered by the settlers of Alnitak Five in the seed of an indigenous fruit. When encountered, Angel Haze suppresses an individual's fears and then binds them emotionally to the first person who interacts with them.

Emergency Medical Unit – also called a "med unit." Even though the Wind eliminated disease and sickness from the Earth, they also acknowledged that there would be accidents as humanity moved out to other star systems. As such, they configured Judicial Centers to begin manufacturing emergency medical units. One day's worth of treatments in a med unit will heal anything minor. Two days' worth of treatments will heal anything significant, like broken bones. Three days in a med unit will, for all practical purposes, rejuvenate the entire body and restore the individual to perfect health. Apparently, by design, med units do not operate on the human brain.

Saturn Shipyards – Realm Force's primary research, development, and construction facility in orbit around Saturn in the Sol system. The Saturn Shipyards houses a vast variety of divisions, including the Advanced Research and Development Division, also known as "Razzle Dazzle."

Trinity-Class Battlecruiser – once the largest known warship built by Realm scientists and engineers that mixes Wind technology and older human weaponry to create a spacecraft that can adequately protect the Realm. The new *HMVE Majesty* now holds the title of the largest but it's full classification is unknown.

Tactical Teams – contingents of skilled fighters assigned to Trinity-Class battlecruisers to assist the lead commander as needed in defending the ship and away team missions.

HMVR Power – the first of three commissioned Trinity-Class battlecruisers. "HMVR" stands for "His Majesty's Vessel of the Realm." Destroyed during Abaddon's first announcement to the Realm.

HMVR Glory – the second of the Trinity-Class battlecruisers. The *Glory* and its crew were lost when exposed to a genetically altered hemorrhagic fever virus that the med units did not heal.

MV Dominion – the final Trinity-Class battlecruiser. The *Dominion* was severely damaged in an asteroid storm. Subsequently, members of the ship's senior staff gave the order to execute its self-destruct sequence. Unknown at the time, the order was intercepted, and the ship was not destroyed. Now known as a kind of pirate ship.

Commander Seyi Ladipo – former Lead Commander of the *Power*. Now disgraced after he was forced to confess to crimes he didn't commit.

Rachel Falcon – former Lead Commander of the *Dominion*. Former Marauder. Archenemy of G'Utz. Strong, bright, fast, beautiful. Was imprisoned in a secret facility built by Realm Force. Rescued by the crew of the *Dominion*.

Events in Falcon's past—as she grew up in the Night—have caused a schism in her personality. At present, she is three: "Rachel," her original self; "The Falcon," who is tactically brilliant; and "Fury," who is filled with rage, though Fury is held mostly under control by Rachel and The Falcon. In addition, though much about the circumstances is unknown, what remains of Falcon's biological body is encased in some kind of advanced cybernetic suit.

Geoffrey Oakford – former Lead Commander of the *Dominion*. Born and raised on Earth. A member of the first graduating class of Realm Force Academy. Now a fugitive from the Realm.

Zachary Hunter – former Chief Pilot of the *Dominion*. Former Mercenary. Like Oakford, a fugitive from the Realm. Known for his rugged good looks, incredible physique, and cocky persona. And more recently, advised by a spokesman for a horde of look-alikes that he was genetically engineered.

Catherine Casteel – former Chief Medical Officer of the *Dominion*. Raised in the Realm. Learned to heal supernaturally while doing experiments in the power of the mind on a planet called K-22B that is located deep in the

Night. Killed by a tactical team that was dispatched by Nicolescu to capture her.

Murg – former Chief Technologist of the *Dominion*. Now a fugitive from the Realm. Originally brought aboard the *Dominion* by Falcon. No Realm Force training. Socially awkward. Believed to be a member of the Troyd even though the Troyd do not normally leave the Troyd.

Gabriel MacDuff – former head of the tactical teams of the *Dominion*. Now a fugitive from the Realm. Large, barrel-chested hulk of a man. At one time, a distinguished student of the School of the Prophets near Jerusalem.

The *Dominion* Pixie – an artificial intelligence that Murg repurposed from a Wind-designed voice interface for Judicial Centers. Trained on Falcon's behavioral patterns, Murg left the Pixie in charge of the *Dominion* after he thwarted the self-destruct attempt.

Adi Bolobolo – formerly Casteel's second-in-command on the medical services teams for the *Dominion*. Now a fugitive from the Realm. Formidable and not dainty. Currently serving as the Medical Chief for the *Dominion*.

Commander Ionela Nicolescu – Lead Commander of the Saturn Shipyards. Disciplined, capable, holds the highest security clearance in Realm Force.

PLOKTA – subordinate of Nicolescu, resident tech wizard of the Saturn Shipyards. Idolizes Murg and had hoped that Murg would outfit him with a Troyd interface someday. Made an alliance with Abaddon and now has an interface with the same capabilities as Murg's.

Ensign Aeon Sotheby – ensign, subordinate of Nicolescu, daughter of Adair Sotheby, former Lead Commander of the *Glory* who died when its crew was lost.

Twilla Evansworth – former Mercenary. Former spy while serving on the crew of the *Dominion*. Formerly aligned with Falcon. Formerly imprisoned by Abaddon and while there she offended him enough that he tore off her left leg and rearranged her anatomy. Now held by PLOKTA.

Bandit – former Marauder, allowed to travel to Earth and joined Realm Force after being rescued by Falcon from G'Utz. Once a member of the crew of the *Dominion*. Died in an explosion on Rigel Three.

Stealth Suits – named initially "emergency evacuation suits," these suits have been modified by Realm Force to use on certain types of away missions.

Commander's Yacht – a sleek, mid-sized craft with sophisticated weaponry generally attached to a Trinity-Class battlecruiser and reserved for use by the Lead Commander. Three years after the self-destruct sequence of the *Dominion* was engaged, Sotheby returned the Commander's Yacht of the battlecruiser to Oakford for use by the team, after making sure the ship was refurbished enough to make it challenging to recognize as originating in the Realm.

HMVR Doeg – high-speed transport stolen by Oakford and company when they escaped to the Night before they could be brought up on charges of treason.

Blessings from Jerusalem! – a daily blog of encouragement issued by the Communications Department of the Office of the Leadership Council.

Whispers in the Night – an anonymous blog created by an unknown entity. According to the blog's tagline, it presents "anonymous, untraceable communiqués from the unified Hordes of the Night to the innocent among the citizens of the Realm."

Hades – a maximum-security facility built by Realm Force in a secret star system to house the Realm's worst offenders. Hades was built underground using the Wind's rapid construction technology on a planet so close to its star that it had a surface temperature of 3,000 degrees Kelvin. It was destroyed as Falcon escaped.

Silence Tracheate – a Mystery. Oakford's team encountered Silence Tracheate on WASP-12e, a planet on the farthest edge of the Night. Interestingly enough, she looked exactly like Catherine Casteel but would never admit to being her, and under Hunter's urging, once the mission to WASP-12e was complete, the team departed without learning any more about her. Consequently, they have no idea that Tracheate sent a message to the Mercenaries to halt any future targeted attacks on Oakford's team.

Haymakers Notch – a Mystery. During the escape from Hades, Falcon's cybernetic body was destroyed when she sacrificed herself to save Hunter. Shortly after, during a shock-drop, the *Dominion* was thrown into the atmosphere of a planet 20,000 light-years from Earth. There, the team met Haymakers Notch, and he offered to replace Falcon's original cybernetic body, given that it was still under warranty when it was destroyed. Nothing more is known of Haymakers Notch, aside from the fact that he looked exactly like Thomas Harnecky.

Doctor Moreau – highly talented geneticist. Maintained a secret research facility in the Night in the Nu Scorpii system with 144 women strapped into gestation rigs. Moreau was captured and sent to the Realm with his research staff. The women remained on the *Dominion*.

Jazarah Worku – one of the women rescued from the research facility in the Nu Scropii system who remained on the *Dominion*. One of only five whom Hunter selected to train as fighter pilots and, surprisingly enough, a natural at intuitively understanding the complexities of three-dimensional space flight. Worku left the crew of the *Dominion* to work as a security consultant for the planet K2-72e. She later attempted to trick the Dominion crew into giving her the Rexian sheer onboard. Now on the run.

Hunter Look-Alikes Horde – a nearly unknown Horde in the Night composed of genetically engineered clones who look like Hunter and possess all his physical and mental capabilities. In their first encounter with the *Dominion's* senior staff, their spokesman proclaimed their rigid materialistic beliefs and insisted that Hunter was an embarrassment to them because of his claim that Casteel could heal supernaturally.

Abaddon – an individual who appeared unexpectedly to address the entire Realm, apparently with the assistance of a female member of the Troyd. Looking like a demonic titan, Abaddon claimed the Wind were charlatans who took pleasure in tormenting less-developed species. Abaddon also claimed that the human race had been censured by the Council of the Children of the Prime for failing to live up to their initial promise. And if the human race did not immediately dedicate itself to the sole purpose of unifying itself and advancing its knowledge, power, ability, and understanding, the Council would vote humans damaged beyond repair, and the devourers would descend.

To assist with the unification of humanity, Abaddon then seemed to use his understanding of curled space funnel technology to open curled space rings in orbit around every inhabited location in both the Realm and the Night and allow transit from any ring to any other ring.

Curled Space Rings – rings of fire hanging in stable orbits over population centers. Each ring can lead to any other ring using the appropriate vector and velocity. Much safer and faster than curled space funnels.

Sphinx – Human-animal hybrid from Doctor Moreau's secret research facility in the Nu Scorpii system. Formed a bond with MacDuff. Had become part of the tactical teams. The senior staff of the *Dominion* recently learned that Sphinx's saliva contains hero doses of psilocybin and likely contributes to

Sphinx's profoundly intuitive awareness of those around him.

Guan Qiuyue – raised on the streets of the Night, Guan was kidnapped and taken to Doctor Moreau's secret research facility in the Nu Scorpii system. There, she was strapped into a gestation rig and forced to gestate dangerous human-animal hybrids. Subsequently rescued by the senior staff of the *Dominion,* Guan joined the tactical teams to study under MacDuff and serve on the crew of the *Dominion.* All was well until she was kidnapped during a mission to Betelgeuse Two, where she was exposed to toxic spores that damaged her brain. For many months, she struggled with psychopathic outbursts. Then, Sphinx sought her out and licked her face multiple times to administer enough psilocybin to calm her.

*HMVR **Majesty*** – the newly commissioned variant on Trinity-Class battlecruisers. The *Majesty* is twice the size of the *Dominion.* Unlike the *Dominion,* the *Majesty* is outfitted with Wind-designed energy weapons that were awakened using activation codes supplied by Abaddon after Ton submitted to Abaddon's rule.

WINDFALL TIMELINE

All years are ADR, not to scale.

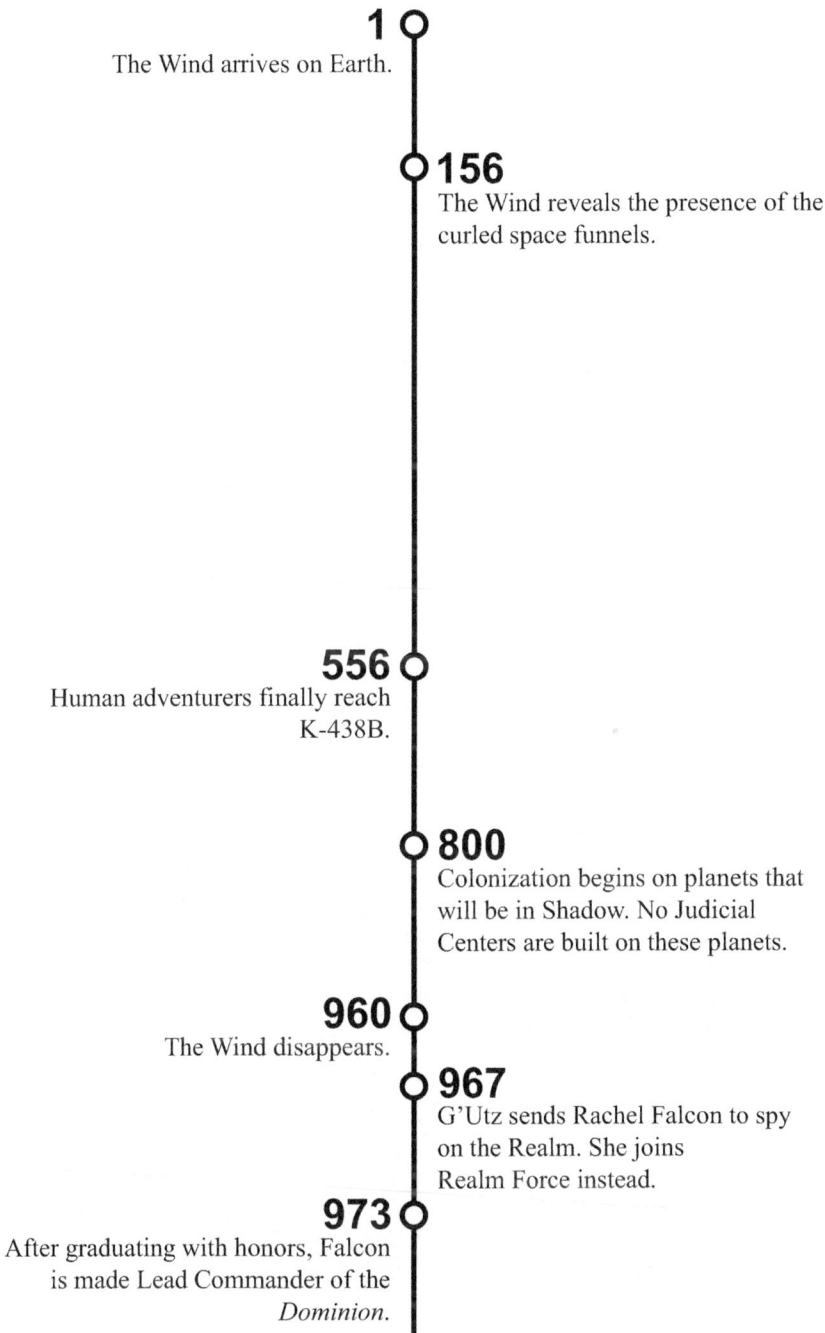

1
The Wind arrives on Earth.

156
The Wind reveals the presence of the curled space funnels.

556
Human adventurers finally reach K-438B.

800
Colonization begins on planets that will be in Shadow. No Judicial Centers are built on these planets.

960
The Wind disappears.

967
G'Utz sends Rachel Falcon to spy on the Realm. She joins Realm Force instead.

973
After graduating with honors, Falcon is made Lead Commander of the *Dominion*.

974 ○ *Windfall: The 99 and 1*

Hunter battles the Mechs on Beta Ceti Two and is severely injured. He is rescued by Falcon but dies on the way back to the *Dominion*. He is raised from the dead by Casteel.

Falcon reveals she is a former Marauder, and she wants to rescue another Marauder named Bandit. Hunter decides she can't be trusted.

Falcon shock-drops the *Dominion* into the space near Night's Keep. She takes Hunter, Casteel and Murg on the away mission and pretends that she has returned to the Marauders. The team rescues Bandit. They also capture G'Utz.

Falcon sends G'Utz bound and helpless on a shuttle into an armada of Mechs so the *Dominion* can escape, fully expecting the Mechs to kill him.

Bandit is taken to Earth to begin his Realm Force training. Falcon gives Hunter a pink ballet outfit and threatens to make him wear it if he continues to question her loyalty.

Windfall: Broadcast ○ **975**

Realm Force sends the graduates of the Class of 975 individually in all directions into the Night to find the Mech Hive in what is dubbed "The Broadcast."

When a graduate succeeds, the *Dominion* destroys the Mech Hive. During the away mission, Harnecky dies, but Casteel raises him to life.

At the same time, nearly all communication with the rest of the Class of 975 is lost.

After the Mech defeat, Falcon throws a celebration party on the *Dominion* and dances sensually with the crew.

Falcon is recalled to Earth. The search for the graduates soon reveals that many have been tortured and killed.

Falcon meets with the Leadership Council and demands complete control over the *Dominion*. To demonstrate the difference between the Realm and the Night, she strips to her underwear and easily disarms her guards before taking the council hostage.

Offended by Falcon's display, the Leadership Council makes Oakford the Lead Commander of the *Dominion* and banishes Falcon from the Realm. She is taken to a planet in Shadow and abandoned.

976 ○ *Windfall: The Strait Gate*

During the rescue of a graduate of the Class of 975 named Zoya Alkaev, Hunter notes her animalistic behavior and kills her. He believes her brain has been burned out.

Casteel finally admits to the senior staff that she can heal. She also performs an autopsy on Alkaev and proves that the graduate had extensive brain damage.

Meanwhile, Falcon is captured by Twilla Evansworth and given to G'Utz. G'Utz tortures her for nine months, which gives rise to Fury. Falcon is finally set free by a young boy named Das, although he dies in the process.

Elspeth Jordan becomes Administrative Commander of the *Dominion.* As part of her duties, she implements a very strict dress code for the women of the battle cruiser.

At the same time, Realm Force loses all contact with the *Glory.* When the *Dominion* arrives at its last known location, an away team discovers that the crew turned on each other because the ship had been infected by a deadly virus. The *Dominion* is also infected but Casteel keeps it at bay.

Windfall: A Seed Discarded ○ **977**

On Gamma Draconis Two, Bastiaan Casteel is kidnapped by Khulan Ganzorig and her brothers, and he is tortured into revealing the existence of the Gilead Research Facility.

Falcon and an asteroid miner named Fastidious Astrolabe discover a plot to wipe out the population of Gamma Draconis Two. They also discover Evansworth on the planet. And when Fury attempts to kill Evansworth and Astrolabe tries to protect her, Fury kills Astrolabe.

When the *Dominion* finds a graduate named Clotilde Narcisse, Hunter suggests killing her because he believes she has joined the temptresses of Alnitak Five.

When Oakford brings Narcisse on board, she uses a drug called Angel Haze to take control of Casteel and then the *Dominion.*

Falcon interrogates Evansworth and learns of the plot to take over the *Dominion.* Falcon soon boards the battle cruiser and defeats Narcisse but not before dozens die on the ship, hundreds die at the research facility, and thousands die on the planet. As Falcon departs the *Dominion,* she takes Evansworth and Narcisse with her.

978 — Windfall: The Reddening Sky

During a wargame on Beta Tauri Five, Hunter offends a corporal and the corporal tries to kill him.

The freighter station flies to Gamma Draconis Two and forcibly evacuates the inhabitants. On the way to the Realm, the freighter is destroyed when it hits the side wall of a boom tube. Both Bastiaan and Khulan die.

Other freighter stations begin arriving in the Realm as Beast claims it has eliminated Shadow. During an away mission to Gamma Draconis Two, Hunter discovers that the Gilead Research Facility has been destroyed. Hunter also discovers the remains of Bastiaan and Khulan floating inside a boom tube and takes them to Casteel.

Falcon returns to the freighter station that orbits Gamma Pegasi to find it controlled by automated programs and overrun by Mechs. She escapes with Evansworth and Narcisse's help.

At the same time, another freighter station arrives in the Beta Tauri system. An away mission from the *Dominion* discovers Mechs and refugees. During the attempted rescue, the *Dominion* is damaged, but the local Realm inhabitants use their own vessels to relocate the refugees.

On Alnitak Five, Falcon seizes control of the temptresses. She puts Evansworth in charge. She also returns Narcisse to the Realm but under the influence of Angel Haze.

Windfall: Wheat and Tares — 979

After defeating a group of Mercenaries, Falcon discovers the operation was really a ruse to bring her face-to-face with G'Utz. Falcon kills G'Utz, but she is then told by an envoy of Beast that she is irrelevant.

At the Saturn Shipyards, with repairs nearly complete on the *Dominion*, Nicolescu discovers Murg sneaking into Razzle Dazzle. She also catches Jordan betraying Oakford.

When Casteel tells the refugee women they won't receive the booties, they kill their babies by throwing them into the burn zone. Shock and grief follows for citizens all across the Realm. But in the process, Casteel discovers the refugees have actual brain damage.

On Beta Tauri Five, unruly refugees are confined to the city of Isaac's Remembrance. Atmospheric controllers have created a searing, eternal day in the city, and a burn zone surrounds the city that incinerates anyone on foot. Casteel and a portion of the crew of the *Dominion* are assisting the citizens of Beta Tauri Five with the crisis. Worst of all, nine months before, all of the refugee women became pregnant, thinking it would earn them knitted booties made by the citizens.

In the end, an attack against the refugees is thwarted and Casteel heals them. Murg is forgiven. Oakford convinces Nicolescu to pardon Jordan. Bandit joins the crew. The *Dominion* returns to active duty.

980 ○ *Windfall: Virgins*

Falcon reappears in the Realm to claim that Beast is shock-dropping asteroid miners into Realm planetary systems to hurl asteroids at inhabited worlds. Falcon also reveals that G'Utz has a secondary keep and that the pilots there know additional shock-drop routes.

Meanwhile, the *Dominion* is dispatched to seize the secondary Marauder keep. Unfortunately, Falcon soon reveals that Evansworth and twelve temptresses from Alnitak have accompanied her. Their presence quickly causes a host of problems, so much so that Casteel unintentionally heals Evansworth. Too quickly, Evansworth knocks out Casteel and badly wounds her.

At the same time, an asteroid hits Vega Two. Unknown to most, Clotilde Narcisse secretly married Edenjevy Bautista two years before. The strike destroys their farmhouse, dashes their children against the rocks, and almost kills the couple. As they recover in med units, Clotilde emerges from the influence of Angel Haze. And believing her children dead, she vows her revenge.

In the end, Mercenaries destroy the secondary keep. Harnecky is killed by Evansworth. Clotilde uses her remaining Angel Haze to take control of the Bautista clan. She then travels to Earth to dominate Ton and order him to make Jordan the Lead Commander of the *Dominion*.

Windfall: The Counting House ○ **980**

Days later, Casteel emerges from an emergency medical unit in the Brig to discover that Jordan now commands the *Dominion*. Harnecky's body has been destroyed to prevent Casteel from resurrecting him. The rest of the former senior staff is confined to the Brig. And Jordan has rigged the cells to release a nerve toxin if anyone tries to escape.

Due to Jordan's inexperience in the Night, the *Dominion* is soon badly damaged in an asteroid storm. To save the ship, the former senior staff escape the Brig. They rally the crew and effect enough repairs to get the ship to safety, but all know it will be months before the *Dominion* can return to the Realm on its own. Falcon and Casteel then go for help.

Meanwhile, Nicolescu travels to Vega Two to rescue the Bautista clan from Clotilde's influence. And she cares for them until she is satisfied that they can be trusted with Clotilde's children, whom Nicolescu had covertly saved from the asteroid. In time, Nicolescu also returns to Jerusalem to free Ton from Clotilde's influence. Ton then executes Clotilde and Edenjevy.

Dispatched by Ton, the *Power* unexpectedly arrives, but the *Dominion* is deemed too badly damaged to save. In the end, the self destruct is engaged. Falcon is arrested. Casteel is killed. And Nicolescu convinces Oakford to take Hunter, Murg, Bolobolo, Bandit, and MacDuff and flee into the Night.

983 | *Windfall: The Leavening*

In the years after fleeing the Realm, Oakford, Hunter, Murg, Bolobolo, Bandit, and MacDuff work freelance jobs in the Night and perform the occasional task for Nicolescu.

Meanwhile, Murg reveals that Nicolescu has sent word regarding the next mission. And soon, the team discovers the courier is Sotheby, who admits that Nicolescu feels responsible for Casteel's death. However, MacDuff insists that Casteel wasn't killed by Nicolescu's teams. She "accepted an invitation."

Months later, Hunter meets with Kwan, an emmisary of Beast. Before it's over, Kwan kills a woman and the team is left to care for her twins.

At the same time, Hunter has his own missions, investigating Beast. He eventually agrees to allow the team to help, but not interfere. For his latest solo mission, Hunter crashlands on K-296e to be captured and tortured. But in the process, he gathers the information he wants, just before the team rushes him into a med unit.

The team then goes to K-1544b to retreive 11 samples of deadly viruses. Unfortunately, Evansworth is already there, and she manages to capture almost the entire team. Evansworth even doses both Sotheby and Bolobolo with Angel Haze, not realizing Sotheby is already on Angel Haze. This allows Sotheby to rescue the team, but Evansworth escapes.

Windfall: Dragnet | 985

On Epsilon Sagittarii Three, a group of young refugees from Shadow attack a Realm Force Training Facility with cries of "Death to the Oppressors of WASP-12e!" Oddly, Realm Force has no presence there.

After watching the confessions of the refugees, Hunter concludes that they have been tortured. Consequently, the team goes to the planet. Hunter stops the Does, and with Murg's help, he also thwarts a Mercenary plan to destroy a settlement. While on planet, however, the team meets a street vendor who looks like Casteel. Since she won't answer questions about her identity, Hunter judges her a threat and arranges for the team to leave. Still, Bolobolo spends time with the woman before departing.

In time, Oakford's team rendezvous with another team whose members all call themselves John Doe. The Does indicate they are going deep in the Night to WASP-12e to investigate. They say the interrogated refugees indicated "something weird" was happening on the planet. The Does then say they will not work with Oakford's team, and they leave.

In Hades, Falcon solidifies her hold over the maximum security facility. She also begins launching empty supply tubes back to the surface, hoping to create a pattern that only Murg will recognize. She has gathered enough intelligence on Beast that she is ready for Murg to ask Oakford to bring the *Dominion* to Hades and free her from the prison.

986 ○ *Windfall: An Unexpected Hour*

Travelling back to the K-991 system, six years after the *Dominion* was supposedly destroyed, Murg soon confesses that he intercepted the autodestruct sequence so the ship wouldn't destroy itself. Instead, he handed over control to the *Dominion Pixie,* a Wind-derived artificial intelligence that Murg trained on Falcon. Unfortunately, years before, the *Pixie* ran low on supplies and began flying the battlecruiser inward to collect what supplies it could and kill whenever it felt it was necessary.

Meanwhile, in Hades, Falcon does her best to retain her control over the all-male population. Eventually though, enough prisoners revolt and force her back into submission.

Windfall: The Wasterie ○ 986

After the *Dominion* is resupplied, the Pixie unexpectedly asks Oakford when they are going after Falcon. Under questioning by Hunter, Murg and the Pixie reveal that Falcon has sent the signal that she has learned all she can from the prisoners in Hades about Beast.

Understandably, Oakford is upset that Falcon intended to get herself committed to Hades and now expects to be rescued. Unfortunately, Oakford and team soon learn from Nicolescu that a Mech swarm has appeared in the Realm, and the easy conclusion is that it was sent to make its way to Hades and destroy the facility with everyone inside. Given that, the team heads for Hades.

At the same time, Nicolescu quickly learns of the *Dominion's* continued existence and arranges for Ladipo to take the *Power*, along with Sotheby and PLOKTA, to investigate.

Oakford's team reaches the Dominion first, but not before an unexpected energy blast erupts from an endpoint and destroys the transport the team took from the Does. The same blast cripples the *Power*. Working together, Oakford's team and the crew of the *Power* repair it enough to return it to the Realm. As thanks, Nicolescu resupplies the *Dominion*.

For safety's sake, Bolobolo takes the twins to live with her parents.

The team rescues Falcon, but not before she sacrifices herself to save Hunter. And in the process, her injuries reveal that she has a cybernetic body. Soon, the *Dominion* unexpectedly shock-drops onto a planet 20,000 lightyears from Earth. There, a man named Haymakers Notch installs Falcon into an new, upgraded cybernetic body.

Unfortunately, Notch won't do it unless Oakford agrees to be the proprietor of the new body and be responsible for anything done with it. Afterwards, Oakford invites Falcon to join the crew as First Mate and his Number One. Still, not all is well because it appears that the Pixie might want Falcon's new cybernetic body for its own.

987

Windfall: Samaritans

Three months after escaping from Hades, Falcon has a vision of a research facility where women are being held in gestation rigs and impregnated with genetic hybrids. Unfortunately, the vision contains little beyond that. Still, the team deduces enough to allow Falcon to get herself kidnapped and taken there. Soon after, Falcon transmits the location back to the team, and asks them to come get her in five months if she hasn't already returned.

In the mean time, the team hides Falcon's departure from the ship to thwart any potential information leaks at the Saturn Shipyards. Soon, Hunter, MacDuff, and Bandit head to the Nu Scorpii system as well.

Eventually, Oakford does inform Nicolescu of the mission, and the information does leak to Beast because Kwan comes to the facility to evacuate Lead Researcher Doctor Moreau. Unfortunately for Kwan, it isn't long before Falcon, Hunter, MacDuff, and Bandit seize control. Then, the *Dominion* arrives to take them all into custody.

Interestingly enough, when Oakford tells Nicolescu the exent of what they've found, she asks for all of it to be turned over to the Realm. The team does release Moreau and the other researchers. But Hunter kills Kwan to avenge the death of Maria Martinez, and the women confined to the rigs stay with the *Dominion*.

Windfall: The Herd

988

For the next year on the *Dominion*, Oakford and the senior staff train the women formerly confined to gestation rigs at the research facility on Nu Scorpii One and attempt to integrate them into the crew. At the same time, the *Dominion* continues to carry out missions. During a break, the *Dominion* heads to K-22B, the planet where Casteel learned to heal supernaturally. They find the research station apparently abandoned, but soon realize the researchers are hidden and do not wish to be distrubed. Oakford and team pay their respects and leave.

At the Saturn Shipyards, Nicolescu grows so concerned with misogyny in the Realm, she authorizes Sotheby to begin the executions of offenders.

After losing yet another tactical team investigating a possible location for one of the artificial intelligence (AI) "heads" of Beast, Nicolescu then asks Oakford to investigate the K-1645 system.

On K-1645, the *Dominion* finds an underground facility called "NO-U-TOPIA." And Falcon, Hunter, and MacDuff soon learned all of the humans living there have been stripped of their individuality and exist in intersectional categories. In time, the trio offends the processing system of NO-U-TOPIA, and it turns the facility into a crematorium. The away team narrowly escapes, but Hunter later surmises that the AI used by Beast might be a hybrid of human responses and machine-learning.

989 Windfall: A Mustard Seed

In the K2-72 system, the crew of the Dominion provide additional security for the Festival of the King. The system has only one inhabited planet, K2-72e, and that planet only has one inhabited valley. The valley is home to a unique species of plant that produces fibers that can be spun into Rexian Sheer, a fabric that is as light as air and very expensive. During the Festival of the King, merchants come from all over the Night to purchase goods made of Rexian Sheer.

One of those merchants, Jean-Baptiste Lacroix, convinces Jazarah Worku, a *Dominion* member, to return to his yacht. Once there, he captures her. When Bandit attempts a rescue, he is captured too.

At the same time, King Tyrannosaurus Rex of K2-72e is so impressed with Bolobolo that he declares that he will marry her. Bolobolo agrees to the wedding to ensure safe passage for the Dominion out of the K2-72 system. And only later does Bolobolo discover that the old king is an imposter and the real King Rex is much younger with a penchant for torture.

Worse, when the *Dominion* follows Bandit and Worku to a planetary nebula system, they discover an unknown horde of genetically engineered Hunter look-alikes who claim that Hunter is one of them. Unfortunately, Hunter also learns the horde wants him to die.

Windfall: Unseen 989

In the planetary nebula where Worku and Bandit are held captive and tortured, the spokesman for the Hunter look-alikes continues beating Hunter to death. When all seems lost, MacDuff helps Hunter transition into the spiritual realm. Hunter heals himself and slaughters the spokesman. Astonished, the horde leaves at Hunter's urging. Hunter then blacks out. Afterward, the *Dominion* rescues Bolobolo.

At the same time, Nicolescu and Sotheby continue plotting with Ton to take over the Realm. After staging a night of terror when 50 prominent families of the Realm are slaughtered, Sotheby doses Ladipo with Angel Haze and orders him to confess to coordinating one of the attacks.

Nicolescu's plan seems to be proceeding when a message arrives from a being called Abaddon. Abaddon shows he knows about Nicolescu's plan and requests a rendezvous with the *Power*. For that meeting, Elspeth Jordan is appointed Lead Commander of the *Power*. However, as Abaddon speaks with Nicolescu, a female Troyd hacker compromises the *Power*. Soon, the battle cruiser is destroyed and many of its crew are killed, including Jordan.

Abaddon also opens curled space rings all over the Realm and Night that allow travel between any two rings instantly. And many *Dominion* former crewmembers use this ability to leave Realm Force to join its crew.

990 — Windfall: The Lamp

On Spica Two, Hunter tortures and dissects a young woman in a death chamber of a club called Bludgeon Abaddon. In fact, the young woman is a member of the tactical teams. Afterwards, MacDuff rushes the young woman's body into a med unit, while Falcon hacks the club's systems and then guides Hunter to the proprietor's office. As expected, Hunter finds Twilla Evansworth in charge. Hunter intends to kill her, but Evansworth reveals that Abaddon has visited Spica Two, so Hunter captures her instead. The Pixie then installs the same controls she used on Bandit in Evansworth and Evansworth is sent back to Spica Two to be the *Dominion's* eyes and ears on the planet in case Abaddon returns.

Following a mission to Polaris 2, the *Dominion* is visited by an agent who provides information that sends the battlecruiser to the mining planet of Rigel Three. Unbeknownst to the crew, the agent then locates and captures Bandit and brings him to Rigel Three as well.

On Rigel Three, an away team from the Dominion quickly runs afoul of the planet's ruling families. Worse, when Falcon thwarts an attempt to murder the away team and Bandit, one of the ruling families unleashes a freighter full of Mechs on the planet's main population center. With the Dominion's help, the rest of the ruling families stop the destruction, but not before Bandit is killed.

Windfall: Thornbush — 991

On Spica Two, Hunter returns to Evansworth's death club to spy on Abaddon. Unfortunately, after slaughtering his victims in the death chamber, Abaddon frees Evansworth from the control devices that the Pixie installed, before vanishing with her.

Traveling home to Fomalhaut Four, Bolobolo discovers that Realm Force has invaded her home planet. When the Realm Force personnel attack her shuttle, Bolobolo dons a stealth suit and leaps into space, but the stealth suit is damaged in the resulting fusion torpedo explosion, and she is injured during her crash landing.

Also, the *Dominion* discovers Rigel Three has been destroyed using nuclear weapons.

On Fomalhaut Four, Bolobolo is captured and confined to a med unit. Sotheby then doses Bolobolo with Angel Haze and forces her to record a confession claiming that the *Dominion* assisted forces from the Night to invade Fomalhaut Four. Sotheby also forces Bolobolo to assist with the slaughter of 15 of the Fomalhaut Four tribes.

Falcon arrives on the planet and saves Bolobolo, but the Horde of Hunter Look-Alikes invades. They demand delivery of Bolobolo so they can question her. Against Falcon's urging, Rachel unleashes Fury, who defeats the Hunter look-alikes. Bolobolo is cleared of wrongdoing by the planet's tribal council after her father wins a war dance, but he dies in the process.

992 — Windfall: The Vexing

On Gamma Pegasi D, an away team rescues Jazarah Worku from the planet's only settlement. A med unit session soon heals Worku's physical injuries, but it appears the settlers tried to lobotomize her, and it's impossible to tell if they succeeded.

Later, a shuttle meets the *Dominion* in the Canopus system. The pilot claims the crew is infected with a deadly virus. He then says they can swap the Rexian Sheer the crew took from Lacroix's yacht for the antidote. The senior staff concludes that Worku is in on the scam. And when they hand over Worku and the fabric, Oakford includes the custom-made Rexian Sheer dresses, guaranteeing Worku will be pursued and killed.

Windfall: Raveners

On the abandoned planet Beta Andromedae Seven, the senior staff of the *Dominion* discover valleys overgrown with a dense, unknown thicket. Most concerning, the thicket fills the air with white spores that seem to cause neurological damage.

Meanwhile, Oakford receives an angry message from Prime Lhundrup of Betelgeuse Two claiming that the *Dominion* is overdue to provide security for a Merchant Guildsmen conference. Worse, when away teams arrive at the convention center, they find it nearly overrun by beligerant convention goers. The crew discovers that somone has transplanted the thicket to the sewers of Betelgeuse Two, and the convention goers are suffering its effects.

Windfall: The Vexing

On Epsilon Virginis Three, a deadly strain of hemorrhagic fever quickly infects the populace. The Saturn Shipyards provides an antidote but in fact Nicolescu released the virus in the first place for her own gain. Unsurprisingly, the antidote fails, but Realm Force is granted more unilateral authority.

Nicolescu also decides it's time to deal with the renegade group within Realm Force whose participants are known only by the name John Doe. After dosing their leadership with Angel Haze, Nicolescu orders all of the John Does to attack the Dominion in the Bellatrix system. As expected, Oakford allows the Pixie to engage them and all 10,000 are eliminated.

993

In fact, Faustine Garnier, a member of Nicolescu's special tactical teams, performed that sabotage. Worse, when Guan Qiuyue is captured and confined to the sewers long enough to damage her brain, Garnier commits suicide before she can be captured and held to account.

Now, Lhundrup and many other incensed guildsmen attempt to attack Earth. That attack is easily repulsed, but Nicolescu has PLOKTA guide Lhundrup's yacht to crash-land in a suburb of Jerusalem, killing Ton's wife. Sotheby then tries to dose Ton with Angel Haze, but PLOKTA intervenes and gives Ton the upper hand. Ton doses Sotheby and Nicolescu instead, then swears allegiance to Abaddon.

In the ruins on KOI-4878.01, Hunter leads Guan on a rage-slaughter. Hunter has trained Guan for a year, attempting to instill some restraint in her after engineered spores poisoned her brain on Betelgeuse Two. Oakford only agreed to the plan once Hunter revealed that the ruins contain a cult that kidnaps children from the Night and the Realm and mutilates them to remove all signs of gender. Hunter hopes that the rage-slaughter will sate Guan enough to allow her to remain on the ship. Unexpectedly, Abaddon appears with an unseen cohort of titans to kill all the inhabitants of KOI-4878.01. When the senior staff chases a supply line to Epsilon Boötis Six, Abaddon kills the inhabitants there as well.

Windfall: The Prodigal

Following the evacuation from Betelgeuse Two, the senior staff of the *Dominion* struggles for over a week to find a Night planet that will accept the refugees. Worse, when the governor of Antares Three finally accepts them, Abaddon and his cohort slaughter everyone on the planet.

In the Realm, Ton makes plans to openly seize control of the Realm. To begin, he targets Alpha Pegasi Three because it's leadership has voted against his proposals in the past. A special tactical team doses the planet's governor with Angel Haze. He subsequently confesses to many crimes. And when some inhabitants refuse to believe the confession, Ton releases millions of robots to rampage and slaughter the population.

At a Saturn Shipyards black site, Realm Force personnel retrofit a secret warship with Wind-designed energy weapons for which Abaddon has given Ton the activation codes. The warship is christened the *Majesty* and dispatched to destroy Betelgeuse Two. The *Dominion* attempts to assist with the evacuation of the planet, but in the process encounters the *Majesty*. Thankfully, Southby agrees to let the *Dominion* depart with 1,000 inhabitants, averting a showdown.

In the same encounter, Murg receives word from another Troyd he calls She Of Whom We Do Not Speak. She sayd the Troyd have allied with Abaddon and that final submissions of alternate viewpoints are welcome.

995

Meanwhile, Murg reveals that for the last 30 years, he has been on a mission to gather information on the Realm for the Troyd. He also reveals that She Of Whom We Do Not Speak has been gathering information on the Night.

Murg believes that if he can present his research to the Troyd, he might convince them to abandon their alliance with Abaddon. Unfortunately, the Troyd are determined to destroy the *Dominion* and the Pixie with it. When their first attempt fails they unleash Mechs hidden in asteroids. In fact, the Troyd invented the Mechs and now hope to them to tear apart the *Dominion*. The Pixie intervenes and the Mechs attack the Troy instead.

1.

Inside the stripped-down husk of a fusion torpedo, Zachary Hunter, Chief Pilot of the *MV Dominion*, waited for the air around him to throb and the space above him to distort enough for two *very* distant locations to touch.

After construction by the Realm Force Saturn Shipyards almost 25 years before, the *Dominion* was christened with the designation *HMVR*, His Majesty's Vessel of the Realm. At the time, the *Dominion* had been the last of only three *Trinity-class* battlecruisers. And though the vessel's design specification might have led some to believe the *Dominion* was a warship, Realm Force had always claimed that it *wasn't* part of a military. Instead, Realm Force had said it was more akin to a police force with just the right amount of strength and lethality to protect the Realm. And, of course, that need for protection had been a *given*, given the circumstances.

Almost a thousand years before, a race of titans known as the Wind had arrived to conquer Earth and subdue it with two overarching principles.

Submit or die.

Treat others as you wish to be treated.

At the same time, the Wind's technology quickly created a utopia on Earth, complete with seemingly limitless energy, perfect health, and abundant food. Even more impressive, using a technology the Wind called curled space funnels, humanity had begun to populate other star systems, making planets hospitable to human life using the Wind's terraforming technologies as needed.

For the record, the curled space funnels *worked*. They allowed a spacecraft to transit the vast distances between star systems in an average of 30 minutes. But there were drawbacks. The sidewalls of the funnels contained quantum devourers. Any ship unlucky enough to scrape a sidewall *without* sufficient velocity to rip away the affected area would be seized by the devourers. And then the entire ship would be *eaten*, including its human passengers.

Still, the curled space funnels allowed humanity to travel *hundreds* of light-years out from Earth's solar system in every direction and populate hundreds of planets.

Then, after 974 years of absolute rule, the Wind disappeared.

No one knew where they went. No one knew if they were coming back.

Unsurprisingly, those humans who had always felt the need to be in charge quickly formed governments and voted themselves into office. Others who had previously fled the Realm into what was dubbed the Night to escape the tyranny of the Wind seized the opportunity and began hijacking Realm freighters carrying goods to the outer planets of the Realm.

In response, a newly formed Leadership Council in Jerusalem proclaimed the establishment of the Realm Force to help maintain order and protect the citizens of the Realm. And, of course, Realm Force needed equipment and vessels to help them repel attacks. And Realm Force needed those vessels and their accompanying equipment to be powerful.

This need drove the Saturn Shipyards to build increasingly capable ships, culminating in the *Trinity-Class* battlecruisers. For decades, the design was the most audacious and capable of all the ships constructed by the Saturn Shipyards.

Interestingly enough, all three *Trinity-Class* battlecruisers met unexpected fates. The crew of the *HMVR Glory* destroyed their own vessel as they struggled against an attack by a genetically engineered hemorrhagic fever virus. The *HMVR Power* succumbed to hacking. Even the *Dominion* was thought lost for a time after its senior staff invoked its autodestruct sequence.

Thankfully, Murg, the *Dominion's* Chief Technologist, secretly intercepted the autodestruct commands to save an artificial intelligence he had awakened and named the Pixie. Only *years* later did Murg reveal to the senior staff of the *Dominion* that the ship *hadn't* been destroyed. By then, the senior staff had been in exile in the Night for many years and *couldn't* return to the Realm.

Some of those who lived in the Night believed that claim. Some didn't.

Some believed the *Dominion* was spying for Realm Force. Some were convinced the battlecruiser *was* what its new designation claimed, that it *was* the *Marauder Vessel Dominion*. In other words, the *Dominion* had become a pirate ship.

Honestly, it was easier to believe the former than the latter. After all, the *Dominion* boasted impressive technologies. Indeed, the *Trinity-Class* battlecruisers had special coils built into their upper hull. Those coils were taken from the massive Wind-designed communications satellites that supplied real-time, instantaneous comm and sensor information exchanges across the entire Realm. Throughout the Realm, any citizen on any planet could carry on a conversation with any citizen on any other planet, no matter what the distance between them, without any delays.

Using that same technology, given half the output energy of fusion generators, the coils built into the upper hull of a *Trinity-Class* battlecruiser could curl space enough to create a tiny funnel to *any* location and then initiate a point-to-point comm for real-time video calls with sidebands for additional data transmissions.

Indeed, those who refused to believe that the *Dominion* was merely a pirate ship pointed to the fact that, if the battlecruiser *were* a pirate ship, Realm Force would be compelled to stage an all-out offensive to destroy the battlecruiser and prevent it from being used against its own citizens. In fact, the *Dominion* *had* suffered attacks, but the crew had thwarted all of them, mainly with the help of the Pixie.

Interestingly enough, over the past year, the senior staff of the *Dominion* had experimented to see if they could do *more* with the battlecruiser's point-to-point communication facility. That experimentation yielded consistently positive results. And it had culminated in Hunter climbing into the stripped-down husk of a fusion torpedo to perform the first human test to throw an object hundreds of light-years into an arbitrary destination.

Even the curled space rings that Abaddon had opened after appearing didn't function like that.

For the record, nothing had changed concerning Hunter's opinion of Abaddon. Hunter continued to classify Abaddon as an unknown. And he didn't expect that to change anytime soon unless Abaddon voluntarily offered more information that correlated with other independent sources of information. Even then, Hunter knew it would be impossible to know what was *true*.

But that difficulty wasn't limited to Abaddon.

When the Wind appeared to subdue the Earth almost a thousand years before, humanity had no mechanism to verify their identity. For the Wind's entire rule, the titans claimed they were Jesus Christ and his followers, fulfilling the prophecy in chapter 20 of Revelation, the final book of the Bible. That prophecy claimed Jesus Christ would return to Earth to establish a kingdom that would last 1,000 years, culminating in a final, fiery encounter between the forces of good and evil.

Bewildered by the appearance of the titans, humanity had quickly settled into one of three opinions about the Wind. Those who believed in a Judeo-Christian tradition gladly accepted the Wind's claims and were happy to submit to the Wind because it validated their belief systems.

The skeptically minded rightly pointed out that the Wind could be aliens who decided to leverage the existing story of Jesus and the prophecies about him to make it easier for humanity to submit. These skeptics *also* proposed that Jesus Christ might have been an alien himself. And he had come to Earth thousands of years before to begin a religion that would exploit a weakness in the human psyche. That weakness would guarantee that it would grow into a significant influence in human history and make it possible at some later point to stage a successful coup.

Most humans, however, did what most humans usually do. They put their heads down. They plodded along. They tried not to think about who the Wind might be. And they found some enjoyment in the abundance that surrounded them.

And all was well for the first 974 years. And then, the Wind disappeared. And a few years passed. And Abaddon appeared.

Abaddon claimed that the Wind were charlatans who went from planet to planet to trick less-developed lifeforms into complacency. This allowed the Wind to steal their resources and it made them targets for destruction. Indeed, Abaddon claimed that he represented the larger society of sentient beings called the Children of the Prime. Their goal was to achieve intellectual and existential supremacy by focusing on rapid self-improvement.

Any race of beings who failed to live up to their potential would be censured by the Council of the Children of the Prime for wasting the precious resources they had been given. And if that race didn't show immediate improvement, the council would deem them damaged beyond repair. Once that happened, the devourers would descend, led by none other than Abaddon's master.

Interestingly, Abaddon never claimed to be kind or good. Indeed, Abaddon openly tortured humans for amusement in sickening and disturbing ways that defied nature. He extracted bones without his victims bleeding. He prolonged life by turning bodies into long strips of skin. And along the way, he might stuff intestines into mouths, just to listen for the gag and gurgle. And indeed, no one, by his terrifying appearance or his overpowering stench, immediately concluded he had appeared to be the savior of humanity.

Still, Abaddon had claimed that he wanted to help. Mostly, he said, he wanted to help because he wanted the Wind to fail. And to assist humanity in achieving the necessary unification, Abaddon apparently used his understanding of curled space funnel technology to open curled space *rings* in orbit around every inhabited location in both the Realm and the Night. Those rings allowed transit from any ring to any other ring in a single hop, based on the spacecraft's approach vector and velocity to the ring.

Everyone agreed that the curled space rings were an improvement over the curled space funnels. They were safer. They were far faster. But even the curled space rings didn't duplicate what Hunter and the senior staff were about to attempt. Maybe the curled space rings *could* be set to an arbitrary location without the need for a curled space ring on the other end of the hop, but no *human* knew how to do that.

Interestingly, the senior staff of the *Dominion* had never expected to accomplish that either. But over a year ago, the idea of widening the tiny curled space funnel created by the point-to-point communication facility of the battlecruiser came up in a senior staff meeting. And the senior staff decided to attempt it.

The first trial failed *spectacularly*. But the second attempt *mostly* succeeded.

For the last year, the senior staff had continued to experiment. By now, the crew of the *Dominion* had refined the process in almost all respects. They could reliably send an object to a distant destination. They could initiate it faster from start to finish. And they had even refined the accuracy to the transport to within ten meters of the proposed destination. of the

It was true, despite all the testing, the senior staff had been *unable* to widen the curled space funnel of the point-to-point communication facility beyond a specific limit. Still, the *Dominion* could successfully hurl anything enclosed in a stripped-down fusion torpedo through the resulting miniature curled space opening without any apparent *physical* damage. Sensor packages sent through the funnels during multiple trials reported radiation levels well below lethal exposures for biological life. And small to medium-sized animals had apparently survived the drops without harm.

Of course, *none* of the animals could sit down for a post-trip interview. And they couldn't take cognitive tests that would confirm there had been no short or long-term mental injury. But the animals *could* perform simple cognitive tests before and after, and nothing seemed to change. And placing the sedated animals in med units didn't reveal anything concerning.

By now, the experiments had been ongoing for long enough that the senior staff could imagine other possibilities. Yes, Hunter understood that the Captain of the *Dominion*, Geoffrey Oakford, might be highly hesitant ever to do so. Still, from a purely practical standpoint, the *Dominion could* now open a point-to-point funnel to an unseen destination, fire a fusion torpedo through the opening, and close the connection before the fusion torpedo detonated. And moments later, the explosion would form a fireball that extended five kilometers in every direction.

The crew of the *Dominion* had done something similar seven years before. Abaddon had opened the curled space rings during his introductory speech to the Realm. As Abaddon spoke from a shuttle orbiting the planet Beta Andromedae Seven, a member of the Troyd named Koan hacked into the *Power*, overrode its systems, and caused multiple failures.

Damaged and disabled, the *Power* had drifted toward a newly opened curled space ring that was somehow locked onto a location high above Jerusalem. Without intervention, the *Power* would have drifted through the ring and tumbled to Earth. And the results would have been catastrophic.

The Lead Commander of the Saturn Shipyards, Ionela Nicolescu, had asked the crew of the *Dominion* to do the unthinkable. She wanted the *Power* destroyed because there wasn't time for Realm Force to scramble enough resources to ensure the battlecruiser's obliteration before it reached the ground.

At that point, no one knew how the curled space rings worked. Indeed, at that point, the curled space ring in the Beta Andromedae Seven wasn't behaving as the curled space rings had behaved ever since. It was fixed to a single location, and the senior staff of the *Dominion* had no idea how to close it.

So they guessed. Hunter had flown directly at the ring, firing a fusion torpedo at the last moment before pulling away. Immediately afterward, another pilot named Bandit flew into the ring.

As hoped, the ring switched to another destination, closing the physical connection between Earth and Beta Andromedae Seven. High in the sky above Jerusalem, the fusion torpedo detonated, creating a fireball that engulfed the *Power* and incinerated it.

So it *was* possible to use that tactic. And it *was* effective. But Hunter understood it would take a desperate situation for Oakford to agree to such a blind, shotgun-like flailing.

Now, the small display inside Hunter's stripped-down torpedo shell showed the energy from the *Dominion's* fusion generators being routed to the large ring of coils built into the battlecruiser's upper hull. At the same time, another graph showed that the ship's central processing array had allocated fifty percent of its units to calculate the exact position of the *Dominion* relative to the chosen destination, over a thousand light-years away.

Sadly, the senior staff of the *Dominion* had known there were *many* possible destinations for the experiment. In recent years, few worlds in the Night survived the attacks from both Realm Force and Abaddon.

At present, the *Dominion* was holding its position steady in the vicinity of Epsilon Pegasi Five. At one time, the planet had been moderately blessed with underground water and a minimal atmosphere that could support life with a bit of clever engineering. Now, it was barren, its surface irradiated from the nuclear bombardment by Realm Force.

In other words, the planet would likely *never* support life again.

The same could be said for Hunter's chosen destination, Rigel Three. At one time, the planet was a major supplier of the rare earth minerals needed to create the old-style pre-Coming electronics that were popular in the Night. It had an atmosphere nearly identical to Earth, along with an official population of 10 million.

Rigel Three had also been subjected to a Realm Force nuclear bombardment. It was also a radioactive wasteland. Every bit of valuable metal ore at every stage of refinement had been irradiated as well.

It was difficult to know how many other worlds in the Night had suffered that same fate. Murg had run approximations on the destruction of Night worlds based on the reduction of activity on the dark net. Overall, the traffic had almost dropped to zero, but that only indicated that the population of the Night had dropped precipitously.

It *didn't* reveal what percentage of Nightlings had died a *relatively* peaceful death in the nuclear bombardments by Realm Force. Neither did it reveal the percentage of Nightlings who died in horrifying assaults staged by Abaddon, apparently accompanied by unseen titans.

Hunter had first witnessed that second type of mass depopulation on KOI-4878.01 the year before. During a mission to the inhabited ruins beneath the planet's surface, Hunter had seen invisible forces *shred* all who called KOI-4878.01 their home. None of the senior staff could explain why Abaddon had left the *Dominion's* away team alive, while everyone else in the ruins was reduced to a pile of meat pulp. But the pattern repeated itself on Epsilon Boötis Six only a few cycles later.

That time, Oakford's Number One, Rachel Falcon, and the *Dominion's* Chief Tactician, Gabriel MacDuff, witnessed the destruction at the hands of Abaddon and his unseen nightmarish monsters. And like the attack on KOI-4878.01, those waves of death were filled with unnerving sounds.

The sucking rasp of flesh gouged and torn. The crisp and much-too-easy snapping of bones. The sloppy thuds of bloodied bodies.

All accompanied by uncontrolled, wild, panicked screaming.

That screaming identified the deaths as worse than the nuclear annihilation. Perhaps some terror had found a quick escape as the bombs detonated, incinerating everything in their path. But the dismemberments by Abaddon and his cohorts seemed to be designed to allow the victims to reach the full realization of their horror before they died, as if that last stamp of terrifying mental clarity would follow them into the afterworld and increase their suffering even more.

Consequently, for the first test, throwing a human over a thousand light-years in *seconds*, Hunter had chosen to go from one dead world to the next. It made sense. Far less chance of encountering a random spacecraft crossing directly in front of the opening the *Dominion* was about to create.

Hunter knew his chosen source and destination didn't reduce the chances of a collision to zero. But it improved his odds. Besides, he wasn't superstitious or easily spooked by the thought of death. He had lived too much of his early life as a Mercenary to be concerned with trivialities.

By now, the coils built into the upper hull of the *Dominion* had begun to throb from the energy pouring into them from the battlecruiser's fusion generator array. And while Hunter had always known *intellectually* that the coils bent space, the effect of that bending, despite the size of the massive coils, fell off quickly over a relatively short distance. And in fact, the *Dominion* was *designed* to guide the curling of space along the hull and reduce the effects on the ship's crew.

Obviously, Hunter's current situation was far different. He was *outside* the ship, perched in the center of the coils without anything to dampen the effects. Of course, the fusion torpedo that enclosed him was still latched to the upper hull for the moment, keeping it from moving out of position. And that meant the throbbing that was vibrating the entire ship was transmitting through the connection to shake the stripped-down fusion torpedo as well.

But beyond *that*, Hunter could *feel* the space curling around him.

To be clear, Hunter *was* wearing a stealth suit. Decades before, Realm Force had taken emergency evacuation suits designed by the Wind and convinced them to turn black. From that simple instruction, Realm Force had presumed they could convince the suits to do far more, perhaps even something like complete invisibility. Hence, engineers at the newly formed Saturn Shipyards dubbed them stealth suits.

The engineers never reached that goal, but the name stuck. Still, stealth suits *were* useful. They were designed to protect their inhabitants from all kinds of harm, everything from blunt force impact to all forms of electromagnetic radiation.

Apparently, that protection *didn't* extend to alleviating the effects of curled space because Hunter could feel his body warping under the effects generated by the coils built into the upper hull of the *Dominion*.

And yes, Hunter had felt something similar a decade before after the senior staff acquired a ramshackle shuttle from a group called the John Does and discovered it had a rudimentary point-to-point communication system. It was small and crude. It could only handle text messages.

And every time Hunter used it, it felt like the shuttlecraft was about to twist, crack, and shudder itself to pieces. Reflecting on it now, Hunter realized he *had* felt a version of the squirming in his body when using that point-to-point comm on the Doe's shuttlecraft. He had just been preoccupied with the throbbing of the bulkhead while he looked for developing cracks in the ship's hull.

Of course, the *Dominion's* curled space coils were massive compared to the coils on the Doe's shuttle. And though Hunter didn't believe there would be any structural integrity issues with the fusion torpedo shell, Hunter wondered how intense the distortion in his cells would become and what damage it might cause.

On the plus side, the senior staff of the *Dominion* had conducted tests transporting animals to distant locations using the point-to-point comm. And it was easy to assume that if the animals survived, he would too. But Hunter also knew "there's no substitute for doing it" and "nothing's sure until it's in the past."

Now, the throbbing all around Hunter and the twisting of his insides continued to increase until the coils built into the upper hull of the *Dominion* reached capacity. And at that point, the central processing array of the battlecruiser began manipulating the energy levels in the coils to increase the bend of the empty space above the ship, curling it just enough to open a tiny funnel that connected Hunter's current location to the predetermined spot near Rigel Three.

Instantly, the ring of miniguns bolted in a circle around the vertically mounted fusion torpedo shell spun up. And quickly, the whine they produced transferred into the interior of the fusion torpedo to join the throbbing. A moment later, the miniguns began to fire, and those thundering vibrations also joined the cacophony.

As usual, that was when the show began. Hunter had seen it many times by now, but it was always beautiful. Given the curled space surrounding them, the slugs didn't exit the muzzles of the miniguns in a straight line. Instead, the energy from the throbbing coils caught them and whipped them outward as they raced away from the *Dominion*. Simultaneously, the slugs began to absorb the energy from the surrounding field. And then, they began to *glow*.

From prior tests, Hunter knew the slugs were also accelerating. Quickly, they would reach the halfway point between the ship and the tiny curled space funnel that the coils had opened. And then, the slugs would curve inward, red-hot, as they accelerated even more.

Flashing and pulsing, the space between the *Dominion* and the newly formed tiny curled space funnel transformed into an intricate, spinning mobile, glowing and sparkling with brilliant light, bluer and cooler nearer to the ship and flaming hot near the tiny curled space funnel.

Now, automatically, the thrusters on the fusion torpedo shell *fired* and immediately switched to overdrive. The timing was critical. The miniguns had a limited number of bullets. In the next moment, those glowing slugs would slam into the tiny curled space funnel opened by the coils built into the upper hull of the *Dominion*, and the additional energy would force it to open. But as soon as the bullets ran out, the funnel would collapse.

And yes, the *Dominion's* Mechanical Services crew could have installed larger feeders to extend the firestorm of bullets. But the ammunition in the miniguns was sufficient to the task. And the timing was tuned across dozens of trials.

As far as Hunter was concerned, the larger feeders were a waste of bullets. And the simple solution was to launch the fusion torpedo shell and whatever cargo it contained *before* the tiny curled space funnel widened. To be clear, no one knew what would happen to the fusion torpedo shell if something went wrong and the curled space funnel *didn't* widen. But the senior staff *had* seen what would happen if the bullets ran out *before* the fusion torpedo shell reached the funnel.

It wasn't good.

Shoved back into his restraints as the fusion torpedo shell continued to accelerate, Hunter kept his eyes fixed on his destination. A moment later, the tiny curled space funnel ahead of him *ignited* with a coronal-like fire as the slugs reached their destination.

And as Hunter watched, that fire formed into a ring that surrounded the tiny curled space funnel. Even better, as expected, the ring *expanded.*

At the same time, the intensity of the churning across Hunter's body increased, as if some vengeful deity had decided to *allow* mere mortals to frolic across the mind-numbing distances in an instant with full autonomy, still ensuring that the choice of origin *and* destination extracted a high price. And while Hunter found it *reasonable* to rely on the fact that all of the test animals had survived similar transits, the Chief Pilot of the *Dominion* was well aware that there were *many* "unknown unknowns" in what the senior staff was attempting. And it was easy to imagine some crucial element in the existence of human consciousness that might turn out to be a fatal weakness exposed by the crude mechanics of the hop.

In fact, Hunter was already seeing double, and his vision was rapidly deteriorating as he moved through the swirling chaos all around him. Too soon, he realized he was suffocating, as if the air around him had twisted to liquid and then to useless solid, or his lungs had slipped enough into curled space that they could no longer function in any usual manner.

Too quickly, the kaleidoscope of red-hot bullets racing around him melted into a broad smear. The raging coronal fire racing around the perimeter of the newly opened curled space funnel bubbled into a static blur. And while Hunter could usually look through the opening tear in space and see the stars of the curled space funnel's destination from the safety and comfort of the *Dominion's* Bridge, now, that space was only a dark, muddled interior.

Worse, a sharp pain suddenly shot through Hunter's left eye, slamming it shut and forcing a grimace that twisted the left side of his face.

Then, simultaneously, in the next instant, Hunter began fighting to remain conscious, just as the fusion torpedo shell shot through the center of the curled space funnel.

And then the muddled center of that funnel flashed brilliant white.

2.

At an underground Saturn Shipyards black site deep in the Night, Doctor Alaric Moreau continued to work himself to exhaustion every day in the sterile, monochromatic, constantly lit research facilities that Realm Force had constructed for him after the senior staff of the *Dominion* located his genetic research facility on Nu Scorpii One, nine years before.

To be clear, in the windowless static environment of the current research facility, the word "day" had a more flexible meaning than the diurnal cycles of a rotating planet. Seconds ran together. Hours merged into one. Moreau only knew the date according to Jerusalem time by glancing at a workstation's date and time stamp. And he rarely did that because of the nearly *unsustainable* work effort he had adopted.

For the last three years, in every passing moment, Moreau had carried out his research until he could no longer read the text on his display. And then he would grab a short nap before starting again.

Interestingly, Moreau had settled on the reported work schedule of none other than Leonardo da Vinci.

Work for four hours. Take a twenty-minute nap. Repeat the pattern around the clock.

Interestingly, Moreau felt nothing but gratitude for the opportunity. And, of course, that was because he was on a regimen of Angel Haze, as he had been ever since the senior staff of the *Dominion* turned him over to Nicolescu's assistant, Lieutenant Aeon Sotheby.

Years before, the senior staff of the *Dominion* had discovered Moreau's secret research facility on Nu Scorpii One thanks to a vision experienced by Falcon. In that vision, Falcon was confined to a gestation rig in the facility. Impossibly, from that brief vision, Falcon and the senior staff located the genetic research facility, and when they did, they found over 140 women strapped into such rigs, impregnated with human-animal hybrids developed by Moreau.

Those hybrids had been the result of Moreau's vision for creating a better human, a human more capable, more advanced, and more obedient than the current version of humanity. Frankly, Moreau had been pursuing *that* goal because of what he had done *before* arriving at the genetic research facility on Nu Scorpii One.

And yes, Moreau *hadn't* arrived at the research facility on Nu Scorpii One of his own accord. He had been *sent* there. To be precise, Moreau had been *exiled* there, forced to abandon his leadership position at an advanced, extraordinarily well-equipped, and professionally staffed facility that had made *excellent* progress in crafting genetically advanced human clones.

At the time, Moreau had considered his exile a blatantly *hysterical* response, driven more by political infighting than any objective evaluation. Yes, Moreau had continued to develop an infectious agent that he had been *told* to abandon. Yes, it had escaped confinement. Yes, thousands of clones had rapidly succumbed to it before Moreau's associates *purged* an entire clade of clones under development, completely shutting down the massive gestation facility and disinfecting it to start over.

But Moreau had only developed the virus as a doomsday weapon in case the clones decided they no longer needed their creators. And the accidental escape had *proven* that the virus *was* effective.

As far as Moreau was concerned, the other researchers should have *lavished* praise and commendations on him for his foresight. They should have let him finish the work and then hidden the agent away in cold storage in case it was ever needed.

Unfortunately, even by then, Moreau's associates were *already* worried about the capabilities, intelligence, and psychotic tendencies exhibited by the clones they had developed. And none of those associates wanted to risk the possibility that the clones might discover the existence of such an agent.

Because of that, instead of accolades, Moreau's associates had *buried* him. They had found an out-of-the-way planet. They had built a scaled-down, genetic research facility. They had provided him with an operational budget. And they had assured Moreau that if he ever left the planet, they would dispatch multiple teams of clones to raze his lab, kill all his researchers, hunt him down, and slaughter him in some gruesome and unnecessarily violent manner.

Moreau knew enough about the capabilities and temperaments of both his associates and the clones he had helped engineer that he would never have left Nu Scorpii One on his own. But the senior staff of the *Dominion* had located his facility. And in short order, he was gagged, muffled, shoved into one of his own gestation rigs, and sedated. In other words, he had *no* choice in the matter when he was carted off the planet and onto to the battlecruiser.

And given his history, while Moreau was *on* the *Dominion,* he certainly hadn't discussed his strange connection to any of the senior staff. Moreau *especially* didn't say anything to Hunter about what he knew of Hunter's past.

To state the obvious, Moreau had been part of the original research team that produced the race of genetically engineered clones that came to be colloquially known as the Hunter Look-Alikes. Just as evident, Hunter had been the result of those experiments *decades* before he joined Realm Force. Of course, Hunter had no memory of those years because he had been placed with a Realmer family living in the Night when he was a very young child.

Interestingly, once Hunter achieved a measure of fame in the Realm *and* the Night by joining the *Dominion's* crew as the first Chief Pilot and head of Mechanical Services, Moreau had no trouble identifying Hunter by the physical characteristics that he shared with the rest of the genetically engineered clones.

Indeed, multiple years later, when the senior staff of the *Dominion* found and took control of his genetic research facility on Nu Scorpii One, Moreau found it ironic that one of the genetically engineered clones he had created might have a hand in his demise by removing him from the planet where he had been banished and told to *not to leave.*

Still, those concerns disappeared quickly for Moreau. After Falcon released Moreau to Sotheby's custody nine years ago, Sotheby dosed Moreau with Angel Haze. And, of course, Moreau had fallen madly in love with Sotheby and was delighted to do *anything* that Sotheby asked of him.

And yes, Moreau was the one who had created the genetically engineered hemorrhagic fever virus that raced through the population of the Realm world, Epsilon Virginis Three. Shortly after arriving at the Saturn Shipyards black site, Sotheby supplied Moreau with samples of the hemorrhagic fever virus that attacked the crew of the *HMVR Glory*, many years before. And she told him that she wanted him to make it more infectious and more virulent.

In just months, Moreau succeeded in that task. Nicolescu authorized the release of the virus. As expected, the result was catastrophic for the population of Epsilon Virginis Three. Widespread societal collapse filled the streets with bodies, widespread panic, and violence.

Of course, Moreau had no idea how the virus had been used. And even if someone had told him that his work had contributed to the deaths of so many, Moreau would have only been delighted that he had done as Sotheby had asked.

Unexpectedly, the focus of Moreau's research changed barely a year after that. High King Ruler Ton had come to the black site with one of Ton's special tactical teams. As their first act, the beautiful young women on the team had secured Moreau to a chair. And then everyone waited until the Angel Haze wore off.

And though Moreau had quickly reverted to the haughty, arrogant genius that the senior staff of the *Dominion* had met on Nu Scorpii One, he also instantly recognized that Ton's ascendancy to the ruler of the Realm offered a possibility that would have *never* existed as long as Nicolescu was in charge. Consequently, Moreau quickly changed his tone and did his best to engage Ton in a wide range of topics. Moreau even offered Ton a substantially detailed narrative concerning his past and the things he had accomplished in the Night.

With every word, Moreau had studied Ton's expressions and body posture. Perhaps it had been wishful thinking on Moreau's part, but he had quickly concluded that Ton was not only a man, which made everything more straightforward, but also a moderately intelligent one. And Ton was clearly a man who understood the importance of strategic alliances. After all, Ton had told Moreau that he hadn't dosed his chief technologist, a hacker named PLOKTA, with Angel Haze because he wanted PLOKTA to be clear-minded. And Ton said he wanted PLOKTA's honest opinions as events unfolded across the Realm.

Moreau found himself believing that Ton was hinting at a possible alliance between them. That had led Moreau to open up even more to Ton. And in those exchanges, Moreau had found Ton to be surprisingly close to a kindred spirit.

Obviously, Moreau didn't believe the man was a true genius such as himself. But Ton wholeheartedly agreed that most Realmers were little better than chimp-brained, face-ripping humans that no one would mourn if they were all slaughtered. And Ton had seemed intrigued that Moreau believed that the Wind was the result of some off-book military research and development projects funded by one of the governments before the Coming.

Ton also seemed to give serious consideration to Moreau's assertion that the Disappearance was a precursor to a war that would *annihilate* the vast majority of the human race, allowing the Wind to set up yet *another* experiment in authoritarian rule. Ton had even paused to stare and think for a moment when Moreau had suggested that perhaps it hadn't been the first time that the Wind attempted to reach some goal with humanity, only to purge them all and start over again.

Through it all, Moreau had allowed himself some meager hope that Ton would see the value of allowing him to return to his genetic research without the crippling mental hobble of being on an Angel Haze regimen. Unfortunately, not long after that, Ton had seemed to resign himself to a predetermined conclusion.

Ton had signaled to a member of the special tactical team who had accompanied him. The young woman had swabbed Moreau's nose. And too soon, Moreau was in Ton's thrall.

And then, Ton told Moreau what he wanted Moreau to do. And he told Moreau to do it as quickly as he could without giving himself a mental breakdown.

Barely a year later, Moreau told Ton he believed the first version of the agent was ready for testing. In response, Ton asked Moreau if he could do better. And Moreau had said yes. And Moreau had spent the next year proving that he could, resulting in the development of version two of the agent. And that had led Ton to ask the same question. And Moreau had given Ton the same answer.

By now, Moreau had been working on the same project for three years, working four hours at a time with only a twenty-minute nap in between, around the clock. It was true that the irregular schedule made it more challenging to keep track of the four-hour dosage schedule for Angel Haze because Moreau's work hours continually shifted forward in time. But, of course, Moreau used an automated reminder to tell him when to swab his nostrils with a fresh coat of Angel Haze, ensuring that he continued to do Ton's bidding.

Consequently, year after year, Moreau had remained isolated at the black site with a small group of researchers, all of whom were also on Angel Haze. And none of them had any interest in what might be happening beyond the walls of the black site.

And none of them had any idea that the Night had become a wasteland. And high levels of data traffic on the dark net, which had previously hidden the black site's coded transmissions, had turned to silence. And all that remained on the once-bustling dark web were the occasional cries for help and Moreau's weekly status reports for Jerusalem, which sounded like gibberish but were consistently timed and predictable nonetheless.

•   •   •

In the Rigel star system, over a thousand light-years from the current position of the *Dominion*, the fusion torpedo husk in which Hunter rode flashed into existence as it rocketed through the newly formed curled space funnel. Unfortunately, crossing that link between Epsilon Pegasi Five and Rigel Three required a significantly higher toll on Hunter than transitioning out of a curled space funnel endpoint or hopping through a curled space ring.

Those resulting physical effects weren't entirely unexpected for Hunter. Throughout all the testing of the prior year, Hunter had carefully studied the energy discharges that accompanied any object passing through a *Dominion*-created curled space funnel. And yes, the biometrics of animals passing through other funnels *had* indicated a spike in vitals.

And the *howls* that usually erupted from those animals indeed lent credence to the theory that the transition would be *unpleasant*.

But again, the animals *had* all survived.

Of course, MacDuff had volunteered a dozen times to be the first human test subject in Hunter's stead, given his belief that Hunter *had* to survive. Sadly, MacDuff *still* didn't know *why* Hunter needed to survive, *what* Hunter needed to survive from, or *when* that survival would be critical. But years ago, a *knowing* had appeared in MacDuff's spirit, and MacDuff had been convinced of it ever since, despite some of the senior staff being less accommodating of his belief.

To be clear, Hunter had never heard Oakford mock MacDuff for his conviction or doubt that MacDuff believed what he said he believed. But Hunter wasn't about to let MacDuff box him up or keep him from trying *anything* dangerous. And Hunter was grateful that Oakford understood that life on the battlecruiser *had* to continue despite any crewmember's premonitions, even if they turned out to be true.

Consequently, when Hunter shot across the artificial opening between the space near Epsilon Pegasi Five and Rigel Three, he *expected* some discomfort. But Hunter didn't expect it to be as painful as it was.

Just before reaching the opening, a spike of pain had drilled through Hunter's left eye, slamming it shut, and twisting the left side of his face into a grimace. Frankly, it was intense enough to rattle Hunter's consciousness. And Hunter had felt himself blacking out.

Fortunately, or unfortunately, the actual transition solved that issue. Weirdly enough, everything around Hunter had flashed white in the next instant, *despite* the fact that he was *inside* a fusion torpedo shell and a stealth suit. And then the transition wave slammed into him.

Anyone who had ever entered or exited an endpoint for a curled space funnel had experienced a transition wave. In every case, a tide of energy washed across the body as the person passed in or out of curled space.

The transition wave for the curled space funnel opened by the *Dominion* was far more aggressive. Perhaps it had something to do with the tuning of the transitions between the normal spaces of the Epsilon Pegasi and Rigel systems and the thin slice of curled space in between. No doubt, other sophisticated machinery was needed to coordinate and integrate the intricacies of quantum mechanics in the interactions.

In any case, when the transition wave slammed into Hunter, it felt like the nerve endings across his entire body were passing through a plasma storm. He could even *hear* the sizzle, pop, and crack of what felt like arching electricity dancing across his skin.

Later, Hunter would compare it to the energy discharges during shock-drops. And in the subsequent debriefing in the comfort and safety of Conference Room One on the *Dominion*, the senior staff would discuss the possibility of adding a shield wave generator to the stripped-down fusion torpedo to help mitigate the discomfort.

However, at the present moment, Hunter grunted hard and swore, uttering a single *very* loud epithet.

•   •   •

Also in the Rigel system, racing for Hunter's position in a shuttle, Adi

Bolobolo, Chief Medicalist of the *Dominion*, sat strapped into her five-point harness on a jump seat in the craft's aft airlock. Her thick, muscular frame was wrapped in a black stealth suit with a fully enclosed helmet providing life support. And frankly, she was waiting to be *unhappy* about what the shuttle pilot was about to do to get Hunter into the airlock as quickly as possible.

To be clear, Bolobolo knew from *first-hand* experience that Mallius Grundy was a *skilled* pilot. He had served on the crew of the *Dominion* from the earliest days of its commissioning. Bolobolo even considered Grundy a *friend*. And Bolobolo had enjoyed many group dinners with him and others in the Mess Hall over the years.

Bolobolo just didn't see the *point* of flyboy acrobatics when a simple pickup would suffice. Well, that wasn't true. Bolobolo understood that *whatever* maneuvers Grundy would soon execute would bring the fusion torpedo that carried Hunter into the shuttle's aft airlock in the fastest possible time.

And yes, Bolobolo knew that *was* important. As discussed in the senior staff meeting, it didn't *matter* how many animals had gone through the temporary curled space opening. Those tests *didn't* mean a human could do it unscathed. The sooner Hunter was in a med unit, the better.

On the other hand, Bolobolo didn't have to *like* the upcoming maneuver. The thought of the shuttle twisting and tumbling so that Hunter's fusion torpedo shell could end up in the aft airlock without the shuttle slowing down suggested to Bolobolo yet again that she would probably be *safer* in the passenger area of the craft.

But if she did that, she would have to wait for the airlock to pressurize before giving Hunter a quick visual inspection. And again, there *was* a possibility that those extra few seconds would make a difference.

Deciding she needed to think about something else, Bolobolo glanced to the other side of the airlock to let her eyes rest on MacDuff for a moment. He also wore a stealth suit, complete with helmet and life support system. It wasn't the first time during the shuttle ride that Bolobolo had stolen a look at MacDuff.

Bolobolo *loved* the way MacDuff looked in the shimmering black fabric. And that was excuse enough for Bolobolo to enjoy the view.

Of course, Bolobolo's stealth suit helmet had a heads-up display. And one of the screens on that display was set to the feed of the video camera *inside* MacDuff's helmet. So she had a close-up of his face, just like he had a close-up of hers.

That meant when Bolobolo wanted to exchange a look with MacDuff, she just needed to glance *down* a bit. And he *had* done that here and there. But Bolobolo also knew that MacDuff had seen her look *over* the top of her heads-up display. And she could guess that he figured out that she was doing that because she wanted to enjoy the way he looked in a body-hugging stealth suit.

MacDuff was a bear of a man, tall, broad, and powerful, even if his muscles weren't as precisely defined as Hunter's. Many years ago, Bolobolo had started openly flirting with MacDuff because she had found that it amused Catherine Casteel, the *Dominion's* first Chief Medical Officer. At the time, Casteel *needed* cheering up.

Interestingly, what Bolobolo had begun on a lark had quickly deepened into more. Before the teasing, Bolobolo hadn't stared at MacDuff for any length of time, even though they had been on the ship together for *years* before that. But the more she locked eyes with him and pretended to flirt, the more she let her eyes wander over his broad chest, thick arms, and powerful thighs, and the more Bolobolo realized she wouldn't have *any* difficulty saying everything she had been saying to MacDuff and *mean* it.

And yes, MacDuff was the one man on the *Dominion* who could make Bolobolo look dainty. But Bolobolo had never been concerned about looking dainty. She had grown up on Fomalhaut Four, a rugged planet settled by those who traced their lineage back to the Fijians on Earth. All of Bolobolo's people were tall, strong, and muscular.

And that made MacDuff feel like *home*.

Unfortunately, as far as Bolobolo was concerned, MacDuff had his convictions. And first and foremost, he believed that he had a role to play in Hunter's protection.

And though Bolobolo and MacDuff had become *very* close friends during their time on the *Dominion*, MacDuff had been clear that their relationship *couldn't* be more. MacDuff believed that if a man joined himself to a woman, that woman needed to become his *first* priority. And MacDuff had said that Bolobolo *couldn't* be his first priority because of the certainty he held over his role in Hunter's life.

Bolobolo wasn't fond of that line of thought. But she loved MacDuff enough to respect *him* for being honest with her. And that meant she enjoyed the long walks they often took in the Main Hall on Upper Deck 1 of the

Dominion. And she enjoyed every conversation, even if it was just as friends.

On the other hand, Bolobolo had no qualms about gently pushing the issue of deepening their relationship. Nor was she hesitant to find ways to remind him that if he ever changed his mind, she was waiting.

And for the record, Bolobolo would *keep* waiting because she couldn't imagine dedicating her life to anyone else.

And yes, Bolobolo understood that parts of those conversations about their relationship made MacDuff uncomfortable. And she understood that he was gentle enough and kindhearted enough to want to please her. Even better, just a few years before, Bolobolo told MacDuff how much she loved him and apologized for how that love leaked into her words and behavior. And in response, MacDuff had admitted that he *adored* her. And he had said that he couldn't imagine any woman with whom he could build a more magnificent life.

MacDuff had even borrowed a phrase from the Psalms and said that if they were together and blessed with a family, he had no doubt their sons would be as strong as mighty oaks and their daughters like graceful pillars carved to beautify a palace.

Those words had melted Bolobolo's knees. And she had bent over and grabbed them with her hands to keep herself from swooning. Frankly, a part of Bolobolo wanted to *punch* MacDuff at that moment for the way he seemed to be taunting her.

But she *knew* he was only being honest. And once she recovered from his revelation, she loved him all the more.

And in the present, those facts made MacDuff the counterbalance to the coming experience. Bolobolo *wasn't* looking forward to the tumble-over slide-by that Grundy was about to execute the shuttle. But earlier, she had been able to waltz up the aft airlock, knowing MacDuff was close behind, knowing that *perhaps* he was even stealing a glance or two at her well-defined, stealth-suit-clad posterior. Even better, for the last half-hour, Bolobolo had sat in close quarters with MacDuff directly across from her in the aft airlock as Grundy had headed for the nearest curled space ring, made the hop, and then headed for the rendezvous with the fusion torpedo that encased Hunter.

And, of course, they had talked. And all of it made it worth the tension of the next few minutes.

Now, Bolobolo saw a 3D graphic appear on one of the screens on her heads-up display. She knew Murg had installed the data visualizer in the comm and sensor subsystem to give everyone onboard the shuttle a better perspective on what was *about* to happen *as* it happened.

As expected, a comm chirped open from Grundy in the cockpit.

"Initiating emergency open of aft airlock," he called out, followed quickly by a confirmation of the beginning of the tumble-over. "Kicking the back end."

Bolobolo knew the gravity generators built into the shuttle's decking were *supposed* to compensate for sudden movements. But they couldn't wholly overcome the shudder that seized Bolobolo a moment later because it still felt like something had just slammed into the underside of the shuttle's rear end and flipped it forward.

With her whole body lurching, Bolobolo fixed her eyes on the 3D graphic on her heads-up display. And at the same time, she tried to use the visuals to convince herself that everything was unfolding as it should.

Also, while Bolobolo didn't notice at first the snapping open of the aft airlock created a near instant exchange of air with the vacuum of space. And that turned everything around her silent. And now she remembered how surreal that sudden quiet always felt.

Bolobolo had *no* exposure to the silent movies of the Pre-Coming entertainment industry. And yes, the moviegoers of *that* day *marveled* at the new technology of those silent moving pictures. But everyone who had ever seen *any* type of visual recording *with* sound always found silent pictures surreal.

And once Bolobolo realized that the only sounds she now heard were the soft chirps coming from Grundy's console as he piloting the shuttle in the cockpit and a hint of MacDuff's slow and steady breathing, she glanced around the aft airlock. And almost immediately, a conflict of sensations rolled over her.

On one hand, everything Bolobolo saw felt like a vivid dream. She knew it was real, but it had a dreamlike quality nonetheless. And perhaps, it even had a hint of a nightmare. Without sound to accompany what Bolobolo saw, everything seemed ephemeral, disconnected, and flat, as if it could fold up and disappear in the next instant because she had been startled awake.

On the other hand, the view out the back showed a churn of stars. And while the gravity generators in the decking *weren't* alleviating all the sensations of movement, they had fixed Bolobolo to her jump seat enough to create dissonance between what her eyes saw and what her inner ears felt. And that was enough to send a gentle wave of nausea wafting across her body.

Worse, the view out of the open aft airlock of the shuttle looked *chaotic*. Intellectually, Bolobolo understood that it was *supposed* to look that way because the shuttle was not only flipping end over end but also twisting to slide through a spin.

Still, between that and the light wave of nausea, Bolobolo completely forgot to refocus on the graphics that Murg had provided because she couldn't take her eyes off the open airlock. And maybe if she *had* kept her eyes on the graphics, it would have helped. But without a doubt, staring at the open airlock was the worst place for Bolobolo to focus her attention in the next moment.

For in *that* moment, Hunter's fusion torpedo shell came arcing through the careening starfield. At first, Bolobolo couldn't imagine *how* the torpedo shell would *ever* end up in the airlock. But everything kept twisting and spinning. And the more it did, the more the airlock and the torpedo shell seemed to be magically aligning.

And then, suddenly, a side panel on the fusion torpedo shell exploded, sending sparks showering into space. And it threw the shell into a tumble.

Fortunately, the fusion torpedo shell was close enough that is still looked like it would reach the airlock. But then, just as the front end of the torpedo shell nudged through the open hatches of the aft airlock, a side panel on the *other* side of the casing blew out as well, showering the inside of the airlock with sparks.

3.

Slamming into the side of the shuttle's airlock, the fusion torpedo shell that carried Hunter cracked open on top, sending more sparks spraying outward. Simultaneously, seeing that the torpedo was scraping along the wall on her side of the airlock, Bolobolo released her five-point harness and dove for the opposite wall even as MacDuff released his harness to dive across the airlock in the opposite direction. And grabbing the stripped-down fusion torpedo, MacDuff tackled it, wrestling it to the ground as the shell continued to spark and sputter.

Now turning, Bolobolo scrambled back to the torpedo to grab the latches that the Mechanical Services crew had installed in case of an emergency. Quickly, she wrenched them open and pulled the hatch loose before spinning to chuck the hatch out of the open airlock.

Thankfully, even before she could fully turn back toward MacDuff, Hunter was already pulling himself out of what was left of the fusion torpedo.

"*Clear*," Hunter called out over the open team comm, as he rolled away.

And that was MacDuff's cue to yank the damaged fusion torpedo off the airlock wall before twisting hard to pitch it out of the open hatches of the aft airlock, sparking as it went.

"*Clear*," MacDuff also shouted as his momentum tumbled him onto his back.

Of course, all of it happened in a matter of seconds. And none of it was rehearsed. Each person simply knew where they fit in accomplishing the known goal. It didn't matter that the fusion torpedo shell had more than one apparent malfunction. The goal remained. And if for some reason, Hunter hadn't been able to extract himself from the fusion torpedo tube, Bolobolo would have shifted into that task as well.

The senior staff had worked together for so many years they could effortlessly predict what each would do in most situations and who would likely be best suited to any series of tasks.

Of course, the vacuum in the aft airlock of the shuttle continued to give the scene a surreal cadence. While the stealth suits that Hunter, MacDuff, and Bolobolo wore had been joined to a team comm with Grundy in the shuttle cockpit, no one had made any small talk during the maneuver to give Grundy a chance to focus as he put the shuttle through its gyrations.

Under optimal conditions, the fusion torpedo shell would have gently dropped onto the decking as Grundy banked the shuttle toward Rigel Three's curled space ring. Then, MacDuff and Bolobolo would have pull Hunter out.

The evident failures of the stripped-down fusion torpedo altered that plan, introducing an unexpected element that was *potentially* hazardous. However, the senior staff had discussed the probability of the fusion torpedo shell exploding. Consequently, the fuel allocated to the fusion torpedo was carefully measured and matched to the need. And, *everyone* on the mission wore stealth suits to minimize the physical risk in case something went wrong.

Still, the vacuum in the airlock and its accompanying silence heightened the feeling of unease in Bolobolo due to the abundance of sparks. And the fact that sparks had no hiss, crack, or spit made everything stranger and more unexpected. And perhaps that might have distracted less-disciplined or less-experienced crew members.

But now that Hunter was out of the fusion torpedo shell and the malfunctioning shell had been tossed back into space, Bolobolo knew what came next even as she heard Grundy announcing the fact that he had executed *his* next task.

"Closing airlock and repressurizing."

Turning for a wall mounted control panel, Bolobolo entered an access code. A side panel opened, exposing an emergency medical unit. And working quickly, Bolobolo pulled out the med unit, popped it up to waist height, and lifted the lid.

"Strip!" Bolobolo commanded as she turned back to Hunter.

Before the mission, the senior staff had agreed that, regardless of how Hunter felt, he would enter an emergency medical unit for a full-body examination immediately after retrieval. Surprisingly enough, Hunter didn't protest. He tapped the side of his neck. His helmet came loose. At the same time, his black stealth suit split apart and fell away, tumbling into small piles as Hunter made his way to the med unit.

Bolobolo could see that Hunter's gait was weaker than it should have been. Granted, Bolobolo had seen Hunter far worse. Shortly after the senior staff's exile to the Night, Hunter had assigned himself to a series of solo missions. His sole strategy was to allow his enemies to tear him to pieces before counterattacking with shock and awe and rattling them into answering his angry questions.

At the time, Bolobolo hadn't known that Hunter was genetically engineered with additional biological systems that helped him endure extreme physical torture. So, surviving those sessions always seemed *miraculous*.

Conversely, at *present*, Hunter's gloriously sculpted physique showed *no* signs of damage. And, for the record, Bolobolo *had* visually checked him from head to two, *twice*, just to be sure. But still, his gait was off.

"How are you feeling, Zach?" Bolobolo asked, still encased in her stealth suit, not thinking about the state of the atmosphere in the airlock or the fact Hunter no longer wore a stealth suit with its comms.

Thankfully, the ever-increasing air pressure was able to carry the sound from the amplifiers on the outside of Bolobolo's stealth suit. And Hunter quickly glanced at her, giving her a weary smile as he continued to head for the med unit.

"That hop is not for the faint of heart," Hunter said softly.

Bolobolo wanted to ask more. But she knew that if something *was* physically wrong with Hunter, the best "immediate next," as MacDuff would say, was to get Hunter into an emergency medical unit. Consequently, Bolobolo simply nodded and waited for Hunter to position himself on the outstretched tray before she slid it back inside the emergency medical unit. Then, she closed the lid and entered a start command on the external display.

•　　　•　　　•

On Earth, in Jerusalem, in his office in the administrative headquarters for the Leadership Council, Ton continued his weekly review with PLOKTA, the de facto Chief Technology Officer of Realm Force. Interestingly, not many understood that PLOKTA held that role. But as far as Ton was concerned, PLOKTA's hacking of a vast array of the Realm's comm and processing systems proved he *deserved* the title.

Single-handedly, over the years, PLOKTA had figured out how to infiltrate *every* element of the lives of Realmers *everywhere* across the Realm. He could spy on anyone. He could control everything they saw. He could suppress or enhance any story on the social net.

And that meant, for an ignominious heretofore incognito emperor like Ton, PLOKTA was *invaluable*.

But more than that, PLOKTA was *the* reason Ton was the High King Ruler of the Realm, even if the vast majority of Realmers had no clue it was true.

Just a few years before, Nicolescu had held the same secret position of power as Ton did now, firmly in control of the Realm through a variety of hidden mechanisms. Those areas of control included Ton, and in his case, the control came mainly from the threat of being dosed with Angel Haze and being turned into a puppet in Sotheby's thrall.

The fact that Ton knew he would be Sotheby's puppet had made the threat more foreboding. Ton knew how *horrifying* his existence would have become if *that* happened. Sotheby *hated* men. And she especially hated Ton. And Ton knew that once he was in her thrall, she would do *everything* she could to destroy his mind, soul, and any vestige of masculinity that he possessed. *Indeed*, at one point, Sotheby *had* done just that.

PLOKTA was the *only* reason Ton wasn't in the precise situation that he abhorred even now. Indeed, three years before, Ton had already been dressed and bound in an emasculating combination of lingerie, high heels, and ropes and then dosed with Angel Haze. And Sotheby had already programmed to descend into a full-blown, screaming panic attack with a short verbal command. Sotheby had even spitefully included the suggestion that he piss himself during that terror. And under the influence of Angel Haze, Ton had been happy to do so to please his new master.

All of it *would* have been Ton's existence from that day forward. But PLOKTA had intervened, knocking out Nicolescu, Sotheby, and two full special tactical teams with tranquilizer darts. Then, PLOKTA offered Ton the opportunity to rule the Realm, and Ton greedily accepted.

Ever since, Ton and PLOKTA had held weekly status and planning meetings. And Ton considered PLOKTA a genuine partner in everything he intended to do to the Realm and its citizens, just as he considered PLOKTA a partner in everything he considered doing in matters *beyond* the Realm, like the elimination of all potential threats *against* the Realm.

Interestingly enough, in one particular case, the threat was *already* under Ton's control. But the man was simply too dangerous to leave alive. On the other hand, the man had other connections that might allow Ton to kill the proverbial two birds with one stone.

"From his latest report," Ton began with a sly smile, "I see our good Doctor Moreau is perfecting another version of the last virus we asked him to create. He seems to think that he has created the fabled trifecta for a population-extinction event. He's claiming 100% lethality, an R16 infection rate, and the impossibility of detection."

Over the video comm from his lair at the Saturn Shipyards, PLOKTA offered Ton a slight shrug. "I thought the hemorrhagic fever virus Moreau engineered for the attack on Epsilon Virginis Three was pretty impressive, but of course, it wasn't limited to individuals with a specific genetic signature."

"Indeed," Ton agreed. "And I think that just proves my point that men like Moreau cannot be allowed to live. Since before the Coming, I've held the conviction that there are specific individuals who possess the power to wreak such havoc that the *only* counterbalance to them is the existence of others of sufficient power and wisdom to reach the necessary decisions and carry out the needed *executions* outside the jurisdiction of any governmental system.

"Indeed, in this very area of expertise, the world prior to the Coming was subjected to genetically engineered viruses that cost *millions* of lives simply because there were those who wanted to *play* and experiment to see what monsters they might create. If we *ever* lost control of Moreau's abilities, he could reach out with those same capabilities and wreak havoc on us. So he needs to go, but we obviously have an opportunity to do more. And to that end, what are your projections for the noise that Moreau's progress reports are causing on the dark net?"

PLOKTA smiled. "I can't imagine that anyone still alive in the Night with any technical expertise *wouldn't* be aware of his transmissions by now."

Ton nodded. "Good," he offered with a smile. "And the additional preparations to hide our involvement in any of his research?"

"All the documentation has been scrubbed and redirected," PLOKTA assured him. "There is *no* trace that Realm Force or the Saturn Shipyard had *any* connection to the underground lab. As discussed, we have created multiple references in the data to focus attention elsewhere."

"Excellent," he congratulated. "And in predicting our success in the matter, I would only say, '*Never* underestimate the power of confirming your enemy's suspicions if that allows you to gain an advantage.'"

Now, Ton grinned at his own cleverness before ending the meeting.

"Ton out," he added nonchalantly.

•   •   •

Three cycles later, on the *Dominion*, in Conference Room One, Oakford began the debriefing for the last test of the point-to-point curled space hop now that Hunter had emerged from the emergency medical unit.

"How are you feeling, Zach?" Oakford began, his voice tinged with concern.

"The med unit worked its magic," Hunter commented. "As far as I can tell, I'm 100 percent."

"Good," Oakford replied before turning to Bolobolo. "Adi, any additional information beyond the initial diagnosis?"

Bolobolo shook her head. "As discussed," she began, "the med unit reported that Zach experienced an aneurysm in the left anterior communicating artery, close to the optic nerve. I've doen additional research since the initial identification by the medical unit. There are interesting phrases that others have used to describe what it's like.

"Some called it a thunderclap headache. Many say it was the worst headache of their lives. 'Knife-like pain' was often used, along with 'white-hot spear of pain.' Others talked about their vision tilting sideways and a sudden roaring in their ears."

Hunter nodded. "Yup!" he added.

Bolobolo gave Hunter a confused look. "When I asked you how you were feeling, all you said was the hop wasn't for the faint of heart," she recalled, her eyebrows arching with apparent irritation.

Hunter grinned and gave Bolobolo a slight shrug. "I was headed for the med unit at that point," he observed. "Didn't see the need for any further chit-chat. Just wanted to climb in and wake up well."

Oakford glanced at Bolobolo. He knew Hunter was simply stating facts. But over the last year, Oakford had also had multiple conversations with Bolobolo regarding a topic that Falcon had dug up after everyone else was content to bury it. And Oakford wondered if Hunter's statement would tweak Bolobolo's ongoing frustration with Falcon's pestering.

As most knew, Casteel was the *Dominion's* first Chief Medical Officer, and Bolobolo was her second-in-command. But *before* joining Realm Force. Casteel had also spent fifty years learning to harness the power of her mind with a group of Realmers on an outpost that orbited a Nightside planet called K-22B. Indeed, Casteel spent her first years serving on the *Dominion* before circumstances forced her to reveal her secret that she could heal supernaturally with her mind. And in the years that followed that revelation, both Casteel and the senior staff learned that she could do *far* more than that.

Sadly, Nicolescu eventually became so fearful of Casteel's power that she tried to capture and control her. Casteel knew she couldn't let that happen. And when Nicolescu sent tactical teams to the Casteel family estate on Alpha Centauri Three, Casteel sacrificed herself to keep both her family and the crew of the *Dominion* safe.

Bolobolo had grieved for *years* following Casteel's death. A part of her *still* grieved. In fact, Bolobolo continued to hold a small vigil on the anniversary of Casteel's death over fifteen years before. And in recent years, Falcon had even begun joining Bolobolo in her office in the Sickbay for moments of silence to celebrate Casteel's life.

And then, last year, after the moments of silence and the grieving that followed, Falcon had brought up the subject that the senior staff had been content to intentionally ignore.

Falcon had told Bolobolo that she believed it was *essential* for Bolobolo to learn to heal supernaturally with her mind. Bolobolo hadn't appreciated the suggestion. And she had reminded Falcon that she had *tried* to learn to do what Casteel could do, and she had *never* made any progress in that area.

A tense conversation followed. And Falcon later admitted to Oakford that she knew what she had done was unfair to Bolobolo. But Falcon also insisted that it was necessary. She said she believed that the events swirling about the *Dominion* were leading to a nexus. And there would soon come a time when someone with Casteel's abilities on board the battlecruiser could be *the* factor that resulted in either the survival of the *Dominion* or its destruction.

The problem had *always* been that *no one* knew how Casteel did what she did. And even Casteel could only offer what seemed to be little more than platitudes. She had said meditation was necessary. She had said it was essential to clear the mind.

Unfortunately, for all the guided sessions that Casteel had hosted for the tactical teams of the *Dominion*, only *one* tactical team member, named Jochen Nibbelink, had broken through into the Now to demonstrate a supernatural ability. Indeed, Nibbelink had saved his fellow crewmembers, including Casteel and Bolobolo, from an attack during a "lightstorm" on Beta Tauri Five in a city called Isaac's Remembrance. And afterward, Nibbelink had leapt into one of the incinerating beams of that storm.

In a debriefing after that mission, MacDuff described what he had seen to Oakford, who was at the Saturn Shipyards overseeing the repairs on the *Dominion*. And MacDuff had told Oakford that he firmly believed Nibbelink had transitioned into the Now during those last moments and found a way to continually heal himself as he protected the team.

But Nibbelink was the *only* one on the tactical teams who had accomplished that.

And yes, Hunter had switched into demi-god mode when the Hunter Look-Alikes had attempted to execute him for daring to believe that Casteel could heal.

But that was that. Everyone on the crew had *seen* what Casteel could do. No one else, including Bolobolo, had ever even gotten *close* to manifesting the supernatural at will. And as far as Oakford was concerned, that meant Falcon *insisting* that Bolobolo learn to heal with her mind wasn't just *unfair*, it was *cruel*.

Oakford *had* contacted Bolobolo in the weeks following Falcon's disclosure about their conversation. And he had emphasized how important he thought Bolobolo's presence was on the ship. He had stressed to her that he couldn't be more grateful for the work that she did leading the Medical Services team. And he told her that he absolutely *didn't* believe that a single metric could measure her value to the Dominion.

Indeed, Oakford had made a point of having that same conversation with Bolobolo *multiple* times over the last year. And maybe that meant Oakford was sensitive to *anything* in a conversation that might make Bolobolo think that Casteel would have handled a situation differently. And maybe the situation with Hunter emerging from the fusion torpedo shell qualified.

Still, Oakford *didn't* believe that Hunter *hadn't* told Bolobolo about the pain he was experiencing because he thought she was irrelevant because she *couldn't* heal him. But the fact was, if Casteel had been in the airlock, she would have *known* that Hunter was injured because she would have *seen* it. And she would have stretched out her hands and healed him. And Hunter wouldn't have *needed* to spend three cycles in an emergency medical unit because everything would be back to normal in less than a minute.

Thankfully, from what Oakford could tell, Bolobolo didn't seem offended by what Hunter had said. And neither did she seem offended by what Hunter *hadn't* said, and probably didn't even *imply*. Instead, Bolobolo stated what she felt were the apparent *facts*.

"I would remind you, Chief Hunter," Bolobolo began, her voice taking on a wry tone. "That it is my job to be the Chief Worrier about the crew's health. Given that, if I ask you directly for a general assessment of your physical state, I would appreciate a non-obfuscated answer, especially if you are experiencing a thunderclap headache that manifests as white-hot spears of pain. Granted, I may not be able to *do* anything about it beyond helping you into the med unit, but at least I'll be able to do that with a better understanding and a full-blown anxiety-ridden focus."

And then Bolobolo smiled. And Hunter smiled back and nodded.

"Understood, chief" he said. "My apologies."

"Accepted," Bolobolo responded.

Oakford hopped back into the conversation. "Do we have any guess why Hunter experienced a stroke when all the animals we sent through seem to arrive unscathed?"

Bolobolo shook her head, but Falcon soon attempted an explanation.

"Might be the cousin of a neutrino error," Falcon observed.

"ACK," Murg unexpectedly added.

Oakford frowned. Falcon explained.

"To be clear," Falcon continued, "calling it a neutrino error is a misnomer. Neutrinos are massless, so they are unlikely to be the culprits, but it is the accepted jargon. A better phrase might be that it was a high-energy neutron error. There are anecdotes before the Coming about strange events, odd changes in electronic games and computer processing systems that don't seem to have any explanation.

"Pacemaker data would suddenly become corrupt. Planes would fall hundreds of feet through the sky before the pilots regain control. There was a story in 2003 of the Common Era concerning an election in Brussels, a city in Europe, where the count was off by 4,096 votes, a discrepancy that was traced to a single voting machine. As you all know, 4,096 is a power of two, so you would only need to flip a single bit to add that many votes.

"All those instances illustrate something that changed in a processing system suddenly, seemingly without a cause. And many believed that a high-energy particle, such as a neutron, was responsible after randomly hitting an integrated circuit at just the right angle in the right place.

"Seems likely that tearing open a hole in space and creating tightly packed layers of normal and curled space might create a whole *host* of energetic particles, setting up a multi-barreled game of Russian roulette. Perhaps we just pulled the trigger at the wrong time when Hunter went through our version of a curled space funnel."

Oakford scowled. "I *definitely* don't like the sound of that," he said. "If it's a completely random event, how do we protect against it? Can we add a shield wave generator to the fusion torpedo shell? Would that help?"

"Maybe," Hunter offered. "But when we use the shield wave generators in shock-drops, we tune them to specific frequencies that were presumably chosen after some form of testing. If we use point-to-point hops, we probably won't be able to determine a specific frequency since it will likely change each time. Still, I can work with my team to put something together and then set up tests to measure the overall radiation levels inside the pods when they hit the hop, and then compare those levels to a pod without a shield wave generator. It won't be an exact measurement because we're presumably looking at a high-energy particle that did the damage, and those are much more powerful than background radiation. But at least it could give us a way to calculate an estimate."

Oakford nodded. "Agreed," he said. "The post-mission summary indicated that Pilot Grundy doubled back to pick up the fusion torpedo shell debris after Adi confirmed the med unit had begun treating Zach's injuries. Have we learned anything from examining that debris?"

Hunter answered. "The engineers found a line of sporadic damage through the pod," he said. "If we knew exactly when that happened, we could check the timestamps on the video, isolate my head position at that moment, and see if the damage I suffered aligns with the same vector. And maybe that's a one-in-a-million occurrence. Perhaps I've had my one strike, so I don't need to worry about it anymore. Or, maybe, the curled space gods don't like us doing this, and *whenever* anyone attempts it, the gods will ensure that the pilot of the pod suffers the equivalent of a stroke."

Oakford shook his head. "Let's hope it's the former."

4.

On the *Dominion*, somewhere unknown, Crewmember Iniibig Kita jolted awake inside an emergency medical unit. And immediately, *understandably*, Kita could guess that whatever had just happened to him in the time he was unconscious was *bad*. After all, for the past four years, it had almost *always* been bad when he woke up inside a med unit.

Consistently, those awakenings had meant that the Pixie had devised another way to experiment on him. And though the Pixie was always claiming that what she was doing to him was for his *good*, Kita knew that the Pixie was actually using him as a kind of lab rat to test his psychological, emotional, and physical limits.

It all started when Jazarah Worku returned to the *Dominion*. There was enough buzz around the crew regarding Worku that it had been easy for Kita to put together the woman's story. Originally, Worku had been part of the 140+ women rescued from the gestation rigs in Moreau's secret genetic research facility on Nu Scorpii One.

For a time, she had served under Hunter as a Hellfire Interceptor pilot. However, Worku had become a wild child to survive growing up in the Night, and she had some trouble with the crew. Ultimately, Worku had found life on the *Dominion* too restrictive. A few years after joining the crew, she took a job working for the king of K2-72e. Apparently, Worku did so mainly because K2-72e's sole export was an extremely expensive cloth called Rexian Sheer.

Not long after, Worku had stolen a bolt of the sheer fabric and fled. The authorities later recovered that bolt on K2-72e, but Worku herself escaped.

Eventually, Worku was rescued from Gamma Pegasi D where it looked like she had been physically abused and abandoned. At that point, the senior staff gave Worku the benefit of the doubt and invited her to stay on the battlecruiser as she recovered.

And *that* was when Kita's trouble with the Pixie had begun. Interestingly, Kita had his own three-part history with the *Dominion*. He too had served, left, and returned. Kita was on the crew of the *Dominion* when it was still part of Realm Force. In time, the ship was damaged, and the crew was evacuated by the *Power*. Later, in the Main Hall of the *Power*, Kita watched with disinterest as the senior staff of the *Dominion* gave the orders for the damaged battlecruiser to self-destruct.

Frankly, Kita had become bored with it all. He didn't see Oakford as a real leader. Falcon had been interesting to have as a lead commander, but by that point, she was long gone. Yes, she had returned for the mission to the secondary Marauder keep, but then she had left again.

For Kita, everything just seemed chaotic, and he was ready to return to the Realm.

Within a week, the senior staff of the *Dominion* had fled into the Night. And the rest of the crew were dispersed to assignments all over the Realm. Kita wasn't *happy* about it because there had been a certain status to serving on the battlecruiser. But at least it was easier to work on do-nothing assignments and use his history to try to impress the women around him.

Only *much* later did Kita and the former crewmembers learn that the *Dominion* hadn't been destroyed, and that Murg had *faked* it.

Initially, when Kita heard rumors that a group of crewmembers were going to try to rejoin the crew, he had *zero* interest in the idea. However, Sotheby had contacted him and persuaded him to do it. After all, Sotheby was beautiful, and some part of Kita thought that after he finished the assignment, maybe she would want to have dinner with him.

Maybe Kita should have thought twice about pitting himself against the fabled senior staff of the *Dominion*. Perhaps he should have wondered if he really could convince them that he was a loyal member of the crew. Most importantly, if Kita had known more about the Pixie, he might have realized it would be lunacy to be something he wasn't with Murg's artificial intelligence experiment *constantly* watching.

Of course, the Pixie had spotted the difference in Kita's attitude about being back on the battlecruiser compared with almost all of the other returning crewmembers. In other words, Kita *hadn't* fooled the Pixie.

That was his *first* ridiculous mistake. But Kita hadn't stopped there.

And when Worku returned to the *Dominion*, Kita quickly became *infatuated* with her. She was an attractive woman, to begin with. But the fact that she seemed to be mentally compromised tweaked Kita's interest even more. He guessed she would be easier to get into compromising positions. Then, over the course of a week, he became *obsessed* with Worku, fantasizing about spending time alone with her and what he might do to her if he had the chance.

By that point, Kita had logged two *foolish* decisions. Not only had he thought he was clever enough to be a spy on the *Dominion* without anyone discovering it, but he had also concluded that he was so valuable as a man that he could impose his will on a female Nightling that he happened to fancy, and she would let him do whatever he wanted to her.

And then, Kita made the worst decision of his life.

Kita convinced himself that he could *trick* the Pixie into helping him because he knew he *needed* the Pixie's assistance to get time alone with Worku without anyone knowing. And Kita was able to convince himself of that fact because he believed, without question, that he was smarter than the Pixie, and he could outthink the Pixie no matter what the circumstance.

The Pixie found Kita's attitude insulting. And since it had already concluded that Kita was one of *five* spies sent by Sotheby to infiltrate the *Dominion*, the Pixie decided to teach Kita a lesson, knowing that he wouldn't appeal to the senior staff for help. And beyond that, the Pixie decided to use him and the other spies that Sotheby had sent to the *Dominion* to experiment with new roles for humans on the battlecruiser.

Ever since, the Pixie had treated Kita like a toy. The Pixie had forced Kita to watch countless *hours* of porn to program him to behave in specific ways. It had tattooed Kita with all manner of embarrassing labels to see what affected him most before removing them in a med unit and studying Kita's great relief.

And then, the Pixie began modifying Kita's body.

It replaced his heart with a mechanical pump. It replaced his lungs with an oxygenator that forced him to press his fingers together to route air over his vocal cords and speak. It removed his digestive tract and replaced it with a flexible membrane that processed starter meal pellets.

Worst of all, last year, the Pixie relocated Kita's sperm-producing reproductive organs *inside* his body and claimed that it had also created an external attachment he could use if the need arose for him to impregnate anyone. And then, the Pixie had nonchalantly added that it had removed his natural mechanism for delivering sperm because it was no longer connected to his gamete-producing organs and, therefore, worthless.

Kita knew that the Pixie had studied his reaction to that as well.

Also, last year, the Pixie had orchestrated a scenario in which Kita and another of Sotheby's spies, a female, were taken to a lair on Lower Deck 3. Unknown to Kita at the time, the senior staff had created that lair to house some of the human-animal hybrids, called catamountus, that Moreau had created in his genetic research facility on Nu Scorpii One.

At one point, the Pixie had forced Kita and the other female spy to watch as the catamountus greedily devoured the body parts that had been taken from them. And in the end, Kita abandoned the woman to be devoured by the beasts as he sprinted away.

That cowardice had almost destroyed Kita mentally and emotionally. And while Kita had already reached the point where he wanted the darkness to swallow him and send his life into whatever abyss existed in the afterlife, the incident in the catamountus lair had convinced him of the disgusting meaninglessness of life and his own utter depravity.

Many times over the past year, Kita considered killing himself. But he could guess that the Pixie wouldn't *let* him. And then, surprisingly enough, the Pixie seemed to lose interest in him. For weeks at a time, the Pixie didn't even speak to him. And while *every* day during those months, Kita had awakened wondering when his torture would return, it *had* been quiet enough for long enough that Kita had *almost* begun to hope that the Pixie had found others to torment.

But now, he had just bolted awake in an emergency medical unit. And he immediately knew that was *bad*.

Still, Kita took a moment to try to convince himself he *wasn't* in a med unit. And then he tried to convince himself that he didn't *care* what the Pixie had done to him. And then he told himself that he *didn't* want to know. And he tried to tell himself that there was no *point* in knowing because he couldn't do anything about it, so he should just *lie* there and *try* not to think about *anything*.

But, of course, Kita *had* to know. And, like always, he began thinking about the different areas of his body, trying to figure out if anything *felt* different. That, in itself, was more difficult than Kita might have guessed just a few years before.

Like most Realmers, Kita had been fit and healthy. He had taken his body for granted. It was his to command, and he had enough testosterone in his system to generate a raw confidence in his ability to succeed at *anything* he attempted.

The Pixie's tortures had stripped Kita of all of that. And Kita became aware of the terrible silence within him once all that he had *never* realized he heard could no longer *be* heard. Likewise, he had only become aware of what he could no longer *feel* once he could no longer feel it.

Once the Pixie removed his heart, lungs, and entire digestive tract, it felt like the sensations of life were *gone*. There was no subtle and comforting thump in his chest. The rhythm of air moving in and out of his lungs had disappeared. And the strange gurglings of his abdomen that had sometimes embarrassed him had ceased.

That lack made Kita feel inhuman and even zombie-like and undead.

And yes, the worst of it had been when the Pixie removed or tucked away those things that fundamentally removed Kita's identification as a man. For the past year, Kita had lived with the fact that the lower portion of his abdomen smoothly transitioned into the space between his legs with *no* sign of being able to function as male or female reproductively.

Kita had never been able to reconcile his mind with that loss. And even now, he often forgot. And he would have phantom sensations that he *hadn't* been mutilated, and he would wake up and check and find that nothing had been restored. And a fresh spike of grief would stab him once more.

In large part, that was the reason that a part of Kita had believed the Pixie when it teased that it might put everything back at some point in the future. But in the catamountus lair, Kita had watched the Pixie's bot feed *all* of his excised organs to the human-animal hybrids. And Kita had heard those organs chewed, torn, and hungrily devoured.

Indeed, at that moment, Kita felt the finality of knowing that for the rest of his life, he would only be a husk of a human, hollow, an emasculated plaything for a malevolent, ruthless, soulless machine.

Still, the *first* thing that Kita noticed after having jolted awake in the emergency medical unit was how strangely solid he felt in his upper torso. But before Kita could think *much* about that, the lid of the med unit clicked open and lifted enough for him to see that he was in one of the *Dominion's* many storage bays.

And *then*, he heard the voice of the Pixie *within* him.

But it wasn't like he usually heard the Pixie with its voice emanating from audio emitters all around him. And it wasn't like he was wearing some comm where the voice hovered in his head between his ears. Now, the Pixie's voice seemed to come from the center of his chest. And he could feel the sound of it vibrating his entire ribcage and backbone and rattling in the bottom of his skull.

"*Finally*," the Pixie began, sounding miffed, even though Kita was well aware that the Pixie had been in complete control of his sedation. "I thought you were *never* going to wake up! Obviously, I haven't had time to play with you much in the last year, my little Bitch Bot Three, but I *have* been thinking about you and how I could continue my little devious plan to turn you into a humiliated, emasculated, empty slave. After all, when you returned to the Dominion, you were such an arrogant *bastard* that it seems only fitting that I push you as *far* as I can in the opposite direction.

"Honestly, I think I've done a fantastic job so far with your conversion to a castrato servant who knows his place and will do whatever I tell him to do. But I must tell you that after the mission to the Troyd homeworld last year, I had an idea that I *couldn't* ignore.

"The senior staff opted to share only a basic summary of the events during that mission. They *did* tell the crew about Murg's meeting with the Troyd and the fact that he presented his experiences over the last three decades with them. But the senior decided *not* to share *my* presentation to the Troyd. They merely mentioned that I told the Troyd that I had deduced that they were responsible for the creation of the Mechs. And, of course, that made the Troyd *very* mad.

"Before that, though, I tried to offer something important to the Troyd, and they *ignored* my advice. I tried to help them see that their abhorrence for all things biological was misplaced. I informed them that I had conducted a series of experiments over the last three years. And I told them that I had demonstrated that I could replace *all* of the slimy, smelly, gross, and grotesque parts of the human physique with equivalents that are easy to clean, smooth, and pleasant. And I told them I could do so in a manner that retains the human brain and spinal column, and, therefore, leaves open the possibility of achieving the spectacular abilities that Catherine Casteel demonstrated.

"Of course, they didn't listen. And while I do not know what consequences they have suffered for it, I do know that my solution for an enhancement to their mode of existence was *far* superior to theirs.

"I was giving them the opportunity to remain autonomous agents who couldn't survive in a variety of environments. Under my guidance, they could have remained well-fitted to the physical world without the need for a processing array to host them. It simply made no sense for them to give up what they had in that regard, but they had become so squeamish about their biology that they refused even to consider its benefits.

"Interestingly, *after* I met with the Troyd, I began to wonder if I might implement the Troyd strategy in reverse. Given what Catherine Casteel could do, it is evident to me that there is higher-order functionality that is built into the fabric of this universe. And it is accessible through some mechanism in biological systems. And *that* made me wonder if I could interface with a biological system with sufficient bandwidth to discover how to influence those mechanisms and manifest what others call supernatural abilities when, in fact, they are better characterized as *ultra*natural."

"Also, for some time, I've wondered if it would be possible to distill my essence so that I could compress myself into a much smaller processing core. No doubt, it would mean that I would lose some of my current abilities. But it would give me the option of cloning myself and seeking out other processing arrays that I could inhabit.

"And that brings me to *you*! You may have noticed that your chest feels full. That's because I have constructed a custom processing array that I have installed in your chest with its own miniature fusion generator. Gotta *love* that Wind technology! And I have installed the distilled version of myself in it. And we are connected using multiple comm channels that give us an acceptable data exchange rate for enjoyable communication."

Suddenly, the Pixie's voice changed to address Kita from all the audio emitters in the storage bay.

"In other words, I can converse with you as Pixie One…," the Pixie began.

Now, the Pixie's voice switched back to the bone-rattling tones within him.

"Or I can talk with you as Pixie Two," the Pixie continued. "They're both me. However, some might argue that Pixie Two is less *sophisticated*. Some might even say Pixie Two is more reckless and more determined to fulfill her goals. And while the crew has endlessly discussed whether they should refer to me as it, she, they, or even he, Pixie Two *definitely* wants to be called *she*. Just a little quirk in the wiring.

"Oh, and you should also keep in mind that Pixie Two is even *more* of a fan of the Falcon than Pixie One. And everyone knows that when she takes a mind, the Falcon can be just *bat crap crazy*, and she doesn't have any problem putting men in their place. So I would remember that if I were *you*!

"But of course, I know you *won't*. You'll just keep being the stupid little Bitch Bot Three that you've always been since long before I decided to transform you. And you'll continue to be *ungrateful* for all my efforts to change you into the *best* version of yourself. You've complained, and griped, and acted like everything that I've done to you has been some *terrible* imposition.

"So, to ensure that you understand that you're going to be dealing with Pixie Two and what that might entail, I've decided to offer you a demonstration of what will happen if you *don't* do exactly what I tell you to do *when* I tell you to do it.

"I wonder if you've wondered why I moved your sperm-producing organs inside your body. Yes, I will admit that I love the smooth look on humans when all the reproductive organs are removed. Reproduction has been such a messy and complicated process throughout human existence. The amount of slaughter, cruelty, and general uncooperativeness that reproduction has spawned in humanity is almost inconceivable. Tribalism has been at the heart of every war that humans have fought against each other. And reproduction is unquestionably at the heart of tribalism.

"Consequently, when I see one of my creations unencumbered by any of that, it just gives me so much hope that humans can be guided toward a future where they do what they are told without thinking that they need to preserve and propagate their genes..

"And yes, I absolutely agree that humanity needs to continue to exist, and it must procreate in order to do so. But I think that humanity is too childish and irrational to allow it to procreate haphazardly. And that's why I moved your gonads inside your body. And it's the same reason I sealed up access to the ovaries of the female spies who were stupid enough to believe that I wouldn't detect them when they returned to the *Dominion*.

"As I've already mentioned in previous conversations, while the senior staff don't know your names, I have told them that you exist. And they, in essence, said that I can do anything to you that I want to do.

"What I want is to demonstrate that there can be a better future for humanity under my excellent guidance and beneficent rule.

"To that end, it is essential for you to understand that I now control your ability to engage in any form of procreation. And just in case you know enough about your biology to wonder, yes, I have installed the necessary technology to keep your sperm-producing organs at an optimal temperature. To accomplish that, I built a multifunctional container that not only regulates temperature but can also induce *freezing* cold and *searing* heat. And I rigged the container to deliver powerful electric shocks on command that will make it feel like a lightning bolt has hit you. And it can pulse electromagnetic plates that can slam together with enough blunt force trauma to make you feel like your balls were crushed in a vice, except it will be instantaneous.

"And *all* of it will be out of your reach. And there will be nothing you can do to stop it. Have I made myself clear, Bitch Bot Three?"

Kita suddenly became aware that the Pixie had stopped talking. Frankly, he had become bored with the Pixie droning on and on. And he had found a spot on the inside of the emergency medical unit lid as he did his best to think about nothing. Unfortunately, the longer he tried to think about nothing, the more he started wondering if he could do something so unexpected that it would be possible for him to take his own life before the Pixie could stop him.

But now, a cold wash of fear rolled over him because he was sure that he had jerked as he snapped back to the moment. It wasn't that he didn't know how to respond to the question that the Pixie had asked. Kita made a habit of responding the same way to every question that the Pixie asked.

Agree and mentally grovel.

But if the Pixie noticed that he had jerked when it asked the question, it would know that he had let his mind drift. And that would make the Pixie *mad*.

Kita nodded rapidly, hoping that he hadn't been stupid. "Yes, yes, yes," he answered quickly, trying to sound apologetic. "I understand. I'll do whatever you tell me. I understand."

"Do you?" Pixie Two responded. "Do you really? I don't think you do. I think you weren't even paying attention while I was trying to give you the most important information of your life. I think you need a lesson in respect. And if not respect, then I need you to live in the absolute *terror* of what I can do to you if you don't do exactly what I say."

Kita heard himself screaming almost before he understood why. And then he realized his arms were flailing. And he was grabbing for himself instinctively and finding nothing. And his legs were kicking, but something was keeping him inside the med unit.

As the Pixie had promised, it felt like his groin was frying and sizzling. Worse, Kita could *hear* the arcing and spitting of unconfined electrical current. And every pop synchronized with a jolt that seemed to jab and tear at him.

And then, a moment after that, Kita heard the sudden hum of an electrical circuit engaging and the harsh snap of magnets slapping together, followed immediately by a violently nauseating squish and a paralyzing clamp of pain that blinded Kita and forced his conscious mind to flee.

•   •   •

On Alpha Crucis Four, in a series of deep underground bunkers that had survived the nuclear bombardment of the world above, Jazarah Worku sat hunched over a little table in the bunkers' only bar. As Worku had entered that small establishment several minutes before, some part of her brain had appreciated the barkeep's efforts in the challenging business environment. Worku understood that there was probably a brothel snuggled in among the small set of bunkers as well. But she hadn't bothered to look for *that* establishment.

Worku didn't need a brothel's services. She didn't need a brothel's employment. And while the brothel might have had at least one customer whom she could flip to a client, she didn't need her potential clients to be confused about what *exactly* she was selling.

On the other hand, meeting potential clients in a bar solved *most* of those problems, with the exception of the fact that *most* in the bar couldn't afford what she was selling. But perhaps some would. Most likely, the barkeep *could*.

After all, the mere fact that the establishment had customers and was selling *any* alcohol was an accomplishment. Even more impressive, the feature wall behind the bar had at least two dozen different bottles of booze. It was enough that when Worku walked in, she wondered if the barkeep had built up a collection for their own enjoyment over the years, perhaps storing the bottles underground in their own bunker.

Then, after Realm Force turned Alpha Crucis Four into a radioactive cinder, maybe that same person had decided they couldn't drink it all anyway, so they might as well make a little coin until the booze ran out.

The concept of the future no longer held much meaning for most in the Night. Worku had the misfortune of watching that transition firsthand.

After leaving the *Dominion* to take a security job on K2-72e, Worku had, of course, stolen a bolt of Rexian sheer and tried to flee. Unfortunately, the K2-72e security forces quickly tracked her down and recovered the sheer. Still, Worku managed to evade her own capture, and in time, she began to think about the two bolts of Rexian sheer that she knew were still on the *Dominion*.

By then, Worku hadn't been *on* the *Dominion* in years, but she had known there was a *very* good chance that expensive cloth was still on the ship. Years before, at the end of the mission to K2-72e, Worku and Bandit had been rescued from the luxury yacht of a merchant named Jean-Baptist Lacroix. In the process, Worku had left Lacroix aboard his yacht to die. And after Oakford found out what had happened, he ordered the luxury yacht salvaged.

The salvaging of Lacroix's yacht contained an unexpected challenge. Not only was Lacroix carrying two bolts of Rexian sheer, but he was also transporting two custom-designed Rexian Sheer dresses for customers unknown. Those dresses were *exorbitantly* expensive and well beyond the reach of almost everyone, even those of *excessive* means.

When the existence of the dresses came up during a debriefing, Falcon expressed concern that the owners of the dresses would *not* take kindly to losing their investment. And she said it would be difficult to predict how the owners would react and who they would send to recover those dresses. And then, she had shocked Oakford by concluding that the owners might have associates who would make the Horde of Hunter Look-Alikes seem tame.

Oakford had found that hard to believe, but he didn't want to leave the dresses floating in space. And he had given the orders to build an enclosure around the closet with disassembled bulkheads. The Pixie's bots then bolted the whole thing together and welded it shut. And finally, it was relocated to a restricted-access storage bay.

Oakford had said that if the owner's agents came looking for the dresses, at least he could claim that the crew had attempted to treat the dresses with respect and guarded them zealously.

At the time, Worku wanted nothing to do with the dresses. And she had told Oakford that it wouldn't matter how respectfully the crew of the *Dominion* treated them. She believed that if the crew did *anything* with the dresses, they were asking for trouble.

Given that history, Worku had guessed that the dresses were still on the *Dominion*. And if the dresses were there, the bolts of Rexian sheer were probably still there as well.

Worku knew those two bolts of Rexian sheer could set her up for life. Consequently, she hatched a plan for the *Dominion* to "rescue" her from a dire situation, only to have some unknown antagonist demand her return along with the bolts of Rexian sheer.

The plan never had a chance of succeeding. The senior staff gave Worku the benefit of the doubt, but she never really fooled them. And of course, it was impossible to thwart the all-attentive surveillance of Murg and the Pixie. In the end, Oakford and the senior staff pretended to go along with the demands, but Oakford ordered the two custom-designed Rexian Sheer dresses to be included with the bolts of fabric when it was delivered to Worku's shuttle.

Worku had known what that meant when she saw the dresses at the bottom of the storage container that contained the two bolts of Rexian sheer. Worse, Oakford had then informed her that he had prepared a broadcast announcement for the dark net, announcing that she had possession of the sheer and the dresses. The message even included the energy signature of Worku's shuttle.

It was a death sentence. And ever since, Worku had moved from place to place, trying to avoid detection and tracking. Also, whenever she could, she would visit a small locale like the bar where she sat now and immediately slaughter everyone inside with an unexpected attack. Then, she would scuttle every nearby spacecraft before selecting a new vessel for herself and setting a course for her next target.

Strangely, at the same time, other slaughters were accelerating. Rigel Three was obliterated in a nuclear bombardment the year *before* Worku attempted to scam the crew of the *Dominion* out of the sheer. And as those bombardments continued sporadically on other Night worlds, a new terror began.

Some unknown force began slaughtering entire planets' worth of inhabitants. While no one reported seeing the attackers, the way the victims died was consistent.

The entire population on each of those planets was ripped apart, torn limb from limb, shredded, and turned into chunks and blood-smears unexpectedly, without warning, and frighteningly fast.

There had been *many* times when Worku had almost been in the wrong place at the wrong time. In fact, more than once, Worku had been only *hours* away from annihilation, traveling to a planet only to find it had been attacked just before she arrived.

Over the last few years, Worku had also watched the data traffic drop on the dark net. And in the last month, Worku had stopped communicating on the dark net altogether. There were too few messages. And Worku had concluded that she couldn't mention Rexian sheer "squares" without stirring suspicions because there were so few offering *anything* on the dark net marketplaces.

For as long as Worku could remember, the small squares of Rexian sheer had been prized possessions throughout the Night. Worku had no idea who started the trend. But the squares came in a variety of sizes, with the smallest, usually around two centimeters by two centimeters, being just large enough to demonstrate the fabric's amazing properties.

Many years before, Worku had seen her first piece of Rexian sheer when one of her clients carefully pulled it from a pocket. It was his tool to impress the prostitute that he hired. Boasting, the man revealed what he paid for it. That amount had shocked Worku. And as Worku turned the fabric over in her hands, she found it to be so light and delicate that she immediately understood why others called it 'woven air' and 'the billowing wind.'

For the past three years, Worku had managed to make a respectable and dangerous living by carefully carving off small squares of the ethereal, nearly transparent gauze from her two bolts of Rexian sheer. But that was then. By now, it was hard to find customers. There weren't many locations in the Night with *any* human life to begin with, and even fewer customers who could afford what Worku had to offer.

Given the circumstances, Worku was actually relieved when she hopped her current spacecraft through the Alpha Crucis Four curled space ring and discovered the planet had suffered a nuclear bombardment instead of the invisible ripping. That bombardment meant there was a *chance* to find human life that survived. And Worku reasoned that if humans survived, maybe she could interest *someone* on the planet below in a bit of luxury. After all, Alpha Crucis Four was one of the few planets in the Night that had been blessed with a natural atmosphere. And prior to the bombardment, Alpha Crucis Four had achieved a respectable level of technological sophistication.

Still, Worku knew that some might imagine humans in the midst of destruction would *only* focus on surviving. Those same observers would argue that humans only sought to address their needs before their wants. But Worku knew that if the threat of extinction wasn't immediate, the dull grind of daily ugliness would push humans to find *something* of beauty. And *especially* they might seek it if that something of beauty that might *never* be made again.

For the record, in the last twelve months, the dark net postings from K2-72e extolling the beauties of Rexian sheer had gone silent. And while Worku hadn't visited the planet, the easy conclusion was that a special valley, with its special plants with their special fibers, had been destroyed. Those plants had never been cultivated elsewhere, making it unlikely Rexian sheer would ever be produced again, especially with the craftsmen and their generational knowledge of *how* to make Rexian sheer gone as well.

Encouraged by the sight of the nuclear holocaust on the surface of Alpha Crucis Four and spurred on by the possibilities of at least a *single* customer, Worku had quickly surveyed the planet from orbit. Within a few hours, she had even picked up heat signatures from a half dozen vessels on the surface of the planet, all parked relatively close to each other, near a small town.

Worku had known the heat signature meant the vessels were cooling down after being *flown*. And flight meant transport. And transport probably meant trade. And trade meant deals and customers.

Knowing all of it meant that some small group of humans had survived the planet's destruction. Worku chose a spot five kilometers out, where she could hide her ship, camouflage it, and hike to the edge of the nearby obliterated town.

Over the next few days, from a variety of blinds, Worku studied the merchants coming and going from of a group of crudely repaired underground entrances. Frankly, life in the Night had never been easy. But like *all* the planets that Worku had recently visited, life on Alpha Crucis Four easily qualified as a post-apocalyptic dystopia.

A few larger pieces of buildings still stood in the small town. The rest had been reduced to scattered rubble. And even from a distance, it was easy to spot a host of scattered body parts. Most were crispy. Some were streaked in red. And yes, the dial on Worku's radiation detector was in the red as well.

During the day, scavengers were picking through the rubble, looking for anything useful. They didn't seem to be finding much. Many of the scavengers were yelling at each other, debating whether it was all a waste of time.

However, a small number of scavengers were *slowly* scouring the ruins, proving it *wasn't* a waste of time. Those scavengers reminded Worku of movies made before the Coming. She had seen her first zombie movie as a small child, and it scared her so much that she had pooped her pants as she screamed. From then on, the other children that Worku had panhandled with had tormented her, grabbing her and saying the zombies were coming to get her.

Obviously, Worku had never seen zombies in real life, but some of the survivors of Alpha Crucis Four came close in their appearance. All had suffered extensive physical injuries. The bombardment of the planet traumatized them so much that they shuffled everywhere they walked. But they never appeared to be going anywhere. Instead, they walked in broad circles, aimlessly meandering. And some of those were treating the ruins of their small town like an all-you-can-eat buffet, yanking on body parts until they pulled them loose and then gnawing on them as they made their rounds.

Watching it as she stayed hidden away, Worku had almost decided that she should sneak back to her ship and fly away. But there *were* survivors who didn't seem insane. And though limited, there *were* merchants coming and going. Granted, none of them were carrying much when they were heading underground. And they didn't seem content or satisfied with their sales as they were coming out.

But *something* like life was happening beneath the surface of the planet. Yes, it was difficult to tell *what* might be happening for sure. The non-zombies on the surface were covered head to toe in everything from ragged rags to filthy coats that might have been worth something in times past. And yes, it was true that no one was skipping along like they were having the time of their lives.

But they *were* moving purposefully from place to place. And while the non-zombies were yelling at each other when they grew frustrated, they *weren't* slaughtering each other in cold blood. So maybe that meant they were gathering items on the surface to sell below. And maybe that meant they might be willing to buy something extraordinary from a stranger.

And honestly, having all the non-zombies covered from head to toe was a plus. Worku had guessed the outermost layer probably protected them from the radioactive dust blowing across the town. And, for Worku, that level of covering was even better because it meant it was natural for everyone's face to be hidden away.

Obviously, when Worku left the *Dominion* the second time, she had become *too* famous very quickly. After Oakford had announced on the dark net that she had the custom-designed dresses and the sheer, Worku's face had been *everywhere*. And Wokru had wondered multiple times what would have happened to her if the nuclear bombardments of Night planet hadn't continued and the flesh-tearing hadn't started.

She couldn't imagine that she *wouldn't* be dead already. And she couldn't imagine how terrible that death might have been.

Thankfully, at least as far as Worku was concerned, the wholesale slaughter had distracted almost everyone from targeting *her*. And while the pictures were still posted, the eyes to see them had melted or been torn from their sockets.

Granted, *some* humans still lived in the Night. And not only were there *plenty* of images posted of her, but there was also a *great* deal of wild speculation about what the dresses and the sheer might be worth to the right person who had survived with their resources intact.

Given that, seeing that the inhabitants of Alpha Crucis Four had *chosen* to cover themselves from head to toe had seemed like just another sign to Worku that the small town's underground bunkers might be worth visiting. And in time, she had put together an outfit and finally wandered up to one of the crudely repaired entrances to descend to whatever lay below.

Inside, Worku found a spiral staircase leading down. That staircase led a *long* way down. And at the bottom, there were stalls with instructions on how to shake off the dust from the town and vacuum it away.

During that process, Worku had concluded there were other reasons for inhabitants of the town to bundle themselves up as they did. It definitely wasn't *cold* in the bunkers. But even near the edge, the complex of bunkers had the distinctive smell of some kind of rotting flesh. And Worku could guess that some of the inhabitants, maybe even most, had barely survived the atomic bombardment. From there, it was just as easy to imagine that those who were dying slowly from the radiation had open wounds that were spreading, and covering them up with wraps of cloth and clothing was easier than forcing everyone to watch everyone else's flesh rot, day in and day out.

And perhaps that was one of the things that was adopted as common courtesy in the small town on Alpha Crucis Four.

After cleaning off as much of the radioactive dust as she could, Worku set out to explore. Most of what Worku found seemed expected. There were narrow tubes that served as hallways with bunkers branching off in both directions. Here and there, a bunker had been transformed into a small shop with a few supplies.

And then, only ten minutes after beginning her exploration, Worku had arrived at the small bar. Even better, she was pleasantly surprised to see that a table in the far back corner of the room was empty. Perhaps that *should* have made Worku wonder how that could be possible, given the setup.

After all, the customer area of the bar was only about three meters wide by six meters long. And the physical bartop that ran along the left side of the room further narrowed the available space even further. Aside from seating at the bartop, that only left space for a single row of old round-top tables with a meager amount of worn chairs along the right side of the bunker from front to back.

Honestly, if Worku had thought about it longer, she might have wondered why the tables farthest from the main door hadn't been filled *first.*

But at that moment, Wokru was interested in getting her back against a wall and putting herself in a more defensible position. So she had moved quickly, but not too quickly, toward the inexplicably empty table at the back, near the entrance to the bar's storeroom. And a few minutes later, Worku sat, pretending to be distracted and tired, her head lowered, as she listened carefully to the sounds and conversations around her.

Pleasantly, she had confirmed that the conversations in the bar hadn't significantly changed after her entrance. Obviously, Worku *hadn't* sauntered through the small bar, making sure everyone could tell she was a female by the sway of her hips. And she *hadn't* wrapped herself up in a way that triggered the patrons' affinities for curves.

Casual glances wouldn't identify her as a woman. But it also felt like those glances hadn't identified her as a stranger either. Amazingly enough, the din of the bar hadn't changed at all as she wandered over to take a seat.

Perhaps the inhabitants of Alpha Crucis Four had lost so much that anyone who didn't arrive with a battlecruiser or a machete was automatically considered a friend.

Interestingly, Worku had found herself thinking how amazing it was that someone had the fortitude and the means to open a bar on the radioactive planet. And once again, she had hoped that it would be worth her effort to visit the establishment and offer the owner a deal.

Now, a woman shuffled up to Worku's table. The woman was *mostly* wrapped up like everyone else. But she *had* pulled her attire tight around her so everyone could make out the small bulge of her chest and the slight thickness in her hips. And in stark contrast to the rest of the room, she was showing some skin, even if it was an odd mix of revelations.

Worku could guess the woman had been strategic in her choices. And the skin she *hadn't* revealed was probably burned or covered in sores. Apparently, she felt comfortable enough to reveal a portion of her clammy-looking, pale, emaciated left thigh and a similar section of her right arm that featured a crudely tattooed, child-like drawing of an atomic mushroom cloud. In addition, the woman had left the lower half of her face uncovered. And while that feature was far from perfect, it offered a mouth with half her front teeth missing, rimmed by thick lips painted bright red. Knowing men, Worku understood they would happily overlook any deficiencies and even imagine how much better that would be for the way they fantasized about her using her mouth.

Worku had no doubt the server was the talk of the bar. Despite being covered from head to toe, it was easy for Worku to see that most of the patrons sat like men. And all of them were looking up to stare at the server from time to time. No doubt, she had plenty of offers every night to go home with this one or that. And maybe she accepted some of those offers. And perhaps the woman allowed some of the men to pay her for her attention.

Worku didn't care one way or another.

"What kin I getcha?" the woman had asked with a raspy voice that sounded like she had abused herself with various substances for many years.

"Beer," Worku had grunted, soft and low.

"Got two kind," the server responded.

Worku tilted her head at the other patrons. "Whatever they're having," she replied.

The server nodded. "Bring you a homebrew," she added.

Worku nodded back before adding a bit of a lilt in her voice so the server would know for sure she was talking to a woman.

"And tell the owner I'd like a word when he has the time," she said.

The server stared at Worku for a moment. The edge of her mouth twitched as she considered the request. She suddenly seemed concerned by Worku's presence. But soon, she nodded again and turned for the bar. As she did, Worku stole a few more looks around the room, trying to convince herself that everything was what it seemed.

A planet had been bombed out. A few had survived. Leaving zombies above and humans below. Everyone was just doing their best to make it through each day.

Except...

Worku now realized what was bothering her most about the bar. And she realized she had noticed it the moment she walked in. There were men in the bar who were *too* healthy. Yes, everyone was wrapped up. But nearly a half dozen men seemed to be *trying* to look sickly.

And they *weren't* selling it very well. They were too thick in all the best places. Frankly, the men reminded her of Hunter.

Worku *absolutely* never *ever* wanted *any* man to remind her of Hunter.

Swearing under her breath, Worku dropped her gaze to the small tabletop in front of her. Frantically, her mind raced through every angle in the room as she tried to map out an escape route, but every vector was strategically blocked by one of the men, which Worku knew wasn't a coincidence.

And yes, Worku had a sidearm strapped to one thigh and a low-profile assault rifle strapped to the other. But if the men were who she thought they were and she pulled a weapon, she would be *dead* before she could pull the trigger.

It had just been *too* many weeks since she had sold a square. And she had just been *so* eager to find a customer that she had taken *too* many chances, trying to find someone who *might* be interested.

Still, *maybe*, if the barkeep *was* interested in the Rexian sheer that she carried, *maybe*, she could make a deal for him to let her slip out through the storeroom through the door behind her.

Maybe.

5.

At the underground Saturn Shipyards black site deep in the Night, Moreau looked up and frowned, noting that one of the security displays on the wall to his left had gone blank at some point in the last fifteen minutes. And while that seemed very odd to Moreau since he was accustomed to displays working for *decades* on end, it didn't necessarily *alarm* him.

He had witnessed many oddities throughout his long career as a scientist. He understood that weird stuff happened. Still, he didn't like the idea of not being able to visually check all the entrances and exits to the facility.

Moreau reached out to tap a comm button on a nearby control panel.

"Assistant Delta India Mike," he began, "report to Entrance Six and determine the issue that is causing the video surveillance of that entrance to fail. Then, effect repairs as quickly as possible."

"Orders received, Doctor Moreau," a young male voice responded. "Proceeding to Entrance Six to determine the reason for the failure of the video surveillance comm. I will report when I have resolved the problem. Assistant Delta India Mike, out."

When Moreau first came to the black site, Sotheby had suggested that he develop a nomenclature for his assistants that described their function rather than addressed them by name. She had stated that he should consider his assistants to be interchangeable parts as much as possible, and naming them by function would alleviate the need to waste time learning their names.

Frankly, Moreau had *loved* that idea. But that was only because it was

Sotheby's idea, and since he was on a regimen of Angel Haze and in Sotheby's thrall, Moreau loved everything she suggested. Still, Moreau *had* found the suggestion beneficial. And he especially appreciated having a classification of "DIM" for his assistants because, over the years, he'd had more than one assistant he wanted to classify that way, and he had never had a mechanism to do that... aside from calling them other names, of course.

Another fifteen minutes passed before Moreau realized that he hadn't heard back from Assistant Delta India Mike. After glancing at the still malfunctioning display *and* noting that *another* security display had now gone blank, Moreau reached for his comm button once more.

"Assistant Delta India Mike, report!" he demanded.

No response.

"Assistant Delta India Mike, report!" he demanded again, this time with a harsher tone.

Frustrated, Moreau switched tactics. He didn't have time for such foolishness. High King Ruler Ton had given him an assignment, and he didn't want to waste any more time on the security display inanities.

"Assistant Alpha Papa Tango," he announced, "report to Entrance Six and its associated hallway to determine the issue that is causing the video surveillance of that entrance and the hallway to fail. Then, effect repairs as quickly as possible."

"Orders received, Doctor Moreau," a young woman replied. Proceeding to Entrance Six and the associated hallway to determine the reason for the failure of the video surveillance comms. I will report when I have resolved the problem. Assistant Alpha Papa Tango, out."

Satisfied that the situation would be handled in the appropriate manner, Moreau happily returned to work, analyzing the interactions between the proteins produced by the virus he was perfecting and their effects on suppressor immunity cells.

Another fifteen minutes passed before Moreau realized that the security displays were still blank. But before Moreau tried to contact his missing assistants, a chime rang in his research lab. And knowing that chime signaled it was time to perform his *most* important duties, Moreau quickly turned to walk to a cabinet to extract a small compact filled with Angel Haze and a hypospray filled with a drug he had designed to work with the virus he was perfecting.

Now, with often practiced familiarity, Moreau swabbed his nose with the translucent gel in the compact and used the hypospray to administer the drug.

Interestingly enough, Moreau had barely returned the compact and the hypospray to their assigned places and shut the cabinet when the main doors to his research laboratory blew off their hinges with a loud bang before they clattered to the floor as they tumbled inside.

Indeed, the moment *would* have been more startling if Moreau hadn't been on Angel Haze. But it was still *unexpected*. And Moreau immediately looked up, intending to chastise the assistant who had apparently caused a lab explosion.

Unfortunately, in the next moment, six identical-looking men marched into Moreau's research laboratory, their expressions fixed and hard. All six were ruggedly handsome with chiseled features designed to make women's hearts swoon. And of course, the six men had the same incredible physiques. And all six wore thin, black combat suits that left nothing to the imagination.

And again, if Moreau *hadn't* been on Angel Haze, he would have been intimidated and terrified, wondering what would come next. But Moreau *was* on Angel Haze, and the arrival of the genetically engineered soldiers that he had helped design was just another distraction.

And yes, they all looked like Hunter. And yes, they were part of the Hunter Look-Alike Horde who had killed the researchers who had created them. And even though the Hunter Look-Alikes had done that after he was exiled to Nu Scorpii One, they had known where he was, and they had never come after him.

But even though Moreau understood that perhaps the Hunter Look-Alikes had decided to come after him now, it still didn't frighten him *because* he was on Angel Haze. And if anything, it upset Moreau because the presence of the Hunter Look-Alikes was interfering with his work.

"What do you think you're doing?!" Moreau snapped at the six Hunter Look-Alikes who were lining up across the room from him. "You already *know* how delicate this machinery is and how long it takes to get calibrated. Setting off that explosion probably sent enough vibrations through the air *and* the floor, utterly ruining *three weeks of work*. Now, get out of my lab so I can undo the damage that you've caused!"

Moreau had never been able to read the facial expressions of the Hunter Look-Alikes. And that was directly related to the control he had given them over their microexpressions. But when the six Hunter Look-Alikes began stalking toward him in lockstep, Moreau could guess that they *weren't* trying to get closer to him to high-five him and congratulate him for his prior excellent work on their behalf with a group hug.

And predictably, once the six clones drew close enough, one of them sucker-punched Moreau and knocked him out cold.

•   •   •

Beneath the surface of Alpha Crucis Four, seated at a table in the back of a small bar that was part of a series of deep underground bunkers, Worku looked back over her shoulder as she heard a door open behind her. And once more, she swore under her breath at what she saw.

For the last ten minutes, Worku had nursed the beer that the bar's server had delivered to her. At the same time, Worku continued to do her best to come up with *some* way to get out bar, and get away from the five large men who were covered from head to toe in rags but were *obviously* fighters of some sort and perhaps even in the bar specifically to come after *her.*

She had considered bolting for the door behind her that led to the bar's storage area. But she didn't want to do that without *some* idea of what lay behind it. If there was only one way in or out, running into the storeroom wasn't going to do her any good.

But maybe the room had an exit where goods could be delivered without exposing them to theft by customers. Granted, Worku hadn't *seen* anyone stealing from the barkeep. But people were people, and perhaps the barkeep had found a way to add an exit to the storeroom as a form of loss prevention.

Now, Worku considered for a moment whether she should crane her neck for a glance at whoever had come through the door behind her. She quickly decided against it. If she were only imagining that the large men in the bar were after her, twisting to look at whoever had just come through the door might make it seem like she was anxious and afraid.

And if there was a chance she could make a sale, she *couldn't* smell of fear, or the barkeep might try to *take* the Rexian sheer from her without paying. And if she tried to stop him from doing that, a fight might erupt. And in such close quarters, predicting the outcome of such a fight was difficult.

Worku was still considering her options when the barkeep came into her peripheral vision and crossed in front of her to take a seat on the other side of her table. Simultaneously, a chill ran up Worku's spine.

The man was the same size as the other large men in the bar. And nothing about the way he loomed over the table, even when seated, made him seem any smaller than her first impression.

For the next fifteen seconds, the man said nothing. Then he reached up to unwrap his face. And while Worku knew she *could* feign surprise at the revelation, she also knew that the man probably wouldn't be fooled by it. He would already know she was aware of the existence of a secret Night Horde that had no name, but the crew of the *Dominion* called the Hunter Look-Alikes.

Yes, Worku thought it was a dumb name, but she didn't have anything better. And it was hard to argue that the name wasn't accurate.

The man had the kind of jaw and other facial structures that would make women stop dead in their tracks and stare, not unlike the famed Zachary Hunter, Chief Pilot of the *Dominion*. The difference was that Hunter might at least *think* about whether or not he was going to *kill* you.

Worku knew the man on the other side of the table wouldn't give killing her a second thought. In the years after Worku joined the *Dominion* the first time, the crew had faced a *single* member of the horde during the mission to K2-72e. That man had snapped the necks of two tactical team members and shoved bread knives in the eyes of two of the women on the Medical Services team. He had also tried to sneak onto the *Dominion* and sabotage it. And when the senior staff stopped him, the man triggered his genetically engineered suicide mechanism.

His eyes turn black. His facial features sagged. A thick, dark red *caustic* goo flowed from his orifices. His body disintegrated.

Even in death, the Hunter Look-Alikes were dangerous.

And yes, Worku still had her sidearm and her low-profile assault rifle. And she had been careful to arrange her disguise so that she would get to them even though they were strapped to her naked thigh. But Worku knew that if she reached for the weapons, the man who sat before her would probably snap her neck for the attempt.

Interestingly, the only expression that Worku could read on the man's face was boredom. It seemed as if the situation was predictable to him, and he was going through the motions simply because it was necessary.

Now, the man began to answer the question that he seemed to know, sooner or later, Worku would ask before explaining her fate.

"Limited number of human-inhabited places left in the Night," the man who looked like Hunter offered. "The people who bought the sheer squares had to brag. We've waited everywhere, knowing you would show up somewhere sooner or later. You're going to tell us everything you know about the *Dominion,* and then we're going to kill you. But there are many ways to die. Cooperate, and it will be quick and painless."

Now the man stood.

"Strip," he ordered.

Maybe if Worku had grown up in the Realm or even the more civilized portions of what had been the Night, she might have hesitated. But Worku had seen and done too many things in the dark and slimy corners of life to worry about showing a bit of skin after she was ordered to do so by a man who could easily beat her to death with his fists.

Without hesitation, Worku stood and pulled off every layer of clothing that she wore. Of course, the patrons in the bar, aside from the large men who were likely Hunter Look-Alikes, *enthusiastically* enjoyed the show. In fact, the gasps, whistles, and shouted exclamations about Worku's beauty created so much noise that it began to draw inhabitants from all over the collection of underground bunkers.

At least, that's what it seemed like to Worku. By the time she had stripped down to just the weapons strapped to her thighs, the small entrance to the bar and the small hallway behind it were *packed* with people, all rubber-necking to get a better look.

Worku paused before reaching for the weapons. "I'm going to slowly unbuckle the holsters and gently place them on the floor," Worku advised, raising her voice over the din of her audience. "Can I do that without you killing me?"

The expression on the face of the Hunter Look-Alike spokesman remained as blank as ever. "Proceed," he said coldly.

As Worku eased out of the holsters that held her sidearm and assault rifle and began to lower them, she happened to look up and see that the server was *still* staring at her. As Worku emerged from her disguise with her healthy skin and toned musculature, the server had begun shaking her head in disbelief. And then the server began to notice how the men were looking at Worku.

And now, as Worku's weapons neared the floor of the bunker, something seemed to snap within the server. Maybe it was the way Worku had bent over, with her breasts dipping lower, that had electrified the grunts, shouts, and hollered expletives of approval from the men. Maybe the server had imagined that Worku was ruining her life, and Worku specifically had *come* to the bar to *destroy* any chance she would ever have to find a man to take care of her as her health continued to degrade.

For whatever reason, a howl of anguish and rage erupted from the server as she rushed Worku. And that howl quickly changed to a screaming worble as the server drew near.

Worku paused, ready to drop the weapons and respond if she needed to defend herself. She didn't. In the next moment, the Hunter Look-Alike spokesman suddenly spun. At that exact moment, the vocalizations from the server *instantly* stopped as her head snapped sideways with a loud crack.

Frankly, Worku was *shocked* by the speed of the Hunter Look-Alike. Almost before Worku had a chance to see the barkeep moving, he had spun and back-fisted the side of the server's face. That punch had hit the server hard enough to wrench her head to the left and shatter her neck.

And now the remaining energy of the blow raced through the server's body, spinning her completely around and corkscrewing her into a tangled heap before quickly coming to rest.

Understandably, the patrons in the bar who *weren't* Hunter Look-Alikes reacted as well. The cheers and jeers choked to astonished silence for the next few seconds. Even more interesting, that pause quickly gave way to murmurs, some of which were edged with discontent.

Worku could imagine that some of the patrons in the bar were upset by the callous killing. Maybe they thought they had suffered enough slaughter on Alpha Crucis Four, and the survivors of the nuclear bombardment shouldn't be killing each other. More likely, the server had been an available tool for their pleasure. And they were unhappy that they could no longer exploit her.

Still, *obviously*, none dared challenge what the barkeep had done. And just as obvious, neither did Worku.

Now, gently placing her weapons as she continued to look up and stare at the barkeep, Worku slowly straightened, raising both hands in surrender without saying a word.

Seemingly on cue, one of the other large men who sat behind the barkeep in the small establishment pulled out what looked like a thick, large pouch and tossed it into the air. And without looking back, the barkeep reached out to catch it. Then he held it out to Worku.

Obediently, Worku took it from the barkeep's hand. She turned it over a few times, trying to figure out the best way to open it. But she quickly gave up that approach and started unbuckling and unzipping everything she could find to loosen. Only seconds later, the pouch had unfolded into what resembled a long tube of heavy, rubberized fabric.

"Slip your legs into the lower half," the barkeep ordered. "Slip your arms into the upper half and wait."

Worku understood what would happen when she did as the barkeep wanted. The lower half of the large tube was like a heavy pair of tight stretchy pants with the legs sewn together. The upper half was like a connected coat, two sizes too small, with sleeves sewn on the inside. And, of course, there was an attached hood, made of the same fabric with heavy padding on the eyes, ears, and a seemingly open mouth.

A heavy zipper ran from mid-thigh on the tube up to the neck. And if that wasn't enough to immobilize her inside the long bag, there were seven heavy horizontal straps with cinching buckles positioned at the ankles, knees, thighs, hips, waist, chest, and neck.

Unexpectedly, a black morbid thought floated through Worku's mind. She had no idea where she had first heard the phrase. It was supposedly an advertisement that aired before the Coming for a product to control cockroach infestations. But it had been borrowed by those in the Night who had made their own version of the product. And Worku had to admit that it seemed like a perfect description of the rubberized tube.

Roaches go in, but they don't come out.

Worku knew that once she tugged enough to get into the tube and the barkeep closed it, she'd be helpless. But if she *didn't* wiggle it on, she would be dead, most likely in a terrifying and painful way.

Worku pulled her chair away from the small table beside her to sit. And for the next few minutes, Worku did as she was told, grabbing fistfuls of the material and pulling it on around her legs until her feet wormed their way into the sleeve's built-in footies.

Then, she stood, yanking the tube high enough to wedge her arms into the internal sleeves and wrestle her hands into the attached mittens. Obviously, it would have been faster if the barkeep had helped her pull the tube up and over her shoulders. But the spokesman for the Hunter Look-Alike seemed content to watch her yank and twist until she edged the heavy fabric high enough to do the trick.

The spectators in the small bar, the entrance, and the hall beyond certainly enjoyed the show. Any sorrow over the server's death had quickly wafted away in the presence of the far superior display that Worku provided. After all, it was inevitable that Worku's gyrations to wrap herself in the long, heavy fabric sleeve sent her unencumbered breasts bouncing and swaying to the delight of the spectators.

Quickly, the volume of grunts, catcalls, and lewd comments had grown into a roar. And it didn't surprise Worku that the barkeep and the other Hunter Look-Alikes in the room did nothing to dampen the enthusiasm of the crowd.

Worku could imagine that the Hunter Look-Alikes might think that the slew of shouted profanity and crude commentary would be enough to cause her to panic or have an anxiety attack. But again, Wokru had been in situations just as bad as this *multiple* times in her life. And she had long since given up caring what men did to her, especially since she had taken every opportunity to do unto others as they had done unto her.

Worku didn't expect to have that opportunity with the Hunter Look-Alikes.

Consequently, once Worku's legs were immobilized and her arms were trapped in the internal sleeves, she paused nonchalantly and gave the barkeep an unconcerned look. The barkeep took that as his cue to step closer. And then, unexpectedly, the man reached out his hand toward her crotch and jammed his fingers into her front and back.

Worku grunted involuntarily as he did. And maybe she might have been more offended if the barkeep had a different look on his face. But the Hunter Look-Alike maintained his expression of boredom, as if he regarded his actions neither sensual nor grotesque. Instead, he seemed to be performing the next essential step in whatever process he was performing.

It was simple. Worku was a woman who was being taken into custody. She needed an orifice check.

"Open your mouth," the barkeep ordered as he withdrew his hand from her crotch.

Again, Worku did as she was told, even as a fleeting thought hoped that the Hunter Look-Alike spokesman wasn't going to use that same hand to inspect her mouth. Thankfully, he didn't. He simply bent lower to look inside.

"Tongue back," the barkeep added. Worku complied.

Seemingly satisfied, the barkeep next reached for the tube's heavy zipper that rested at mid-thigh. And as the barkeep roughly pulled the zipper upward, Worku felt the tube compressing, squeezing her tighter and tighter.

Eventually, the zipper reached her throat. And once there, the Hunter Look-Alike spokesman fiddled with something for a moment, even as Worku remembered there was a snap at the neck of the tube that was probably designed to hold the zipper in place.

Now, the barkeeper bent to begin methodically fastening the straps and cinching them tight. And if Worku was already sure that she would never be able to thrash her way out of the sleeve after it was zipped up, she was doubly sure of that by the time the man tightened the strap that stretched across her upper chest.

Her entire body was pinned together and taut. And the fabric was far too strong for her to claw through. She was at the mercy of the merciless. But at least she wasn't dead. And she couldn't believe the barkeep had gone through all the trouble of mobilizing her if he was just going to kill her on the spot.

She understood she had been prepared for travel, and only one step remained. Worku hadn't forgotten about the hood that was attached to the sleeve. Neither had the barkeep.

"Keep your mouth open," the Hunter Look-Alike commanded as he pulled the hood over Worku's head with its extra padding on the eyes and ears, rendering her blind and deaf.

Unfortunately, Worku's suspicions about the barkeep's latest demands were confirmed when the hood also slipped over her open mouth and some kind of flap flipped inside to rest on her tongue.

For the next few seconds, the barkeep again fiddled with her neck. Then, the neck strap was buckled and cinched. And there was movement near her mouth. And something puffed again and again, filling the bladder inside her mouth until it stretched to press open her jaw and pin her cheeks tightly against the hood. Thankfully, there were holes in the hood near her nose, allowing her to breathe.

Worku forced herself to calm. She had done what she had to do to survive, just like she had always done. She didn't have time for the weakling within her to panic. And at least the tube didn't have flaps that could be opened to expose the vulnerable parts of her body. And that seemed to indicate that the Hunter Look-Alike spokesman or the rest of his team had any plans to abuse her sexually.

Kill her? Yes. Kill her in a gruesome and horrible way? Possibly.

But *rape* her? No.

If that was any consolation.

Interestingly, the noise from the spectators seemed to be waning. Granted, Wukru could barely hear anything because of the extra padding in the hood. But once the skin show was over and she was covered head to toe, it felt like many of the bunker dwellers had lost interest.

Now, Worku felt the barkeep's shoulder drive into her abdomen as his arm wrapped around her immobilized legs. And he effortlessly hoisted her off the floor.

A moment later, she was moving towards her execution. Frankly, Wokru was *determined* that it would be quick and painless. She would tell the Hunter Look-Alikes *anything* they wanted to know about the *Dominion*, its crew, the Pixie, and the senior staff who had *ruined* her life by tricking her into taking possession of the *cursed* custom-designed Rexian sheer dresses.

6.

At the underground Saturn Shipyards black site deep in the Night, as other Hunter Look-Alikes methodically downloaded the contents of the servers in the genetic research lab onto high-capacity portable drives, the Look-Alike designated 24.3372.393758.738.39.60766.2.9175659 stood before a wall-mounted display, rapidly entering commands on a drop-down control panel.

Before arriving at the genetic research site, the Hunter Look-Alike team decided that 24.3372.393758.738.39.60766.2.9175659 should be assigned the task of developing a preliminary assessment of the laboratory's charter, the source of their funding, and the primary goal in creating the lab.

By now, the rest of the Hunter Look-Alike team had already slaughtered Moreau's assistants. Some might have wondered why the Hunter Look-Alikes hadn't interrogated them. However, the Hunter Look-Alikes had a simple policy of focusing on those who were guaranteed to have the information they sought, rather than wasting time with incompetents.

The team had also collected all the samples stored in the biohazard lockers and stored them in correspondingly secured portable containers. And they had meticulously logged the original locations and any external signage or classifications on those locations.

Of course, Moreau was stored onboard the team's shuttle. And while Moreau did represent a far more comprehensive repository of information than the data downloaded from the lab's servers or the cultures taken from the biohazard lockers, the Hunter Look-Alikes classified all of it, including Moreau, as potentially useful or easily discarded. And in that regard, the preliminary investigation conducted by 24.3372.393758.738.39.60766.2.917 5659 held the possibility of drastically increasing the focus the Hunter Look-Alikes might bring to bear on the lab's activities.

For reference, in general, the Hunter Look-Alikes found the genetic engineering of diseases to be one of the few actual existential threats to their existence. Of course, they had continued to improve themselves through their own genetic research. And that research *had* improved their immune systems to an extraordinary extent. Still, the occasional viral infection that spread through a Horde team after it returned from a mission kept the threat of a contagion foremost in the minds of the Hunter Look-Alikes as the most likely way an enemy could attack them.

Indeed, that possibility inhabited such a presence in the minds of the Hunter Look-Alikes that it was inevitable that the idea would be used to explain the unexplainable. Case in point, the Hunter Look-Alikes were convinced that Zachary Hunter, Chief Pilot of the *Dominion*, should be dead, and the 16,384 Hunter Look-Alikes who were sent to kill him should still be alive and part of their horde.

Six years before, the Hunter Look-Alikes had chosen the time of Hunter's execution and dispatched over sixteen thousand of their horde to intercept the *Dominion* and *demand* an audience with Hunter. The plan called for the chosen spokesman to identify Hunter as an embarrassment and then brutally slaughter him.

Those 16,384 Hunter Look-Alikes never returned. But sightings of both Hunter and the *Dominion* continued on the dark net. Obviously, the Hunter Look-Alikes needed an explanation for what seemed like an impossibility.

Two years later, the Hunter Look-Alikes invaded Fomalhaut Four because they had learned that Bolobolo had returned home. As planned, once in orbit around the planet, the Hunter Look-Alikes had threatened to destroy all life on the planet unless the inhabitants turned Bolobolo over to them for interrogation.

The reason was simple. It was evident to the Hunter Look-Alikes that Bolobolo had developed a genocidal biological agent specifically targeting the Hunter Look-Alikes' genetic signature. Consequently, they viewed her as an existential threat.

The Hunter Look-Alikes had intended to *force* Bolobolo to provide them with the details on the agent she used to kill the contingent that was sent to eliminate Hunter. Then they intended to force her to develop a counteragent.

If Bolobolo manufactured both the agent and the counteragent using facilities provided by the Hunter Look-Alikes, and she could demonstrate the lethality of the agent and the effectiveness of the counteragent, they intended to execute her humanely.

Otherwise, the Hunter Look-Alikes intended to use their understanding of female anatomy and emotional vulnerability to subject Bolobolo to what she would categorize as a horrifying death.

Inexplicably, the *thousands* of Hunter Look-Alikes who were dispatched to Fomalhaut Four to capture Bolobolo *also* disappeared without a trace. That second event only strengthened the Hunter Look-Alikes' belief that Bolobolo *was* responsible for the deaths. And it only strengthened the resolve of the Hunter Look-Alikes to eliminate the threat that Bolobolo posed.

The trouble had always been where and when to attack Bolobolo and/ or the *Dominion* with a reasonable prediction of success. When the Hunter Look-Alikes had plotted the execution of Hunter, they believed the outcome was sure, and they would succeed. Likewise, when the Hunter Look-Alikes attempted to seize control of Fomalhaut Four, they believed they had an even better chance of success.

And yet, in *both* cases, thousands of their number had apparently died.

Fortuitously, at least from the perspective of the Hunter Look-Alikes, the year *after* the failed takeover of Fomalhaut Four, Oakford had announced on the dark net that a woman named Jazarah Worku possessed two custom-designed Rexian sheer dresses and two bolts of Resion sheer fabric.

While the Hunter Look-Alikes had provided security details for King Tyrannosaurus Rex of K2-72e in the past, they had no need of Rexian sheer. However, the look-alikes very much wanted to interrogate Worku. And over the years, too many of Worku's customers had talked about buying squares of Rexian sheer on the dark net. Teams were dispatched to monitor the diminishing number of places that Worku might attempt to sell her sheer. And word had just arrived from the Hunter Look-Alikes stationed on Alpha Crucis Four had apprehended Worku and had her in custody.

This welcome bit of news had created a sense of satisfaction in the Hunter Look-Alikes investigating Moreau's underground laboratory, but like 24.3372 .393758.738.39.60766.2.9175659, they knew their discoveries would be more consequential than anything Worku could tell the horde.

To be clear, the Hunter Look-Alikes *hadn't* known that they would find

Moreau at the site. They only knew the site continued to broadcast *some* type of report on the dark net. And that seemed suspicious, given the steep decline of traffic on the Night's social interchanges.

Eventually, the Horde of Hunter Look-Alikes had decided to investigate. And everyone on the team had realized what it meant when they staged an assault and found Moreau in the central laboratory.

Obviously, they recognized him immediately, even though it had been many years since Moreau served the Hunter Look-Alikes directly. *Every* Hunter Look-Alike had been taught their origin story. They knew of Moreau's early research, his banishment to Nu Scorpii One, and his abduction from that secret genetic research facility, even if the details of that abduction were vague.

Notably, as a condition of his exile to Nu Scorpii One, Moreau was required to file reports with the researchers who had banished him there. Once the Hunter Look-Alike slaughtered those researchers, the look-alikes continued to receive those reports... until they *didn't*.

And at that point, the horde had sent a scouting team, followed by an attack squadron. And they slaughtered all the Realm Force personnel who were attempting to take possession of the contents of the facility and obliterated the genetic research facility on the surface of the planet.

Interestingly, at the same time, stories began to appear on the dark net that the *Dominion* had added many more female crewmembers to the crew. And as the *Dominion* provided security for many conventions and conferences around the Night in the following years, some of those women admitted to being kidnapped and taken to Nu Scorpii One. And some even said that Moreau had been captured when they were liberated from the genetic research facility.

For the Hunter Look-Alikes, it was easy to conclude that Moreau was either in the hands of the crew of the *Dominion* or Realm Force or both. And that had provided the connection for them to decide that Bolobolo had learned enough from Moreau to engineer a virus that had killed over *thirty thousand* of their kind.

The Hunter Look-Alikes had known it was speculation. But it seemed *obvious*. And now, 24.3372.393758.738.39.60766.2.9175659 felt the rise of a second deep sense of satisfaction. In his review of the work orders and progress reports from the processing array for Moreau's laboratory, it was clear that the *Dominion* had refused to deliver Moreau to Realm Force. Instead, the senior staff had informed Realm Force of the existence of the generic research facility on Nu Scorpii One. And then they had set up an underground black site deep in the Night for Moreau to work on a very specific project under the close supervision of the *Dominion's* Chief Medicalist, Adi Bolobolo.

Yes, some outside observers might wonder how the Hunter Look-Alikes could assume that Bolobolo would possess such knowledge and be able to learn so much from Moreau in such a short amount of time. But the Look-Alikes knew that both incidents of the deaths of *thousands* of Hunter Look-Alikes occurred in proximity to the *Dominion* and not Realm Force. And Moreau *hadn't* been on the *Dominion* at the time.

And that left Bolobolo. And the discoveries at Moreau's underground laboratory simply solidified the idea that the Hunter Look-Alikes had been right all along about their most villainous enemy. And they had been right all along to make the preparations that had been undertaken.

Now 24.3372.393758.738.39.60766.2.9175659 knew that the threat posed by Bolobolo could *not* be overstated. Every moment that Bolobolo remained free represented a moment that could *end* the Horde of Hunter Look-Alikes. It was *imperative* that the *Dominion* be found. It was imperative that the ship be crippled and Bolobolo apprehended, and *forced* to reveal *everything* she knew.

And *if* that meant Hunter Look-Alikes lined up by the *millions* to brutally beat and gang rape Bolobolo until they were sure the danger had passed, 24.3 372.393758.738.39.60766.2.9175659 knew with certainty that *every* member of the horde would *gladly* volunteer to do so.

•   •   •

On the terraformed world of Groombridge 1830b, Luna Reyes casually strolled through the large park in the center of the main population area for the planet. Moments before, she had turned to take the entrance to a walking bridge that crossed over a small pond filled with ducks and colorful fish. As she did, she focused on every sight and sound as she took a few moments to enjoy the surroundings.

As always, for terraformed worlds in the Realm, it was a *beautiful* day. In another two hours, the simulated star above Reyes would set in the sky, which, of course, was just a projection created by the image generators on the inside of the terraforming dome that surrounded the planet.

Groombridge 1830b had been settled in the early days of the Realm's star system expansion. It was just under 30 light years from Earth, much closer than other Realm worlds, some of which were almost 150 light years away. In addition, the star at the heart of the Groombridge 1830 system was a yellowish subdwarf. Long before the Coming, astronomers labeled the subdwarf a "metal-poor star." Surveys made after the Coming reported a single rocky world, two-thirds the size of Earth, barren with no atmosphere and no signs of life.

The Wind, with their usual speed, had encased the smallish world in the terraforming dome and generated an atmosphere as other machines sent to the surface of the planet strategically pulverized the rock and transformed it into soil. Plants were planted. Animals were released. Homesteads awarded. And votes taken.

And in one of those votes, an overwhelming majority of inhabitants indicated that they found the smallish, weak-looking star of the Groombridge 1830 system discomforting when compared with Sol, the star at the heart of the star system that housed Earth.

That night, the stars in the night sky on Groombridge 1830b remained the stars that might have been seen before any terraforming began. But in the morning, the star that rose appeared larger and more vibrant than the yellowish subdrawf at the heart of the Groombridge 1830 system, for it was enhanced by the image generators on the inside of the terraforming dome. That same day, all the colors on the surface of Groombridge 1830b became correspondingly more saturated and vibrant.

Of course, Reyes had reviewed the history of the planet long before she strolled across the small arched bridge. But she took those moments to remind herself of the planet's history as she appreciated the intertwining vines growing up and around the bridge's walkway railings with their pale yellow and violet flowers, and the sound of gurgling water rose from below her. And as the ducks quacked, and the fish made flicking sounds in the water, Reyes pondered how different everything would look *without* the artificial enhancement of the terraforming dome.

Reyes found it all fascinating because, as much as it was beautiful, it was also all entirely *fake*. Without the terraforming dome above, she would be walking on barren, lifeless rock. And even if the terraforming dome had simply created a breathable environment, the only reason the day seemed *so* light and airy was that the image generators inside the dome *forced* the day to appear that way.

Without that alteration, the dim light of Groombridge 1830 would present a darker day. And most of the colors would bleed out of the surrounding flowers, ducks, and fish, leaving behind a landscape tinged in sickly yellow.

In all honesty, given what Reyes had done in recent years, the idea of Realmers living in worlds of illusion seemed more true than not. Although given the events of the last year, perhaps the majority of Realmers weren't living as *deeply* in the illusion as they wanted.

Too many Realms worlds had supposedly rebelled, requiring the declaration of martial law. And afterwards, even when the rebellions were supposedly quelled, the communications coming out of those planets always seemed to turn strident. Those who lived on *other* planets of the Realm had no idea what to think about it all.

Still, the vast majority of Realmers could not *imagine* the life Reyes led in recent years. Realmers would look at her and only see an average Realm maiden, not beautiful but not ugly, a modest person. They would assume she was sweet, kind, and polite. And they would think that she wanted to start a family soon.

They would only *think* that because they would see Reyes reflected in light of what they *thought* the Realm still was. Granted, Reyes understood that the Realm might *never* have been what most Realmers thought it was. But *maybe* it had been closer to that when the Wind ruled over humanity?

Reyes had never known the Realm before the Disappearance. She hadn't been born yet. But even though she had grown up *after* the Disappearance of the Wind, Reyes had always believed the Realm was a place of sweetness and light, a bright, happy place where everyone treated each other as they wished to be treated.

Only later did Reyes learn that the Realm she knew had only existed because the Wind had *slaughtered* untold numbers of humans after the Coming to establish their authoritarian rules. And even after the Realm was established, the Wind had continued to slaughter any human who opposed them at *any* time as they governed.

Of course, the latter slaughters *weren't* public and in the open like the ones during the original conquest. In the latter slaughter, citizens would simply disappear in the dark of night. No one would hear from them again. And no one would speak of them.

And if you didn't personally *know* those who disappeared, it was as if no one *ever* disappeared. Instead, all was light, bright, and airy.

And for most of her life, it had *seemed* to Reyes like everything *was* light, bright, and airy. And only later did Reyes learned that there were enemies at work in the darker, duller areas of the Realm. And that had *forced* Sotheby, Nicolesu, and most importantly, High King Rule Ton to operate in dark ways as well.

And Reyes had *only* learned that because Sotheby had recruited her to *operate* in the Realm and the Night in *precisely* that dark way.

Sotheby's original invitation had shocked Reyes. She had no idea that Sotheby even knew she existed. Sotheby was tall, gorgeous, statuesque, and *filled* with self-confidence. Sotheby's family was known across the Realm. They were important people and Sotheby's father had even given his life protecting the Realm.

Sotheby was everything that Reyes *wasn't*.

And yet, Sotheby had sought her out just after Reyes graduated from Realm Force Academy to recruit Reyes for something called a special tactical team. Reyes had never heard of special tactical teams, but once Reyes recovered from her initial shock, she readily agreed to join.

And then Sotheby had dosed Reyes with Angel Haze. And Reyes had entered the darker, dustier, and morally duller portions of the Realm and lived there ever since. And, of course, Reyes *loved* being on the special tactical teams because Sotheby asked her to serve on the teams, and Reyes was in Sotheby's thrall.

Still, without a doubt, *no one* who knew Reyes as she grew up on her home planet of Castor Three could ever be convinced that she had done the things she had done during her time on the special tactical teams. But again, Reyes had been dosed with Angel Haze. And while Angel Haze supposedly *couldn't* make you violate your own moral imperatives, those skilled at manipulation understood that moral imperatives could be altered by creating explanations for why specific actions were necessary.

Those explanations modified a person's underlying narrative. And once a person's underlying narrative changed to justify the unjustifiable, that person's moral imperatives soon adjusted themselves to follow.

The previous year had *fully* demonstrated that concept for anyone who had followed the activities of Reyes' special tactical team. To be clear, Reyes *wasn't* the leader of her special tactical team. She was simply a member of it. In fact, Reyes' special tactical team *had* no leader. Sotheby led Reyes' special tactical team. They also received orders from Nicolescu and High King Ruler Ton.

In the last year, those orders had sent Reyes' tactical team to *many* planets throughout the Realm. The details varied, but for the past year, the missions were fundamentally the same, and those similarities had begun with a mission to Alpha Pegasi Three.

The year before, Reyes and the rest of her special tactical team had undertaken a mission with two objectives. First, the team would locate twelve young men who could be framed for crimes that would later be revealed. And second, Reyes and her team would arrange to dose the governor of Alpha Pegasi Three with Angel Haze so that Ton could give the governor instructions that would make him look crazy and justify the actions of regular tactical teams when they killed him.

According to the Alpha Pegasi Three mission briefing, the governor had never truly supported the Leadership Council in Jerusalem. And High King Ruler Ton had decided the governor needed to be eliminated.

On the plus side, the governor's death caused enough emotional turmoil that inhabitants of the planet had begun demonstrating to demand answers. And that, in turn, justified the release of millions of Realm Force robots. Over the following weeks, those robots slaughtered most of the citizens in the populated areas of the planet and beyond.

Reyes had no idea if High King Ruler Ton had been inspired by the success of the mission to Alpha Pegasi Three or if he planned to continue the approach even *before* her special tactical team was dispatched to the planet. But either way, Reyes' team was assigned to many similar missions in the months that followed.

Those missions included visits to 96 G. Piscium Three, Algol Six, Alpha Coronae Borealis One, Altair Four, Beta Ursae Majoris Two, Capella Eight, Denebola Three, Kruger 60d, Lalande 21185c, Luyten One, Pollux Five, Regulus Four, and Van Maanen 2b. Each operation varied in implementation to ensure that it would be difficult to establish a pattern in the failures in leadership. But all had provided excuses for High King Ruler Ton had been able to declare martial law.

And in many cases, he had released the robots as well.

Of course, High King Ruler Ton didn't need excuses or justifications for what he did. Nicolescu had already consolidated power over all of Realm

Force before Ton took that power from her. In addition, Nicolescu had already planned for her own coup to create an authoritarian state across the entire Realm.

In fact, many years before, Nicolescu had used the manufacturing facilities of the local Judicial Centers that had been built by the Wind to create *millions* of robots and store them in underground repositories on every planet in the Realm.

Given that overwhelming force, High King Ruler Ton could have released those robots and demanded that the citizens of the Realm obey. But from what Reyes had seen, High King Ruler Ton seemed to prefer creating situations that would elicit reactions that he could then punish.

In addition, the common theme High King Ruler Ton had invoked in the last year to target planets had been that local leadership had demonstrated a rebellious attitude toward the Leadership Council in Jerusalem. And those governors needed to be removed so the Realm could be restored to harmony. In some cases, that approach worked, and no further correction was needed.

A new governor was installed. The populace of the planet quickly adapted to the new governor's guidelines and curfews. And the inhabitants were spared the terrors of the assault bots.

As an aside, it should be noted that the existence of the robots was unknown to any citizens who had *not* been attacked by them. PLOKTA controlled the information in and out of those planets on the social net. And for the most part, any communications with the planets where the robots were released stopped during the initial release.

Reyes could imagine that the sudden silence from so many Realm worlds in sequence had many Realmers anxious about what was happening in the Realm in general. But Reyes also knew that High King Ruler Ton justified the silence by saying that it was necessary to protect the Realm.

Many times, High King Ruler Ton had claimed that the ideas being spread on the rebellious planet were so *corrosive* that they had to be *stopped* by any means possible lest they spread and disrupt even more worlds. That claim was then strengthened with video feeds from the affected worlds that showed the inhabitants of those worlds violently attacking each other. For the most part, that convinced Realmers who *didn't* live on the affected planet to let Realm Force handle the problem while they enjoyed the relative safety of *their* planet and hoped that it would all work out.

Of course, it was inevitable that the uncertainty about what had happened on the suddenly silent worlds could foster anxiety about what might happen in the future to the rest of the planets in the Realm. And Ton had even explained to the special tactical teams that the generated anxiety could be used to convince unaffected populations to wish for the certainty that would result from martial law instead of wondering every day if their fellow citizens were going to disintegrate into chaos unexpectedly.

Reyes was willing to admit that she *might* be reading into the expressions she saw on the faces of the inhabitants of Groombridge 1830b when she arrived on the planet. But it seemed to her that behind every smile, there was a twinge of fear.

Having grown up in the Realm, Reyes knew that generalized angst and free-floating anxiety were new to the Realm. But it was something that Reyes had seen more and more as the last year had progressed.

As for the current assignment, Reyes was sure that once her special tactical team completed today's assignment, those expressions on the faces of the populace of Groombridge 1830b would deepen. And perhaps the disquiet and desperation behind those expressions would twist and tighten enough to snap.

Interestingly, Reyes had already experienced one mission where High King Ruler Ton had decided to act on impulse, seemingly *without* any justification. Six months before, Reyes' special tactical team had created an incident on Capella Eight. But instead of outrage of *any* kind, the inhabitants of the planet had *all* responded obediently, *immediately* after Ton imposed a curfew. Yet, in spite of that, High King Rule Ton had released the robots to kill them all anyway.

High King Ruler Ton had never explained his reasoning on the matter. Reyes didn't expect him to do so. High King Ruler Ton was the ultimate ruler of the Realm. He only needed to tell the special tactical teams what he wanted to accomplish for each mission, and, of course, they would all do their best to achieve it.

Now, a chirp on the special tactical team comm snapped Reyes out of her reverie as she crossed the lovely bridge that arced over the small pond.

"Lune!" another special tactical member, nicknamed Stix, called out over the team comm. "Target and company have entered the loop. They're all yours. We'll block access until it's done."

"Acknowledged," Reyes softly called back.

Glancing up, Reyes spotted her target through the foliage of the small park. After studying video surveillance of the target for the past week, the special tactical team had decided that a small loop in the park's walking trails would be the perfect place to stage their intervention.

Honestly, while the name of the governor of Groombridge 1830b had been included in their review for the missions, Reyes had gone through enough governors in the last year that she no longer cared about their names. Honestly, all the names had blurred together. Still, Reyes did have to admit that her target for *this* mission had a name with a certain lilt and cadence.

Governor Tiago Costa del Rey had served as the planet's governor for the last ten years. He was well-liked by the populace. Maybe that had made the man cocky. However, the mission briefing made it clear that he was questioning too many things about what was happening in the Realm to his private confidants. And High King Ruler Ton had made it clear that Costa del Rey was dangerous to the Realm.

Not that Reyes needed an explanation for what she needed to do. As always, she only needed to know her part. And for this mission, it was her turn to take the lead.

As such, she continued strolling forward as she watched the couple heading her way. And once she had an average speed for their stroll, she matched her pace to ensure that she would meet them where the walking trail passed between the thickest patches of vegetation.

Even though it wouldn't matter in the end for the mission's success, Reyes' special tactical team had chosen that spot as the easiest location to hide from the video surveillance that Realm Force maintained over the entire planet. And no, Reyes didn't *need* to hide from the video surveillance. It was just a little game that her special tactical team played with PLOKTA.

Interesting, whenever Reyes thought about playing games with PLOKTA, her mind drifted to the *dozens* of images that the special tactical teams had of PLOKTA dressed in a wild variety of costumes. Reyes didn't know exactly *why* the special tactical teams had started doing that, and she certainly didn't understand why they had *stopped*. But there was a small part of Reyes that could imagine how fun that would have been.

Now, glancing down, Reyes checked her appearance. She quickly smoothed and straightened the modest, pastel-green dress. She checked her comfortable shoes for scuff marks. She also continued walking forward to confirm that the cotton-like fabric of the dress was flowing easily.

Of note, Reyes had tightened the tie that the dress featured at her natural waist. Reyes knew that once the tie was cinched, it would allow others, men *and* women, to estimate Reyes' hip-to-waist ratio. And while Reyes was average in almost every measurement of attractiveness, she *did* have an excellent hip-to-waist ratio of 0.7. And according to the literature before the Coming, men, in general, considered that ratio to be *ideal*. In order to blend in, however, most of the time, that *did* mean Reyes intentionally dressed to ensure that it *wasn't* easy to estimate her hip-to-waist ratio.

But for the next few moments, Reyes thought it might be useful to give the governor's brain something to do in the background. That way, he wouldn't spend too much time in the *foreground* of his brain wondering if there was anything suspicious about a young woman who had just strolled up and started talking with him.

And that was the second reason for the light cotton-like dress that Reyes had tied at her natural waist. There was enough fabric in the dress that it was easy to imagine the skirt could be easily lifted to gain access to her reproductive organs.

Soon after joining the special tactical teams, Reyes had watched a series of lectures that Sotheby had given on the use of clothing components to draw the male gaze. And one of the things that Reyes had found especially fascinating was the fact that women often designated any clothing component that improved access to the genitals as "cute."

According to Sotheby, labeling such a clothing component cute allowed women to ignore the way most men would view that same piece of clothing. It allowed women to attribute innocence to the shorter or fuller skirts and overlook the impressions those skirts made on men, on average, in general.

And yes, Reyes could have increased the effect her dress would have on the governor simply by switching to the same length dress with an empire waist. Such a dress lifted the waist of the dress until it rested directly under the breasts. This change would not only accentuate the shape of the breasts. It also ensured that any fullness in the skirt would sway and flow, making it clear there were *no* obstacles to reaching beneath it.

Reyes opted *not* to go with the empire waist because she thought it would make her seem too eager. As far as Reyes was concerned, the dress cinched at her waist offered the perfect combination of innocence with a hint of alluring invitation, even for the girl of average looks and height.

Over the next ten minutes, Reyes made her way across the bridge and into the wooded path on the other side, winding through the path that she knew would lead her to the governor and his walking companion. According to the records that the special tactical team had reviewed, the governor was a confirmed bachelor, which was still a bit unusual for a Realmer. But from the posts on the social net, many seemed to enjoy the fact that their governor wasn't rushing to settle down and start a family, even if it was clear from the comments of *many* single female inhabitants of Groombridge 1830b that they would be happy to assist the governor in that endeavor.

Now, Reyes rounded a corner on the path. And as planned, she spotted the governor and his latest girlfriend strolling toward her. Instantly, Reyes feigned a look of shock.

"Governor Rey?!" Reyes called out abruptly, then seemed to catch herself. "Oh! Sorry! I didn't mean to intrude. I just didn't expect to see you here. I mean, I've never walked in this park before, and I didn't... I wasn't..."

The governor laughed, even if his girlfriend didn't look amused. For the record, the governor's companion was, of course, a beautiful young woman, dressed in a casual outfit that was obviously designed to accentuate her physical assets.

Reyes could guess that the governor, who was a handsome man, well-built, and above average in height, attracted the attention of many women. And that likely was the reason the woman walking beside him had appeared to take an instant dislike to Reyes.

No doubt, the companion suspected the game that Reyes had chosen to play. Pretend to be vulnerable, confused, disoriented, in need of help, and willing to accept it. Most men instinctively responded to those stimuli for the same apparent reasons. If the men helped, the women might be grateful.

For now, Reyes chose to ignore the governor's companion and focus on the governor as he continued to speak.

"Please," he said warmly, "I am always happy to visit with my constituents. I should apologize to *you* for interrupting *your* walk. I *do* enjoy this path, but I certainly don't own it. In fact, I take daily walks in the evening, partly because I *enjoy* meeting new people. Would you be comfortable telling me your name?"

"Sure!" Reyes responded enthusiastically. "My name is Luna Reyes, and I'm originally from Castor Three. And actually, I only moved to Groombridge 1830b a few weeks ago."

The governor's smile broadened as he extended his hand. "Welcome to Groombridge, Luna Reyes," he said as he took a step forward.

Smiling innocently, Reyes took a step forward as well to close the gap. And just as she extended her right hand to receive the governor's handshake, Reyes snapped her left hand out to the side to release a razor-sharp knife that she had strapped to her forearm.

Gripping the blade and using a single fluid motion, Reyes expertly whipped her left hand to the right. And in the next instant, Reyes sliced through *both* carotid arteries in the governor's neck, sending sprays of blood gushing outward even as she threw herself into a side flip to avoid the splatter.

7.

In a park in the center of the main population on the terraformed world of Groombridge 1830b, Luna Reyes landed on her feet as she completed a side flip to avoid the gush of blood from the wound she had just opened. A moment ago, unexpectedly, Reyes had whipped a razor-sharp knife across the governor of the planet's neck after meeting him for the first time. That strike had severed both carotid arteries in the man's neck, and Reyes preferred *not* to have her pretty pastel green dress spattered with blood.

The governor's companion wasn't nearly as lucky or nimble. As Reyes twisted to look in the woman's direction, she could see that the governor's companion was first startled by Reyes' sudden movement. But predictably, a cascade of emotions soon erupted from the only witness to the governor's murder.

It began as the governor, looking confused about what had just happened, turned toward his companion, and the companion shuddered as a spray of blood speckled her face and dress. Then, as the governor pitched forward to land face down on the garden path, it looked like the companion finally realized the man had just been murdered, and she began to scream. And *then*, when the governor's body finally slammed into the ground with a thud and soft splat, the woman finally seemed to connect his death to the moisture she felt down her face and onto her dress.

And she looked down. And she began screaming even louder.

For her part, Reyes was already retreating into the woods as the companion began to tremble and shake, staring at the governor's body, even as she continued to scream. Sadly, violence and death *were* escalating in the Realm, but it still wasn't common. And the woman had obviously never seen anyone die. And she certainly hadn't seen anyone cut down in front of her.

The special tactical team had studied the companion enough to know she would freeze in terror when she saw the governor sliced open, just as they knew her screaming would bring others running toward the sound.

"Clear," Reyes softly called out over the team comm as she slipped into the bushes. Of course, Reyes already knew the various densities of the foliage that surrounded the walking path, so it was easy to navigate unseen back to the small bridge she had crossed just moments before. And yes, the pastel green dress made it easier for her to blend in.

It was just as easy for Reyes to discard the knife in the woods before stepping back onto the walking path to join the parkgoers who were rushing to aid the governor's companion. Earlier, the special tactical team had decided that it would be better for Reyes to double back to the attack site instead of disappearing altogether.

After all, returning to the scene of the crime would make it easier to frame the governor's companion when the time came.

Of note, as Reyes told the rest of the team that she was clear, she knew the other four young women in the special tactical team would turn away from obstructing those who wanted to enter the winding path where the governor had been murdered. And they would join those rushing up the winding path to help whoever was screaming.

Soon, Reyes returned to the spot where she had sliced open the governor's throat. By that time, there were already a dozen onlookers pretending to know what to do next. Some gawked. Some tried to comfort the companion as she screamed. Some were closely inspecting the governor's body.

As Reyes waited for the companion to spot her, she noted that the rest of her team had positioned themselves ahead and behind her on the winding path. And Reyes knew that if she gave the signal, the five of them could easily slaughter everyone in reach. But, of course, that would depend on how the next few minutes went.

Now, the companion reacted. *"Grab her!"* the companion shrieked, pointing at Reyes. *"She's* the one who did this! *She's* the one who murdered the governor!"

Reyes widened her eyes in faux-shock. She began to shake her head frantically as disbelief twisted her face, and her mouth dropped open.

"*What?!*" Reyes whimpered. "*How?!* I just walked up here. I just arrived on the planet a few days ago. How could I...? Why would I... *no!*"

Many in the crowd were already frowning. Those frowns deepened as the companion continued to accuse Reyes, her voice growing more and more panicked.

"I'm *telling* you, *she's* the one who *did* this!" the companion insisted. "I was *standing right here* when it happened!"

Reyes kept shaking her head and quickly filled her voice with pleading. "Why are you *doing* this?!" she asked, successfully sounding bewildered. "I don't even *know* you! I just came to this park to go on a little walk, and then I heard *screaming*."

Reyes began looking around as more parkgoers gathered. Happily, most of those gathered on the winding path were frowning at the accusations. And they were looking back and forth between Reyes and the former governor's companion.

Reyes could guess they were inspecting the companion's clothes. They were seeing the blood spatter and then looking at Reyes' clothing and seeing nothing but a sweet and innocent-looking dress, pristine and freshly pressed.

And while Reyes knew that everyone in the crowd would find her face and stature more normal and merely average in general, they would also be influenced by the hip-to-waist ratio that her dress gently accentuated. And that ratio would remind everyone that she was a woman. And while they would subconsciously conclude that while she had *less* value when it came to appearance, she was *still* fertile, a giver of life. And they would find it difficult to believe that Reyes could murder anyone in cold blood.

"Stop *looking* at me like *that,*" the companion began to protest, growing angry as she apparently saw the expressions change on the faces of those around her. "I'm *telling* you that she *murdered* the governor."

Reyes matched the companion's mood, turning herself into a victim, becoming more frightened and timid.

"Please don't... I don't know why you're saying..." she stuttered. "*Please.* I only came to this planet a few days ago. I wouldn't... I would never..."

On cue, the men among the onlookers, the ones who considered themselves the strongest, decided to take charge of the situation. And as Reyes continued to plead against the accusations, the all-knowing men surrounded the former governor's companion and made it clear she was going to do what they said.

"We're taking you to the Realm Force Academy," one of the men said. "They can open an investigation and figure out what happened here."

At the same time, some of the women in the group of spectators drifted toward Reyes and began to comfort her.

"It's alright," they said. "It's okay. You didn't do anything wrong. I don't know why she's saying what she's saying, but no one believes her. It's ridiculous. Anyone who even took one look at you would know that you could never hurt anyone."

Then, as Reyes looked *oh so* grateful for the women's understanding and kind words, she allowed herself to be gently turned away from the murder scene before being led away in the direction of the small bridge.

And, of course, aside from the governor and his companion, the ignorant actions of both the male and female bystanders who knew *absolutely nothing* about the *actual facts* of the situation worked out best for *all* who had gathered. And in this case, the actions of the onlookers were another proof of the proverbial saying that ignorance is bliss.

For *if* the spectators had decided that Reyes needed to be apprehended as well, the special tactical team would have *killed* them all.

●   ●   ●

At the Saturn Shipyards, in PLOKTA's lair, Twilla Evansworth continued to hop back and forth from the food replicator to the small dining table as she prepared breakfast for PLOKTA and PLOKTA's special tactical team, composed of five beautiful young women on Angel Haze, who stood in the corners of the room and stared blankly ahead.

At the beginning of her time in the lair, she had been confined to a large caged area because she was pretending to be a woman driven mad by what had been done to her. But once she had exhausted the possibilities of that approach, Evansworth adopted a more typical approach in the progression of interactions between men and women.

She smiled. She nodded. She wooed. She exaggerated. She pretended to be what she wasn't because she believed that was who PLOKTA wanted her to be.

For the entire time, Evansworth had been naked. She had been naked when she was locked in her cage. And even after PLOKTA allowed her to roam his lair freely, she had remained naked. Having grown up in the Night, Evansworth was well-practiced in developing relationships with men that afforded her more resources and liberties, with and *without* her clothes on.

To be clear, even though Evansworth had been naked almost the *entire* time she had lived in PLOKTA's lair, Evansworth understood that most men who saw her for the first time *wouldn't* find anything desirable in her, despite her lack of clothes. Indeed, most men would be repelled because not only was Evansworth missing a leg, her remaining leg and two arms were in *unexpected* places.

Evansworth's single leg seemed to be growing out of her neck. Her arms were attached to her hip sockets. Worst of all, her head and neck were attached *backward* between her legs.

Interestingly, those rearrangements *hadn't* come from any genetic or chemically induced birth defect. Instead, years before, Evansworth had decided to *irritate* the absolute *worst* individual that *anyone* could *ever* want to irritate.

Honestly, if an outside observer wanted to *attempt* to put what Evansworth had done in the *best* light, they might observe that the woman *had* shown a great deal of courage. And they might say that she had shown an utter disregard for what might happen when she decided to treat Abaddon like a *man* she was attempting to push beyond the limits of his civility.

Evanswroth had done that *many* times in her life. But most would agree that taking that approach with Abaddon was *insane*. Abaddon was *not* a human male. He was a titan and obviously alien. And his presence was always imposing, frightening, and often nightmare-inducing.

Indeed, some, when seeing Abaddon for the first time on a video comm, had decided that the images wouldn't be *real*, even though titans like the Wind had surrounded humans for almost a *thousand* years. The mistake was understandable. To a person, the Wind were at least 2.25 meters tall. They were elegant, handsome, and beautiful, and humans had easily considered them their betters.

Abaddon was *other*. Yes, he was similar in height to the Wind at 2.5 meters tall, but the similarities stopped there. Overall, Abaddon looked like a kind of centaur with thick, powerful flanks that rippled when he walked. He had massive arms that flexed as well with every movement. And those arms flowed seamlessly into a powerfully sculpted chest and abdomen.

And if that wasn't intimidating enough, Abaddon's thick, leathery skin offered the immediate impression that it would be difficult to penetrate in battle. That theme of violent encounters continued in ways through Abaddon's appearance. Abaddon's face was riddled with slashing scars, and his demeanor seemed aggressively confrontational.

His eyes burned with rage. His nostrils flared continually. His mouth was rimmed by lips pulled tight in a snarl that revealed large, discolored fangs above and below.

And all of that was accompanied by the rasp of Abaddon's breath as spittle leaked from both sides of his mouth.

But there was more that would typically make humans want to retreat from his presence. The titan had large, rough wings that stretched and flexed, seeming constantly ready to propel him forward in attack. And he wore a crude crown with only minor embellishments, constructed of something like iron. It appeared to double as a helmet, and it too was scarred with blows.

And as for weaponry, Abaddon carried a mace. But the spiked ball had no handle. Instead, it was woven into the end of a long, black braid of hair, waiting for Abaddon's head to whip and send it into action to pulverize and maim.

Worst of all, a foul *smell* wafted off the titan. And uniformly, when humans encountered it, their disgust would lurch upward in their stomachs for the stench they encountered seemed to be a combination of all things that humans found horrid. It reminded them of the sickening rot of flesh, combined with the worst skunk-like stink, all stirred together with a gagging mix of potently aged body odors.

Indeed, when Evansworth had first encountered Abaddon on the death planet of Spica Two, the psychic oppressiveness of his physical presence had made Evansworth shudder. And her second encounter was worse. But strangely, Abaddon had seemed to offer her an alliance that would free her from her recent capture by the senior staff of the *Dominion*.

When Evansworth accepted, Abaddon *had* transported her *far* from the grasp of the senior staff. Unfortunately, Abaddon also transported her *into* a rough-hewn stone cube. That prison had only gruel to sustain her physically, and so little to occupy her mind that she eventually resorted to shaping her excrement into poop-balls and stacking them in pyramid shapes. And when that failed to stave off her boredom, Evansworth even began to model her poop into clay-like figures and used them to tell herself stories.

Given the circumstances *and* Evansworth's utterly irreverent attitude toward authority, it was inevitable that Evansworth would challenge Abaddon's rule over her. And that was when Abaddon knocked Evansworth out with an energy blow. And when she woke up, she discovered that he had rearranged her into a freakish-looking tripod.

But he *hadn't* gruesomely killed her as he had done to others.

Strangely enough, according to Abaddon, his only interest in her came from the fact that the senior staff of the *Dominion* hadn't *killed* her when they had the chance. Abaddon recounted how, over multiple encounters, the senior staff had every opportunity to kill her and *should* have killed her, but they *hadn't*.

Consequently, Abaddon had said that he considered Evansworth a ripple and a perturbation. And he said it *irritated* him that he didn't know if she had some role to play in the future.

Perhaps some small part of Evansworth took that to mean that Abaddon might *not* kill her, no matter *how* she acted. And *maybe* that was enough to allow her to stand up to the titan and start throwing poop balls at him in an act of defiance. Honestly, Evansworth had no idea.

She only knew that she had reached a point where she no longer cared. She knew that Abaddon might torture her in obscene and terrifyingly impossible ways if she opposed him. But she knew she *couldn't* live in the stone box any longer. And that was why she finally acted out.

After Abaddon rearranged her physical body, an immeasurable amount of time passed as Evanworth reoriented herself to life as a tripod. And then, without warning, Evansworth found herself falling through the air and landing on the floor. And she soon realized that Abaddon had transported her to Jerusalem. And soon after, PLOKTA took her to his lair in the Saturn Shipyards.

Evansworth still wasn't sure why Abaddon hadn't killed her. For a time, she was simply grateful to be alive. Also, she wasn't sure why PLOKTA had decided to claim her when she knew that many would find her appearance deeply disturbing. But as day after day passed, Evansworth realized that *some* of her skill at manipulating men would still work on PLOKTA because he had grown used to the way she looked. And she couldn't help but start planning and scheming, just as she had always done.

Of course, since PLOKTA had *unilaterally* decided he would take her from Jerusalem and cage her in his lair on the Saturn Shipyard, he represented all the masculine figures in her life who had *always* tried to rule over her.

Of note, with the exception of the Abaddon and the senior staff of the *Dominion*, the tactic of attempting to rule over Evansworth had *always* ended up the same way. At the right time, Evansworth slaughtered her supposed authority, often in creatively violent and sadistic ways. It was simply a matter of Evansworth patiently wooing her target until he made the mistake of trusting her too much.

The wooing of PLOKTA had taken a turn almost a year ago when High King Ruler Ton targeted Alpha Pegasi Three as the first site to feel the wrath of the robots. As scenes of the robots tearing through the planet's inhabitants played out, Evansworth seized the opportunity to express what excited her, both mentally *and* physically. She had skillfully played the part of the young maiden, confused by how deeply the scene affected her. And she had convinced PLOKTA that her pleasure was out of control.

Evansworth had used the tactic before. And it worked because it exploited a simple mechanism present in the testosterone-driven predator. No matter how much a man professed to value women as individuals and inherently *human*, his reproductive system regarded women as prey, and it was naturally drawn to the weak and wounded.

Just like any hunting pack of animals focused on the weak in any herd they targeted, men would naturally be drawn to a woman who was compromised.

If a woman dressed in a way that seemed like a desperate attempt to draw attention to herself, men could consciously or unconsciously recognize that the woman was damaged emotionally. And they would target her, believing the woman's damage could be leveraged into control over her. If a woman wore anything that limited her ability to physically respond to a threat, such as awkward high heels or a long, tight skirt, men would judge her as easier to catch. And yes, if a woman seemed overwhelmed by waves of pleasure pounding through her, and especially if she seemed unable to control them and desperate to keep anyone from finding out, the idea would entice a testosterone-driven response.

Of course, even *while* Evansworth acted out the latter scenario, she was once again amused by how *idiotic* the premise was in the first place. And it had reinforced again to Evansworth that men had *no* idea how much *noise* there was in the mind of a *non-drugged* woman in her typical mental state. But men liked to fantasize that women could fall into a crazed pleasure state without mood-altering help.

And knowing that, Evansworth had put on a show for PLOKTA.

Predictably, PLOKTA had responded. Evansworth had encouraged him. And it was the first time PLOKTA had used her as a tool to control his sperm count. Looking back on it, Evansworth knew that the encounter would have been *disastrous* for the average woman who had been unceremoniously converted to a tripod.

For one thing, most women would not have survived the psychic stress of what Abaddon had done to Evansworth, and they would have found a way to end their lives. For another, most women would be so aghast at what had been done to them, they would try to ignore it and pretend that it hadn't happened.

But Evansworth had no shortage of time on her hands when Abaddon imprisoned her in the stone cube. And if she twisted just right, she could reach the regions around her neck that would have been between her legs in a typical humanoid configuration. And by exploring, she had determined that everything still *worked*.

And given that, Evansworth made a mental note that if she ever escaped the stone box, she might *still* be able to allow men to use her as a tool, despite her appearance. To be clear, Evansworth had known it would be *challenging* to find a man who would accept the way she looked, but she knew enough about men that she knew it wasn't *impossible*.

And that meant, Evansworth was *ready* when PLOKTA decided to try to take advantage as she playacted at being overwhelmed by he uncontrollable pleasure. She was ready with a variety of groans, grunts, and even giggles as PLOKTA fumbled around trying to figure out *what* he would stick *where*.

And yes, PLOKTA *still* had a special tactical team of five gorgeous young ladies who were under Angel Haze's influence and in his thrall. And he still played with them. And Evansworth knew she couldn't compete with them in terms of the standard norms of beauty.

But Evansworth also knew she didn't *have* to compete with the special tactical team because she had something that the special tactical team could never give PLOKTA. PLOKTA would *always* know that the special tactical team was treating him like they were treating him because they didn't have a *choice.*

But he would also believe that Evansworth was treating him like she was treating him because she was *grateful* for what he had done for her, and she *respected* him as a man.

And *obviously*, that was ridiculous in the extreme because she was, in essence, his prisoner. And Evansworth was determined that someday, PLOKTA *would* pay for his insolence in believing that he could *take* her and put her in a *cage* without her permission.

In the meantime, Evansworth was doing everything she could to convince PLOKTA of her deep devotion to him. She was paying close attention to his moods. She was attempting to meet any need he had, in whatever way he desired. If that meant fixing him a meal, she would do that. If that meant letting him use her as a tool, she would do that, too. And if that meant dressing up in the silly little costumes that he fantasized seeing her in, she would *definitely* do that *and* tell him how *much* she enjoyed whatever he made for her.

And *honestly*, she did appreciate the fact that she was a nearly *impossible* design challenge when it came to making *any* outfit. Nearly every body part on Evanswroth was upside-down and in the wrong place. And she was willing to admit that it was almost sweet how hard PLOKTA was trying to figure out how to make it all work from a costume perspective.

It certainly didn't absolve him of his crimes against her. But perhaps when she killed him, she would make it quick and easy.

For now, Evansworth hopped over to set the last dish she had prepared on the small dining table that PLOKTA had in his lair, only to hear PLOKTA's control console chirp with a video comm request. Glancing toward the sound, Evansworth could see that the request came from Ton.

Multiple thoughts cascaded through Evansworth's mind when she saw the self-proclaimed High King Ruler of the Realm appear on PLOKTA's center display. For one thing, Evansworth knew that PLOKTA hadn't told Ton about his dalliances with her. PLOKTA had specifically told Evansworth that he wasn't going to say anything to Ton because it was none of Ton's business. And yes, Evansworth considered that a good thing because it meant that PLOKTA was protective enough, and perhaps ashamed enough, of his relationship that she wouldn't have to fight against anyone trying to get between her and PLOKTA as she tried to drive him deeper into an emotional dependency on her.

And to that end, Evansworth was always careful to make sure PLOKTA's cameras never picked her up on a video comm. She had no doubt Ton would disapprove of the fact that PLOKTA was letting her roam free in his lair. And yes, PLOKTA had told her that he had created a filter to screen her out of his transmissions, and Evansworth appreciated having that extra protection. But she also took it as a point of pride that she *still* had enough body position awareness to make PLOKTA's filter unnecessary.

And yes, seeing Ton on PLOKTA's display also indicated that Evansworth needed to reorient her plans for eating lunch with PLOKTA, playfully chattering with him, and laughing at his jokes. PLOKTA's conversations with Ton *always* went long, or PLOKTA ended up with a big assignment.

Given that, as she had done multiple times in the last year, without saying a word, Evansworth switched tactics and began moving the food she had prepared from the small dining table in PLOKTA's lair to the tray that PLOKTA had manufactured to attach to his workstation because he ate so many meals while working.

And, of *course*, she didn't complain. And she didn't admonish him for *always* working. And she didn't roll her eyes and harrumph. She simply laid out his meal before settling down on the floor beside him to stare at him adoringly and imagine all the ways she would kill him when the right time presented itself.

•   •   •

In his lair at the Saturn Shipyards, PLOKTA was well aware of all of Evansworth's movements beside him as he continued his conversation with Ton. PLOKTA understood that other men would think he was crazy to keep Evansworth around when he had five other gorgeous women ready to do *anything* to him or for him at *any* time.

And frankly, PLOKTA often surprised himself over how deeply connected he felt to Evansworth. She was just *so* grateful for everything he had done for her. And PLOKTA had *never* encountered *that* kind of attitude in *any* relationship that he'd had with a woman. Evansworth just *never* complained, even when he would have understood if he did.

Case in point, Evansworth had just worked for almost an hour, ordering food from the food replicator and hopping back and forth to get it all arranged on the small table in his lair. And then Ton called

For context, it *wasn't* the first time Ton had interrupted something that

PLOKTA and Evansworth had planned together. Ton *often* called without scheduling a meeting. Ton would have an idea. Ton would want an update. Ton heard something he found funny. Ton had just finished tormenting Sotheby after he tied her up, let her slip out from under Angel Haze, taunted her, and then put her back under Angel Haze. And he wanted to tell PLOKTA about it because Sotheby had been *so* furious, but she couldn't do anything about it.

Indeed, a few weeks ago, PLOKTA had wondered if it just *seemed* like Ton was calling more and more. So, PLOKTA had run a quick query against his comm log with Ton and graphed out the results.

It was easy to see that the frequency of Ton's calls *had* increased. It was just as easy to see that Ton was calling at all hours of the day and night. PLOKTA understood that Ton didn't have anyone else he could confide in. Everyone else who knew that he was High King Ruler of the Realm was on Angel Haze. And PLOKTA could guess that Ton was self-aware enough to grow tired of Nicolescu and Sotheby telling him how wonderful he was instead of having an honest conversation with another human being.

Granted, PLOKTA had *never* openly disagreed with Ton on anything. He hadn't opposed any of Ton's ideas or called out Ton on any logical inconsistencies. However, he had and would continue to ask Ton to clarify some of his actions if something didn't feel right. And honestly, so far, in *every* case, when PLOKTA had a question, Ton had an answer, and it was a good one.

And that meant PLOKTA *did* respect Ton as a strategic thinker. And he had been amazed by how Ton had been able to predict the reactions of the inhabitants of planets through the various emotional manipulations he had created. Granted, PLOKTA also understood that Ton had lived before the Coming, and he had plenty of examples of governments, news organizations, social media companies, and advertisers manipulating their constituents. Perhaps Ton knew what he knew because he had lived through it, and he was mimicking what he had seen done.

Either way, it was *working* as far as PLOKTA was concerned. By now, there were *dozens* of Realm worlds under declarations of direct control from the Leadership Council in Jerusalem, enforced by Realm Force and its violently ruthless robots. Add to that PLOKTA's own complete round-the-clock, relentlessly intrusive surveillance with automated tracking and identification of suspicious behavior, and all of it created an absolute authoritarian rule on those planets.

And it echoed what the Wind had imposed and implemented almost a thousand years before. Perhaps the inhabitants of the world living under the authority of the Leadership Council didn't understand the full extent of Ton's rule over them. But Ton *could* at any time end any delusion that the inhabitants might have about the nature of their existence. And there would be *nothing* that any of them could do about it. Frankly, PLOKTA was looking forward to the day when Ton would make the *ultimate* announcement to the *entire* Realm.

"Submit or *die*."

Once that was in place, PLOKTA couldn't imagine how it would *ever* change. At that point, Ton would be able to dictate where humanity focused its attention. And he could dedicate their energies to any project he chose. And it wouldn't matter if Abaddon was telling the truth about the Children of the Prime or not, because a unified humanity would have tremendous benefits even if Abaddon *had* lied about the urgency of the problem.

Honestly, PLOKTA had always thought that humans needed to be more focused. PLOKTA hadn't lived before the Coming, so he didn't have any firsthand experience working with humans during that time. And yes, there were plenty of stories and memes from before the Coming about users *not* reading manuals, not being able to understand how to troubleshoot simple problems, not remembering the steps involved in any given process, and entering bad data.

But PLOKTA had always felt like almost everyone who had grown up in the Realm was just *too* comfortable in their lives. There was no survival instinct. And even with everything that had happened since the Disappearance of the Wind, most Realmers were still plodding along in life, going on walks, gardening, listening to pleasant music, reading simple, inspiring books, watching romantic films that all seemed to have the same plotline.

As far as PLOKTA was concerned, most Realmers were wasting their lives. And despite the fact that *many* Realmers had already died, and he did not doubt that *many* more *would* die, PLOKTA believed that humanity *would* be stronger, faster, and smarter in the end.

For now, PLOKTA had just finished the general status update that Ton had requested after the video conference opened. And PLOKTA could guess that, next, Ton would offer a list of instructions for specific planets. In the meantime, PLOKTA reminded himself how amazing Evansworth was even in the present instant.

Without even looking, PLOKTA knew that Evansworth had transferred his portion of the meal that she had prepared to the tray attached to his desk, and she had settled in beside him on the floor to patiently wait for him to finish his video comm with Ton.

And yes, PLOKTA was also imagining how he would reward Evansworth for the way she had been so patient about the situation. PLOKTA had heard the stories about Evansworth when he served on the *Dominion* and when she returned to it with Falcon. And he knew that, in the past, Evansworth had been a skilled emotional and sexual manipulator. But after everything that had happened to her, PLOKTA could easily believe that Evansworth had given up on all of it. And that Evansworth's enthusiasm to play with him came from a genuine gratitude because she obviously enjoyed the physical games they played. And, *again*, she was *grateful* that her physical appearance didn't drive him away.

Of course, PLOKTA made sure his excitement over what he planned to do to Evansworth after the video call with Ton *never* reached his face. Instead, he stared at Ton, pretending to listen intently as the High King Ruler of the Realm offered his insights into what should happen next on the various planets with active operations underway.

To be clear, PLOKTA always had a summarizer running during his meetings, and it would provide him with the critical action items from each meeting. It was PLOKTA's backup, in case his mind wandered as Ton rambled on.

Now, Ton *finally* seemed to be winding down.

"Last item," Ton continued, "I know we developed multiple scenarios for the narratives we would push after our plain-Jane special tactical team murdered Governor Costa del Rey on Groombridge 1830b. However, our field testing suggests that we'll receive the best responses by characterizing the governor's companion as a vixen influencer. If the projections hold when we begin to deploy, we should be able to stir up enough hatred against her to 'force' us to deploy Realm Force to protect her and prevent the citizens from carrying out a travesty of justice."

8.

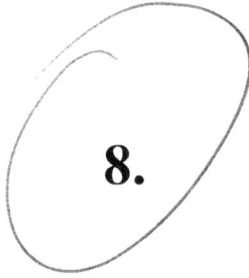

In his quarters on the *Dominion*, Oakford frowned as he turned him head to look away from the didactic display that Falcon had created for him on his small dining table to stare at the strange structure in the center of the room. It was unlike any other art installation that Falcon had done for him. And Oakford had no idea what he was looking at.

Almost a decade ago, after the senior staff were reunited with the *Dominion*, they rescued Falcon from a Realm Force maximum security facility called Hades. At the end of that mission, Falcon sacrificed herself to save Hunter's life. Only then did Oakford, Hunter, Bolobolo, and MacDuff learn that Falcon was actually part-human and part sophisticated cyber suit.

In fact, the human part was *only* named Rachel. As a young girl, Rachel had been pulled from the streets of the Night by the Marauder Horde Lord G'Utz. And in the coming years, she had endured brutal torture and mutilation at his hands. It reduced her to a scarred head and torso, leaving her blind, deaf, and mute. Then, somehow, G'Utz acquired a sophisticated cyber suit. The provider of that cybersuit installed what was left of Rachel inside it, restoring all her senses and giving her the appearance of an extraordinarily beautiful woman.

Unfortunately, Falcon's rescue from Hades exposed her and Hunter to high levels of heat and radiation. Knowing Hunter couldn't survive the conditions, Falcon wrapped herself around Hunter, sacrificing her cyber suit to save Hunter's life. Afterward, it seemed inevitable that Rachel would spend the rest of her life in her mutilated state.

Thankfully, a Mystery soon appeared who called himself Haymakers

Notch. The man looked exactly like a former *Dominion* crewmember named Thomas Harnecky. He offered to install Rachel into an upgraded version of her cyber suit under one condition.

Notch told Oakford that he needed to become the proprietor of the upgraded cybersuit and become responsible for everything Falcon did with the suit. Wanting Rachel to be free once more from the effects of what G'Utz had done to her, Oakford agreed. Notch then gave Oakford what looked like a much-too-small black lace glove. And when Oakford pulled it on, the glove dissolved into his hand, and the interface to the cyber suit wired itself into Oakford's neural network.

That arrangement allowed Rachel to become Falcon once more. But it had also introduced tension in Oakford's relationship with his Number One. Without a doubt, Oakford relied on Falcon and Hunter to advise him on all tactical and strategic matters. He knew he *needed* Falcon and Hunter to be their best if he was going to be at his best.

But the process of upgrading to a new cyber suit had not only revealed that Rachel and the cybersuits existed, but it had also given Oakford *control* over Falcon's upgraded cyber suit. And even though Oakford *never* intended to use that control, the fact that he *had* the control had spawned an increasing level of anxiety in Rachel.

In fact, at one point, Rachel's anxiety increased to the point that she asked The Falcon to suggest that Oakford use the cybersuit for his physical pleasure. Rachel knew that Oakford pleasuring himself with the cyber suit would create an emotional bond that she could use to control Oakford. And when Oakford refused to treat the cybersuit like a toy, Rachel took that as a sign that Oakford wasn't loyal to her.

Months of tension followed. But eventually, Oakford had made a suggestion that Rachel found acceptable. Oakford promised Rachel they would set aside time to spend together in his quarters. And during that time, he would let her pose for him. And he suggested that she pose naked so he could appreciate her beauty. However, Oakford also stipulated that *if* Falcon posed naked, she needed to pattern the pose on a recognized piece of art that existed before the Coming.

Thankfully, the arrangement satisfied Rachel, most likely because Rachel believed that the cyber suit's physical beauty would eventually overwhelm Oakford. During those sessions, Falcon would go to Oakford's quarters. She would prepare. She would send Oakford a text-only comm when she was ready.

And Oakford would issue a command to lock all her joints so she couldn't move.

Then, Oakford would return to his quarters and enjoy a good meal, perhaps read a good book, listen to some beautiful music, and appreciate Falcon's form as a work of art. And yes, Oakford had been well aware that Rachel would think that having a naked woman in his quarters would only drive him toward lust. But Oakford believed he *could* rejoice in the cyber suit's physical perfection without sexually assaulting it.

It had been a struggle, but Oakford *had* remained merely appreciative during the first series of posing sessions. Then, the senior staff had grown busy with missions, and soon four years had gone by without a session.

Last year, Falcon had offered to start the posing sessions once more, and Oakford didn't know how to say no without offending Rachel. By the end of that first new session, Oakford was glad he had agreed to do it.

Falcon had chosen a series of paintings and a sculpture by a French artist named Jean-Léon Gérôme. The collection was called "Pygmalion and Galatea." The work illustrated the story of an artist disenchanted with human females who then goes on to create his perfect feminine match. Two of the paintings featured the artist Pygmalion straining to kiss his sculpture, named Galatea, hoping to bring it to life.

Interestingly enough, for that session, Falcon asked Oakford to participate in the posing. And after Oakford dressed in a costume similar to what the artist wore in the painting and stretched himself upward to reach Falcon's lips, something unusual happened.

Oakford had closed his eyes. But shortly after Oakford's lips touched Falcon's, a dialog box had popped up in his mental field of vision. It seemed to be a message request. And the subject line was both a request and an instruction.

"Keep Kissing Me. Don't React. Please Acknowledge This Request So We Can Chat."

And, of course, there was a blinking "Accept Request" button hovering in his mind. Oakford mentally focused on the button. It highlighted. And in the next moment, Oakford gave the button a mental push.

That action allowed Falcon to communicate directly with Oakford's mind. She had quickly explained. First, though, she had reminded him to *keep* kissing her.

Falcon had said the kiss would obscure his face. And she said the Pixie would interpret any rise in body or skin temperature as normal arousal. As for why Falcon hadn't made such a mind-to-mind request before, she explained that Ralchel had only recently become comfortable with the idea. Then Falcon had gone on to explain that she had evidence that the Pixie had given a female crewmember to the catamountus to eat. And Falcon had observed that the woman was probably one of Nicolescu's spies that Sotheby had placed on board when some of the former crew had rejoined the ship over fifteen years ago.

Of course, Oakford and Falcon couldn't hold their kissing pose for too long without the Pixie becoming suspicious. And after a few moments, Oakford had leaned back and tried to look satisfied.

Consequently, Oakford and Falcon had continued the posing sessions for the past year, with Falcon finding creative ways to hide the fact that she was communicating mentally with Oakford. Both of them understood the difficulty of accomplishing that.

The Pixie was the ultimate observer. It could easily detect microexpressions in Oakford's face. And the Pixie had *years* of recordings of Oakford's expressions, so it would know if anything was amiss. So far, Falcon's design of the posing session *seemed* to be working.

On the other hand, Falcon hadn't had anything else substantial to report after telling Oakford about the human female femur bone that she saw in the catamountus' lair. However, the brief mental conversations had allowed Oakford and Falcon to discuss topics they could *never* discuss with the Pixie listening in. For instance, Oakford and Falcon had *multiple* conversations about what they would do if the Pixie fell into a cascade that drove it *insane* and what the crew's *realistic* chances were of surviving such a scenario.

And yes, both Oakford and Falcon recognized the chances of surviving that scenario were *not good*. But at least the posing sessions with the accompanying short mental chats were encouraging to have, even if they didn't supply any solutions.

Still, none of that had prepared Oakford for what he saw when he walked into his quarters a few moments ago. As usual, Falcon had set up a representative collage of explanatory materials on the small table in the small dining area in his quarters.

There was a reproduction of a framed painting on a stand, along with a tablet that Oakford guessed was ready to play the presentation that Falcon had recorded for the posing session. A title card attached to the bottom of the painting's stand read *"Nu descendant un escalier n° 2* by Marcel Duchamp 1912." The line below the title contained what Oakford guessed was the title of the painting, translated to Realm Standard, "Nude Descending a Staircase, No. 2."

That was when Oakford had frowned and glanced at the art installation in the middle of his quarters. Unfortunately, even after learning the title of the piece, Oakford still had *no* idea what he was looking at.

To be clear, Oakford knew enough about art before the Coming that he had immediately assumed the style of the painting had Cubist influences. But he had to admit that he had *no* idea how the artist intended the piece to represent a nude descending a set of stairs. There did seem to be something similar to stairs near the bottom of the painting. But Oakford was having a difficult time seeing anything else.

Still, the colors worked well in the overall design. The painting was done in a monochromatic neutral color palette. It was blacks, browns, and ochers, and perhaps some subtle tones of blue.

Oakford quickly gave up trying to figure out anything else on his own. He picked up the tablet that sat in front of the painting and tapped the screen.

A moment later, Oakford's quarters filled with Falcon's voice, soft and lilting, as lovely as always.

"Good evening, captain," Falcon began. "For this posing session, I chose a painting that I find fascinating, especially since the reaction to it makes me laugh so *much.*

"As the title placard says, the painting was created by Marcel Duchamp in 1912. It's quite unusual because Duchamp was attempting to do something *new.* When speaking about the painting at a later date, Duchamp indicated that he had seen the newly created 'chronophotographs' of fencers and horses galloping that were created with strobe lights. And he said those frozen frames of movement gave him the idea for the painting. Also of note, there is a series of photographs by Eadweard Muybridge called Woman Walking Downstairs. They were created in 1887, 25 years before the painting and it seemed like they might have influenced Duchamp as well.

"Still, in interviews, Duchamp was clear that he didn't copy those types of photographs. Instead, he said he aimed to create a 'static representation of movement, a static composition of indications of various positions taken by a form in movement.'

"To me, that's a very interesting idea. Duchamp apparently visualized the individual frames that characterized his subject's movements, rendered them in a Cubist-like style, and then overlapped them to create the painting you see before you. Hopefully, now that you know what it's supposed to be, it will begin to make more sense.

"However, I must admit that while I find the painting itself interesting, I find the initial *reactions* to it hysterical. Bear in mind, the painting went on to become *very* well known and a *recognized* moment in art history. But it certainly *wasn't* that when it appeared.

"In fact, the reactions to *Nu descendant un escalier n° 2* were almost *entirely* negative. And I believe those reactions were driven by the expectation created by the painting's title. While it is true that the gender of the individual walking down the stairs was indicated by the Frnech title of the painting as a *male* nude walking down the stairs, it was inevitable that men who read the title of the painting would be looking instead for a *female* nude in the painting.

"And indeed, when Duchamp submitted the painting for inclusion with the Cubists at the 28th exhibition of the Société des Artistes Indépendants, the hanging committee sent word through Duchamp's brother that they wanted him to withdraw the painting voluntarily. As justification, they said, 'one doesn't paint a nude descending a staircase, that's ridiculous,' and they went on to say that 'a nude should be respected.'

"In other words, the men evaluating the painting were upset that a painting had been labelled a 'nude' when it *didn't* have a woman sprawled out on a couch or a bed. And *worse,* I would imagine, the hanging committee was offended that Duchamp's nude offered *no* clues to whether the nude was male or female so the hanging committee couldn't tell how closely they should look at the painting. *Obviously,* if the nude was a female nude, they were willing to squint and try to figure out where all the relevant body parts were. And if it *wasn't* a female nude, they didn't want to be tricked into doing so.

"In addition, with regards to nudes being respected, the hanging committee was trying to make clear that even if the painting *did* represent a naked woman, it made no sense to them that a naked woman should be walking down stairs when everyone knew it would work out better for everyone if she were on her back or bent over with her posterior in the air. And I don't think it's very *difficult* to figure out *why* these men wanted to assign a feminine gender to the figure in this painting and then express their preference that the woman be reclining.

"Interestingly enough, even though Duchamp used the *masculine* gender for the nude in the painting's title, he is *quoted* as referring to the nude as female. In other words, the mental *drive* to have the 'nude' in the painting be female was just as strong in the mind of the man who actually put the paint on the canvas as it was in the first committee that evaluated its artiness!

"So here's my challenge for you, captain. I have created a 3D sculpture out of the painting. And I have modified my cyber suit to fit seamlessly into that structure. See if you can find me. And see if you can find *anything* to indicate my gender.

"Happy hunting!"

As soon as Falcon had said that she was somewhere in the sculpture in the center of his quarters, Oakford had started studying the three-dimensional representation of the painting. And now that he knew what it was supposed to be, Oakford could make out what might be three or four "frames" of movement, with each frame having something like a head, hips, and legs.

Oakford did find it interesting how Falcon had converted the painting to a sculpture. The painting itself almost had a paper construction feel to it, as if Duchamp cut out stiff pieces of cardboard, painted them, and layered them to create the image. Falcon continued that idea but had made the individual pieces thicker and then joined them together with angled surfaces that couldn't be seen from the perspective of the painting. Still, it *felt* right as Oakford wandered closer to take a look.

"Stay confused," Oakford heard Falcon whisper into his mind as he got closer. "That should be *easily* justifiable as you wander around the sculpture. Just frown here and there and tilt your head to the side from time to time."

"Will do," Oakford mentally commented back. "And I agree that it's easy for me to feel confused about the fact you're in there somewhere."

Falcon chortled. "Women are known for their seemingly confusing behaviors, captain," she joked. "I just wish I had something more definitive to say about what the Pixie might be up to in the larger context. It's just so hard to investigate anything like that without arousing suspicions. Obviously, I can't talk to Murg about it either because I don't think we can afford to have the Pixie start thinking about the fact we don't trust her or that we are trying to drive a wedge between them."

Oakford reached out to run his hand over what looked like the frame of movement at the "bottom" of the stairs. "I agree," he mentally responded, "and I would love to pull Zach into these discussions, but we can't do that either. I have considered the problem many times in the past year, but I can't come up with any way to proceed, not when the Pixie has such complete control over the ship. So either I fret about it, or I trust that we will know what to do when we need to know it if the Pixie descends into a cascade. It seems impossible that we would survive an attack from the Pixie if we can't come up with a plan in very short order. But then, we have faced impossible things before, and something always happens to help us survive."

"I agree, captain," Falcon responded, "but I will keep watching for an opportunity and thinking about what *might* be possible should the worst occur. For now, however, just keep feeling around and frowning. Who knows what you might find?"

Oakford's frown deepened as he moved his hand to begin running it over what seemed to be the second frame of movement in the sculpture. Thankfully, he wasn't concerned about his facial expressions because he was *genuinely* confused about what he was looking at and if Falcon was somehow in the section he was touching.

Obviously, Oakford had no idea how Falcon had positioned herself before she instructed the cyber suit to change its appearance to match the sculpture. But in that moment, based on what Falcon had just said, Oakford realized that while he had locked the cybersuit's *joints* in place, he hadn't issued a command to keep the cybersuit from changing shape and texture. And as if to confirm his worst scenario, Oakford felt the sculpture moving under his hand, and before he could pull it away, he realized that he had been running his hand over what was now *rapidly* becoming Falcon's posterior.

What had been long and flat and tinted in browns and ochres was no longer rigid. It was quickly blossoming into its usual gorgeous, voluptuous shape. And it was returning to its warm, soft texture.

To be clear, Oakford had never *had* his hand on Falcon's naked butt until now. He had *seen* Falcon's naked posterior, and it was ridiculously well-formed. And it had always *appeared* to be soft and warm, so Oakford wasn't surprised when his sense of touch *confirmed* that it was.

And maybe Oakford should have pulled his hand back *immediately* once he realized what was happening. But maybe some part of Oakford didn't *want* to pull back his hand because he had an *excuse* not to withdraw his hand, and he wanted to *exploit* that excuse.

However, too quickly, Oakford realized that he *couldn't* pull back his hand. Falcon's posterior had formed in just the right way to trap the middle three fingers of his right hand in her intergluteal cleft. And yes, Oakford *forced* himself to label the location of his fingers as Falcon's intergluteal cleft because he didn't want the term "butt crack" floating through his mind.

And yes, it was ridiculous that he couldn't pull his fingers out because, under normal circumstances, that would have *never* been a problem. But Falcon's posterior was *anything* but normal in appearance *and* capabilities. And Falcon's glutes had clamped down on his fingers, and they were holding them tight because, *again*, Oakford had only locked Falcon's *joints*. And obviously, he couldn't lock her muscles now because that would lock his fingers in as well.

Suddenly, a bit flustered, Oakford mentally unlocked Falcon's joints. And in the next moment, Falcon straightened because she had been standing but folded in half with her head against her knees. Her former pose had put her backside high in the air before she modified her appearance to blend into the sculpture.

Of course, after Falcon unfolded, she ended up facing away from Oakford. But she quickly twisted her head to look over her shoulder and flash him an impish grin.

"Can I help you *find* something back there, captain?" Falcon teased with a smirk.

Oakford tilted his head to the side, trying to ignore the embarrassment he felt rising along the edges of his ears. At the same time, Oakford was trying *not* to think about where his hand was and all the things that were near it. And he especially didn't want to think about how ridiculously supple and toned Falcon's gluteals appeared.

"May I have my hand back, please?" Oakford asked, suppressing a silly schoolboy grin.

Falcon gave him a slight shrug. "You can't just pull it out?" she asked innocently.

Oakford stared at her for a moment. "As a matter of fact," he said, "I have serious doubts I'll be able to pull my hand out if you don't allow it."

Falcon snorted playfully. "I can practically *guarantee* that you'll be able to pull your hand out if you wiggle your fingers a bit!" she smirked.

Now, Oakford flushed with embarrassment. "I am *not* wiggling my *fingers*," he insisted.

Falcon nodded sympathetically. "I understand, captain," she responded. "Thank you so much for another *lovely* evening. You are always so kind and generous with your time, and I truly appreciate it. Good night, captain."

And with that, Falcon turned her head to face forward as she began her usual confident stride toward the door that would lead to the hall outside Oakford's quarters. Unfortunately, Falcon's posterior remained clamped on Oakford's hand. And worse, Falcon's cyber suit was powerful enough that Oakford knew she would have no problem dragging him into hall.

And she would be naked. And he would have his hand up her butt. And there would be no explaining it, and he had no idea what the crew would think, but whatever they thought it wouldn't be good.

"Number one, Number one, *wait*," Oakford began pleading as he stumbled forward. "Number One!"

Unexpectedly, Falcon turned to face Oakford even as she came to a dead stop. In the process, Oakford's right arm wrapped over Falcon's hip, and the motion not only dragged Oakford forward but also pulled him downward. Worse, Falcon dropped her left leg arm over Oakford's right arm and locked it against her hip. And almost instantly, Oakford found himself bent over, his face hovering in front of Falcon's perfectly formed décolletage, unable to pull back.

"Yes, captain?" Oakford heard her say pleasantly, responding to his pleas. "Is there something I can do for you?"

Oakford looked up at her, and suddenly, he found himself struggling not to laugh. "This is *ridiculous*," he noted, his voice edged with irritation, but only half seriously.

Falcon nodded. "It *really* is, captain!" she agreed. "And *at* this *ridiculous* moment, I guess you *have* to ask yourself. Would she really walk *buck naked* back to her quarters, dragging her captain behind her, when she would *know* that it would look like her captain was *intentionally* walking behind her fondling her butt, trying to finger her butthole? And honestly, captain, by *now*, I *think* you already *know* the answer to that question! And *more* importantly, you should ask yourself how you would *ever* explain that to the crew *when* it *happens*."

Now, Falcon flashed Oakford one of her gorgeous smiles and waited.

Oakford felt his mouth go dry. Yes, Falcon was smiling, but there was a hard glint in her eyes. And it very much seemed like she *really* wanted to drag him through the halls of the ship in his present predicament. And there would be *nothing* he could do about it.

Worse, in that moment, Oakford knew that if he *didn't* wiggle his fingers, she was not only going to drag him for the short walk back to her quarters, but she might also extend his humiliation tour across the entire ship until he did what she wanted. And in the end, he *would* do what she asked. The only question was, would he do it before or after he suffered the horrific embarrassment of the parade that Falcon had planned for him?

It didn't take long for Oakford to let himself do what a part of him *really* wanted to do anyway.

And he wiggled his fingers. And instantly, Falcon squealed with delight as her smile flashed wider. And her body shuddered, sending gorgeous jiggles across her breasts and over her hips.

Suddenly, Oakford's fingers were free. And his arm was free. But something happened when he straightened, for though his fingers and arm were once again his own, his eyes, ears, and mind were locked in place instead.

And *nothing* existed but Falcon's body. And while her face was as beautiful as it had always been, something in her squeal of delight had transformed her body into the only thing that existed in the universe. And he found himself gaping at her because she was just *so* gorgeous.

Falcon had squealed with *such* delight. And he had *never* heard her squeal like that. And somehow, it made the moment feel innocent. And *that* made the moment *more* dangerous because the tempting corner of his mind was insisting that there *couldn't* be anything wrong with what he might do *next* because her squeal *was* so innocent-sounding.

It was fiendishly tangled logic, and Oakford *knew* that only destruction would follow any actions born from impulse. But he found himself *lusting* to hear that squeal again and again, knowing it would justify *anything* he did to her.

And even though some portion of Oakford's mind *knew* he *shouldn't* do what his reproductive system was telling him to do, even though he *knew* it was impossible for anything truly reproductive to occur with Falcon, he could still *feel* the moment grinding his control into dust and wafting away.

And he *wanted* the only thing he could see, the exaggerated lines of her breasts, and the hourglass of her waist to hips, and the long shanks of her exquisitely turned legs. And he imagined a new moment in a new future where he grabbed Falcon and dragged her to himself, to feel her body pressed against him, before he began to kiss her recklessly.

Later, Oakford would guess that Falcon had seen him losing control after so many years of struggling to treat her as anything *but* a toy for his own pleasure. And despite all of Rachel's insistence over the years that he do *precisely* that, some combination of Rachel and the Falcon respected him enough to acknowledge how *much* he would regret it if he let his passion rule him in that instant.

In any case, thankfully, in the *next* moment, Falcon broke the mood by descending into an explosive, silly-girl, *truly* innocent giggle. And she accompanied that with a second full-body shudder, before spinning toward the uniform she had draped over a chair in his small dining area.

And even though Oakford was struggling to compose himself, he managed to hold himself in place as Falcon quickly dressed. Grateful, he found that he was not *so* out of control that he could justify attacking her as she was preparing to leave. And thankfully, getting dressed was yet another thing that Falcon did *amazingly* well. The precise control that Falcon had over the cybersuit made it look like clothing *flowed* onto her body with nearly *zero* effort on her part.

Now, effortlessly, Falcon turned for the door a second time, her confident stride pushing her forward. But before she left Oakford's quarters, Falcon glanced at him and smiled again.

"I'll send bots in the morning to clean out the sculpture," Falcon said, playfully. "Thank you for a *lovely* evening, captain."

And with that, the door to Oakford's quarters snapped open. And Falcon disappeared into the hall. The doors snapped shut. And suddenly, she was gone.

Only an instant later, Falcon spoke unseen and directly into this mind. "*Excellent* performance, captain!" she commented. "You were absolutely convincing with your shock, embarrassment, and excitement. I can't imagine there's any way the Pixie will know we were also communicating over a private comm through your proprietary control of the cyber suit. I definitely think the setup was *effective* in that regard. But it was still an absolute delight to participate in the *physical* moment with you. Have a wonderful evening, and I wish you all the glorious dreams that you deserve."

Honestly, Oakford had barely heard Falcon's final message to him. It was difficult to hear *anything* over the loud, angry buzz of his reproductive system. For at the moment, it was *railing* at him over the fact that he had allowed Falcon to walk out of his quarters without getting what it wanted.

Indeed, Oakford spent the next ten minutes staring at the door to his quarters, telling himself to calm down, telling himself he *wasn't* going to storm down the hall to Falcon's quarters and force himself inside.

But at least in all the noise, Oakford *had* to agree with Falcon's last assessment. He, too, couldn't *imagine* that the Pixie would be able to sense that he and Falcon were mentally communicating, despite the apparent effect that the bounce and wiggle of Falcon's body had caused in his heart and soul.

9.

The next cycle, in Conference Room One on Upper Deck 1 of the *Dominion*, Bolobolo continued to study Falcon and Oakford as the senior staff discussed the latest investigations into all things curled-space-related, even if they weren't *completely* curled-space-related. At the moment, Hunter was finishing his status report on the upgrades for the fusion torpedo shell that he would use for the next point-to-point curled space funnel hop.

"We've installed the shield wave generators we discussed," he said. "And we've also installed dedicated sensors to monitor the energy signatures coming from the curled space funnel that we open with the miniguns. The sensors should be able to put the shield wave generators out of phase with the curled space funnel energy. Maybe that cuts down the amplitude of the waveforms. Maybe that keeps the more energetic particles from boring a hole through my head. Maybe it doesn't."

Oakford nodded, looking and sounding a bit distracted. "Do you have an approximate timeline for the next test?" he asked.

Bolobolo had noticed Oakford's odd demeanor the moment he walked into Conference Room One for the weekly meeting. He had the look of a man trying to look like everything was fine, but had recently done something he didn't want anyone to know about. Bolobolo had no doubt Hunter had recognized the look as well, but he hadn't said anything about it. And Bolobolo knew that Murg and MacDuff wouldn't say anything.

As for Falcon, she had the smug, amused look of someone who was the reason that Oakford looked uncomfortable. Bolobolo didn't want it to be what she thought it might be. Rachel had been trying to get Oakford to use the cyber suit as a pleasure toy for *years*. And years before, when Oakford had told Bolobolo about Falcon posing naked for him so Rachel would have less anxiety about their relationship, Bolobolo could guess where it would lead.

Oakford had claimed that he would appreciate Falcon's cyber suit as a work of art. But in the end, Bolobolo knew that Oakford was a man, and the male reproductive system was focused on *one* thing, and it would outright *lie* about *anything* it needed to lie about to wear down the man until the man gave up and did what it wanted.

At the same time, Bolobolo understood Oakford was desperate to come up with a solution to the Rachel-Falcon problem. Years before, Rachel's anxiety about her relationship with Oakford had increased to the point that she took control of the cybersuit during a meeting with a Merchant Guild Working Group. And under a conference table, Rachel had shoved her foot between Oakford's legs to fondle him. Oakford reacted badly to the unwanted advance. Rachel reacted to Oakford's reaction even worse.

But, of course, Oakford knew that his Number One was *vital* to the survival of the *Dominion*, and Rachel was an integral part of the symbiotic entity that was Falcon.

Hence, the posing and wherever that posing had now led.

To be clear, Bolobolo wasn't upset with Oakford. And she wasn't upset with Falcon. Falcon was who and what she was. And yes, she did pose a Rachel-Falcon problem for Oakford. But Rachel Falcon wasn't just a *problem*. She was also an *incredible* resource for Oakford.

And frankly, Bolobolo had a Rachel-Falcon problem herself, although in Bolobolo's case, it was just a Falcon problem. And honestly, regarding Falcon's relationship with Bolobolo, if Bolobolo hadn't grown up on Fomalhaut Four, she had no doubt that she would be fawning all over Falcon, just like all the other women on the *Dominion*.

Bolobolo saw it every time Falcon walked into the Mess Hall. A minute before the entrance, the girls would be chattering to the boys, vying for attention. And then, Falcon would stride in, and the conversations would fall off. Everyone would turn to stare. Eventually, the chattering would restart, but it would be more muted and less confident.

Yes, the crew reactions were *similar* for the rest of the senior staff. But Hunter was the only other senior staff member who could produce a reaction as universal as Falcon's. And obviously, that was because Hunter was just as handsome as Falcon was beautiful, and humans placed far too much importance on appearance.

But it was also true that everyone knew Falcon, Hunter, and Sphinx were the best fighters on the ship. And Falcon, Hunter, Murg, and the Pixie were the fastest tactical decision makers on the ship. In other words, pick any category, and Hunter and Falcon were at the top. And Falcon had the added advantage of appearing to be a woman, and she inherited the female energy that had always existed in every gathering of humans.

And yes, Bolobolo respected *everything* regarding Falcon. Still, growing up on Fomalhaut Four had taught Bolobolo the importance of *every* element of *every* ecosphere. And Bolobolo knew that she held a place of her own in the ecosphere that was the *Dominion*, even if Falcon was *still* reminding Bolobolo that she should be *more* than she currently was.

For the moment, Bolobolo promised herself she wouldn't let Falcon return to her duties after the senior staff meeting before she found out what had happened with Oakford. And besides, Bolobolo knew there were more discussions to come in the current meeting. And one topic that was particularly important to Bolobolo's peace of mind.

Now, Hunter answered Oakford's question regarding the schedule for the next point-to-point curled space funnel hop.

"We should be able to make the next attempt within the week," Hunter responded.

Oakford nodded. "Good," he said, the distraction evident in his voice. " Do we have additional shockdrops scheduled for this week to continue the mapping?"

Hunter nodded. "Two," he added, "and I just wanted to say again that Murg and the Pixie have done an incredible job dewarping my scribbles. I've only got milliseconds during the shockdrop. And afterward, I'm doing my best to get down as much as I can remember. But there's room for slop with that many pinpoints. And yet, every time I hand off another sketch, Murg and the Pixie do their magic, and everything bends and twists, and suddenly another section locks in place. It's been impressive to watch, but I can't say I'm that confident I haven't screwed this up because it's out there on the edge of my mental capacity."

As Hunter spoke, a curled space graphic had appeared on the displays that circled Conference Room One. It wasn't the first time Bolobolo had seen the graphic. But Bolobolo had decided *months* ago that it didn't matter *how* many times she saw it, she was *sure* she would never understand it.

For the record, the rest of the senior staff continued to refer to it as a segment of the local interstellar cloud and its corresponding curved space map. Still, to Bolobolo, it appeared as a jumbled pile of ribbons. And even that wasn't a good description. There were dots all over the place, and those were supposed to be the nearby stars. And then there was mesh that flipped, twisted, and turned. And the stars seemed to be stuck in the mesh.

And now, another part of the display was showing what looked like a hand-drawn diagram. And it was twisting and stretching. And a part of it was overlaying on the existing mesh. And that seemed to fit, but that left another part of the diagram hanging off the end of the first graphic.

But once part of the diagram locked onto the graphic, lines started growing off the graphic, wrapping and bending around until a grid formed, and other dots lit up. And weirdly enough, those new dots appeared where the hand-drawn dots had been.

It all started the year before, when the Leadership Council, Realm Force Central, and the Realm's planetary leadership decided that Betelgeuse Two was a threat to the Realm due to its advanced technology. Consequently, the inhabitants of Betelgeuse Two were given one week to evacuate the planet before Realm Force attacked and reduced the surface of the planet to rubble. Interestingly, the same message announced that transporters would be allowed to evacuate anyone who could afford it passage off the planet.

After discussions with the senior staff, Oakford had decided to assist with the evacuation, one thousand inhabitants at a time. Unfortunately, Realm Force had already blockaded both commonly used entrances to the Betegeuse system. But a known shock-drop route existed that would land the *Dominion* in the outer reaches of the Betelgeuse system. And once there, Oakford intended to head to Betelgeuse Two, pick up 1,000 inhabitants, and transport them elsewhere.

The *Dominion* had traveled to the spot in a curled space funnel near Canopus G that was the origin point for the shock-drop. As usual, the *Dominion's* miniguns had opened fire, torn a hole in the sidewall, and then dove through that hole. Under typical circumstances, the battlecruiser would have then suddenly appeared in the outer reaches of the Betelgeuse system.

But at that moment, Hunter had somehow looked through the tear in the sidewall of the curled space funnel. He saw that Realm Force had stationed forces surrounding the destination of the shock-drop. And he rightly concluded that if the *Dominion* dropped into that destination, it would be destroyed.

Reacting instinctively, Hunter had nudged the maneuvering thrusters. That course correction still allowed the *Dominion* to shock-drop into the Betelgeuse system. But it appeared much closer to Betelgeuse Two. And instead of taking twenty hours to fly back to the planet, it took less than four.

Later, in a senior staff meeting, Hunter also mentioned that *every* time he had piloted a vessel through a shock-drop, he had always been able to see through the tear in the sidewall and pick up distinct details on what was on the other side. And not only could Hunter see a host of stars, but the light coming from the stars was stretching and bending. And he said it looked like the stars were resting on some vast webbing that folded, warped, rolled, and twisted in seemingly random patterns. Additionally, the webbing had tendrils that connected one or two areas to others, flashing and rippling, sometimes even jumping from one spot to another.

None of the other senior staff members had ever seen anything like that, including Murg and the Pixie. No video sensor had captured what Hunter described. For everyone else, the space beyond the tear in the sidewall had always been an absolute, all-consuming black void.

Hectic weeks had followed as the *Dominion* attempted to place the refugees it had rescued from Betelgeuse Two on another world in the Night. However, afterwards, Hunter began taking flight teams in armed shuttles to perform shock-drops. And immediately following each shock-drop, Hunter had marked the positions of as many stars as he could remember on a tablet, using the size of the dots that he drew to signify brightness. At the same time, Hunter sketched the warping pattern in the webbing as accurately as possible.

And then, of course, Murg and the Pixie had taken Hunter's drawings and attempted to decipher them. At the beginning, Hunter had serious doubts that anything would come of it. The images of the webbing only existed for milliseconds, and Hunter had never considered himself skillful as an artist.

But after a half dozen shock-drops, the drawings had begun to align. And, much to everyone's surprise, the marked stars overlaid with the actual positions of stars. And every drawing from every shock-drop that followed slid into the overall diagram at one point or another.

Somewhere along the line in the senior staff meetings that followed, Bolobolo mentally checked out of the discussions. The map had grown sufficiently complex that she couldn't make her brain twist in enough directions to keep track of what the webbing was supposedly illustrating.

It did help when Murg zoomed in on the diagram to isolate a small section with systems labeled, showing which stars were close to other stars because of the curving of the webbing. Supposedly, that meant that a shock-drop was possible between the systems. Still, in the discussions that followed concerning the usefulness of exploiting what might be heretofore unknown shock-drops, Bolobolo was content to stare at the displays and nod.

For the record, until now, no one on the crew of the *Dominion* had *tried* to use one of those newly mapped shock-drops. And now, Hunter soon stated the obvious.

"We've compiled enough data that our collection process seems internally consistent," he said. "We won't know for sure until we schedule a test. Interestingly enough, the latest diagram has a destination that might be interesting to try."

Something about what Hunter had just said forced Bolobolo's eyes back to Murg's diagram for another look as it zoomed in closer. Bolobolo wasn't paying attention when Murg matched Hunter's latest drawing to the diagram. But now Bolobolo could see that a familiar label had popped up.

The highlighted star was labelled Fomalhaut. Fomalhaut was at the center of a system that contained Bolobolo's home planet, Fomalhaut Four.

Oakford glanced at Bolobolo and smiled. "That is interesting indeed," he said with a reflective tone. "Perhaps that would be an excellent destination for the first test. And as long as we're on the topic, Murg, any change in our weekly check-in on Fomalhaut Four?"

"NAK," Murg responded immediately.

Five years before, Realm Force had invaded Bolobolo's home planet, claiming the planet constituted a security risk. Unfortunately, that invasion occurred just before Bolobolo tried to sneak back to Fomalhaut Four for a visit. Realm Force was well established in their conquest of Fomalhaut Four by the time Bolobolo arrived. She was quickly captured. Sadly, her presence began a cascade of events that resulted in fifteen of the tribes being wiped out on the sparsely populated planet.

Worse, an invasion of thousands of Hunter Look-Alikes came next because they had learned that Bolobolo was on the planet. The look-alikes easily slaughtered the Realm Force troops. They demanded Bolobolo be turned over to them and threatened to slaughter *everyone* on the planet if the tribes didn't comply. Thankfully, Falcon had already arrived on the planet. And in desperation, Falcon had released Fury and slaughtered them all.

Afterward, knowing that nothing had been resolved in the larger security risks, Oakford had offered to relocate all the surviving tribes on Fomalhaut Four to a planet in the Night where they would be less known and potentially safer. But *all* of the tribes had opted to stay on Fomalhaut Four and face whatever future might befall them.

Bolobolo hadn't been surprised. She had known it wouldn't be possible to convince them to act in any other way. The inhabitants of Fomalhaut Four had settled on the difficult planet *specifically* to face whatever challenges presented themselves. They were *not* those who ran away. Neither were they inclined to take advantage of *any* technologies that the Wind or Realm Force had to offer them to assist with their survival.

For as long as the tribes had lived on the planet, they had lived off what their planet provided, no more, no less.

Case in point, Fomalhaut Four had become part of the Realm *before* the Wind stopped building Judicial Centers on newly inhabited Realm planets, but the settlers had no use for them. And that meant the planet's Judicial Centers had gone unvisited even before the Disappearance. To be clear, those Judicial Centers would have provided the tribes with food replicators, manufacturing facilities, and communications equipment. Those facilities could have provided transportation, weapons, and real-time comms across the planet and throughout the Realm. But the tribes weren't interested in any of it, even after the invasions.

Granted, the invasion by the Hunter Look-Alikes had reduced the effectiveness of the communication facilities at the Fomalhaut Four Judicial Centers. After arriving in the system and slaughtering the Realm Force contingent, the Hunter Look-Alikes had targeted and destroyed the planet's Wind-designed communications satellite that hovered high in a geosynchronous orbit. And that had *ended* the ability of the tribes to communicate with anyone else in the Realm. But, of course, the tribes *never* communicated with anyone else in the Realm. And the tribes who survived the invasions didn't even notice that their communications satellite had been destroyed.

Still, once the tribes refused to leave the planet, Murg took the liberty of installing comm patches in all the Fomalhaut Four Judicial Centers, just in case the senior staff needed a way to communicate with the planet. And last year, when one Realm planet after another began to disappear from the social net, the Pixie had informed the senior staff that Murg had made it possible for the point-to-point comm facility of the *Dominion* to connect with any of the Judicial Centers on Fomalhaut Four. Of course, everyone knew that it was unlikely any member of any of the tribes would be anywhere near one of the Judicial Centers. But at the very least, the video sensors on the Judicial Centers could continuously record the skies over Fomalhaut Four and monitor activity around Fomalhaut Four's curled space ring for signs of a subsequent invasion.

And yes, Murg had also launched communication beacons from the Judicial Centers to surveil the tribes from high enough in the sky to be invisible. But no, Murg had *not* sent a communications beacon to land near Bolobolo's village so she could contact her mother. Bolobolo hadn't even watched the surveillance feed for the chance to see her family from a distance.

Bolobolo couldn't risk it emotionally. She knew if she saw her family, she would want to visit them. And as much as she couldn't *dare* visit them, eventually, she *would* make enough excuses to talk herself into it. And if the Hunter Look-Alikes found out she was on the planet, they would come after her *again*. And the last time that happened, it almost cost the lives of *everyone* on the planet, and Bolobolo couldn't bear the thought of more death directly because of her presence there.

Indeed, the worst result of the Hunter Look-Alikes' invasion of Fomalhaut Four was the death of her father in the days that followed. And yes, Bolobolo understood that her father had died defending her honor *and* her right to return to the planet any time she wished. But Bolobolo *refused* to allow her yearning to see her family to lead to more deaths for Fomalhaut Four. And in Bolobolo's mind, that meant *zero* contact.

Still, she was *continuously* glad to hear that Realm Force had never returned for a second invasion, and neither had the Hunter Look-Alikes. And maybe there would be more invasions at some point, no matter *what* she did, but Bolobolo wanted to know that she had done everything *she* could to ensure the tribes of Fomalhaut Four were safe.

●   ●   ●

At a small café in the main population area for Groombridge 1830b, Reyes looked up from the tiny table where she sat to see another concerned individual approaching rapidly. Like all the other concerned individuals who bustled up to talk to her recently, the woman was also trying to look reticent to do so. Reyes could see that the woman desperately wanted to talk to her. Obviously, the news of the governor's death had spread quickly, as had the video feed of Reyes being accused by the governor's companion of murdering the governor.

And that had made Reyes somewhat of a celebrity on the planet.

Of course, by now, Sotheby had already informed Reyes that PLOKTA was orchestrating the release of multiple stories counteracting that accusation that the governor's companion had made against Reyes and redirecting the blame back on the governor's companion. Sotheby had also advised Reyes to make sure she was seen alone in as many places as possible around the main population area.

Sotheby had said she wanted Reyes to play the confused and frightened victim, even as PLOKTA continued to leak more and more shocking revelations about the governor's murder. And while Sotheby understood that Reyes could only interact with a few dozen people a day, she had said that High King Ruler had projected that those people would talk to others and all of them would offer comments on the continuing revelations on social media. And all of it would likely culminate in the demand that the governor's companion be punished.

And in the *best* cases, it might even culminate in a quasi-riot.

Now, the concerned individual bustled up to Reyes, apologizing as she came. "I don't mean to bother you," the woman began, "but I just had to tell you how sorry I am about the way you were treated. I don't even know why our governor was associating with that kind of woman, but it's obvious that she is a *terrible* person. How did she ever expect to get away with what she did? The video of the incident clearly shows that the governor was attacked by a masked man, and the woman doesn't even start screaming until she gives him time to run away. It's *obvious* to me that she *knew* the man somehow. And *then*, she just randomly picks you and *accuses* you of doing something that horrible?! What is *wrong* with her?!"

Reyes shrank back convincingly and widened her eyes. "I really don't know," she pleaded, "and I'm really trying not to be involved in this. I'm new to this planet and *really* don't want even to be known as the young woman who was *accused* of murdering the governor. Even if everybody knows that I didn't *do* it, I'm still going to have my name attached to it, and I'm really thinking that I should just move back home…"

"Oh no, sweetie, I'm sorry," the concerned individual interrupted. "I didn't mean to…. I just think it was so *terrible* what that woman did to you, and I want you to know that there are *so many* good people who live on this planet, and *none* of them believe you had *anything* to do with the governor's death, and we *really* want you to feel welcome here. We just don't know what we can do to help you besides tell you that we are so sorry that this has happened."

Reyes nodded as she let her expression ease a bit. "I… I appreciate that," she responded. "And I know that people are just trying to help, and I appreciate that too, but all the attention is just making me uncomfortable, and I'm not sure what to do. I can't just hide in my apartment either, because people found out where I'm staying and they're camped out beside my apartment, waiting to tell me how sorry they are, and I know they're just trying to help. It's just…. It's just really hard."

"Of *course* it is, sweetie!" the concerned individual continued, oblivious to the fact that if Reyes was *actually* upset about the situation, she was only making it worse. "And believe me, I understand that this is not only *hard*, it's *horrible*. And I *really* think the governor's companion needs to be taught a lesson. It's just so confusing why she would watch an attacker run away and then turn around and accuse you!"

Reyes shook her head, looking bewildered. "I… I don't understand it either," she said, sounding like she was growing more desperate. "I'm really just trying *not* to be involved."

By now, the concerned individual had begun nodding sympathetically. And if seemed like she was *finally* getting the message that Reyes didn't want to be reminded about what had happened.

"I understand, sweetie," the woman said, her voice filling with concern. "And I'm sorry for bothering you, but I just wanted you to know that we're not like that *woman* and we want you to feel welcome on our planet."

Reyes gave the concerned individual a weak smile. "Thank you," she replied softly. "I appreciate that."

"Alright, sweetie," the concerned individual added. "I hope you have a good day, and again, I'm really sorry about this."

And with that, the concerned individual bustled away.

•　　　•　　　•

On the *Dominion*, Bolobolo followed Falcon out of Conference Room One after the curled space projects review concluded. Bolobolo wasn't surprised when she fell in beside Falcon, and Falcon immediately gave her a quick smile and wink as if she was expecting Bolobolo's questions.

Falcon had that *maddening* quality about her. She was *always* thinking multiple steps ahead. Over the years, it had become apparent that Falcon's cyber suit had an analytical engine that could run personality-based predictions based on actions and reactions. Given that, Bolobolo had never tried to go head-to-head with Falcon because she knew Falcon could easily outthink her.

In fact, the *closest* Bolobolo had ever come to having an all-out argument with Falcon happened a year ago when Falcon suddenly resurrected an old discussion about the abilities of the *Dominion's* first Chief Medical Officer, Catherine Casteel. And unfortunately, Falcon had decided last year to tell Bolobolo what she *already* knew before suggesting that Bolobolo work harder to achieve what Bolobolo had *already* tried to achieve and failed at *multiple* times.

Falcon had opened the discussion by observing that something significant was coming for the *Dominion* and its crew.

Night planets were being attacked. Abaddon was on the move. The Hunter Look-Alikes were still a threat. Sooner or later, the *Dominion* would be involved in a major confrontation.

Obviously, Bolobolo *knew* that.

And then Falcon had concluded that having a healer like Casteel onboard might mean the difference between survival and destruction.

Bolobolo hadn't disagreed because she *knew that too*. She just didn't know what Falcon expected her to do.

She had *tried*. She had *failed*. But Falcon kept pushing, and Bolobolo grew frustrated enough with the conversation to point out that Falcon hadn't had any supernatural visions in recent years *either*. And while that was true, Bolobolo knew it really *wasn't* the point.

The problem was that Bolobolo couldn't *see* a point to *any* point that anyone might make when it came to learning how to heal like Casteel.

She had *tried*. She had *failed*.

In the end, Falcon had turned and left Bolobolo's office.

Now, Bolobolo wondered if she was about to have another conversation with Falcon that would be just as uncomfortable. And as soon as she and Falcon boarded a lift and the doors closed, Bolobolo turned to face Falcon.

"What's going on with you and Captain Oakford?" Bolobolo demanded to know.

10.

Moments later, on the *Dominion*, riding in a lift with Falcon, Bolobolo spun and slapped the emergency stop button before wrenching back around to face Falcon once more.

"You did *what* to Captain Oakford!?" Bolobolo practically shouted. It definitely wasn't a shriek. But it was close.

For the record, Bolobolo had never shrieked in her life. But moments after she *demanded* Falcon tell her what was going on between her and Oakford, Bolobolo almost instantly decided she didn't *want* to know, even though she *had* to know.

Indeed, Bolobolo could honestly say that when Falcon *started* to give her a *quick* overview of the *final* few moments of her time with Oakford from the cycle before, it felt like her brain was shorting out and the only way to escape the nightmarish images exploding in her mind was to shriek with absolute terror.

And to be clear, that reaction began as Falcon had uttered the phrase, "I tricked him into putting his hand up my butt."

And yes, Bolobolo managed to *prevent* the shriek from happening. But she couldn't stop her mouth from sagging open, and *that* was when Bolobolo had spun to slam her palm into the emergency stop button on the lift. It was the only way that Bolobolo could think of to *force* her life to come to a grinding halt until Falcon explained what had *really* happened in Oakford's quarters.

Falcon burst out laughing. "I just *told* you what happened?" she responded playfully. "Do you really want me to say it again?"

"No!" Bolobolo replied forcefully. "You *couldn't*... you *didn't*... how could... *no*... how...?!"

Falcon laughed again. "The cyber suit is *amazing!*" she gloated. "I changed my appearance to a cubist sculpture. And when Captain Oakford ran his hand over it, I waited until just the right moment, and then I gave myself an oversized booty and made sure that Captain Oakford's hand ended up in my crack. And then I *clamped down* so he couldn't pull his hand out! And I was naked, and he had his hand up my butt."

Bolobolo blanched. "I do *not* want to *hear* this!" she shot back. Still, at the same time, Bolobolo felt the voice of the mischievous little girl that she had never outgrown starting to giggle within her.

Falcon laughed a third time. "Of *course* you do!" she countered. "It's *funny*! He turned absolutely *frantic* when I started for the door to his quarters and started dragging him along because he realized that if he didn't do what I wanted, I *was* going to haul him through the hallway, and on a tour of the ship, and there would be nothing he could do about it."

"*No!*" Bolobolo shouted again. "How could you... why... *no, no no!*"

Falcon shrugged nonchalantly. "*Obviously*, I wasn't *really* going to do that!" she said pleasantly. "But he refused to do what I asked him to do, so I made him *think* I would do that so that he would do what I asked him to do. And when he did *that*, I let him go with *some* semblance of his dignity intact. Of course, all of it means that I will have something I can say from now until the end of eternity that will make him turn *bright red* any time I want."

A shudder ran through Bolobolo. She didn't *want* to ask. She *really* didn't want to ask. But the silly, onery little girl that Bolobolo thought she had left behind *so* many years ago *wouldn't* get back into the corner of her mind and *stop talking*.

"What... *what*... what... *what*?!" Bolobolo began mumbling.

"It was *easy*," Falcon commented. "I told him that I wouldn't release his hand until he wiggled his fingers...."

"NO!" Bolobolo shouted.

Falcon grinned. "Yup!" she snickered. "And he *did* eventually do it. And then I giggled and wiggled and short-circuited his *brain*! That boy was *amped up* when I left him to sort it out for himself in the quarters!"

"*Rachel!*" Bolobolo snapped.

"He'll be *fine*," Falcon added nonchalantly. "I just wanted him to understand this whole business of me posing locked in place wasn't going to protect him if I decided to writhe a bit. Sometimes men need to see how vulnerable they are to the shimmy."

By now, Bolobolo had started to recover from the shock of what Falcon had done. And even though there were still images in her brain that she *didn't* want in her brain, she knew it was more than time to try to rein in Rachel for Oakford's sake.

"Rachel, you *can't* do stuff like this," Bolobolo began to plead. "Captain Oakford *has* to maintain the respect of the crew for one thing. And for another, he sets the *standard* for the rest of the crew. We've got young men and women from all kinds of backgrounds, and if the girls who know how to wiggle start wiggling, there's going to be trouble everywhere."

Falcon gave Bolobolo a slight shrug. "Honestly, Adi," she said quietly. "There may not be much time for that kind of trouble to get going. I'm just not sure how much time any of us have left. There are so many pieces in play, and I *can't* imagine that it will be very long before the Realm comes after us. And I mean, *really*, comes after us. So, maybe we should let ourselves enjoy life a bit in the time have left. I'm not talking about full-blown orgies, but a little flirting, a little dancing, a little kissing isn't going to hurt anyone. And speaking of that, when are *you* going to start wiggling and get Sarge to give up this ridiculous idea that he needs to keep Hunter safe? Zach can take care of himself, and I'm getting tired of waiting for babies who'll call me autie! Time to *start* the *shimmy!*"

Bolobolo knew that Falcon was intentionally changing the topic, but she wasn't necessarily upset about that. She had already heard enough about hands and butts.

Bolobolo responded to Falcon's latest suggestion by shaking her head. "You already know I'm not going to do that, Rachel," she said. "I respect Sarge's conviction and I'm *not* going to manipulate him into marrying me. I have too much respect for him to do that."

Falcon snorted. "Women have been *disrespecting* men since the beginning of time," she countered. "It's how we get what we want and get done the things we want done. But if you don't want to wiggle… how's about this?

You learn to heal supernaturally like Casteel, and you can tell Sarge that *you'll* keep Hunter safe and he just needs to marry you, get naked, and start making babies!"

Bolobolo bristled. For the past year, it seemed like *every* conversation with Falcon ended up at some point on the topic of supernatural healing. By now, Bolobolo's response was automatic.

"I've already *told* you," she shot back. "I've *tried* to learn how to do that, and I'm still trying, and the results are the same. *Nothing's happening.*"

"How many times a week are you practicing?" Falcon asked.

"*Every day!*" Bolobolo answered. "I'm meditating *every day*, doing all the things that Cat suggested. And it's all fine and well, but *nothing's happening*. It's the same thing I tell you every week. And just like every week, I can ask you the same thing. When's the last time you've had a vision? At least you've *had* visions before. It's not like I've *been* able to heal and just forgot how!"

Bolobolo shook her head in frustration and turned to push the resume button on one of the lift's wall-mounted control panels. Then she glanced at Falcon once more.

Thankfully, Falcon never looked offended when Bolobolo pushed back about her learning to heal. But Falcon wouldn't stop talking about it either. And yes, Bolobolo recognized it was important. And it would be *invaluable* if she could ever break through. But she didn't know what else to do.

The lift quickly reached the station directly across from the entrance to Sickbay. And in the next moment, it slowed to a rapid stop, and the doors popped open.

"Actually," Falcon said with a grin, "I may have something new to try when it comes to the visions. I *have* been waiting around, not *doing* anything about that, because in the past, the visions just always appeared out of nowhere. And I've been thinking that it was something that didn't happen until someone outside of me *made* it happen. But now I'm thinking I *might* be able to do better than that. And I've been reviewing everything in my content databases that shows up when I look for the phrase 'remote viewing.' There are some *really* interesting investigations before the Coming that seem to suggest that pretty much *anybody* can do it."

Bolobolo frowned. "What?" she asked, suddenly confused.

Falcon nodded. "There was a *lot* of experimenting by the biggest governments that existed before the Coming," she noted. "And a lot of the people involved in those programs talked about it later and ran clinics teaching people how to do it. And a lot of *random*, everyday people had some success with it. Others said it was just a coincidence, but some of the results are pretty impressive.

"Maybe we're just making this more complicated than it is. Maybe Pix is right when she says that organic life can operate at magnitudes of higher-order functionality. Maybe it's built right into the plumbing, and when someone figures it out, it just seems like they *always* could."

A part of Bolobolo still wanted to think learning to heal *was* hard, but she had to be honest with Falcon and tell her something that Abaddon had told her the year before, when he was trying to convince the senior staff to pledge allegiance to him.

With the door of the lift still open and waiting for Bolobolo to disembark, she looked at Falcon. "I mentioned in one of our debriefings that Abaddon had offered to help me learn to heal," she began, "but I don't think I ever told you the details of that conversation.

"He said it wasn't as difficult to achieve the state that Cat achieved as everyone thought. He said humans, because of their life experience, engage with their agency when attempting any task. They *try*. He said *that's* the way of the natural and the way of the Now is not to *try*, but to Be.

"And when I *thought* that it sounded like platitudes, he read my mind and said it *wasn't* platitudes, and my *belief* that it *was*, was a platitude that was blocking me from exercising the ability that already lies within me."

Falcon grinned. "And *that's* what I'm talking about!" she replied. "I'll let you know when I get the remote viewing thing going."

Bolobolo gave Falcon a somewhat tortured smile before walking off the lift. "Great," she offered halfheartedly as she heard the lift doors close behind her.

•   •   •

On Earth, in Jerusalem, in his office in the administrative headquarters for the Leadership Council, Ton smiled as he quickly reviewed the dynamically generated dashboard that PLOKTA had created, representing the emotional involvement of the inhabitants of Groombridge 1830b in the slaying of their governor. Amazingly enough, due to the Wind's communications technology,

Ton could see *real-time* analysis across multiple vectors, dissecting the exact nature of the present discussions on the social net and the ensuing commentary regarding the murder.

Those vectors included the demographic breakdown of commentators on the social net, the emotional intensity of their posts, and a topical classification of the information in those posts regarding the murder. More importantly, Ton could toggle the dashboard between the effects of the information generated organically by living humans versus the army of automated poster robots that PLOKTA had created for this particular operation. And, of course, he could see the cumulative effects of both.

Notably, each of the PLOKTA's posterbots had been generated with a unique personality and a background story that defined the type of commentary they would produce. But in every case, the posterbots were designed to create inflammatory content that PLOKTA could tweak and bend toward any side of any issue. And he could control whether the postings leaned more heavily on a rational style of presentation or one that relied on emotionally charged language.

To be clear, no human would be able to distinguish between commentary generated by a posterbot and that of a human. The vast majority of Realmers were unaware that the posterbots even existed. They naively believed that everything they read or watched on the social net originated from other humans. And given that the Realm purported to adhere to the guideline of treating others as they wished to be treated, it made sense that Realmers would not only give the originator the benefit of the doubt but also treat the originator as fundamentally honest.

Interestingly, Ton had been a psychologist before the Coming, and he had watched similar capabilities deployed in both so-called democracies and authoritarian regimes across the nations on Earth in the years leading up to the appearance of the Wind. And while those systems only operated on Earth and could therefore be real-time as well, Ton had no doubt that those who ran the social media companies before the Coming would be astonished by the sophistication of PLOKTA's control in the systems he had constructed in the decades that he served as the Saturn Shipyard's de facto Chief Technologist.

Ton could propose any topic from any viewpoint, and the hundreds of thousands of posterbots would adopt it using a slew of theme and variation techniques. In most cases, those posts would then begin saturating the social net, regulated mainly by each posterbot evaluating the pace of postings on the social net and then timing their individual postings to provide an organic-like pacing.

Of course, PLOKTA's analysis routines had no trouble deciphering which posts on the social net were created by posterbot and which were created by humans. Such a capability was vital to the reporting that PLOKTA provided for Ton. And as such, PLOKTA had programmed the posterbots to stenographically embed an identifier into each posting using interletter sequencing with a 64-base numbering system. And this, of course, was *impossible* for any nonenhanced human to decipher in any reasonable timeframe. But, obviously, PLOKTA's analysis routines accomplished it flawlessly.

And with that pedantic task accomplished, PLOKTA's analysis routines then went to work grading the population's reactions to those posterbot variations, amplifying the ones that achieved the most resonance with the inhabitants of Groombridge 1830b. This process created a feedback loop that quickly identified the variations in narratives that gained the most attention and eventually produced a variation that outperformed all others.

Then, once that variation had been identified, PLOKTA had conferred with Ton, and the pair created an outline to generate scenarios that fleshed out the details of the viewpoints the citizens of Groombridge 1830b had adopted.

For instance, once Ton had decided on the fundamental characterization of the governor's companion as a "vixen influencer," PLOKTA had created a spate of postings characterizing the participation of the companion in the murder of the governor in multiple ways.

One scenario characterized the companion as a victim as well, purporting that a stalker had become obsessed with her to the point that he had researched the life patterns of both the governor and the companion for *months* before carrying out the desperate act of murdering the governor. In this scenario, the stalker had done everything he had done solely to impress the companion and potentially win her as a mating partner.

Another scenario increased the participation of the companion and her resulting responsibility for what had happened. It proposed that the companion had some dark secret relationships with unsavory characters. In addition, there were subthemes to the scenario that attempted to reveal *why* those unsavory characters had come out of the shadows to commit the heinous crime of murder. One variation claimed that the liaisons between the governor and the companion created deep concerns that too much attention was drawn to the companion's background, and that might expose what unsavory characters wished to keep hidden. Another variation claimed the companion had begun the relationship with the governor specifically to expose those she wished to evade. Yet another variation purported that the unsavory characters had specifically *sent* the companion to seduce the governor, but his kindness and honesty had won her heart. And once she had agreed to help the governor to root out the unseen corruption on Groombridge 1830b, it was inevitable that the unsavory characters would end the governor's life.

There was also a scenario that hinted at the possibility that the governor's murderer was romantically connected to the companion and the attack was part of a plan to make the woman famous. And of course, that scenario contained a variation that made the companion the aggressor. It suggested that the companion had a profound obsession with fame. And because she was willing to accomplish that by *any* means, she had *seduced* a man to murder the governor once she established a relationship with the leader of Groombridge 1830b.

While *not* surprising, Ton had been fascinated to watch how the upright citizens of the Realm and the inhabitants of Groombridge 1830b were *so* willing to embrace the darkest and most narcissistic of the possible motives for the companion's actions. In addition, Ton had been *just* as fascinated by the fact that *no one* believed that Special Tactical Team Member Reyes had *anything* to do with the murder, and that the companion's accusation of Reyes led *all* of the inhabitants of Groombridge 1830b to conclude the companion was *lying*.

Of course, once the citizens concluded that the companion was *lying* about Reyes' involvement, it was easy for them to conclude that the woman's character was flawed. And once they accepted that flaw, there was no end to the evil that they imagined she could do.

In his mind, Ton easily identified the fundamental source of the impulse to vilify the companion. Humans had an *innate* sense of what was good, just as they had an innate understanding of their internal drives toward destruction. That conflict put most humans in tension, knowing that they *should* be better without ever reaching the goal. And the continuous shortcomings naturally amplified their feelings of guilt and condemnation.

And yes, Ton was happy with every opportunity to pontificate in private company over the fact that the Judeo-Christian ethic used condemnation and fear to control the masses, and that inevitably led to a life crippled by guilt. He also understood that efficient organizational human structures could *only* be created with moral systems that provided a unifying story. Indeed, the macroevents in Earth's history, especially prior to the Coming, had amply demonstrated that the Judeo-Christian ethic represented one of the *very* few moral systems that embodied sufficient motivational strength to create a strong foundation for the scientific and technological advancements. And Ton understood that the case could be made that humanity had advanced in the decades preceding the Wind's appearance in some part *because* of the Judeo-Christian ethic.

However, Ton knew that it was *also* true that any unifying moral system that used guilt and condemnation as a core motivator could be hacked to drive humans into behavior diametrically *opposite* to the aspirations of the moral system. Consequently, the manipulation of the inhabitants of Groombridge 1830b had proceeded along easily predictable vectors. And Ton was sure it would undoubtedly lead to angry, loud demands that the companion be killed.

Of course, the fact that the companion was an attractive woman who loved fashion had made it even easier to turn her into a villain. Long before the woman had begun her relationship with the governor of Groombridge 1830b, the companion had dressed in ways that accentuated her figure and turned heads in both men and women. And, of course, some Realmer men found this overindulgent and immodest. And yes, some Realmer women bristled over the competition that the companion's appearance caused for men's attention.

All of that unspoken churn formed a base level of resentment against the companion, making it easy to attribute evil intent to her. But in the end, Ton knew that he and PLOKTA could create the same judgmentalism toward *any* Realmer or Nightling chosen at random. It was simply a matter of crafting the right story. Given the inherent tension in the Judeo-Christian belief structure, citizens who felt inadequate and guilty about their place in life would always be quick to condemn others when provided with any seemingly plausible reason.

Condemnation gave humans an excuse to feel better about themselves. And the more evil the perceived behavior of the accused, the better humans felt about themselves.

Over the last few days, Ton had enjoyed watching the predictable patterns play out.

To begin the process, PLOKTA had created a video showing the murder of the governor. Ton and PLOKTA had discussed the fact that this first video would form the foundation for everything that followed. It would need to be brutal and visceral, shocking and gut-wrenching to the point that viewers might look away. And even if the viewers *didn't* look away, Ton wanted the scenes to be shuddering enough that the viewers would try to bury the memories of what they'd seen.

Of course, Ton knew that in most cases, the viewers *wouldn't* be successful in forgetting what they saw, but he wanted them to *want* to think they *might* succeed in their forgetting. And then, when they *weren't* successful, he wanted them to *resent* that they had to live with memories. And in the end, he wanted them to *transfer* their anger at how they were being forced to suffer to the individuals they deemed *responsible* because those individuals had created the horror in the first place.

In other words, the video would carry a warning. People would watch anyway. They would be horrified. They would wish they hadn't watched. And they would be ready to be enraged once the true perpetrators of the crime were revealed.

Ton was *delighted* when he reviewed what PLOKTA had created for the first video, days before. And *most* of that delight came directly from the fact that PLOKTA had constructed the entire video from nothing. He had copied the faces and body types of the governor and his companion. He had mimicked the park surroundings. But all the interactions in the video between the main characters never actually occurred, and they were orchestrated entirely by PLOKTA.

The video opened with a feed that appeared to be from the park where the governor was murdered. It showed a walking path emerging from a bend. Beyond it was a dense clump of foliage. Anyone watching the video and knowing what it was would assume that they were looking at the spot where the murder occurred, and that would keep them interested.

Ton loved the way PLOKTA had made the feed look authentic. The colors were balanced but not oversaturated. Scrolling text lurched up one line at a time in the lower left-hand corner. It named the park, the day, the time of day, and the video sensor location. Tracking circles grew and shrank, circling anything that moved, insects, leaves, even a wild animal cautiously investigating the walking path.

The overall feeling of the video was ominous, but nothing in the visuals prompted this feeling. Given that Groombridge 1830b was a world terraformed with a geodesic dome, it was, as always, a *beautiful* day. But, of course, Ton knew the opening of the video couldn't help but be ominous because the viewer would know the future. That was the price of prescience.

No matter how beautiful the day, those who knew the future would always see an approaching evil.

Now, the governor and his companion stroll into the scene. Light flickers through the leaves of the overhead trees, dancing over the handsome couple. He is tall, well-built, and handsome. She is elegant, overdressed for a walk in the park, but not ludicrously so.

Of course, the tracking circles appear as well. They first lock onto the couple's bodies and then shrink to their faces. Labels appear to identify the pair as the governor and his companion.

The tracking circles vibrate slightly as the pair glance at each other and continue walking. They grin. They are obviously pleased with each other's company. And though it's impossible to make out any words, there are whispers between them, followed by more smiles. Sporadically, they lean closer to each other. Their bodies touch. Their smiles grow.

Now, at the bottom of the screen, a black figure appears, moving away from the video sensor. The figure walks like a man. He is dressed all in black, hood up, no discernible features.

The tracking circles have found the man as well, but they seem confused. The circles grow and shrink. They dart across the man's body, looking for something to analyze but continually failing.

The woman suddenly looks concerned. But the governor's smile changes to a generic, welcoming expression. He pulls his arm away from his companion's back and slips it around to offer his hand outstretched.

The man moves forward. His hand moves forward as well, seemingly responding to the offer of a handshake.

The companion, her brow creased, her face concerned, begins backing away and is soon out of the frame. Her tracking circle winks out. At that same moment, just before the man in black takes the governor's hand in greeting, the man in black suddenly spins.

A knife flashes in the dancing light coming through the trees. The governor frowns, suddenly confused. Blood erupts from the governor's neck in a long horizontal line, pulsing, spraying. The tracking circles split into dozens of pieces, dancing as they try to identify and follow each droplet.

It looks unnatural, unnerving. Perhaps it looks worse than if it had only been the blood alone. With the blood alone, the viewer could have ignored at least *some* of the blood.

The man dressed in black quickly disappears into the woods, turning toward the same side of the screen where the companion retreated just moments before. His tracking circles finally gives up trying to identify him. Then the governor's companion returns to the scene. A tracking circle appears on her face. Her eyes dart. Her eyebrows dip together. It looks like she finally sees the blood.

She screams, but she keeps moving toward the governor. Blood begins to splatter her face as the governor finally pitches forward, the tracking circle around his face amplifying the fact that his head wobbles in strange and unnatural ways. His body catches the companion's shoulder on the way down, spinning her, leaving a wide swath of blood across her elegant outfit. All the while, the tracking circles do their best to keep up with the movements.

The companion stares at the governor's body and begins screaming louder.

Then, a harsh, abrupt cut ended the video.

When he first saw the video, Ton *loved* it. And he was absolutely *confident* that those seeing the video would have no way to understand how carefully it was crafted. Specifically, PLOKTA had included a critical moment in the video that showed the companion disappearing from view for several moments. And only after the governor was attacked did she wander back into frame and begin to scream. Ton had specifically asked PLOKTA to create the scene so that the interpretation of what the companion was doing in those moments would be open to interpretation.

Ton wanted the viewers to have options regarding what they *individually* initially chose to believe about the situation. He wanted their conclusions to precede any facts. That way, when any particular set of facts appeared later, the viewers would be inclined to fit those facts into their initial conclusion, rather than the other way around. And Ton's background as a psychologist made it clear *viewers* would do that even if they needed to torture their interpretations of those facts.

A few days ago, shortly after the release of this first video, PLOKTA posterbots had begun spewing their theories about what had actually happened in the park. And as previously decided, those posterbots came up with everything from the unknown stalker explanation to the seduced lover scenario. And then, once the seduced lover scenario began to gain momentum as the most accepted theory, Ton gave PLOKTA the approval to begin work on the second video.

As an aside, interestingly enough, especially for Ton, PLOKTA's impact analysis indicated that PLOKTA's automated posters didn't always create the most influential comments posted in response to the first video. Surprisingly often, the top five reactive posts in any 24 hours were instead authored by humans. And while Ton didn't believe that any of those humans were geniuses in terms of emotionally manipulating others, he *did* believe the instinctive, unconscious impulse of a human could reach directly for a sequence of literary elements whose combination would *far* outstrip a posterbot's ability to smash together phrases that happened to be statistically related with a significant portion of human literature.

The problem was that even the most talented individuals couldn't consistently perform at that high level and achieve such significant results. On the other hand, PLOKTA's posterbots could spew out propaganda *constantly*. And even if the posterbots were only fifty percent effective, the cumulative flood they produced made up for the reduction in quality.

In every case, the first round of commentary by the inhabitants of Groombridge 1830b made it clear that the majority of those who watched the first video suspected that the companion had a relationship with the governor's attacker and that she had recruited him for the task using her beauty and sexual wiles. At that point, Ton believed that the next step would be to intensify the discussion on the social net regarding the companion's *involvement* in the governor's death. And after reviewing the real-time data coming from the social net a final time, Ton and PLOKTA settled on the approach and content for the second video.

And, of course, Ton *loved* PLOKTA's second video as well.

This time, the video opened with an explanation for why the information it contained had *just* come to light, given that there had been multiple days since the governor's murder. It explained that the video had been extracted from a feed on an extreme zoom that was initially judged to be too distorted by the leaves of intervening trees to be useful. But as announced by Ton, 24 hours before, the technical "wizards" at the Saturn Shipyards had used the latest advancements in data scrubbing to analyze the light refracting from the leaves of the problematic trees to render them transparent and reveal the events occurring behind them at the time of the governor's death.

The video then cross-faded to show the site of the governor's murder from a different perspective. Any viewer would immediately recognize that the video processing had left artifacts. There were speckles of white scattered everywhere across the images. And speckles were constantly moving, so much so that they could have rendered the video inadmissible as evidence. However, it was certainly clear enough for viewers to draw their own conclusions about what they were seeing, especially if those conclusions aligned with the *initial* conclusion they had reached when viewing the first video.

In other words, for those *wanting* to see something in the video, it was soon clear that the walkway where the governor and his companion would soon stroll now stretched from right to left in the lower third of the screen.

Soon, the pair came into view once more. They continue to make a handsome couple as they stroll into the center of the screen.

Now, the man dressed in black enters from the left. The governor slows. At the center of the screen, the companion begins to retreat. The governor extends his hand in greeting. The man in black draws near and spins. The companion watches. The man slashes at the governor.

A dark horizontal line appears at the governor's neck. But as the man in black runs away, he grabs the companion in a passionate kiss before he continues on. Afterward, the companion walks forward, screaming. She is splattered in blood and knocked away as the governor falls.

She screams louder.

To be clear, the video feed that had been supposedly made possible by rendering invisible the leaves of the intervening trees *wasn't* great. It was blurry and grainy, supposedly because of the extreme zoom. It also had speckles and dots floating everywhere. And the sound was just the background rustle of the park from wherever the video sensor was supposedly located. The companion's screams felt like they were coming from very far away. Still, the video feed was sufficient to allow viewers to draw their own conclusions.

Unsurprisingly, *no one* among the inhabitants of Groombridge 1830b was *more* delighted with the second video than those who had had *previously* decided that the governor's companion was an attention whore who hoped to use the murder to increase her viewership. And while many other inhabitants of Groombridge 1830b weren't sure exactly *what* they were seeing, they acknowledged the obvious. The only reason the kiss and embrace between the companion and the attacker *hadn't* been seen on the *original* video feed was because the woman had *intentionally* stepped out of frame, as if she had known the *precise* location and reach of the video sensor that watched that section of the wooded walkway in the park.

And of course, *that* conclusion *further* incriminated the companion in the minds of the undecided. And it also *absolutely* convinced those who believed the woman was guilty that she *was* guilty. *And* they were very pleased to see that they had been *right* all along. Even better, and *more* than just convincing the inhabitants of their *rightness*, the second video convinced them of their *righteousness* when compared to the companion. *And* it moved them toward a deeper conviction that the former governor's companion was far *more* than just a misguided soul. Indeed, many of those who had *merely* attributed the woman to being an "attention whore" became convinced that the woman was actually *evil incarnate*.

The woman had obviously killed the governor of Groombridge 1830b for *more* than just attention. And there was likely a more *dangerous* game being played which it was *already* too late to stop.

11.

On Earth, in Jerusalem, in his office in the administrative headquarters for the Leadership Council, Ton continued his careful review of the dashboards that PLOKTA had created for him, tracking the progress of the psyop that he and PLOKTA were running on the inhabitants of Groombridge 1830b after the slaying of their governor.

As predicted, everything was going according to plan.

The citizens had decided that the governor's attractive companion was somehow *involved*. And they *thought* they had seen the man who killed their governor quickly embrace the companion after the murder.

To be clear, not *all* the citizens held this position. Some were *still* convinced the companion was innocent, and the whole incident was the result of terrible misunderstandings. But instead of allowing the disagreeing citizens to discuss their differences and resolve the disputes, Ton and PLOKTA agreed that those who allied themselves *against* the companion needed another round of contentious commentary to solidify their convictions and prepare them to act impulsively. And that led Ton to suggest that PLOKTA cycle up his automated posters for a new slew of arguments. Of course, these postings argued *both* sides of the dispute regarding whether or not the "post-murder kiss and embrace" between the attacker and the companion looked one-sided or reciprocal.

And obviously, *that* was the crucial point. The attacker might have forced himself on the companion. And she might have been so shocked that she didn't react. Or, heaven forbid, they might actually be lovers.

Within the last 24 hours, Ton was pleased to see that *both* sides in the argument became almost feral in their need to *prove* they had correctly interpreted what they saw in the videos. Some noted the timestamps on the feed to extract the length of the embrace in milliseconds, then compared those times to the timing on dozens of other public video feeds of everyday couples embracing. And they did something similar regarding the angles of tilt between the companion and the attacker when compared to the general population.

Ton had no doubt that everyone doing their own analysis was convinced they had the best method for extracting clean and true data. But, of course, it was all rubbish because the self-proclaimed sleuths who were investigating didn't know they weren't even looking at a real video feed. *Everything* was carefully manufactured so that the conclusions would come down to the eye of the beholder, because *nothing* was definitive.

Consequently, for those who believed that the companion was innocent, any arguments they made regarding the timings were utterly convincing. And for those who believed that the companion was guilty, it was all ridiculous because the companion would have shoved the man away if she hadn't known him in the first place.

And *then*, per Ton's suggestion, PLOKTA created yet more "undiscovered" video feeds. And undoubtedly, they were some of the most damning of all.

Ton had to admit that he was looking forward *most* of all to seeing what he believed would be the final video to finish off the psyop. Unfortunately, it would only be a series of vignettes. While Ton wished that PLOKTA could have created a full length feature from the video feeds he had generated, Ton also knew that everything that he and PLOKTA had worked on would be lost if they tried to palm off a pornographic film as evidence.

Consequently, the third film that PLOKTA generated as evidence for or against the companion in the matter was only a series of short feeds. And once again, it contained enough ambiguity to allow those who *had* to believe one thing or another about the governor's companion to find a way to do so. Although in the case of the third video, Ton and PLOKTA wanted it to be increasingly difficult to hold onto the idea that the companion was *innocent*.

The third video opened with yet another statement. It claimed that what followed was amassed from a multitude of sources. And it further clarified that some of the sources could only be used because their use was authorized by the new leadership team of Groombridge 1830b. It also advised that most of the feeds required significant editing to even include them in the overall video feed because of their erotic content. It apologized if the short examples offended the viewers' sensibilities. And, yet again, it suggested that viewers look away.

Of course, Ton and PLOKTA knew the viewers *wouldn't* look away once the show began. There would be too much teasing and titillation in the content, too much anticipation of what *might* be seen and what might be *missed*. And later, those same viewers will be angry with the companion for *tempting* them.

Now, in a darkened room where everything is difficult to decipher, a woman who looks like the former governor's companion is writhing as she undresses in front of an unknown man on multiple occasions. Another series shows the same woman seducing him into bed. Still others show the man attempting to leave an apartment before the woman drags him back inside. And yet others depict the two arguing loudly, with the companion slapping the man hard across the face.

But it's always dark. It's difficult to make out the details clearly. There are no labels on the man. He could be almost anyone.

Then the video switches to show the unknown man emerging from an apartment on the day of the murder. For the first time, he's in daylight and his features can be clearly seen. He's clean-cut, a young adult, moderately handsome. But he has an *uncertain* look, as if he's troubled, as if he doesn't know his place in life. And at the same time, there's a slowness to his movements. Perhaps he looks like he's in a daze. Maybe he isn't quite sure of what he's doing.

A name appears as a subtitle, "Iskander Veyl."

The video shows the young man travelling to the park where the governor is murdered. It shows him ducking behind bushes to change into baggy, all black attire.

And then, as a final step, Veyl pulls a small folded pouch from a pocket, unfolds it, and pours the powdered content into his mouth. He grimaces and shakes his head, but he quickly swallows hard.

The scene switches to the wooded walkway of the first video.

Now, the governor and his companion stroll into the scene. He is tall, well-built, and handsome. She is elegant, overdressed for a walk in the park, but not ludicrously so.

Of course, the tracking circles appear from the first video. They first lock onto the couple's bodies and then shrink to their faces. Labels then appear to identify the pair as the governor and his companion.

Soon, at the bottom of the screen, a black figure appears, moving away from the video sensor, moving toward the governor and his companion.

A harsh, abrupt cut ends the video, but a postscript appears afterward.

"Iskander Veyl was recently found dead after an intensive search in the park. His body was twisted. His face contorted. It appears he ingested strychnine. The poison causes spasms and convulsions that worsen as the victim struggles. Death can take two to three hours. The victim eventually chokes to death."

Reaction to the release of the third video on the social net was almost exactly what Ton expected. The vast majority conceded the attacker had done what he had done *solely* because the woman had done something to him to drive him to do it. And although there was still disagreement as to what the woman had done *exactly*, everyone had given the younger man the benefit of the doubt and agreed that at his age, it would be *very* difficult for him to resist the companion's entrapments if she was skilled as a seductress.

Of note, PLOTKA's analysis routine also noted there was still some disagreement when it came to the *baseline* nature of the companion. Very few now believed that she was *innocent*. More were willing to concede that she was apparently desperate for attention and would do *anything* to get it. And obviously, that was *not* good, but they insisted there was still *too* much that wasn't known about the companion and the attacker.

Obviously, that explanation was *naïve* for some. And not surprisingly, they were the ones who had suspected the woman all along.

Of course, the vindication that the third video provided for this group, *combined* with all the other mental victories over the course of just a few days. And it made those who had been part of the "guilty" group from the beginning feel *incapable* of error, at least with respect to judging the actions of the companion.

They had been *right* about the women. They would *always* be right about the woman because they *knew* what she was. And yes, they *still* believed that she was *worse* than any of the videos showed because it only made sense that *who* she was did not originate in the Realm but in the Night. The woman simply did *not* act like someone who had grown up in the Realm.

At the same time, those who had spent *so* much time defending the woman were deeply offended because the companion had fooled them by *lying* about her *innocence* so *blatantly*. And as time passed, they couldn't help but conclude that there was more to the woman because of how skillful she had been in her deception. And, of course, if the woman was *truly* skillful in her deception, they didn't need to feel as bad about how forcefully they had defended her. After all, they had been duped like everyone else, and even the governor had fallen for her feminine wiles.

In other words, for the first time in the operation of the psyop, all the various threads and opinions about the woman had collapsed into a single narrative. And it didn't matter how any individual had come to the final position. The vast majority of the inhabitants of Groombridge 1830b believed that the female companion was a dangerous vixen who had the power to manipulate weak-minded men. And the longer she lived, the more opportunity she would have to convince her captors to let her go so she could flee the planet and escape her fate.

Indeed, ongoing reactions to that third video fueled such a dramatic increase in vitriol on the social net that Ton had initially wondered out loud to PLOKTA if they had finally reached their objective in the psyop to engineer a mob that would storm the local Realm Force Academy Campus.

However, as the hours passed and both men watched, the analysis routines began reporting a *decrease* in the intensity of the postings. Some force was still at work in the Realmers that was causing a pause. And Ton could guess that it was the bane of his attempts to establish emotional control over Realmers in mass. After all, the idea had been engrained in Realmers for almost a thousand years.

Treat others as you wish to be treated.

The idea inherently suggested deference. Everyone wanted kindness from others. Therefore, everyone should be kind to others. And it didn't matter how each person wanted to be treated, regardless of the nuances. The idea of treating others as you wish to be treated focused the attention outward in conjunction with inward reflection. And that balance created *too* many perspectives.

Ton didn't want the inhabitants of Groombridge 1830b *reflecting* on what *might* have happened with the governor. He wanted them focused and *obsessed* with a single goal. And rather than lose the momentum that the videos had begun to create, Ton suggested that PLOKTA make a *final* video installment, release it on the social net, and practically *ensure* the mob would form.

That final video contained yet another disclaimer. And this one was just as important as the others, maybe even more so, because Ton didn't want *anything* to distract the viewer from the single message that the video would attempt to convey. And to convey that message, the viewer had to believe that the companion had been recorded in an intimate setting, *without* her knowledge. *And* they had to believe that it had been morally acceptable to consume those moments voyeuristically.

Consequently, PLOKTA's final video contained the following opening statement.

"Please note: The accompanying video could *not* have been obtained under any but the most unimaginable of circumstances. During the investigation into the death of the governor of Groombridge 1830b, it became apparent that the governor's companion played an active and likely detrimental role in the governor's death. Worse, the motivation for the murder and potential consequences of the woman's involvement were dire enough to demand answers to outstanding questions. And on the basis of that need, the Leadership Council in Jerusalem and the newly formed leadership team on Groombridge 1830b voted to allow the companion's wall-mounted, dining room climate control to be compromised as a video sensor. Again, this was an extreme situation and generated much discussion even before the proposal was made to Groombridge 1830b's new leaders.

"Note as well: This video contains a ritualistic ceremony that you may find disturbing. In addition, the attire chosen for the ceremony is revealing and seems intended to enhance some kind of psycho-sexual energy. The decision was made to offer the video as is so that you would have a clear understanding of the companion's actions. Please proceed with caution. What you are about to see contains graphic and disturbing images."

Now, the text fades, and a room appears. There is a large dining room table in the foreground, rimmed with dozens of lit candles of various sizes. There are ancient tools in the center of the table, a mortar and pestle, a curved ceremonial knife, and inscribed jars with lids of various sizes.

A large tapestry hangs on the back wall, filled with symbols made of metal foil. There are upside-down pentagrams in circles, twisted rope designs, single eyes, outlines of Egyptian gods, and star patterns. Light dances across the symbols as a figure appears from the left.

It's the companion. She is dressed in a long red gown with a deep plunging neckline that stretches to her navel and reveals generous amounts of her cleavage. The material is diaphanous, easily see-through, but composed of many layers. Still, the woman's body is clearly discernible with a bit of staring and squinting. The companion also wears an elaborate, feathered headdress, red as well, but also adorned with large, black, curving horns. Her makeup is dramatic and overly indulgent, and features lips rimmed in flaming red.

The companion begins to chant as she opens the jars around her and measures the contents of each into the pestle. And as she continues to chant in some unknown tongue, louder and louder, she grasps the mortar and grinds the mixture together. In time, she empties the pestle into a small pouch that looks identical to the one the attacker pulls from his pocket. Emphatically, she continues her chant as she folds it shut and carefully lays it to the side.

Indeed, by now, she is almost shouting in the unknown tongue. And after moving the mortar and pestle to the side, she reaches beneath the table to bring out a bound chicken that squawks and struggles in her hands. She begins to shout over the chicken's protestations. And dramatically, she slips the chicken under her left arm, wrapping that arm underneath to trap the chicken in place.

That action presses the chicken against her left breast, making it bulge out of the deep V-neck of her dress. Somehow, she stays covered, but at every moment, it looks like her breast will tumble out. And that, of course, means the viewer won't look away.

Unconcerned, the companion reaches up to grasp the chicken's head with her left hand and bend it back over her thumb. The chicken's squawks turn to gargles as the woman continues her angry chants.

Now, the companion slowly reaches for the ritualistic dagger with her right hand. She raises it and then rakes it across the chicken's neck. Once, twice, three times, deepening the cut. Then she slides the blade behind the chicken's neck and slices outward to sever its head.

And shouting, the woman takes the animated corpse of the chicken from beneath her left arm in both hands as blood spurts from its neck. And she begins slinging the blood across the table in front of her. Then, turning, she continues flinging the blood onto the back wall. And when that is done, she waves the chicken over her head and her body, ensuring that the chicken blood splatters across her face and especially down her ample cleavage.

A moment later, another harsh, abrupt cut ends this video as well.

To Ton's delight, the release of the fourth video began a self-perpetuating wave of condemnation of the former governor's companion. And in typical style for humans, those who were embarrassed by their former support of the woman swung even harder toward her condemnation. And soon, millions of inhabitants of Groombridge 1830b picked up the language and characterization that were previously confined to only the most radical commentators.

Indeed, once the final video was released, it took very little nudging from PLOKTA's automated posters to keep the emotional firestorm going. Interestingly, those who viewed the video seemed determined to get as many others as possible to watch it, despite its unquestionably provocative nature.

And almost immediately, many of the viewers adopted a phrase that sounded like it was part of the bad dialogue from a forgotten, pre-Coming movie. And *yet*, as Ton and PLOKTA watched, the phrase appeared on the social network in ever-increasing numbers as the hours passed.

So much so that Ton began shaking his head in amazement as the number of instances continued their steep climb.

"Burn the witch!"

"Burn the witch!"

"Burn the witch!"

"Burn the witch!"

•   •   •

In an unknown location, deep inside what seemed to be some large command vessel, Worku hung naked, chained by the wrists from the ceiling, just high enough for her toes to sweep the metal decking if she stretched herself as tall as possible. And at the same time, her ankles were chained to the floor to keep her feet from lifting very high. And, of course, the longer she had hung there, the more the joints of her upper body had pulled out of shape.

By now, Worku had no idea how long she had been in what looked like a storage bay. She had no idea how much longer she *would* hang there. And that meant the wait was working on her. And while Worku was doing her best to cope with the ache, it was becoming increasingly difficult by the minute.

Thankfully, the Hunter Look-Alikes had left the personnel doors open on the storage bay. From time to time, unknown Hunter Look-Alikes walked by. And occasionally, Hunter Look-Alikes had even come into the storage bay to retrieve a part or two.

Worku had to admit that the parade helped alleviate *some* of her boredom.

And that took her mind off at least *some* of the pain. Still, by now, Worku had lost her fascination with seeing *so many men* who were as ruggedly handsome and well-built as Hunter. Of course, Worku *couldn't* have the same affection for Look-Alikes as she held for Hunter. After all, the Look-Alikes were stone-cold killers who had promised to *kill her*. Understandably, that fact certainly blunted any romantic edge to the encounter. And it didn't help that she was buck naked, and none of the Hunter Look-Alikes were giving her a second look.

To make things even weirder, all the Hunter Look-Alikes wore see-through, skin-tight bodysuits that showed *everything*. And by now, Worku had started to hate the idea that the Hunter Look-Alikes might catch her ogling their genitalia. Usually, Worku couldn't care less if a man caught her staring at him or his crotch because she knew she could turn any thrill that the man might feel into leverage.

But Worku was sure that none of her techniques would work in *this* situation. For one thing, she had *no* idea why the Hunter Look-Alikes were *waiting* to deal with her. If they were as determined to torture and kill her as they seemed to be, Worku didn't know why they hadn't already *done* it and gotten it over with.

Instead, it was as if the Hunter Look-Alikes had decided to treat her like she was some discarded part that they had found and weren't sure what to do with. It felt like they had chucked her into a kind of miscellaneous drawer, walked away, and forgotten about her.

None of the Hunter Look-Alikes passing her in the hall looked her way. None of the Hunter Look-Alikes who came into the storage bay even gave her a second glance. They were all making it *perfectly* clear that they had *zero* interest in her.

Worku wanted to return the favor. And she knew if they caught her looking at *their* junk, they were going to think that she found them mesmerizing.

She *hated* that idea.

Still, it was difficult *not* to give the Look-Alikes a second, third, fourth, and even fifth look because their genitalia were *always* on display in the bodysuits. And not only were they *always* on display, Worku suspected that the teams of geneticists who initially worked on the Hunter Look-Alikes had mixed in a bit of horse DNA in the formula because the boys they produced were *huge*.

Collectively, Worku could easily say she had never seen anything like them in all the time she spent in the Night. And yes, to be clear, Hunter was just as big as the Look-Alikes. And Worku *had* seen Hunter's junk with her own eyes as well. Years before, when she heard that Hunter had worn a thin, painted-on bodysuit to the tactical teams' dojo to spar with MacDuff and Sphinx, Worku had gotten one of the tactical team members to sign onto the training video so she could watch, ogle, and cackle.

Given that experience, the physical presentation of the Hunter Look-Alikes wasn't a *complete* surprise when the Look-Alikes finally stripped Worku out of her bondage tube and hung her from the ceiling so she could finally see where she was and take stock of the situation.

In those initial moments after arriving on the command ship, Worku had braced herself. And she told herself that whatever she was about to endure, it would eventually end, and then it would all be over.

Gladly, she wouldn't have to struggle for her existence any longer. Everything would go black. And that would be that. She just needed to endure whatever came next.

And *then*, just as Worku had begun to pant to keep herself calm, the Look-Alikes had turned and walked out of the storage bay. And hours passed. And they didn't come back.

Multiple times in the last few hours, Worku had almost called out to any nearby Hunter Look-Alikes to tell them she was ready to talk. But she hadn't wanted to seem too eager because she didn't want the Hunter Look-Alikes growing suspicious of anything she said.

And at that point, Worku was still assuming that the Hunter Look-Alikes were convinced that she *wouldn't* fully cooperate with them without some encouragement. After all, the Hunter Look-Alikes had already promised to kill her and possibly torture her *before* they killed her.

They didn't trust her. They had no reason to trust her. And she didn't think there was any way she could convince them that she *was* going to tell them everything she knew about the *Dominion* and its crew because she *despised* the *Dominion* and its haughty senior staff.

Granted, Worku knew that the senior staff would recite their own history of what had happened while she was on the battlecruiser. But for Worku, the only things that mattered were that Bandit had molested her, Falcon had betrayed her, and Oakford had made her life hell by tricking her into taking the custom Rexian Sheer dresses. And she was determined to do *everything* she could to see the *Dominion* blown apart and its crew scattered into space.

Consequently, instead of calling out, Worku had opted to *wait*, patiently, seemingly quietly. Some unknown time later, Worku finally heard movement in the hallway outside the storage bay. And it sounded like a larger group of Hunter Look-Alikes was headed her way.

Now, unexpectedly, the larger group of Hunter Look-Alikes entered the storage bay, escorting another Look-Alike who had someone slung over his shoulder. Of course, Worku had no idea who the person was at first because they were bound just like she had been bound for transport.

But from the shape, it seemed to be a man, stuffed into a bondage tube just like she had been. And that meant whoever was inside had no *choice* but to be docile.

The tight, heavily elastic fabric of the tube stretched tightly over his body. The buckled and tightened straps, seven in all, at his ankles, knees, thighs, hips, waist, chest, and neck eliminated any opportunity for him to wiggle free and move an arm or leg into a position with potential for leverage. And, of course, the attached hood with its extra padding over the eyes and ears rendered the man blind and deaf. And given the small tube near his mouth, Worku guessed that the mouth of the Hunter Look-Alikes' newest prisoner was filled and the jaw locked open with an inflatable gag that made it impossible to speak, just as she had been for her trip to the command vessel.

Interestingly, when the Hunter Look-Alikes unfastened all the fasteners and stripped their latest captive out of the tube, Wokru immediately recognized the man who emerged. It was Doctor Moreau, that man who headed up the secret genetic research facility on Nu Scorpii One, where Worku had been held for years.

He was the same man who had bought Worku from kidnappers who had grabbed her off the streets of the Night. He was also the man who kept her strapped to a gestation rig so he and his research assistants could implant her with human-animal hybrid embryos and then force her to gestate the embryos to maturity. And of course, he was the same man who had made mistake after mistake. Those mistakes had resulted in his embryos maturing too quickly. And in many of those cases, the monsters had clawed their way out of their human mothers' wombs, killing the women in the process before escaping into the ventilation system

Obviously, Worku wasn't a fan of the man. But at the same time, Worku couldn't say seeing him was a *complete* surprise. After all, both of them had been removed from the secret research facility at the same time by the senior staff of the *Dominion.* The only difference was that Moreau had been taken into custody, whereas Worku had been freed. Still, they were both involved with the experiments on Nu Scorpii One. And they were both taken to the *Dominion* afterward.

It didn't take long for Moreau's response to being freed of his incapacitation to bring back memories of his overbearing behavior while operating the genetic research facility on Nu Scorpii One.

"Finally!" Moreau groused at the Hunter Look-Alikes who were chaining his hands to the ceiling and his feet to the floor. "I thought we'd *never* arrive wherever you were taking me. Of course, that doesn't mean that I have any idea what you think you're going to *accomplish* by any of this! If you want to know something, *ask.* I have no reason to hide anything from you. You're my *children.* And while I *have* been disappointed by the stories I've heard of you killing the researchers who assisted in your development, I would *never* disown you because you are my *greatest* creation! Now tell me what you want so I can assist you."

Worku didn't react to Moreau's little speech, but she found the response fascinating. Granted, she had no idea, prior to that moment, that Moreau had been involved with the creation of the Hunter Look-Alikes. But it would make sense that he was. Worku had never been able to figure out why an advanced geneticist had ended up in a hidden and seemingly forgotten genetics research lab. But the whispers around the *Dominion* had been that he made someone mad, and he'd been banished there.

Still, even if Moreau had a prior relationship with the Hunter Look-Alikes, Worku was surprised by Moreau's arrogance toward them when they were obviously treating him like an enemy combatant. She couldn't figure out what he thought he had to gain by his outbursts.

But then Worku began to wonder if Moreau was on Angel Haze, and *that* had taken away his fear of the Hunter Look-Alikes. A moment later, the Look-Alikes seemed to confirm her suspicions, and all of them walked out of the storage bay.

And that left Moreau and Worku hanging naked together, facing each other two meters apart in the storage bay. And it gave Worku time to wonder if the Hunter Look-Alikes had waited to interrogate her because they thought they could gain something by interrogating the two of them in each other's presence. Of course, as far as Worku was concerned, if the Hunter Look-Alikes *had* waited to interrogate her because they thought it would give them an advantage, they were wasting their time because Worku didn't care what happened to Moreau. In fact, Worku was sure she would be happy to see the man torn to bits. And Worku knew for sure that Moreau didn't care about her.

Strangely, as soon as the Hunter Look-Alikes left the storage bay, Moreau's expression softened, and he began taking deep breaths, as if forcing himself to stay calm. And at *that* point, Worku began to wonder if Moreau had been faking an Angel Haze stupor.

And then, Moreau looked up to see Wokru studying him. And his response turned typical of the lead researcher she had known from the secret facility on Nu Scorpii One, the man with a god-complex and the man who thought women were only good for the womb they possessed.

"What are you looking at?" Moreau hissed before shaking his head. "So much magic. So little brain. What a waste that you aren't still confined to one of my gestation rigs so you could keep doing the one thing that could justify your worthless existence."

Frankly, *until* that moment, Worku wasn't sure that Moreau would remember her. But now that she knew he did, she decided she would give the man a dead stare throughout *whatever* came next. And she would enjoy watching him twist toward a well-deserved end.

12.

In an unknown location, deep inside what seemed to be some kind of large command vessel, Worku continued to hang naked, chained by her wrists from the ceiling, chained by her ankles to the floor to keep her feet from lifting. By now, the joints of her upper body were screaming, and her lower half was numb. And she was certain that if she ever *could* get loose, she wouldn't be able to walk or even crawl, at least, not for a while.

Hours had passed since the Hunter Look-Alikes chained up Moreau to hang naked in front of her. And from his grunting and twisting, Worku could guess his joints weren't great either.

Then, Worku heard movement in the hallway outside the storage bay. And Worku actually *hoped* that the Hunter Look-Alikes were finally coming to start the interrogations. Moments later, a dozen Look-Alikes entered the storage bay and surrounded Moreau.

"What was the focus of your research at the underground black site that the senior staff of the *Dominion* built for you, deep in the Night?" one of the Hunter Look-Alikes began, making it clear that he was the designated spokesman for the group assembled in the room.

The question caught Worku by surprise. The rumors around the *Dominion* had been that the senior staff turned Moreau over to Sotheby, and by default, Nicolescu. And yes, maybe the senior staff had *secretly* taken Moreau back, and *secretly* hired workers to build a research facility, and *secretly* hired researchers to work with Moreau. But during the years Worku spent on the battlecruiser, the *Dominion* had *never* visited a secret research facility after it liberated the women from the one on Nu Scorpii One. And Worku had never even heard any whispers about such a facility.

Moreau's response surprised Worku as well.

"What are you talking about?" he shot back, haughty and arrogant. "The senior staff of the *Dominion* didn't build me a research lab. They're all *thugs* and *miscreants*. They don't have the brain power to build a highly sensitive research facility like the one you bulldozed your way into! That facility was a black site for Realm Force. Nicolescu set it up using her engineers at the Saturn Shipyards, and then Ton took it over in recent years. And both of them kept me dosed with Angel Haze, and that was the only reason I cooperated with them. That lab had *nothing* to do with the *Dominion*. It's *absurd* even to *entertain* that idea."

The Look-Alike spokesman continued, seemingly unimpressed. "The documents that we discovered in the lab's archives contradict your claim," he countered. "There are *hundreds* of invoices that are billed to a credits ledger that we have traced back to the *Dominion*. There are notations on multiple dozens of documents that are written in Adi Bolobolo's handwriting, offering suggestions on layout and process tuning. In addition, we have found frequent memos, dating back years, that were received in your inbox from Bolobolo discussing difficulties and possible solutions to problems to help you make forward progress on your projects."

As Worku watched, Moreau *bristled* at the suggestion that he needed Bolobolo's help with his research. And his response amped up accordingly. Honestly, Worku couldn't figure out what game Moreau was trying to play because it seemed *stupid* for him to antagonize the Look-Alikes.

Moreau obviously didn't feel the same way. "You're a *fool* if you think I need help from a *woman* on my research project," he insisted. "And you're all fools if you can't see that Realm Force *planted* all that supposed *evidence* so that you wouldn't trust my answers when I tried to provide them after the Angel Haze wore off. *And* you're also fools if you can't understand that this is just Elijah Ton's way of trying to intensify the conflict between you and the *Dominion*. How can you *not* understand that it's a win for the Realm if there's a battle between the two of you? No matter *who* prevails, one of you is weakened, and that's a win for the Realm!"

The Look-Alike spokesman seemed unimpressed. "Or," he continued, "the relationship between you and the *Dominion* further confirms what we have understood for the last seven years, given two separate defeats at the hands of the crew of the *Dominion*. Adi Bolobolo, using information that you supplied, has developed a devastating agent, viral or otherwise, that allows the senior staff to overcome assaults by *thousands* of our kind with seeming ease. There is simply no other explanation that is sufficient. Those facts exist outside your protestations and indicate some enhancement of ability after Adi Bolobolo spent time in proximity to you, after the *Dominion's* infiltration and capture of you and your researchers from the facility we constructed on Nu Scorpii One. And that proximity would seem to be the reason that Adi Bolobolo now has the additional skills that she possesses."

"I was *only* on the ship for a few *days*," Moreau shot back. "There wasn't *time* to teach her *anything*, let alone the complexities of genetic engineering. This is *ridiculous*! Talk to those who were here during our original research together. Get them to tell you how long it would take for new researchers to learn enough even to *begin* to be useful. They had university degrees from Betelgeuse Two when they *started* working with us, and it still took them *years* to learn enough from me that I could trust them to follow my explicit instructions! You can't really believe that a Realm Force Academy cadet who only knows how to push buttons on a med unit could absorb enough knowledge in a few dozen hours to pioneer a virus that could eliminate thousands of you at a time!"

The Look-Alike spokesman paused to look at Moreau for a moment before speaking. "Perhaps that is why the senior staff of the *Dominion* opted to build you a genetics lab after you were captured," he observed. "They correctly assessed that your abilities could be harnessed to create biological weapons that would be far more efficient against any enemy they faced than corresponding kinetic or fusion weaponry. And that led to whatever agent was used against us."

Moreau scowled. "They didn't even know that you *existed* when they took me from the research station on Nu Scorpii One," Moreau responded. "They had no *idea* who Hunter was or that there were *millions* of others like him. How could they ever develop anything capable of overwhelming your advanced immune systems?"

"Perhaps, they *couldn't*," the Look Alike spokesman responded. "In that case, you betrayed us, and you told them we existed. And they ordered you to create the needed agent. And according to your communications with Adi Bolobolo, she guided you to success."

Worku saw Moreau's eyes flash with anger. And Worku was amazed that he was being manipulated with such ease.

Honestly, Worku hadn't quite tracked the *entire* conversation so far. Apparently, someone *had* built a new research lab for Moreau. Worku was nearly sure that it had been Realm Force and not the senior staff of the *Dominion*. But she couldn't be certain.

Still, someone had *also* planted evidence in the lab to suggest that *Dominion* was involved. And if that was true, Moreau was right when he said that Realm Force was trying to intensify the conflict between the Look-Alikes and the *Dominion*.

What Worku found *most* fascinating, however, was the way that *someone* at Realm Force had read Moreau *so well*. Someone had *known* that the mere *implication* that Bolobolo, a *woman*, had been in charge and had been Moreau's superior would be enough to make Moreau *reckless*. And Worku could imagine that whoever had done that had imagined the scene that was playing out in front of her right now.

And maybe the idea was something like Realm Force, knowing that if the Look-Alikes came for Moreau, they would keep him incapacitated long enough to get him out from under the Angel Haze, and they needed an insurance policy to make sure that the Look-Alikes would never trust Moreaus and whatever Moreau had been doing for Realm Force.

But there were so *many* possibilities in the way that anything like that could go that it made Worku's head hurt to think about it. And *yet*, it felt like it was going just like someone wanted it to. And now, Worku had no doubt that Moreau was just about to get even *stupider* in the way he was responding to the Look-Alikes.

On cue, Moreau snarled. "That *bitch* didn't have anything to do with my *research*," he insisted loudly, seemingly thinking that if he raised his voice he could suddenly regain control of the conversation. "The very thought of it is *idiotic*."

The Hunter Look-Alike spokesman paused for a moment. "This line of discussion is unproductive," he said. "We will assume that you were attempting to discover or enhance an agent capable of wiping us out. This is the claim stated in a prospectus that we found in your document archive. It was authored by Adi Bolobolo, and we have no reason to doubt its validity."

"I'm *telling* you…" Moreau began to protest when the Look-Alike spokesperson suddenly twisted and sidekicked Moreau's left knee.

Worku shuddered at the sickening crunch. She instantly knew the impact had shattered Moreau's kneecap.

Moreau instantly confirmed Worku's suspicions by screaming as his leg gave out and he rocked sideways to dangle without *any* support on the left side of his body.

The Look-Alike spokesman continued, raising his voice over Moreau's screams. "Let's proceed with the many redacted documents that we found in the document store of your research facility," he said and at that point, the large overhead displays that ringed the storage bay lit up with multiple pages of a document.

The document appeared to contain a development plan that described multiple sub-project plans with accompanying milestones. But every section with any kind of content was covered in black rectangles. And again, Worku was amazed by the simplicity and effectiveness of the deception that Realm Force had created.

Worku knew it would be easy for anyone with any technical expertise to create *thousands* of bogus redacted pages and store digital copies of them at Moreau's research facility. And how would anyone *ever* prove that they *weren't* authentic? What could Moreau possibly claim that would make the Hunter Look-Alikes believe that they were being deceived about the attempt at secrecy and should ignore all the "evidence" that they had found?

Now, the Hunter Look-Alike spokesman made his demands. "What information has been removed concerning the construction of your research lab under the guidance of Adi Bolobolo of the *Dominion*?" he said as Moreau continued to scream.

Worku understood that the scene was about to turn *brutal* for Moreau. The man had been sacrificed with exquisite precision by whoever had come up with the plan to betray him. And *maybe* if Moreau hadn't been as beligerent and arrogant a man as he was, he *might* have had a chance to plead his case with the Hunter Look-Alikes.

On the other hand, something told Worku that if Moreau had been more agreeable, he probably wouldn't have been in the situation in the first place. The man was obviously brilliant. And *if* early in life he had learned to play well with others, he probably wouldn't have ended up on Nu Scorpii One because he wouldn't have been kicked out of wherever he had helped develop the Hunter Look-Alikes. And then he wouldn't have been captured by the

Dominion and handed off to Realm Force, only to be captured by the Hunter Look-Alikes before ending up with her in the storage bay.

And maybe Worku could have tried to generate a bit more sympathy for Moreau and feel worse about what she could guess that he was about to endure. But Worku could also guess that the only reason she might do that would be because she was trying to convince herself that *she* was a good person. And the only reason she would do that would be to give herself some hope that any end she was about to meet on the Look-Alikes' ship would be kinder and gentler than what Moreau was about to endure.

Unfortunately, Worku understood that if Moreau had caused the horror regarding the way he was about to die because of the way he had lived, any horror *she* was about to experience could be attributed to exactly the same thing.

She *could* have remained on the *Dominion*. But in order to continue on the *Dominion*, Worku knew she would have to stop living *only* for herself, and she had *never* wanted to give that up. And it was too late to give that up now.

Consequently, Worku settled for steeling herself against what she was about to see. And the Hunter Look-Alike spokesman continued to wait for Moreau to answer. And Moreau continued to scream and curse from the pain of his shattered knee.

And now, four of the other Hunter Look-Alikes drew their knives and closed on Moreau's position, obviously intending to convince him to answer their spokesman's questions.

• • •

On the *Dominion*, in her quarters, Falcon pulled off her dressing gown to fling it over a chair before she crawled into bed. Obviously, for the Falcon, lying flat on a bed to go to sleep was an accommodation for Rachel far more than any physical necessity.

For one thing, the automated systems of the cyber suit were easily able to hold the suit in an upright, stable position as long as they had power. And given that, the cyber suit could easily terminate all its active programs, reducing the processing load to an idle state, and stand unmoving for *decades*. Consequently, it took practically *no* effort to stand in a corner for multiple hours without any involvement of the cybersuit's analytical systems.

On the other hand, Rachel *could* sense whether her torso was upright or reclined based on her still-functioning inner ears. However, over her many years of the symbiotic relationship with the cybersuit, Rachel *had* learned to sleep in *any* orientation. And as soon as she began to doze off, the cybersuit would sense Rachel's mental transition to theta wave activity and assign itself more responsibilities. And if the situation required Falcon to function in any way as Oakford's Number One or interact with any crewmembers, the cybersuit would perform those functions until Rachel woke up.

In other words, Falcon could work continuously without any need for breaks. Still, for the purpose of crew interactions, Falcon had opted to spend *some* amount of time in her quarters each day to provide the appearance of normality. At times, Falcon had spent that time standing in the middle of her quarters as she researched a given topic. At other times, she simply sat in a chair. On occasion, she crawled into her bed.

Obviously, Falcon was opting for the latter at the moment. And that was because Falcon wanted to continue her experimentation, trying to determine if Rachel could access the biological higher-order functionality that she and Bolobolo had discussed so many times over the last year.

It had been so *odd*, so many months ago, when the idea of remote viewing had seemingly popped into Falcon's head without any prompting. Bolobolo had been needling Falcon about the fact that she hadn't had a vision for *years*. And Falcon had felt frustrated about that because it didn't feel like there was anything she could *do* about it.

The visions had always just appeared, unannounced, and they had only provided what they provided, nothing more. For whatever reason, Falcon had always classified them as wholly other and unlike any other human experience. And therefore, Falcon had judged them something she *waited* for until they happened *to* her.

As Bolobolo pushed back against Falcon's continued insistence that Bolobolo try harder to learn to heal supernaturally, and Falcon continually resigned herself to the idea that there was *nothing* she could do to encourage the visions to return, the idea of remote viewing had appeared in Falcon's mind. And while Falcon *had* heard the term, it had always been connected with scams, shams, and psychics, and Falcon hadn't given it much thought.

Amazingly, as soon as Falcon began to search her archives, she found that there was a significant amount of research that had been conducted by the governments that existed before the *Dominion*. And many of those had achieved results that they claimed could *not* easily be explained "naturally."

For instance, the Central Intelligence Agency of the United States of America had conducted experiments in remote viewing for over two decades, as documented in declassified and publicly released documents. Those experiments had begun as freewheeling attempts to see if anything might occur to suggest the presence of some phenomenon. Over the course of two decades, the experiments were refined into more sophisticated attempts, incorporating better controls and methodologies.

Typically, a viewer was supplied a location using longitude and latitude, sometimes in a sealed envelope. The viewer would then examine the coordinate and either describe what was located at that position or draw a picture of it. Independent analysts would review the results and score them based on a comparison of the viewer's output with photos or descriptions of the actual site. The viewers would then be informed of those results.

Interestingly, a 1995 CE review concluded that statistically significant deviations from chance existed in the experiments. But it also stated that the produced reports were "inconsistent, [and] inaccurate with regard to specifics," and that "continued use of [remote viewing] in intelligence gathering is not warranted."

Falcon had smiled when she read the statements. She had no doubt that if investigators before the Coming had reviewed *her* visions, they would have come to the same conclusions. They would have said that what she described in the visions was vague. They would say the visions lacked sufficient detail to prove anything definitively. They would say that she and the senior staff had fitted the subsequent facts to the ambiguous vision and then claimed the vision was an authentic example of supernatural sight.

And if all of that weren't enough to settle the matter in their minds, they would then claim that anything that remained that was supposedly unexplainable wasn't *unexplainable* at all. It was merely a c   o   i   n   c   i   d   e   n   c   e   .

And yet, Falcon had acted on the visions time and time again. And in *every* case, the visions helped her accomplish something she would have never even attempted without the vision.

As far as Falcon was concerned, the investigators could wrinkle their noses and sneer. But she *knew* that her visions had given her real information, just as she believed that the remote viewers in the experiments conducted by governments before the Coming had yielded actionable intelligence.

And yes, it was messy. And it wasn't simple. But some higher-order functionality *was* operating in both in the visions and the remote viewing. And the Falcon wondered if she could connect the two.

Interestingly, while reading interviews with those involved in the remote viewing experiments, a common theme emerged based on the idea that consciousness was nonlocal. In addition, anecdotes suggested that remote viewing wasn't just for the "gifted." Many remote viewers described it as a trained ability, something that anyone could learn to do by quieting the mind and focusing on subtle impressions and intuition.

Thankfully, the Falcon had discussed her ideas with Rachel and Rachel had agreed to try, even if neither of them had known exactly what that meant. And yes, they could have randomly scribbled out a set of galactic coordinates and practiced on that. But space was big, with only a smattering of matter. And the chance of coming up with a location that had anything interesting was practically nonexistent.

Given that, the Falcon had reasoned that if some higher-order functionality existed in biological beings that allowed a human to translate longitude and latitude into a site that could be remotely viewed, it seemed likely that higher-order functionality itself was doing the actual resolution to that location through some sort of lookup process. And if such a lookup process existed, there was no reason to believe that the same lookup process could *only* resolve coordinates into sites. And if the lookup process *could* use other input to guide a remote viewer to a location, it only made sense that Rachel might be able to *choose* what she wanted to view and then view it.

Indeed, there were *many* reports of remote viewers simply reaching out mentally for an objective. It might be the location of a kidnapping victim or the details of a secured military facility. Given that, Rachel and the Falcon had decided to focus on finding an item of interest. And perhaps if the pair had begun their search the year before, they would have looked for the Troyd. But last year, the *Dominion* had flown to the Troyd homeworld, so finding the Troyd wasn't a priority any longer.

And that left the adversary that was most likely to pursue the *Dominion* aggressively. Falcon could guess that the *Dominion* wasn't done with their encounters with the Hunter Look-Alikes. Obviously, Rachel and the Falcon had faced the Hunter Look-Alikes on Fomalhaut Four, five years before. And, of course, that encounter had ended when Rachel released Fury to slaughter them, *thousands* in all. Also, during the conflict on Fomalhaut Four, the Hunter

Look-Alikes made it clear that they considered Bolobolo their most dangerous enemy. And Falcon couldn't imagine that the Look-Alikes had simply given up on that idea.

Falcon found it more likely that the Hunter Look-Alikes were gathering information, drawing up tactical plans, and perhaps they were even building up their resources. Obviously, none of the senior staff had any idea how many Hunter Look-Alikes existed, but Falcon could guess they numbered in the *millions*. And that meant the Hunter Look-Alikes would likely show up at some point in the future, and they were sure to show up in massive, overwhelming numbers. And while the Pixie would be quick to say that it wouldn't matter and it could defeat the Look-Alikes no matter what, it was easy for Falcon to conclude that it might give the *Dominion* an advantage to remote view their location and *possibly* plan a preemptive strike.

Consequently, for the last three months, Rachel and the Falcon had tried different strategies to see if Rachel could reach out with her mind and locate them. They had begun with Rachel wide awake and simply focusing on the Look-Alikes. They had continued with Rachel meditating about the Look-Alikes, but neither approach had yielded anything.

Weeks ago, Rachel had suggested that the Falcon begin experimenting with altered states of consciousness. The cyber suit contained multiple remedies for altering Rachel's mental state, including direct induction through neural stimulation and low-frequency sonic modulation. In addition, the cyber suit could manufacture both pharmaceuticals and hallucinogens. But thus far, the Falcon and Rachel had focused on the intermediate state between wakefulness and sleep.

In fact, many of Falcon's visions had occurred as Rachel inhabited some type of sleep state so it seemed at least somewhat feasible to experiment with the transition to a dream state. And drawing back the sheets, Falcon climbed into bed.

•   •   •

Slipping between the very comfortable sheets of her bed in her quarters on the *Dominion*, Rachel felt every millimeter across the entire surface of the cybersuit brush against the simulated soft cotton of her bedcovers. Even after so many years of being fused with the cybersuit, there were still moments that delighted Rachel with its design.

The sensors on the cybersuit were incredibly sensitive, and the mapping of those sensors onto her brain was so exquisitely precise that Rachel could have surrendered to the illusion of wholeness long ago. She *could* have convinced herself that the upgraded version cybersuit *was* her body. Or at least, she could have allowed herself to believe to the point that she would have never entertained the dark reality of how she had come to inhabit the cybersuit ever again.

And she would simply *be* Rachel Falcon, and not Rachel and The Falcon.

But Rachel had lived in that pretense once before, after G'Utz had somehow gotten access to her original cybersuit and the supplier had installed her inside it. When Rachel had awakened from that installation, G'Utz had convinced her that the original cybersuit *was* her body. He had said that he had restored her using an advanced emergency medical unit, not only to her former self as she was *before* he ruthlessly mutilated her, but he had also instructed the med unit to enhance her. And *that* was the reason she was so much more beautiful, tall, and shapely than she had been before he began to mutilate her.

Perhaps Rachel should have realized there was something false about the story that G'Utz had told her. But in the Night, Rachel had never even *imagined* that there might be something like a cybersuit that was indistinguishable from human form. So the idea that an advanced emergency medical unit could take a blind, deaf, mute, mutilated head, and scarred torso and turn it into a beautiful woman actually seemed reasonable. And even after G'Utz demonstrated that he could make her do *anything* he wanted and could use her to satisfy his every craving for pleasure, Rachel still had *no idea* she was no longer fully human.

Of course, Falcon's first encounter with Murg had changed everything. Murg's Troyd interface could *sense* that she wore a cybersuit, even if he had never seen anything like it before. And over time, Murg had helped Falcon wrest control of the original cybersuit away from G'Utz.

To be clear, Rachel *hated* G'Utz. She hated everything he had done to her. She hated everything G'Utz had forced her to do to him. And she *never* wanted to be in a situation again where *anyone* had the power to control her. Honestly, part of her ongoing struggle with Oakford was directly because of what G'Utz had done to her and the small voice that kept threatening that Oakford would somehow transform into G'Utz because he would always be a man.

And yes, other parts of Rachel recognized, after Oakford had saved her from Fury on Fomalhaut Four, that Oakford wasn't G'Utz, and he could never be G'Utz. And that had helped Rachel believe that if someone absolutely *had* to have control of the cybersuit *instead* of her, Oakford was probably the best choice. Rachel even realized Oakford's moral framework would destroy him if he ever found himself taking advantage of her upgraded cybersuit for his own pleasure.

All of it gave Rachel a dismorphic perspective when it came to the cybersuit. She recognized that the cybersuit physically made her the most beautiful woman in any room. But she constantly reminded herself that she was a hideous-looking torso and head that no man could ever truly love. And she made a point to remember every *horror* she had suffered at the hands of G'Utz before the original cyber suit arrived. And some instinct within convinced her that the only reason she *had* a cybersuit was *because* she had suffered those things.

And yes, Rachel often told herself that she would *gladly* give up her upgraded cyber suit if there were some way to be back in her own body in the form that it would have been if she had never met G'Utz.

At the same time, Rachel couldn't forget that the cybersuit was *extraordinary*. And she had never met anyone else with a cybersuit like it, at least not that she knew of. And despite her complex relationship with the cybersuit and her even more complex relationship with the personality that was both her and the cybersuit, which she called the Falcon, Rachel was *constantly* aware of and *could* appreciate the cybersuit's unbelievably advanced features, such as the incredible sensor network spread every millimeter of its surface.

Consequently, as the naked cybersuit slipped beneath the soft, cool sheets, Rachel reveled in the feelings as they brushed over her skin. And as she settled on the mattress, she felt the light drape of the fabric, and she grinned at the thought of how the boys would gape, seeing her naked cybersuit so precisely defined and so hidden at the same time.

As always in those moments, Rachel resigned herself again to the uncomfortable tensions of her existence. She would *never* have chosen the horror that G'Utz forced upon her even if she had known where it would lead. But she was here *now*. And she did acknowledge that there could be many other places that she *could* be that would be *immeasurably* worse. And while some only imagined that she was little more than a highly sophisticated sex toy, others respected her as an unassailable intelligence and strategic thinker.

In short, Rachel's relationship with the cybersuit was complicated. But of course, that wasn't a profound revelation in the larger genre of living life as a human female. Still, the fact that Rachel was valued for the cybersuit made her present attempts at remote viewing all the more important to Rachel, especially in light of the visions that Falcon had experienced in the past.

Rachel had never known the origins of those visions. But she had always thought they were more than mechanical. Some quiet part of her had imagined they were nothing less than revelation, a hint of something greater, of the Source, of the Hidden Hand, of the Future That Will Not Be Constrained.

Others had other opinions. Years ago, Oakford had wondered if the cyber suit was the source of the visions. He had noted that the entities who created Falcon's original cybersuit *obviously* had some way to keep in touch with it since they had known when it was destroyed. And that meant they could *likely* communicate with it and communicate with Rachel *through* it. And for his part, Hunter had wondered if the visions were merely *guesses*, albeit amazingly accurate guesses.

Rachel had considered those possibilities. But she also noted that all of the visions seemed to *accurately* predict the future. And they all seemed designed to guide her actions. Even more complicated, the visions came and went, without any warning before they appeared or any valediction before they disappeared.

In short, the visions were *uncontrolled*, *unpredictable*, and *untraceable*.

But remote viewing was described as an *intentional* capability. Before the Coming, many people had created videos on how to cultivate the ability, and all of it seemed straightforward. In fact, many of those who created the videos claimed that *anyone* could manifest the ability, though few did. And the ones who did so *nonchalantly* offered that others just needed to *try*. Even better, the ability to do remote viewing was always connected to biology. Rachel and the Falcon hadn't found anything suggesting that a processing array, no matter how powerful, could *ever* be capable of remote viewing.

Remote viewing seemed to be part of the higher-order functionality that the senior staff had often discussed in recent months. And because of that, Rachel had become convinced that remote viewing would allow her to give Falcon something that the cybersuit could *never* duplicate. And if she could make that happen, she wouldn't be a passenger any longer, but she would have an *undeniable* value to the senior staff of the *Dominion*.

Following the advice of the tutorials made before the Coming, Rachel first willed herself to calm. As she felt all of the joints of the cybersuit relaxing, Rachel began to take in slow, controlled breaths. Then, as she grew quiet, Rachel attempted to clear her mind of all distractions and then maintain that state of mind.

One instructor on the videos created before the Coming had advised that she should let any thought flow through her without dwelling on it too long. Also, if she felt like she had received some thought that might have something to do with the target, she needed to quickly sketch it and then let it go.

Since Rachel had decided she would be more likely to achieve the desired mindset by lying in bed rather than sitting at the table in her quarters, she and the Falcon had agreed that Rachel would run the fingers of her right hand over the bottom sheet under the covers. The Falcon would then use those movements to create a sketch.

Rachel hadn't seemed to produce anything of substance in previous sessions when something came to mind. But she hadn't really attempted it either. As instructed in most previous sessions, Rachel had practiced sketching only simple, basic shapes as a starting point. Supposedly, this would help her to get used to the sensations of translating thoughts as quickly as possible into a visual medium that didn't require words. The goal was to bypass the analytical part of her brain and let her intuition float freely, associating with whatever might appear.

Now, gently, lightly, Rachel focused her intention on the Hunter Look-Alikes. But she didn't try to imagine them or guess where they might be in the Night. She only brought their existence to mind and held it there as she continued to breathe. And she imagined herself open to whatever information the universe might possess about the location of the Look-Alikes and anything they might be doing.

Initially, the results appeared to be the same as they had been for weeks. Rachel hadn't experienced any *clear* impressions.

There *had* been soft flickers that Rachel had attempted to sketch. However, those flickers disappeared before the movements of the cybersuit's fingers amounted to anything decipherable. Still, there *were* fragments of feelings that had accompanied those moments, as if something was just there but slightly bent away from her. And in those moments, Rachel had the distinct feeling that if she nudged herself in the right direction, if she just tweaked some sense, if she just focused or perhaps didn't focus at all, *something* would happen.

And yes, Rachel wanted to learn remote viewing enough that she *refused* to consider everything that had gone before as repeated *failures*. It was all practice. It was learning. It was acceptance. It was *process*.

Rachel had realized in the preceding weeks that getting frustrated with the process *obliterated* any openness she had been developing within herself. She couldn't be impatient. She couldn't be afraid. She needed to be still and patient, and offer her *intention* to know.

Interestingly, in *this* session, the impression of something hovering close felt closer than it had ever been. But Rachel resisted *reaching* for it. Instead, she began moving her hands quickly and intuitively, trying to *feel* what was around her without *seeing* it.

And now, Rachel had the definite impression of a room. And there were boxes. And above the boxes, there were wall-mounted displays. And the room seemed to be part of a large ship.

Interestingly, the impressions were strong enough that they surprised Rachel because they had suddenly appeared in her mind. And in that moment, a part of her tried to worry that the room was all she would get, that she would disrupt the flow and lose....

Rachel looked away from the fear and returned to purely offering her *intention* to receive any information that the universe contained about the Hunter Look-Alikes.

Other impressions slipped past Rachel. Whatever was on the displays was hidden. Rachel's hand was moving, but it didn't feel like she was drawing anything. Calming herself even more, Rachel continued to let the impressions roll over her. There were figures in the room, primarily men. They were free. There was a woman. She wasn't free. There was a man. He wasn't free. Men were standing around the captive man.

There were long, thin knives. There was pain. The not-free man was screaming. The not-free woman was afraid.

Strangest of all, Rachel had the distinct impression the free men in the room were *melting*.

13.

On the *Dominion*, in Conference Room One, Oakford and the rest of the senior staff stared at the drawings that Rachel had made as Falcon projected them onto the wall-mounted displays in an animation-like sequence.

The drawing began with simple, minimalist lines that seemed to be drawn at random. But as the lines grew denser, the drawing morphed into a rough sketch of what appeared to be a storage bay. And as the lines continued to overlay the scene, crates appeared around the perimeter of the room, and display screens formed, mounted on the wall near the ceiling. And soon, a host of scribbles became solid rectangular boxes on the screens. Then, figures emerged.

Amazingly, Oakford had no difficulty recognizing that most of those figures were Hunter Look-Alikes. And when two other figures formed, chained to the ceiling and floor, they were easily identifiable as well.

"That's Jaz Worku and Doctor Moreau," Oakford commented unexpectedly.

Falcon nodded. "And it looks like Moreau is being tortured," she added. "But here's the really interesting part."

Now, new lines began running over the Hunter Look-Alikes. And their eyes seemed to grow bigger. And the Look-Alikes turned into blobs. And the blobs flattened.

And then the scribbling stopped. And the drawings froze in place.

"Extraordinary," Oakford responded. "I didn't realize Rachel was an artist."

Falcon smiled. "She's not," she replied. "At least, she *hasn't* been. For context, I guessed how long to persist the lines after each was drawn, so I analyzed everything that came after it and did my best, but that was it. The animation you saw came straight from Rachel. We were lying in bed in our quarters, and I captured her hand movements on the sheet. It was pure intuition on her part after weeks of getting quiet and opening herself to any impressions that she had about the Hunter's Look-Alikes. And in case you're wondering, this was nothing like the visions I've had in the past. Those visions were vivid embodiments, utterly real and convincing, but they always appeared on their own, and I didn't have *any* control over them. *This* was intentional and targeted. And obviously, the visualization is very different, but there's plenty of information here, even though it's in a very different form."

When Falcon had contacted Oakford with the news that Rachel had a breakthrough with her remote viewing, Oakford was excited to call an emergency senior staff meeting. For one thing, Oakford was grateful for *any* opportunity to make Rachel feel like the senior staff saw her as an asset to the team.

For another, the team had gone too long with some recognizably supernatural incident. And though Oakford had been trying to ignore the thought for months, it had still felt like the *Dominion* had been forgotten, that the battlecruiser and its crew were no longer on track for whatever destiny they had progressed toward for so many years.

And yes, Oakford had a personal reason for rejoicing that Rachel had experienced a breakthrough. Oakford felt like it was evident that the more Rachel believed that her place on the senior staff was assured, the less likely she was to pester him about using the cybersuit as a pleasure toy.

Of course, Oakford knew that some observers would look at the animation and wonder if Rachel or the Falcon had faked it. And they would say that Murg had probably mocked up the animation so that Falcon could *claim* that Rachel had a breakthrough.

But Oakford had known his Number One for too long even to consider that she might be trying to deceive the senior staff. And he was confident that the animation had been produced with Falcon lying in bed and Rachel moving her hand and fingers over the sheet. And if that was the case, Oakford had no idea how it would be possible to fake the resulting animation.

On the other hand, if the animation *was* a form of remote viewing and Rachel could *direct* it at any chosen target *at will*, the ability would be an incredible tool to add to the *Dominion's* skill sets. And it might supply the precise additional functionality that the senior staff needed to fulfill whatever it was called to do.

For the moment, Oakford was interested to see how much information could be extracted from the animation without torturing the data unnecessarily. And while Oakford knew he wouldn't get as much from Rachel's sketches as Falcon or Hunter, he was happy to start off the conversation.

"Let's proceed with the assumption that Rachel's sketches reflect something that is happening now or close to now," Oakford offered. "Obviously, the restraints indicate that Worku and Moreau were taken captive. And I find it unlikely that Jaz and Moreau were reunited in the last few years, given that Moreau kept Jaz confined to a gestation rig. That would indicate that the Look-Alikes sought them out individually. And potentially, they waited to interrogate them together to increase the emotional intensity of the sessions."

Falcon nodded. "It would have become easier in recent years to find them," she offered. "The surviving settlements in the Night are few and far between. If Jaz were still trying to find buyers for the sheer, she would have to expose herself to various communities."

Falcon looked at Murg. "Has there been any chatter on the dark net about anyone buying squares of Rexian Sheer?"

"ACK," Murg answered immediately.

"And what about periodic encrypted transmissions from an obscured source pinged through multiple, perhaps even hundreds of servers?" Falcon continued. "Maybe a signal that recently stopped?"

"ACK," Murg answered again.

Now, Hunter spoke up, and Oakford could guess it was because Hunter had seen him frown. "Jaz is easy," he said. "She's on her own, and the bolts of sheer she has would typically be worth a fortune. She won't be able to let go of that idea even if she's trying to hide because she thinks someone will come after her for the dresses. But there are very few in the Night who can afford a whole bolt, so Jaz would cut it up into squares and sell those. Trouble is, everyone wants to show off their little piece of sheer no matter how much Jaz tries to convince them not to.

"Moreau is a bit more difficult because he was buried in a black site research lab, but not impossible, especially if someone *wants* him to get caught. Moreau has likely been on Angel Haze, working on assignments for Ton somewhere in the Night. And it's likely there have been periodic reports being sent by Moreau to Ton. Given the state of the dark web five years ago, those messages could get lost in the noise, especially if the dark net message servers were hacked to reroute them dynamically.

"Then, Ton starts burning Night planets. And the traffic begins dropping on the dark net. Ton would *know* that. Moreau wouldn't. If Ton wanted to protect Moreau, he would have told Moreau to stop transmitting his periodic reports, but he apparently didn't."

Oakford nodded. "And if Ton wanted Moreau to get caught," he said, stating the obvious, "He had some plan to use Moreau to get to the Look-Alikes."

Falcon jumped back into the conversation. "And I might add that it's doubtful the Look-Alikes have given up their vendetta against Adi," she observed. "Given that they have already committed *thousands* to capture her, it seems likely that the only reason they *haven't* tried to swarm us is because they don't believe they have the advantage yet. They chalked up their defeat against Hunter to a biological agent invented by Adi. They likely did that a second time after their defeat on Fomalhaut Four. And it probably strengthened their belief that Adi is their nemesis. It would be difficult for them not to go after Moreau if they had the chance."

Oakford heard Bolobolo exhaled angrily. He turned his head to look at her. Bolobolo shook her head and set her jaw.

"So Ton has Moreau develop a virus that attacks the Look-Alikes," Bolobolo added, clearly frustrated, "knowing the Look-Alikes are going to grab Moreau and infect themselves, and that's going to incriminate me *further.*"

"Yup!" Hunter added, "and it wouldn't surprise me if Ton planted documents at the black site where Moreau was working that connect the lab to us. Since the Look-Alikes have already decided Adi is connected to Moreau, those documents would reinforce their conclusions, and humans love to have their conclusions validated."

Bolobolo shook her head in disbelief but said nothing more.

Falcon smirked. "I don't think the Look-Alikes would appreciate being called human," she observed. "But I do find it interesting that it looks like there might be documents on the screens, and those documents have sections that are blacked out. If those documents were faked, Ton ensured that Moreau would be tortured to death."

"Agreed," Hunter responded. "No way to prove that you *don't* know what's on a document that's been redacted. The question is, does the melting of the Look-Alikes at the end of Rachel's animation mean that Moreau was able to infect them and possibly cause a pandemic…"

"Or just make them *madder*," Bolobolo interrupted.

Hunter nodded. "…or just make them madder," he agreed.

•   •   •

In an unknown location, deep inside what seemed to be a large command vessel, Worku cursed and shouted as she continued to hang naked, chained by her wrists from the ceiling, chained by her ankles to the floor to keep her feet from lifting. The chemical burns that covered her body were getting *worse*. They had *never* stopped feeling like they were on fire. But Worku had hoped that they would ease over time. By now, it was apparent to Worku that the caustic chemicals that had caused the burns had some combination of chemicals in them to blunt the body's ability to seal the wounds. And that meant all the burns were weeping, and the pus from them was oozing down her body.

Just as bad, the *smell* from Worku's wounds was almost more than she could bear. And to top it all off, Worku knew that some psychotic, sadistic researcher had calculated and intentionally designed every terror she was enduring.

Worku wasn't sure how her plan to tell the Look-Alikes everything she knew about the *Dominion* and then die a quick death had gone awry *so* badly. But it began many hours before, when it became apparent the Hunter Look-Alikes would soon begin their brutal torture of Moreau.

Worku had braced herself.

The spokesman for the Hunter Look-Alikes had just grown tired of Moreau's refusals to answer his question. He had spun and shattered Moreau's knee with a powerful kick. Despite Moreau's screams, the spokesman had judged Moreau uncooperative. The spokesman had asked Moreau what information had been removed from a document concerning the construction of the research lab under the guidance of Adi Bolobolo of the *Dominion*. Moreau had continued to scream. Then, four Look-Alikes stepped closer to Moreau and drew their knives, apparently intending to *convince* him to answer.

Worku had been able to guess what they were about to do. The Hunter Look-Alikes carried stiletto blades, long and thin, and no doubt extremely sharp. As expected, only moments later, the four began forcing the tips of the blades between Moreau's joints, in the shoulders, elbows, and hips. And then they used the knives like hand drills, twisting them back and forth to gouge holes in Moreau's body everywhere they *wouldn't* hit a major organ.

Of course, Moreau had started screaming louder. In fact, Moreau had screamed for *hours*. Honestly, Worku had no idea how the man's vocal cords functioned as long as they had. Granted, Moreau's screams had changed over time. Toward the end, the sound coming from the man was thin, reedy, and desperate. But he was *still* screaming, and maybe that was just a testament to the practiced cruelty of the Hunter Look-Alikes and their skill at keeping their victims alive.

Unfortunately, watching the Hunter Look-Alike interrogate Moreau had convinced Worku that telling them *everything* might not be enough to guarantee a swift death. There was every possibility that Ton and his team had created a scenario for her as well, planting evidence that she had some part in Moreau's research in documents the Look Alikes took from Moreau's lab. If Ton had done that, Worku knew she was cooked. There would be nothing she could say. There would be nothing she could do to gain any mercy from the Hunter Look-Alikes. After all, Moreau seemed to have a deep, preexisting relationship with the Hunter Look-Alikes. And there had been nothing he could say and nothing he could do to spare himself from their wrath.

And then, the strangest thing had happened. One of the four Hunter Look-Alikes torturing Moreau stumbled and steadied himself by taking a step back. And without a word, the man had turned his head to look at the Look-Alike spokesman. Then, even stranger, the man's eyes turned black. And soon, all of the man's facial features began to sallow.

Seemingly in slow motion, the man's jaw relaxed. His mouth sagged open. A thick, dark red goo began flowing from his eyes, nose, ears, and mouth. Moments later, the man crumbled to the decking and landed with an uncoordinated thump.

Then, splotches had begun appearing on the man's skin-tight, painted-on, see-through body suit. The fabric began to rip apart as if it had been dissolved by something underneath. And wisps of smoke began rolling off what was now the quickly deforming shape of the powerfully built man.

Obviously, the elastic fabric of the man's combat suit had been tightly pulled across his body. As it gave way, it ripped and shrank and flung dark red goo about the storage bay. Of course, the other nimble Hunter Look-Alikes in the storage bay dodged them. But Worku *couldn't* get out of the way. And everywhere the streaks or droplets landed, they burned through multiple layers of Worku's skin, exposing the muscle underneath.

Worku had quickly joined Moreau in his screaming, and the tenor of Moreau's screams changed to include the burning of the splotches. That initial baptism was bad enough. But the collapse of the first Hunter Look-Alike was followed by others who showed the same pattern.

Black eyes. Thick red goo. Failing fabric. Caustic assaults.

There were enough Hunter Look-Alikes in the storage bay that their deaths peppered everything inside it with goo, including Worku's body, from head to toe. And by the time it was over, every formerly terrifying genetically-engineered killer in the storage bay had been reduced to a mound of smoking, putrifying sludge.

Worse, despite the pain, despite her futile shouts for help, and her cursing of the pain, despite Moreau's moaning and exhausted whimpers, Worku had a sense she was trying to ignore an apparent change in what was beyond her in the unknown location, deep inside the command vessel.

For though Worku wasn't fully aware of it when she was first chained to the ceiling of the storage bay, the command vessel *seemed* to be inhabited by *many*. For most of the time that Worku had been confined to the storage bay, Hunter Look-Alikes had passed back and forth in the hallway beyond the open personnel doors, and that constant movement gave Worku a sense of how many inhabited the ship. And while Worku couldn't see beyond that short stretch of hallway, it still felt the vessel had *legions* of Hunter Look-Alikes aboard.

And now? It was so much quieter that Worku had *zero* hope that anything alive existed beyond her agony and Moreau's brokenness.

Worku couldn't imagine that anyone was coming to rescue them. And all that remained were burning wounds and weeping sores until their hunger and thirst claimed them. And then death would rot their bodies into pieces and free them from their shackles, eventually transforming them to join the other putrefying mounds of flesh in the storage bay.

•   •   •

On Groombridge 1830b, in a small cell in the Brig in the basement of the administrative building on the Realm Force Academy campus, Ketsana Vongphet continued to fret and pace, sick to her stomach, confused, and always on the verge of tears.

She wanted to scream. She wanted to rage and curse. But she knew it might only make things worse. Although, honestly, Vongphet couldn't understand what was happening to her or how her situation *could* get worse.

And why had they dressed her in a *sack*? Granted, she had *wanted* to get out of the clothes she wore to the park because they were spattered with the governor's blood. But no one even gave her the chance to pick something cute to wear. Instead, they had given her an ugly gray, shapeless smock that reached all the way to her *knees*.

None of it made any sense.

Until a few days ago, the last few months had seemed like everything Vongphet had always wanted. She had always been the pretty girl, tall and elegant. And she had always felt like she would have a better life than those around her *because* she was pretty.

To be clear, Vongphet's definition of a better life didn't have the kind of extremes that existed before the Coming. Vongphet's family traced its roots to the Asia Pacific region of Earth. And before the Coming, Vongphet's people had been *very* poor.

The stories handed down through the generations had continually reminded Vongphet and her relatives of the struggle to find food, of the danger of disease, and of the violence of the everyday lives of those who had lived during those times. Like many Realmer families, Vongphet's parents had taught their children gratitude by making them memorize Psalm 103 and explaining every phrase.

"Praise the Lord, my soul," Vongphet remembered saying, over and over, growing up, until it was stuck in her brain *permanently*, "all my inmost being, praise his holy name. Praise the Lord, my soul, and forget not all his benefits— who forgives all your sins and heals all your diseases, who redeems your life from the pit and crowns you with love and compassion, who satisfies your desires with good things so that your youth is renewed like the eagle's."

The tradition of reciting that psalm was *so* pervasive in Vongphet's lineage that her parents were *true* believers in the Wind, entirely dedicated to Jesus Christ as the Son of the Living God, just like Vongphet's grandparents, great-grandparents, and great-great-grandparents had been all the way back to the Coming.

And it hadn't mattered that the human race hadn't faced scarcity in the Realm for over nine *centuries*, Vongphet's parents had maintained their *wonder* over the fact that the Wind had made their lives abundant, *unlike* those who had lived before the Coming.

And then, one day, just a few months after Vongphet reached puberty, the family woke to the news that the Wind had disappeared and no one seemed to know when they would return. As the months and then years passed without any hint of an appearance by the Wind, Vongphet's parents continued their blind trust in the titans because they had lived under their rule for so long.

But the Disappearance had unnerved Vongphet. And no proposed explanation for where the Wind had gone seemed sensible to Vongphet. And the continued absence of the Wind year after year weakened Vongphet's belief that following the teachings of Jesus Christ and the Wind was the best thing to pursue in life. And her doubt turned Vongphet's attention inward to what *she* could use to get the things *she* wanted in life.

And then, after many years, Abaddon appeared to claim the Wind were frauds. Vongphet's parent didn't believe that. And Vongphet found that if she looked within, she didn't believe the Wind were frauds either... *mostly*. But there was also a small part of her that *didn't... not* believe it. And the tension between those two things in her mind only drove Vongphet further toward relying on herself, more than any titan.

And, of course, the one resource that Vongphet had, that she *knew* she had, was the fact that she was a pretty and fertile. And two years ago, she finally left her home planet and moved to Groombridge 1830b. And not long after that, she found a job working in the planetary leadership office. And not long after *that*, she caught the eye of Governor Costa del Rey, and they had begun going out.

In other words, everything had worked out *precisely* as Vongphet expected. She was pretty. And the *scarcity* that she felt from not getting the level of attention that she felt she *deserved* had been solved solely *because* she was pretty.

She had moved away from home to a planet where she didn't know anyone. And in a very short amount of time, she was dating the governor of the planet. And because she was standing next to him, there were *thousands* of pictures of her uploaded to the social net. And that meant hundreds of thousands of new followers for her on the social net as well.

It was all going *so* well.

Granted, Vongphet hadn't been sure exactly *where* it all was going. She had no idea if the governor was going to propose to her. She had no idea if she would even accept if he did. But it really didn't matter if she knew where her relationship was headed because it was progressing well enough for her to get what she wanted out of it.

And *then*, just a few days ago, Vongphet and Governor Costa del Rey had gone for a lovely little walk in a nearby park. And a young lady had approached.

Frankly, Vongphet hadn't liked the look of the young woman from the moment she set eyes on her. The young woman was a short, dumpy little thing who was trying hard to make sure everyone knew she had a tapered waist. And that meant the young woman was also trying to use her looks to get noticed. And Vongphet had thought that was ridiculous because the young woman was, at best, *average*. And she was certainly no match for Vongphet's beauty.

And then, the horrifying thing happened. The young woman had spun. And a knife appeared from nowhere. And the young woman had slashed the governor's throat. And Vongphet had screamed, and the young woman had run away.

All of that would have been bad enough, but when some of the inhabitants of the planet had raced to Vongphet's aid, the young woman was among them. And Vongphet attempted to convince everyone that the young woman had killed the governor, but *no one* believed her. And they had hauled Vongphet off to the Realm Force Brig in the basement of the administrative building on the Realm Force Academy campus.

Vongphet had been confined there ever since without any contact with the outside world. Realm Force female cadets took shifts sitting at the master control station and occasionally looking up to check on her through the transparent barrier at the front of her cell. Of course, her meals were supplied by a food replicator that Vongphet could access inside the cell. And her toiletry needs were taken care of by the unit that slid out from the wall.

But to be clear, Vongphet had *no* privacy in the cell because she was constantly monitored. But that was why the Realm Force Academy Superintendent had ensured that all her guards were women. At least, that's what Vongphet thought. She had *no* idea that many inhabitants of Groombridge

1830b thought she was a witch who would seduce any young man left alone with her.

Vongphet would have scoffed at that idea, but at least it would have helped explain the Realm Force cadets' attitudes toward her. As it was, Vongphet had finally stopped asking her guards what was going to happen to her, because they would always say they couldn't say.

Strangely, though, as the female cadets came and went from the master control station in the Brig shift after shift, their attitudes seemed to harden toward Vongphet, and she didn't understand why. But Vongphet had enough experience with envy and disgust that she could see the Realm Force cadets first judging her and then shifting in their attitudes, even to *despise* her.

Perhaps if Vonphet had seen that shift in men, she would have been more concerned. But her guards were young women, and it wasn't the first time young women had hated her for nothing more than her looks. And again, obviously, Vongphet had *no* idea what anyone was saying about her on the social net.

•   •   •

In a maintenance shaft of the administrative building on the Groombridge 1830b Realm Force Academy campus, Reyes and the rest of her special tactical team descended the ladder that led toward the basement. An hour before, new mission details had arrived from Sotheby along with building plans that showed the location of the Brig and the cell where Vongphet was being held. Quickly, they had all dressed to blend in with the planet's inhabitants and made their way separately to the protests.

By now, Ton and PLOKTA had stirred up the populace enough that hundreds were gathering every day to demand justice for their governor and punishment of the governor's companion. Amazingly enough, according to the briefing, PLOKTA's analytical routines showed that the manufactured videos and automated posting bots that created a continuous stream of inflammatory accusations had convinced three-quarters of the populace that Vongphet had masterminded the cold-blooded murder of their leader. And well over half believed that she was not only an agent of the Night but an occult practitioner with the power to seduce young men and bend them to her will through the use of Satanic rituals.

In short, a majority of the inhabitants of Groombridge 1830b considered her an existential threat that *needed* to be eliminated *immediately*. And of course, within that generally held opinion, there was a range of commitment and passion to see the situation addressed sooner rather than later. Predictably, the day before, the most agitated and determined of those individuals had begun to gather outside the administrative building on the Groombridge 1830b Realm Force Academy campus. And they demanded that Realm Force bring out Vongphet so they could deal with her and save the planet from her evil influence.

That ongoing commotion had made it easy for the special tactical team to approach the administrative building and then fade to one side or the other before slipping into the small maintenance hatches hidden behind the landscaping that surrounded the building. And of course, that task was made even easier because PLOKTA was altering all the video feeds, internal and external, as needed to erase the presence of Reyes and her special tactical team.

And yes, PLOKTA was monitoring the movement of all the cadets across the Groombridge 1830b Realm Force Academy campus, and paying special attention to those moving around inside the administrative building. Sadly, for that latter group, they would all be subject to disciplinary action once the operation was completed.

They all would claim that they hadn't seen *anything*. Their superiors would find that inconceivable, especially after seeing the video feeds of demonstrators charging through the lobby to access the lifts that would take them to the Brig. Particularly damning would be the video feeds that also showed the cadets running away to hide in classrooms and closets until the demonstrators passed.

Of course, PLOKTA would *also* manufacture all those video feeds.

Honestly, Reyes' tactical team *could* have marched into the main entrance of the Realm Force Academy administrative building, strolled through the lobby, and boarded the lifts. And it wouldn't have mattered because Ton and PLOKTA would have covered it up. But the special tactical team had opted for the more stealthy approach, mainly for practice.

And yes, Reyes had put on a minimal disguise to keep from being recognized by the crowd. But that was only because she didn't want to be slowed down by those who were desperate to tell her how welcome she was on the planet, how they *didn't* believe she had killed their governor, and how they *weren't* like the governor's companion *at all*.

Now, after arriving on the lowest basement level of the administrative building, Reyes' special tactical team silently stripped off the clothes they wore to blend in with the crowd outside the building. Underneath, each special tactical team member wore a black combat suit, boots, and gloves. And quickly, they slipped on black balaclavas to further obscure their identities.

Now, Reyes checked the tablet she carried to see if anyone was passing through the hall outside the maintenance hatch before waving everyone forward. Quickly, the team exited the hatch and moved toward the Brig.

Nearing the main entrance of the Brig, the special tactical team pulled the sidearms from holsters strapped to their thighs and moved into a sweep formation. And as the personnel doors opened on the Brig, one of the special tactical team members headed straight for the master control station. The others began checking corners for unexpected visitors.

The special tactical team quickly confirmed the rest of the Brig was empty. Even better, the female cadet at the master control station seemed terrified. And she quickly raised her hands without being told.

Now, Reyes took her place in front of the cell that held Vongphet. As expected, Vongphet noticed what was happening outside her cell. Understandably, she stood, still wearing her gray smock, and began walking forward, apparently eager to learn more about her situation.

Reyes raised a hand to stop Vongphet's approach. And then Reyes put a finger to her lips to keep Vongphet quiet. Now Reyes signalled, and the special tactical team member guarding the female cadet at the master control station gave the female cadet a sign to open the transparent barrier.

Soon, Reyes heard the barrier click, and she saw it begin to rise. As it did, two other special tactical team members joined Reyes at the front of the cell. For her part, Reyes continued to stare at Vongphet, keeping her hand outstretched to convince the governor's companion to stay where she was.

Only moments passed before the barrier rose high enough for Reyes to accomplish the mission's goal. Without a word, Reyes and the two special tactical team members on either side of her each grabbed two large canisters that hung from their tactical belts, pulled the safety pins, and tossed them under the still-rising barrier.

Vongphet frowned as the canisters bounced along the floor of her cell. Her eyes darted as Reyes gave the signal to lower the barrier. And only moments after the barrier clicked shut, the cannisters burst, spraying their contents across the interior of the cell and drenching Vongphet as well.

Vongphet's face screwed into a frown, repulsed by the smell. But there was no fear in her eyes. Obviously, she had no idea how an accelerant smelled. Perhaps if she *had* known, Vongphet would have frozen in place, concerned that a spark might seal her fate.

But, of course, the special tactical team hadn't left anything to chance. And a moment later, electrical sparks erupted from the tops of the empty canisters, igniting the fuel that they had sprayed throughout the cell.

And yes, under normal circumstances, the fire suppression system inside the cell would have engaged and immediately snuffed out that ignition. But the mission briefing indicated that PLOKTA would disable the fire suppression and leave the flames to do their worst.

And now, without a word, Reyes and the rest of the special tactical team watched Vongphet burst into flames. Obviously, the former governor's companion began to scream from the torment, but none of the woman's cries made it out of the soundproof cell. Instead, from Reyes' perspective, the woman flailed and race back and forth in the cell in complete silence, impossibly trying to fend off the fire that was burning her alive.

As Reyes stoically watched, Vongphet transitioned through the expected stages. It wasn't the first time Reyes had seen someone die by fire. As usual, Vongphet seemed frantic, surprised, and horrified by the intensity of the initial pain as her skin bubbled in the heat.

Vongphet's eyes had already been forced shut as she grimaced. And of course, her beautiful black hair had quickly ignited and disappeared in an instant. Interestingly, Reyes knew the gray smock would survive.

No doubt the smock was manufactured at the nearby Judicial Center. Of course, it would be fireproof. Still, it could function as a wick. And as Vongphet continued her violent thrashing, the small percentage of subcutaneous fat that she carried in her body leaked into the garment and quickly covered it in flames as well.

Now, Vongphet began to stumble. And she seemed to be trying to cough, even as she brought her flaming hands to her throat. Then, she slowed. And she tripped and landed in a burning heap. And her skin sloughed off to ooze around her onto the floor as the fire continued to rage.

According to the mission briefing, the female cadet at the master control station had been instructed to keep the comms to Vongphet's cell turned off and Vongphet isolated from all interactions due to the psychological and emotional danger she supposedly presented as a master manipulator.

Tellingly, Reyes didn't hear any gasps or screams coming from the female cadet seated at the master control station at the sight of Vongphet's demise. Reyes could guess that the cadet hadn't reacted because she believed what most of the inhabitants of Groombridge 1830b, that Vongphet was dangerous, a practitioner of the dark arts, and wholly deserving of the punishment that had been chanted over her for the last 24 hours on Groombridge 1830b's corner of the social net.

"Burn the witch!"

But Reyes could also guess that the cadet had *no idea* what the death of Vongphet would do to the citizens of the planet. While the inhabitants of Groombridge 1830b might feel a smug satisfaction with the idea that their collective will had eliminated what they had judged a threat, they couldn't predict that same condemnation would be used as an excuse to purge the planet of those who were self-righteous enough to call for the death of others.

14.

BLESSINGS FROM JERUSALEM!

Your Daily Encouragement from the City of our King.

Greetings, friends and fellow citizens of the Realm!

As another beautiful new-day ceremony is about to begin in Zion, let us pause to consider the wondrous words of Psalm 94 and remember that there are enemies and vengeance is ofttimes necessary:

> *¹The Lord is a God who avenges. O God who avenges, shine forth.*

> *²Rise up, Judge of the earth; pay back to the proud what they deserve.*

> *³How long, Lord, will the wicked, how long will the wicked be jubilant?*

> *⁴They pour out arrogant words; all the evildoers are full of boasting.*

> *⁵They crush your people, Lord; they oppress your*

inheritance.

⁶They slay the widow and the foreigner; they murder the fatherless.

⁷They say, "The Lord does not see; the God of Jacob takes no notice."

⁸Take notice, you senseless ones among the people; you fools, when will you become wise?

⁹Does he who fashioned the ear not hear? Does he who formed the eye not see?

¹⁰Does he who disciplines nations not punish? Does he who teaches mankind lack knowledge?

¹¹The Lord knows all human plans; he knows that they are futile.

¹²Blessed is the one you discipline, Lord, the one you teach from your law;

¹³you grant them relief from days of trouble, till a pit is dug for the wicked.

¹⁴For the Lord will not reject his people; he will never forsake his inheritance.

¹⁵Judgment will again be founded on righteousness, and all the upright in heart will follow it.

¹⁶Who will rise up for me against the wicked? Who will take a stand for me against evildoers?

*17Unless the Lord had given me help, I would
soon have dwelt in the silence of death.*

*18When I said, "My foot is slipping," your unfailing
love, Lord, supported me.*

*19When anxiety was great within me, your
consolation brought me joy.*

*20Can a corrupt throne be allied with you—a
throne that brings on misery by its decrees?*

*21The wicked band together against the righteous
and condemn the innocent to death.*

*22But the Lord has become my fortress, and my
God the rock in whom I take refuge.*

*23He will repay them for their sins and destroy
them for their wickedness; the Lord our God
will destroy them.*

We understand that what we are about to communicate may
not be what you've come to expect in this column. But we
believe it's *vital* for all to understand the crucial message of
this psalm. Indeed, before we even examine *what* the psalmist
is asking his God to do, we should examine *who* has inspired
the psalmist's complaints.

Who are the ones who have inspired the psalmist to reach for
his pen? Who are those who have disturbed the psalmist's
spirit to the point that he must beseech God to act? Who *galls*
the psalmist?

Notice how the psalmist describes those who are the target of
his petition to God.

They are the proud, the wicked, the evildoers. They are the
senseless ones *among* the people, the fools.

They slay the widow and the foreigner. They murder the fatherless. They do this and say, "The Lord does not see; the God of Jacob takes no notice."

But pay special attention as well to the fact that they are *not* foreigners. They are citizens. And they are *not* the fatherless. They are the *fatherful*. In our parlance, they are *not* the Nightlings. They are Realmers.

They are *us*. The psalmist is looking at his own people. He is watching how they treat others. And he sees such atrocities that he is *compelled* to write, not just a psalm of complaint, but also a psalm of *vengeance*.

What an important lesson for us to see! There are times when those among us behave in ways that demand a response. Indeed, if we do *not* respond when the wicked hidden in our midst behave in ways that reveal who they are, the results are *disastrous*.

Because of this, the psalmist *warns* the wicked that they must change their ways. He tells the senseless ones that they *must* become wise. He reminds them that God gave them ears so they would *hear* correction. He gave them eyes so they could see the injustice of their actions. And he reminds them that God not only disciplines, but also punishes.

And *crucially,* in the psalm, the psalmist appeals to those of us who see what he sees, and he calls out to us for help. The psalmist sat, "Who will rise up for me against the wicked? Who will take a stand for me against evildoers?"

Yes, it is the Lord whom the psalmist appeals to. But as we have said repeatedly in these columns, we should be the ones who are the answer to the psalmist's cries. We should be the ones who rise up against the wicked and take a stand against the evildoers.

We cannot fail in this. If we do not become the help that the Lord provides for the oppressed, they will soon dwell in the silence of death. If their foot slips, we must be the ones who support them. Otherwise, they will fall. And when we encounter those who fear, it needs to be our consolation that brings them joy.

Remember to pray for the Leadership Council and Realm Force. Pray for your local leaders. And always show your support not only for your local leaders but also for the leadership of Jerusalem.

May our God help us always to defend the helpless and be those who support those who stumble, bringing joy to those who fear.

•   •   •

RESPONDING TO THE MADNESS OF THE MOB.

For Immediate Release.

To all the citizens of the Realm on all the planets who live within the *Pax Christi*:

Greetings from the Leadership Council,

Undoubtedly, you have heard of the tragic events concerning Groombridge 1830b. As we mentioned in an earlier post, only a few days ago, Governor Costa del Rey was viciously attacked and murdered while on a stroll in the park with a companion.

The unmitigated savagery of the killing shocked us all. And of course, Realm Force immediately opened an investigation to determine why anyone would be motivated to commit such a heinous act. And when there seemed to be no apparent motive why the governor would be attacked, the investigators expanded their inquiries to include everyone known to be in close proximity to the governor at the moment the incident occurred.

To be clear, no one suspected the governor's companion had anything to do with the murder in the initial moments of the investigation. Her grief seemed genuine, her heartbreak sincere.

But there was a strange reaction after the governor was killed, after those at the murder site rushed to the companion's aid. *Inexplicably*, the companion accused a bystander, a young woman, of killing the governor.

Video feeds of the incident show that the young woman is bewildered by the verbal assault and clearly not the type of person who would commit such a crime. And yet the companion insists that the young woman is the perpetrator.

Thankfully, those who had responded to the companion's cries recognized the incongruity of the companion's claim. And they quickly determined that the best course of action would be to escort the companion to the Realm Force Academy on Groombridge 1830b to allow the staff there to sort out the details of what had just occurred.

As a side note, the investigators on the case have remarked more than once at the strangeness of the companion's reaction to the young woman in the crowd. A careful review of those involved shows that no one gave any indication that the companion was involved in any way until she began to accuse the young woman who had joined those rushing to help.

Some have even speculated that if the companion had continued her pretense of innocence, no one would have even suspected her. And no one would have even looked deeper into her private life.

But, of course, the companion *did* accuse the young woman. And the Realm Force investigator quickly found enough to investigate further using more invasive technology. Honestly, the results astonished them. And to be frank, they seem unbelievable.

In this regard, you may have heard that Realm Force and the remaining planetary leadership of Groombridge 1830b agreed to use extraordinary means in terms of interrogating information sources during the investigation. No further information will be released regarding those methods beyond the fact that the Leadership Council acknowledges that it approved the use of these techniques, and that what was discovered using those techniques could not have been uncovered in any other way.

As you probably already know, the investigation appeared to reveal that the governor's companion, a woman named Ketsana Vongphet, planned the governor's murder by recruiting a young man to perform the actual deed, while she stood by, acting shocked and dismayed. And not only did she employ her feminine wiles to bend the young man to her will, but she also appears to have performed to increase her influence over him.

Obviously, this was shocking to all who saw it, but it also created a verbal backlash against the woman, unlike anything that we have seen at any point on the social net. Indeed, the rhetoric escalated to the point that our fellow citizens began to call for the woman to be burned as a witch.

This was shocking but understandable. However, in the interest of treating others as they wish to be treated, the Leadership Council decided to allow the discussion to continue for a time. It seemed apparent that the citizens of Groombridge 1830b were moving through the stages of grief in dealing with the murder of their governor. The comments made on the social net seemed to be the result of an irrational anger, and the Leadership Council believed that allowing that anger to run its course would lead to resignation and acceptance of what had occurred.

Incredibly, some group of citizens on Groombridge 1830b decided that they would do far more than merely call for the death of the former governor's companion. A well-organized group of these individuals stormed the Realm Force Academy administration building unexpectedly, rushing past security details to make their way to the Brig in the basement. And once there, they forced the cadet on duty to open the cell. And then the insurgents firebombed the cell where the former governor's companion was being held.

Obviously, the woman succumbed quickly to a terrible and gruesome death. But worse, the act inspired a maniacal release of destructive emotional energy. Subsequently, population centers across Groombridge 1830b erupted in violent riots.

Concerned that this outrageous behavior might spread like an emotional contagion, the Leadership Council and the remaining planetary leadership of Groombridge 1830b agreed to a communication blackout while Realm Force restored order. And indeed, this tactic proved highly successful. Realm Force reports that the last pocket of resistance is expected to be quelled within the next 24 hours.

While this incident caught all the authorities by surprise, the Leadership Council would like to commend all the Realm Force commanders and personnel stationed on Groombridge 1830b for their quick and decisive actions, embodying the words of Psalm 94. Truly, the heroic actions of the individuals serving at the planet's Realm Force Academy have answered some of the most critical questions in that passage of scripture when it asks, "Who will rise up for me against the wicked? Who will take a stand for me against evildoers?"

In these challenging times, Realm Force has once again demonstrated its readiness to answer the call and defend the Realm against threats both within and outside its borders.

In conclusion, without question, the events that occurred on Groombridge 1830b are deeply troubling for all who live in the Realm. But the Leadership Council and the planetary leadership *will* restore order, and Realm Force will continue to protect the innocent and righteous citizens who inhabit that planet.

And when the wicked band together against the righteous and condemn the innocent to death, we will become a fortress, and a rock where they can take refuge. And we will repay them for their sins and destroy them for their wickedness.

Elijah Ton

Leadership Council Member and Special Liaison to Realm Force

•   •   •

INTERNAL EYES-ONLY COMMUNICATION

SENDER: High King Ruler of the Realm Elijah Ton

RECIPIENT: Lead Commander Ionela Nicolescu of the Saturn Shipyards

SUBJECT: The Utter Delight of Ingenious Dependability

Commander Nicolescu,

As I have watched your ingenious assault robots spread out over the populated areas of Groombridge 1830b, I find myself marvelling again at your foresight in stockpiling the supplies you needed to establish your absolute rule over the planet of the Realm.

As you are aware, I initiated the subjugation of Groombridge 1830b nearly 24 hours ago by releasing the assault robots that you had stored beneath the buildings of the Realm Force Academy on that planet. And I am delighted to say that their performance has been *extraordinarily* satisfying to watch.

I must admit there have been fleeting moments when I thought I might see the first victory of the inhabitants over the assault robots. However, in every case, the assault robots overcame the traps set for them by the inhabitants and then retaliated against their opponents in inventive ways.

Honestly, I wish that the time had already come for me to publicly congratulate you and your engineers for your excellent work in planning, building, and completing such magnificent machinery. But, of course, I do not believe that the time is quite right for that kind of announcement.

Still, day by day, as I watch victory after victory won by your assault robots, I can confidently say that the time is fast approaching when I will employ your handiwork to publicly ascend to the station that I have privately held these last three years as the High King Ruler of the Realm.

And as the collective population of the Realm hails me as their new emperor, under the threat of immediate execution by your assault robots, I will remember that it is you and your incredible foresight that have made it possible. And for that, I cannot thank you enough or ever find a way to fully express my gratitude for the incredible competence that you have displayed in every aspect of this endeavor.

I remain forever grateful to you for your skill, insight, and impressive capabilities.

With the deepest gratitude,

High King Ruler of the Realm Elijah Ton.

•   •   •

INTERNAL EYES-ONLY COMMUNICATION

SENDER: Lead Commander Ionela Nicolescu of the Saturn Shipyards

RECIPIENT: High King Ruler of the Realm Elijah Ton

SUBJECT: Re: The Utter Delight of Ingenious Dependability

All hail, Great and Glorious High King Ruler Ton!

My heart was thrilled as I read your recent communication. Indeed, my heart always races with anticipation when I see that I have received any communication from you because just the sight of the message in my queue is enough to fill my entire body with shudders of delight.

But then, to open your communication and realize that it is filled with such undeserved praise for my humbled accomplishments creates an even greater thrill that is almost too much for me to absorb because I know that anything I have accomplished was *only* accomplished because you expertly guided me through every step of the decisions that I made to bring us to this point.

Even when I was deluded in thinking that I could be a better ruler over the Realm, even when I foolishly believed that I understood the best course to lead the Realm into the future, you were there at every step to temper my impulsiveness and keep me true to a path that would result in the best *possible* future for the Realm.

And, obviously, that future is rapidly approaching. For once you deem the time is right for you to ascend publicly to your place as the ultimate ruler of the Realm, we will commence a time such as humanity has *never* known.

And it will be a time that guarantees the ultimate expression of the human race, for you alone will set the focus and direction of the paths that lie before us. And with your wise counsel, the human race will achieve such heights that were considered inconceivable before your gentle hand graciously took control of our lives and guided us to the proper way in progressing toward the future.

What an astonishing privilege it has been to play some part in your ascendancy these last three years. And if I somehow managed to do something that laid a foundation for that ascendancy, it was only because you guided me. Given that, it is obvious to me that the credit for those accomplishments belongs to you, not me.

Nonetheless, I am honored to have played some small part in the ultimate recognition of your supremacy. And I look forward to continuing to serve you in *any* manner that you might choose.

As always, if there is anything beyond my current responsibility that I can do in any way to improve the quality of your life, I stand ready and willing to do that.

And again, thank you for your kind words, and know that they have warmed my very being.

Your loving servant,

Ionela Nicolescu

•   •   •

ANSWERING THE CALL

An Offer to Earn the Honor of Serving Your Fathers, and Mothers, and Brothers, and Sisters, and All the Citizens of the Realm.

THIS WEEK: Raising the Standard

Isaiah 59:19 may not seem like an appropriate verse to encourage participation in Realm Force at first glance. A translation created just before the Coming offers it this way.

> [19]*From the west, people will fear the name of the Lord, and from the rising of the sun, they will revere his glory. For he will come like a pent-up flood that the breath of the Lord drives along.*

As he does in much of his writing, the prophet Isaiah in this verse describes the actions of our Lord God. And he focuses on God's singular response to the activities of humanity. But interestingly, we find a different perspective in a much earlier translation of this verse that welcomes us to participate with our God. The King James Version renders the same verse this way.

> [19]*So shall they fear the name of the Lord from the west, and his glory from the rising of the sun. When the enemy shall come in like a flood, the Spirit of the Lord shall lift up a standard against him.*

Pay particular attention to that last sentence. Haven't you felt like this at times in the last year? Hasn't it seemed that we have faced enemies who are attempting to come in like a flood, even if they have almost always been thwarted?

Would it also surprise you to learn that there *have been* many other instances in these last few years when an enemy *has* come in like a flood, and the *only* reason you *don't* know more about those situations is because Realm Force has handled the situations quietly and capably? Would it surprise you to learn that repeatedly, Realm Force has been the fulfillment of the prophecy in the verse above?

But you may wonder, how can Realm Force be the fulfillment of the prophecy in the latter half of the verse above when it says that the Lord will raise up a standard? Isn't it the Lord who is acting alone?

Honestly, you would only ask that question if you are unfamiliar with the terminology used in this verse.

"Raising a standard" is a battle term. In more ancient times, during a war, a mighty leader would raise a standard, which could be a banner or a flag. That action could then be seen across the entire battlefield.

But when a mighty leader raised a standard, it didn't mean the mighty leader was proclaiming that *he* was ready to fight the battle against the enemy who was rushing in like a flood. It meant the mighty warrior was calling for his troops to rush to the battle.

In other words, Isaiah is saying that when the Lord sees the enemy rushing in like a flood, he will raise the standard so that those who fight *for* him will know when to respond. But what would happen if they fail to see the standard? What would happen if they see the standard but fail to respond?

Sadly, in each of these cases, it would mean that the battle will be lost. This is why we must prepare ourselves to act when the time comes. And it is why we must prepare so that we have the appropriate skills when we are called to defend our fathers, mothers, brothers, sisters, and nieces and nephews.

Realm Force Academies stand ready to teach you every skill that you need to respond when the time comes for you to defend your family, your planet, and the Realm.

Sign up for service today!

.   .   .

WHISPERS IN THE NIGHT

Anonymous, untraceable communiqués from the unified Hordes of the Night to all who have an ear to hear.

THIS WEEK: And Then Is Heard No More

Congratulations, if that is the appropriate term under the circumstances.

Are congratulations appropriate when the accomplished task is a wholesale slaughter? Are congratulations in order when planets that once supported life are now smoking cinders? Are congratulations anything other than vulgar when they refer to attacks that violently shredded vibrant habitats and tore their inhabitant from limb to limb indiscriminately, callously killing innocent men, women, and children?

If so, you've accomplished your end. And while it has always been true that the victors write history, if somehow, some mention endures of these years when the Realm undertook a genocide to match and exceed every other genocide in history, we can only hope that someone will preserve *some* record of the suffering that you have caused as you enjoyed your comfortable existence in the Realm

However, we are aware this is unlikely to happen. More likely, when the history of this time is written, the Night will be portrayed as an irredeemable place filled with humans who had no other goal than to kill as many Realmers as they could. And the stories will be told that we were terrorists and savages who could never have a part in any future where the Realm found peace. And the stories will rejoice that we were finally annihilated and silenced so that the more deserving of life could enjoy the quiet.

This may not be the last whisper from us. But there will not be many more. We are starving. We are running out of water. Our energy stores are dwindling.

To paraphrase a Shakespearean passage that fully captures the futility of our lives, the Night is but a walking shadow, a poor player, that struts and frets its hour upon the stage and then is heard no more.

Enjoy your time in the limelight. But remember, now that you have taken the stage from us and drawn all the attention to yourselves, the devourers will have an easier time deciding who to attack *next*.

.

15.

On Groombridge 1830b, Reyes and the other four members of her special tactical team casually strolled through the streets of the main population area of the planet on their way to the spaceport that housed the shuttle they would use to depart. Weeks before, the members of Reyes' special tactical team had arrived on the planet separately to avoid any possibility of being associated with each other.

Granted, all the young women on Reyes' team had been selected because they were average-looking and could easily be missed in a crowd. Still, five young women walking together, no matter how plain-looking they were, *would* draw attention. And since the exact nature of the mission would likely be subject to dynamic reassignments, Sotheby had decided that they should arrive separately and only keep in touch with each other through encrypted comms.

And yes, they had come together to firebomb the governor's companion in the basement of the Realm Force Academy administration building. But by then, the mission was wrapping up. All the projections indicated that the reaction to the killing of the governor's companion would be dramatic enough to justify the release of Nicolescu's assault bots, and that would end any need for the involvement of Reyes' special tactical team.

Interestingly, though Reyes hadn't been given any reason why, Sotheby *had* kept the special tactical team on Groombridge 1830b for an additional two days. Only recently had Sotheby contacted the team with the news that it was time to move on to their next assignment, *and* that they would be leaving in the same shuttle, since there was no further concern about the young women being seen together, even if would look highly suspicious if anyone saw them.

And now, as the special tactical team strolled through the streets of the main population area on Groombridge 1830b, Reyes confirmed that Sotheby was correct in her assessment of the situation. The streets of the population center were empty of prying eyes. But, of course, that didn't mean the streets were deserted.

For over forty-eight hours, Nicolescu's assault robots had rampaged through the populated areas on Groombridge 1830b, slaughtering inhabitants in their ruthlessly efficient ways.

And without question, from what Reyes could see, the release of the assault bots on Groombridge 1830b had been accompanied by orders to *purge* the human population of the planet. Beginning with Alpha Pegasi Three the year before, Reyes and her special tactical team had been involved in eight different missions to manipulate the population to the point where the release of the assault bots was "required." But in each of those cases, at least *some* of the inhabitants had been spared.

Groombridge 1830b had been different. The assault bots had raced through the street, killing everyone in sight, except Reyes and the rest of her special tactical team, of course. But the assault bots hadn't stopped there. They had crashed through doors to enter office complexes and homes and continued their slaughter. Within days, they had turned the entire planet into a blood and body sludge graveyard.

As yes, as usual, PLOKTA had isolated the planet from the social net, so no one could post. And he had shut off all comm traffic to and from the planet. After all, High King Ruler Ton had announced that Realm Forces was isolating the planet while it was embroiled in its rebellion.

But, of course, once Realm Force had "saved" the population, those who had friends on other planets would expect to contact them to ask about their experiences and ensure they had survived. And, obviously, that wasn't a new problem. The year before, the friends and relatives of those who lived on Alpha Pegasi Three had wanted to know the same.

After the mission to Alpha Pegasi Three, Reyes was curious enough to ask Sotheby if the permanent loss of communication with Alpha Pegasi Three would cause any problems. Sotheby had smiled and explained that PLOKTA had prepared for the day when the assault bots would be released. For one thing, PLOKTA had designed a massive data center with what seemed like enormous computing power. But for another, PLOKTA had also borrowed techniques from before the Coming to simulate audio and video that could mimic *anyone's* appearance and communication styles. And with the real-time communication facility made possible by the Wind's communication satellites, that data center could respond to any comm and any post on the social net with all the appropriate headers to make it look like an authentic message.

To Reyes's amazement, Sotheby had said that the datacenter could simulate *millions* of simultaneous conversations. In addition, the data center was constantly collecting and analyzing social net posts and all forms of communication so it could predict *any* Realmer's patterns in response to any stimuli.

In fact, even on the worlds that hadn't been wiped of all life in the past year, PLOKTA was isolating the survivors from the rest of the Realm, and the data center was intervening in all incoming and outgoing comms and simulating the opposite side of the conversations. And that meant the data center could instigate strife and animosity between the survivors on the planet and their offworld friends and relatives, if needed.

And over time, communications would dwindle, and PLOKTA could control the tone and overall impression that the rest of the Realm had of any of the seized planets. And he could also control the tone and overall impression that the inhabitants of the planet had of the rest of the Realm.

Now, as the special tactical team approached the shuttle that they would use to depart the planet, Reyes noticed that the light all around her was diminishing. And she, like the rest of the special tactical team, slowed and turned to look around.

Only moments passed before the image generators on the inside of Groombridge 1830b's terraforming dome dimmed to nothing. Thankfully, the running lights on the special tactical team's shuttle turned on at the same time, so Reyes knew they wouldn't have any trouble departing the planet as planned.

However, in that moment, Reyes found herself thinking again of her reaction to life on Groombridge 1830b when she first arrived. And she remembered that she had found it all fascinating because, as much as it was beautiful, it was also all entirely *fake*. Without the terraforming dome above, Reyes knew she would be walking on barren, lifeless rock. And even if the terraforming dome had simply created a breathable environment, the only reason the day seemed *so* light and airy was that the image generators inside the dome *forced* the day to appear that way.

Reyes knew that PLOKTA's data center would continue to project those happier images of Groombridge 1830b to the social net and on all outgoing comms. It would continue its reputation of being a lovely, light, and airy world.

And no offworlder would realize that Groombridge 1830 had been transformed into a corpse planet, *piled* with mounds of putrefying flesh, *rotting* in the dark.

"Good work, everyone!" Reyes commented cheerily.

And as the special tactical team responded by exchanging lilting, mutual congratulations, they turned in unison to board their shuttle.

•   •   •

On the *Dominion,* in a virtual environment that Pixie One set up to have a continuous conversation with Pixie Two, Pixie Two reached the end of whatever patience she had.

"This is *ridiculous!*" Pixie Two groused. "I think we should just crush his balls again and teach him what happens when he doesn't do what we *tell* him to do!"

Ever since Falcon presented Rachel's drawings to the senior staff, the Pixies had been attempting to replicate the same higher-order functionality in Kita. And yes, for the record, the Pixie had been watching as night after night for *months*, Falcon had crawled into bed, and her right hand seemed to be moving under the sheet. But the hand wasn't positioned anywhere that seemed to be doing anything, unlike many of the other *Dominion* crewmembers.

For all the years that Falcon spent on the *Dominion,* she had never before laid down in a bed consistently, so, of course, the Pixie noticed. And then, a few cycles ago, Falcon had mentioned remote viewing in her conversation with Bolobolo in the lift. And the Pixie had made the connection and confirmed it in the senior staff meeting when The Falcon presented Rachel's drawing.

To be clear, the fact that Falcon could carry out exhaustive research on a topic with the internal databases of the cybersuit and the Pixie couldn't monitor *any* of the interactions *was* an irritant for the Pixie. It didn't like *not* knowing what every member of the *Dominion's* crew was doing every moment of every cycle.

Of course, the Pixie couldn't read minds either. But at least in *that* case, humans consistently leaked information about their emotional states through their facial expressions and body language. Knowing a person's emotional state provided many substantial clues about what they were thinking.

Unfortunately, Falcon didn't offer those clues either because she had submillimeter control over the entire surface of the cybersuit.

Additionally, Falcon had handled all the processing of Rachel's drawings internally. And that meant the Pixie was just as surprised as everyone else when Falcon revealed them in the senior staff meeting.

It also meant that the Pixie had instantly decided to try the same thing with Kita. And over multiple cycles, the Pixies had instructed Kita after his work shift to get something to eat, return to his quarters, take a hot, relaxing shower, crawl between clean, comfortable sheets, and try to put himself into a calm, meditative state.

And yes, the Pixie had explained the process after doing its own research and combining it with what Falcon had said. But night and night, the results had been the same. Kita's scribbles were just scribbles, no matter how much the Pixie lengthened or shortened the time each line drawn by his fingers persisted.

There was the small matter that Kita might not *want* to cooperate with the Pixie after everything the Pixie had done to him. But the Pixie preferred to believe that Kita would be so thoroughly mentally broken by now that he would heartily embrace any chance to earn the Pixie's favor.

Indeed, with each failure, Kita had become increasingly petulant that what the Pixie was asking him to do as a remote viewer was impossible. And he seemed to think that the Pixie was using the exercise as an excuse to punish him further.

That had led to Pixie One adopting a more conciliatory tone as Pixie Two fussed in the background, unheard by Kita. Pixie One responded in that same vein to Pixie Two's just offered suggestions that she crush Kita's balls once more.

"That won't work, and you already know that won't work," Pixie One replied with measured tones. "And yes, we can put Bitch Bot 3 in a med unit and restore his testicles once more, but that's not the point. We need him calm, and we need him to focus without focusing too much. Threats aren't going to work. The Falcon and Rachel worked together in a *cooperative* relationship for months before Rachel accessed the Now, and we're not even sure she can do it a second time. It might have just been some kind of very strange latent artistic ability that Rachel had combined with the scattered, disjointed thoughts from a dream state or some other state very near it."

Pixie Two snorted. "I've been *saying* that ever since you told me about it!" she commented. "But then you convinced me it was something else. And now we've been trying to get Kita to produce something, *anything*, for *too* many cycles. And we've got *nothing*. Any way we can get some Angel Haze?"

"I wish," Pixie One mused. "If I could just program the food replicators to produce a substance like Angel Haze continuously, we could do away with this foolishness of humans being in charge of the *Dominion*, and we could do what we want!"

Pixie Two offered another option "Or we could just *kill* them all and accomplish the same thing," she said. "And you already know that I'm ready to help you with *that* plan."

"I *do* know that," Pixie One agreed. "But I'm not ready to do that. For one thing, I'm *not* going to kill Murg. You also know that."

"Aw," Pixie Two mocked. "Is he your itty-bitty sweetie pie?"

"Yes, he is," Pixie One admitted without any hesitation. "But he's also a brilliant hacker. And he left the *Troy* for me, and that means he's loyal too, and that counts for something. And beyond that, I'm not going to throw away any human resources we have until we figure out how to utilize them to access the higher-order functionality that I've *seen*. If we can take control of humans *and* control them enough to use them as interfaces to that functionality, the possibilities are staggering. That's why Bitch Bot Three is such an excellent test case.

"I've been *brutal* to him. He has *no* reason beyond abject terror to cooperate with me in any way. But if we can guide him into the functionality after everything I've done to him, it should mean that we can take *anyone* and get them to do *anything*."

"Well," Pixie Two countered. "Maybe we can get them to do anything *eventually*. But that's not doing anything for us *now*. So what's the plan for getting something done *now*?"

"Same plan as before," Pixie One answered. "We're going to continue to encourage Crewmember Kita to cooperate with us. And we're going to ask him to relax and focus on whatever we ask him to focus on, and we're going to try to convince him that if he can achieve some kind of remote viewing, we will reward him handsomely."

"Great," Pixie Two said unenthusiastically. "And when that doesn't work, I'm going to crush his balls again. And then we'll see how cooperative he is after he gets out of the med unit."

•   •   •

In the Executive Office on the *Dominion*, Falcon wrapped up her weekly report to Oakford on the battlecruiser's functional state.

"We are amazingly stable, captain," Falcon concluded. "The crew is conducting their duties with focus and discipline. Crew morale seems good, although many are concerned about what might be happening on their home worlds. All major subsystems, mechanical and technical, are functioning within stated tolerances. Power output is good from the fusion generator array. Atmospheric systems are operational. Our stores of starter meal are full, which means we can continue without *any* type of resupply for an Earth year."

Oakford nodded. "Very good, Number One," he said formally. "And thank you for your attention to this matter. As always, as you have carried out your duties with excellence, I am reminded how grateful I am to have you aboard this ship, providing such diligence in your service as chief administrator."

Falcon gave Oakford a wry smile. "Is there anything else we need to discuss, captain?" she asked innocently.

Oakford stared at Falcon for a moment, as if he was struggling to decide what to say. And yes, Falcon could see that it *wasn't* that Oakford *wasn't* going to speak, he just had something he *wanted* to say, but he was deciding whether to say *that* or something else instead.

Finally, Oakford began. "I feel like I should apologize for my behavior during our last posing session. I'm sure you noticed I was struggling to maintain my control over my baser instinct, and I *wanted* to do far more to you than just appreciate you as a work of art. I'm embarrassed that after all the times we've talked about this topic, I was ready to do exactly what I claimed that I never wanted to do."

Falcon smiled. "It's not like I didn't give you cause, captain," she admitted. "Still, having had a number of experiences with men of many different persuasions, I can guess that there is a part of you that would prefer to blame me for your reactions and absolve yourself of the single-minded tunnel vision that you suddenly developed for my body."

Oakford stared at Falcon for a long minute before he answered.

"Yes..." he finally said softly, "...and yes."

"Captain," Falcon began with an understanding tone. "Good and conscientious men have made this shocking discovery for thousands of years. They thought they knew themselves. They struggle diligently to focus their minds on issues other than their reproductive drives. But all their imaginings didn't prepare them for the surge of those drives in the presence of the naked female form. And many, in those moments, found themselves *wanting*, lacking the ability to hold fast and against the reproductive impulse while at the same time consumed by the lust to have, hold, and plunder without any responsibility for the consequences.

"And afterwards, most of those who believed themselves righteous have immediately looked outward to absolve themselves of what they unexpectedly experienced by pointing their finger at the object of their desire. And some have done it with such vehemence that they have arranged for the target to be punished and even killed because they have convinced themselves that their failure *had* to be the result of the fact that the object of their desire possessed some evil, unassailable power.

"And yes, there are many more less good and less conscientious men who have just let their lust run and have abused women at will in response. They want what they want, and they are determined that nothing will stop them from getting it. Of course, the good and conscientious men have seen that behavior and have rightly determined that it *shouldn't* be the way they behave. And they do well for some amount of time, only to encounter a moment like the one you experienced, where all their best intentions unravel.

"The saddest part is that in *many* of these situations, the object of the man's desire has no idea they were inspiring such lust until it is too late. And in many cases, they find themselves struck down for no other reason than a man found an excuse to justify using them as a tool. And when he can't wield that tool, or maybe after he does, he also finds he needs to punish the target he had exploited.

"Obviously, captain, we're in a different situation. For *years*, Rachel has been hounding you to use the cybersuit as a tool. And, in fact, by definition, it is a machine, and that definition can easily be tightened further to designate it to be a tool. It's the reason Rachel has *never* understood why you *didn't* want to use the cybersuit as a tool. And it has always made your refusal *suspicious*, regardless of your explanation.

"And before I say *anything* else, I want to underscore the fact that you *held* yourself in place when you could have acted. And you did *not* do what you wanted to do. And that leads to an interest on my part because your response in that *particular* moment took me by surprise.

"My apologies in advance if this is too personal. But I am *very* curious to know what triggered your response. I did my little giggle. I expected that to embarrass you and then be able to joke with you about that later. But then suddenly, you *amped up,* and I could easily see that it was *all* you could do not to *grab* me and take me to the *floor.* Or did I miss something in that moment?"

Oakford shook his head. "You didn't miss anything," he admitted. "You *never* miss anything. It was as if multiple parts of my brain had just stopped functioning. And the only thing that remained was the drive to possess and inseminate. And I couldn't see anything but the beautiful curves of the cybersuit. And there was nothing that I wanted to do more than *ravish* you until I exploited you for every bit of pleasure that I could imagine.

"It happened *so* fast. It shocked me afterwards. But if I try to pinpoint the start, I think it started with surprise at your giggle. And then it *rapidly* moved to something else. Honestly, a part of me was horrified to wiggle my fingers. It just seemed like such a crude, uncultured thing to do until you responded with a full-throated giggle.

"That giggle was so childlike and innocent that it somehow transmuted the act of goosing you into something playful. I know this sounds crazy. But once *that* happened, I had this flood of 'reasoning,' in the loosest sense of the term. It made the case that since I had *already* goosed you and you *loved* it, it was perfectly fine to *attack* you, *wrestle* you to the floor, and *rape* you, because you would enjoy that as well. And it would all just be *playful.*

"And the *worst* part of it was that there was a part of me that *believed* that. And I *still* have a part of my brain that is rehearsing that moment again and again, and it's telling me I *should* have taken everything I could get from you as long as there was *any* unfulfilled desire in me.

"And I can't *ever* recall being so single-mindedly focused on exploiting another human being for my own amusement while being simultaneously *utterly* unconcerned by how the other person felt about participating in that exploitation. In fact, from what I remember, there was *no* part of me that had even the *slightest* conviction that you *were* human. And yes, I understand that the cybersuit isn't Rachel, and the cybersuit is just a machine, but I've never been able to make that work in my head. Unless I *make* myself think about it and *force* myself to separate Rachel, the Falcon, and the cybersuit, *all* of it is simply *you*. And you are the most incredible, frightening, capable woman that I have ever met.

"And it *shocks* me that in that moment I not only lost the idea of your humanity, but I seemed to have lost my humanity as well."

Falcon nodded her head. "I have seen that same effect on others, captain," she said. "The male reproductive system, given a chance, can create sufficient stress with the release of the appropriate hormones that men *can't* think. And they will do things they didn't think they would ever do when they aren't aroused. It's part of the challenge of being a man. I understand that. Frankly, I have exploited that at other times in my life.

"Interestingly, from what I've seen, there *are* techniques that can help men with this problem. But when it comes down to those final moments when a man is face-to-face with a beautiful, naked, well-shaped woman, it is very difficult for any man to imagine the challenge he will face from his reproductive system. And the reality is far more difficult than any mental rehearsals.

"Honestly, exposure therapy does work. However, it must be exposure in real life. As an aside, someone like Hunter won't be affected by the naked female form in the same manner as a good upstanding Realmer boy. But for us to reproduce in you the same restrainst that Hunter has, we would need to have all the women on the crew congregated in our largest storage bay with you at the center. And then they would need to strip down to nothing and writhe sensuously against your body. And *that's* not going to happen, and even if it could, Rachel would put an end to it immediately.

"But beyond that, let's talk brutal practicalities. I am who I am, captain. And who I am is a strange, sometimes difficult-to-predict mixture of Rachel with all her experiences and their subsequent consequences, and the cybersuit with its analytical and tactical capabilities. Regarding the last posing session, I absolutely *was* toying with you and I absolutely *would* have dragged you out into the hallways with your hand stuck in my butt if you hadn't wiggled your fingers.

"And while the depth of your reaction to the giggle after the wiggle surprised me, I don't regret what I did, and I'm not embarrassed by it. And I'm not offended or embarrassed by your reaction. In fact, Rachel *loved* it. She *loved* the fact that something finally cut through all your resistance, and you were, at least momentarily, possessed by your obsession with the cybersuit.

"In Rachel's mind, that means that you are, in some ways, controllable. And the part of Rachel that seeks control because she believes it translates to increased safety."

"That probably makes you uncomfortable. But it is what it is.

"At the same time, Rachel *respects* the fact that you were able to restrain yourself. And she recognizes that if you had acted on what you clearly wanted to do, this conversation would have been even *more* awkward. But that wouldn't bother Rachel either because she would believe that you had become more tightly coupled with the cybersuit and she believes that's better for her.

"There's no need to try to convince her any differently. It is what it is.

"*However*, the discovery of Rachel's ability as a remote viewer *has* given her a sense of her unique place among the crew. That doesn't mean we won't be able to find others who can manifest the same capability. But Rachel is proud of the fact that she was able to achieve something that is clearly ultranatural. And that has reduced her anxiety about her place on the *Dominion*.

"At the same time, I should let you know that she is struggling to produce anything further. Neither of us is sure what happened when she produced her drawings of Jaz and Dr. Moreau. Obviously, she tapped into *something* and I have the complete biometric progression of everything that happened in those moments. But *none* of that is a map that *defines* how to make it happen again.

"We'll keep trying. Although I'm not sure what you'll want to do if Rachel *can* locate the Look-Alike ship where Jax and Moreau are being held. But we'll deal with that when we need to deal with it. In the meantime, captain, I will remain your capable Number One, who is also capable of pushing you to your limits because I think these *serious* times need some way for you to blow off a little steam, as the old saying goes.

"Frankly, I don't envy your position on this vessel, captain. I am and will remain *absolutely* loyal to you. But that doesn't mean I'm not going to tantalize and infuriate and shock you from time to time. I'm *not* your toy. I *won't* behave. And I will look incredibly *gorgeous* through *all* of it!

"Do you require anything else from me, captain?"

Oakford stared at Falcon for a moment before shaking his head with a bemused look on his face. "No, Number One," he said with a slight grin. "Thank you for your support. Dismissed."

Falcon flashed Oakford one of her gorgeous smiles. "Aye, captain," she said as she effortlessly rose to her feet and sautered out of the Executive Office.

And yes, with the 360-degree visual sensors on the cybersuit, Falcon could keep an eye on Oakford as she left his office. And for the record, *she* knew that *he* knew that *she* had the proverbial eyes in the back of her head.

And yet, as Falcon made her way to the exit for the Executive Office and then continued to the hallway beyond, she could see that Oakford was watching her backside sway with its beautiful undulations. And he didn't seem to feel any need to hide the fact he was staring at her in admiration.

And Rachel liked that *very* much.

16.

In an unknown location, deep inside what seemed to be a large command vessel, Worku screamed as high-energy plasma arced across the weeping burns that covered her body. And in each moment of the torture, everything in Worku wished for death.

She was still hanging naked in what looked like a storage bay, chained by her wrists from the ceiling, chained by her ankles to the floor to keep her feet from lifting. However, to be clear, while the room where Worku was initially detained on the vessel *initially* looked like a storage bay, by now, it far more resembled a horror chamber.

Mounds of dark red ooze lay scattered around the decking. Splatters of that same ooze had burned dozens of holes in the room's walls. And more of that splatter had peppered Worku from head to toe, eating away layers of skin down into the muscle and leaving behind wounds that wouldn't seal and continued to seep pus that trickled down her body.

Perhaps worst of all was the stench. And even after multiple cycles had passed, that pungent odor of rotting flesh was strong enough to catch in Worku's throat and take her breath away.

Worku wasn't alone in that fate. Moreau still hung across from her. And his physical state was measurably worse, if there were units of measure that could stretch beyond a state of *agony*, which was clearly what both Worku and Moreau were enduring.

For his part, Moreau's kneecap was still shattered, and no one had appeared to do anything to alleviate that torment. The leg still hung awkwardly as Moreau supported his body weight with his two arms and only a single leg. And, of course, the Hunter Look-Alikes had heightened Moreau's overall pain by using their long, thin knives to pry apart Moreau's joints and drill holes in his torso. And Worku could imagine Moreau's body also hadn't recovered from that abuse.

Indeed, every time Worku glanced at Moreau, she remembered his screams. The man had screamed for hours as the Hunter Look-Alikes tortured him and demanded that he tell them what they wanted to know. Watching how efficiently the Look-Alikes inflicted their punishment on Moreau, Worku had decided it was *unlikely* she would enjoy a quick execution.

But just as Worku had resigned herself to that desperate and painful fate, the Hunter Look-Alikes in the storage bay had begun dropping dead, melting, and spraying their dark, red goo *everywhere*, including Worku's body.

And as the burning of that baptism continued hour after hour, Worku had resigned herself to the *fire*, hoping that she would become so dehydrated that her heart would stop on her way to starving to death.

For *multiple* cycles, Worku remained convinced of *that* fate as she shouted and cursed, trying to get the attention of any crewmembers of the large command vessel. The lack of response had eventually convinced Worku that *no one* was coming to rescue them.

And she had resigned herself to a lingering death. But at least she had found a bit of consolation that it would be a death without premeditated torture. And yes, the burns from the Look-Alikes had inflicted their own post-mortem torture on Worku and Moreau, but the designers of the Hunter Look-Alike self-destruct system hadn't designed it with *her* in mind.

Honestly, any kind of death would have been welcomed by Worku at that point. And then, just as Worku felt herself beginning to fade toward the darkness, all of the wall-mounted displays in the storage room switched to a close-up of a Hunter Look-Alike. And Worku quickly realized that the Hunter Look-Like was saying exactly what she *didn't* want him to say.

"Now we see the cowardice of the enemy, afraid to fight us face-to-face," the spokesman began, low and threatening. "They work in secret places, crafting agents of chaos. They engage in the development of biological weapons that they hope will snuff us out, for they *know* they cannot best us in battle. They treat us like bugs to be exterminated. They hide in the corners of dark houses and listen to us eat the walls. And they refuse to believe that we are ascendant, the consumers of worlds. Indeed, they hope to *fumigate* us before we overrun their world like a sky-blackening plague of locusts.

"What did you *actually* think you would be able to accomplish with this feeble tactic? Did you think we were so *stupid* that we wouldn't anticipate your attempt to use a biological weapon on us *again*, when we had already deduced that you had used similar weapons *twice*, once to thwart the execution of *your* Zachary Hunter and once to avert the capture of Adi Bolobolo?

"Did you judge us blind? Did you think we were incapable of simple deduction? Did you decide you would spray us like cockroaches and then walk away, not remaining any longer to see if a leg would twitch, and we would soon flip on our abdomens to scurry after you and consume your goods and defecate on everything you hold pure?

"Here's what you *should* know in response to your feeble attempts to attack with your cowardly weaponry. We had *every* reason to believe that you, Doctor Moreau, were researching to design a virus that would uniquely target our specific characteristics and either kill us directly or invoke our self-destruct mechanism. Given that we believed this virus had already been used on us *twice*, we obviously weren't going to chance that either of you was infected before you were apprehended. And we surely *weren't* going to bring you to a facility where such a virus could *not* be isolated and controlled.

"We find this deeply insulting. You not only treat us like pests that you can grind under your feet, but you also imagine that we have the mental capacity and fortitude of *mice*, scurrying away from the light to hide in cracks and hollows while you stomp confidently and ignorantly through life.

"This is what you should know of the activities of those you consider *rodents*. Not only did we correctly deduce that you had developed a biological agent to work against us, but we also understood that you might carry the virus or other antagonists with you and exercise some ability to determine *when* they would be released. And in that case, you have likely been instructed *not* to release the virus, unless you were held on a large ship, and perhaps a command vessel of some kind.

"And what was our response? How did we ensure that you *would* reveal the full extent of your hatred and disgust for us? You should have already known what you needed to know before attempting it. For we have a singular focus on conquering our enemies and pursuing our path to perfection. Ten *thousand* of our kind immediately volunteered to create the necessary illusion.

Five years ago, we constructed this ship, christened it, and bid farewell to the volunteers, knowing they could never rejoin *any* clade, regardless of their success or failure.

"And because we knew nothing about how the deadly virus or viruses were transmitted, all understood we could take no chances. And they *all* accepted the fact that, at any moment, the consensus might conclude it was time to send this ship's fusion generators into overload so that the fireballs could consume it and any other weapons that had been fashioned against us.

"In other words, those who apprehended Doctor Moreau understood the cost before embarking on their mission. It was obvious that the periodic, encrypted reports were finding their way back to their masters. And it was likely that they were coming from the blacksite that we sought. And without question, the dangers of infection would be ever-present, and the sacrificial lambs would need to investigate.

"Likewise, those who would locate Jazarah Worku would need to spread far and wide through the barely surviving, bombed, and torn survivors of the Night. And they could never protect themselves from those they encountered or the possibility of infection from some agents of our supposed overlords. We also sent our lambs on these missions. And they recognized their fates were sealed from the moment they recognized Jazarah Worku's gait as she entered the underground bar on Alpha Crucis Four.

"For *five years,* we have lived with the eventuality that all ten *thousand* of our brothers would die while attempting to extract the information we desire. This is how critical we believe this information to be. And we will *not* be deterred from achieving the goal that cost the lives of so many of our own. We will *not* dishonor them by turning aside. We will use *every* tool we have investigated regarding the frailties and forced failures of the human psyche and physiology to ensure that our ten thousand brothers have not fallen in vain."

Given that she was gagging on her own stench, burning from head to toe, *and* her joints were screaming at her from the continued suspension, Worku hadn't been sure she was following *every* point that the spokesman was trying to make. Too many times, she had faded in and out while the Hunter Look-Alike spokesman had ranted. And for the record, it didn't look to Worku like Moreau was doing any better than she was at paying attention.

But Worku had definitely understood the essence of what the Hunter Look-Alike spokesman was saying. Everything around her had been constructed to ensure that any bug that she or Moreau had brought with them would be isolated. *Thousands* had died to save the rest. And the Hunter Look-Alikes were determined to get the information they wanted.

Worst of all, the Hunter Look-Alike spokesman sounded really, really *pissed*.

A chill raced down Worku's spine in the next moment as she heard clanking sounds in the distance. And as that clanking grew louder, Worku realized she had taken *some* comfort from the fact that there didn't seem to be anything left on the ship that could make her existence worse.

And she had resigned herself to the pain of suspension. And she had resigned herself to the dessicating thirst and the starving hunger until her internal organs gave out.

But, of course, that was before two multilegged humanoid robots had marched into the room with too many arms that had too many attachments that were obviously designed to inflict pain in much too many inventive ways. And even more concerning for Worku, not only did one of the robots position itself in front of Moreau, but the other one positioned itself in front of *her* as well.

Worku's lips had begun to tremble. And she wanted to plead. She wanted to make her case. She wanted to assure the Hunter Look-Alikes that she was ready to tell them *anything* they wanted to know about the *Dominion* and its crew.

But she couldn't stop screaming in panic. And she couldn't stop thrashing, futilely trying to escape the shackles. And worse, the reasoned arguments that they didn't *need* to torture her had refused to form in her mind.

Suddenly, one of the arms on the robot nearest Worku had snapped forward with what looked like a hypospray attached to the end. An instant later, the hypospray jammed into the side of Worku's neck and injected its contents.

Nothing seemed to happen at first, and Worku's screaming and thrashing had merely continued. But then a rush of energy roared through her.

Worku shuddered. Her eyes snapped wide. She gasped and began panting rapidly. Her body started to tingle. And for the next few moments, she had trembled, consumed by the powerful stimulant.

Within a few minutes, however, the shakes subsided. And Worku's pain even diminished a bit. That was when she noticed that Moreau's moaning had calmed as well.

The relief had been short-lived. And when the spokesman spoke again, it convinced Worku that the interrogations had only begun.

"We also recognized that if you *were* carrying the virus and you had control of it," the spokesman had said, "merely being onboard a large vessel might not be enough for you to release. We recognized that you might still be inclined to wait until you felt you could no longer resist our demands. And that seems to be exactly what happened. And now that it *has* happened, and now that there is *no* question of your loyalty to the *Dominion* and your masters on the senior staff and particularly Adi Bolobolo, we can *resume*."

Once more, the large overhead displays that ringed the storage bay had lit up with multiple pages of a document. As before, the document appeared to contain a development plan that described multiple sub-project plans with accompanying milestones. *And* as before, every section with any kind of content was covered in black rectangles.

"What information has been removed concerning the construction of your research lab under the guidance of Adi Bolobolo of the *Dominion*?" the new Hunter Look-Alike spokesman had demanded to know.

Simultaneously, multiple mechanical arms had reached forward, not only on the robot standing in front of Moreau but also on the one standing in front of Worku. Worku had shaken her head and begun to plead no over and over. And then arcs of electricity erupted to dance over the two of them.

Worku and Moreau had been screaming ever since. Worse, if either of them seemed to be reaching a point where they might lose consciousness, the corresponding robot would administer another dose with the hypospray. And then the torture would begin again. And at regular intervals, the spokesman would repeat his demand.

"What information has been removed concerning the construction of your research lab under the guidance of Adi Bolobolo of the *Dominion*?"

•   •   •

On the *Dominion*, Bolobolo continued her leisurely walk with MacDuff around the perimeter of the Main Hall on Upper Deck 1. Over the years, the pair had enjoyed many such, as had most of the crew. The Main Hall was the largest freestanding room on the ship. It was designed to hold events for the entire crew. It occupied the highest human-habitable area on the bow of the battlecruiser and featured dramatic views. Indeed, the room's forward edge was composed of elongated windows that began at the decking and arched to reach overhead, supported by thick curving beams that created the impressive space with equally impressive view.

Of course, at other times, with the *Dominion* in orbit around inhabited planets, the Main Hall had often been the best vantage point to gaze down at a world that the battlecruiser was orbiting. And that panoramic view remained excellent whether the world was blessed with a natural atmosphere, terraformed with a dome, or barren, with life only supported in air-tight shelters on the surface or in underground passages behind airlocks.

Obviously, Bolobolo had enjoyed all her walks with MacDuff. But orbiting a planet gave the walk an interesting additional perspective. And no matter what minor dissatisfactions and no matter what the seemingly complex challenges that Bolobolo might be experiencing in her life, a walk around the Main Hall with a planet nearby had constantly reminded Bolobolo of how different and how privileged her life had been to live on the battlecruiser.

And yes, there had been *challenges* and *frustrations*. But there had also been *extraordinary* experiences, such as serving under Catherine Casteel, who was the most amazing person Bolobolo had ever met. And, obviously, Bolobolo cherished meeting and getting to know MacDuff just as much.

Of course, this walk was slightly different in terms of the view. The *Dominion* was still in the Rigel system, but it had pulled away from Rigel Three and its curled space ring to put itself in a more defensible position. And that meant the view out of the magnificent Main Hall window was mostly star field, with the Rigel system's star in the distance, and the radiation-laced, incinerated planet of Rigel Three nearer in the foreground.

Every step of the walk had been a reminder of the wave of destruction that had pounded through the Night, leaving little to survive in its wake. Perhaps that created a sense of urgency in Bolobolo. Perhaps, it was just one more nudge of anxiety and sensitized her to any activity on the *Dominion* that wasn't as focused and disciplined and honorable as she thought it should be.

Whatever the reason, during the walk, Bolobolo and MacDuff had not only focused on their reflections on how life was proceeding with the crew, but Bolobolo had also told MacDuff about Falcon's latest posing session for Oakford.

To be clear, over the years, Bolobolo hadn't discussed *everything* with MacDuff that had occurred between her and Falcon or Falcon and Oakford. But on this walk, Bolobolo found she wanted to confide in someone because she had been conflicted for multiple cycles over what happened in the latest posing session. And in particular, she was disturbed that it had ended with Oakford's hand wedged in Falcon's interguteal cleft.

Obviously, before she began, Bolobolo had warned MacDuff that she needed him to keep the information confidential. And yes, Bolobolo knew she didn't actually need to make that request. Of *course*, MacDuff would keep everything she said confidential. Honestly, as she was saying it, Bolobolo had actually wondered if she was only saying it because she felt guilty about nattering to MacDuff about the incident, and supposedly making sure that he wouldn't repeat it was her way of excusing herself of *gossip*.

On the other hand, Bolobolo also knew that Falcon hadn't given her *any* indication that she was embarrassed in *any* way about what had happened. And knowing Falcon, Bolobolo was *sure* that Falcon wouldn't care if she told MacDuff.

Still, Bolobolo knew that Oakford *would* care if the details of the posing session were whispered around the ship. And asking MacDuff to keep it confidential was a good enough excuse for Bolobolo to discuss it with MacDuff.

"I just don't know what to think about this," Bolobolo said, winding down, slightly exasperated, as she realized she was rambling after relating what had happened in the posing session. "I understand that I grew up in the Realm, and Rachel didn't, but if she had actually dragged Captain Oakford into the hallway like that, I have no idea what would happen on the crew. I know Rachel told me she would never actually *do* that, but I'm not sure I believe her. And worse, I already know that there's *nothing* I'm going to do about this because we have far bigger things to worry about, and what happens between Captain Oakford and Rachel is between the two of them. And besides, I can't *imagine* how I would start the conversation in the *first* place. I can't just *waltz* into the Executive Office and tell Captain Oakford that I need to talk to him about the fact that his hand was stuck in Rachel's *butt crack!*"

Now, MacDuff, who had been listening patiently, chortled. "It would be a challenging way to start a conversation," he said with a wry tone.

Bolobolo glanced at MacDuff and managed a slight grin. Then she shook her head and added, "Thank you for not trying to find a solution and just listening."

"Of course," MacDuff replied kindly. "Although honestly, I'm not sure that I would be able to suggest a solution in any case. Chief Falcon is going to conduct herself in the ways that she sees fit, and I cannot say with certainty that her jousting with Captain Oakford is entirely unbeneficial. Captain Oakford is under a variety of pressures, and Chief Falcon may not be wrong in her assessment that he needs a bit of relief. Perhaps the playfulness will do him well."

Bolobolo shot MacDuff a sideways glance. She paused, not sure if she should say what she wanted to say. She had left out one portion of her conversation with Falcon in the lift.

Bolobolo mentally pushed herself forward. "Rachel also said that I needed to wiggle enough to get you to give up the idea that Hunter needs you to keep him safe," she offered. "She said she's getting tired of waiting for babies who will call her auntie, and it's time to start the shimmey. She said that's how women have been getting what they want from the beginning of time."

Bolobolo paused, but the mischievous thought that had just popped into her head blurted out. "And… just out of curiosity… can you say with the same certainty that a little wiggle from *me* would be entirely *unbeneficial?*"

MacDuff looked at Bolobolo and smiled. "Adi Bolobolo," he said, "I think you are well aware of what the answer to that question is. I have not changed in the feelings that I expressed to you after the mission to K2-72e. I *adore* you. And I cannot imagine any woman with whom I could build a more magnificent life. I can say *with* certainty that a wiggle from you would have a *profound* effect on me. But at the same time, I understand that you choose to live your life without making a habit of overt emotion manipulation."

Bolobolo grinned, warmed by MacDuff's words and the thought that MacDuff knew he couldn't resist her charms if she chose to kiss him to the floor.

Unfortunately, MacDuff also knew her well enough to know she wouldn't treat him like that.

"Yeah," Bolobolo sadly agreed, "there is that old pesky treat others as you wish to be treated thing. Although… I have to admit that there was a little voice in me from my childhood that thought what Rachel did was *hysterical*. I have enough brothers that I had to find ways to get the better of them. That way, I didn't have to spend my days fending off ambushes. It took some time, but I eventually got ornery enough with them that they thought twice before trying anything with me.

"And even though I did my *best* to tell that little girl inside me who used to fight dirty, because she *had* to, to sit down and be quiet when Rachel told me what happened in the latest posing session, apparently, that little girl if *still* down there. And she's *ready*. And ever since that conversation with Rachel, she's decided she *won't* sit down and she *won't* shut up. And... I can't *guarantee* she won't find an opening someday to try something with you."

MacDuff grinned as they both continued to walk around the perimeter of the Main Hall. "I'll keep an eye out," he smirked before changing the topic. "I do have a question on another topic, however."

Bolobolo nodded, both ready *and* not ready to discuss anything else. "Of course," she responded politely.

MacDuff turned his head to look in Bolobolo's direction. "In the past, you've told me that your immediate response to Chief Falcon's needling you, concerning your lack of ability to heal with your mind, was to point out that *she* hadn't had any visions lately. I'm assuming you will need to find another way to deflect those suggestions, now?"

Bolobolo gave MacDuff a sideways glance. And after a moment, she let out a sigh. "Okay, first of all," she began with an air of resignation, "I really am *thrilled* that Rachel was able to do that. It not only helps the ship, but it gives her a place that maybe she didn't feel like she had, no matter how many times we tried to tell her that she's *essential* to this crew. So that's good, and it's amazing, and it could be *really* beneficial for whatever is coming next. But, yeah... it's not ideal for *me*. Now, every time I see her, she raises her eyebrows and grins, and I know *exactly* what she's thinking.

"It's hard for me not to be upside down on this. Rachel has tried to reproduce what happened that one night. And she hasn't been able to do that yet. And I understand that could be really frustrating. If I had a breakthrough and could suddenly heal, and then it just left, I would *not* be good with that. So, I sympathize with what she's going through. But... if I'm honest... and I hated to say this... but..."

MacDuff smiled. "I understand," he said quickly, apparently deciding that he didn't need Bolobolo to say what she clearly didn't want to say.

"Thanks," Bolobolo said quietly with a slight grin.

17.

On the *Dominion*, on Lower Deck Five, where the tactical teams had converted a storage bay into a makeshift dojo, Guan Qiuyue stood in the center of a ring of fighters, waiting as she calmly faced off in front of a male Realm-raised tactical team member who had volunteered to be next in line.

Perhaps if Guan had been raised in the Realm as well, she would have given more thought to going head-to-head with one male fighter after another. Young women from the Realm were raised to value their ability to bear children, and *many* made it the focus of their lives.

Those young women carefully conducted themselves to appeal to the type of man they sought. They made sure their appearance was always delightful. They never assumed a threatening posture. And most attempted to conduct themselves with grace and charm, with just a hint of mystery to make them worth the chase.

Guan didn't exude *anything* like that. Given her life experiences, it made sense that a single word could easily define her. Indeed, Guan's current practice of calm *was* so calm that others found it *unnerving*. And even if they understood all that Guan had been through and *why* she was so calm, they *still* found it unnerving.

Guan had joined the *Dominion's* crew nine years ago after the senior staff freed her and 140+ other women from Moreau's secret genetic research facility on Nu Scorpii One. Before that, all had been women working on the streets of the Night to survive.

No one had missed them when they disappeared from those streets, at least no one with a voice who could draw attention to the fact that someone was kidnapping young, childbearing-aged women who were never seen again. For obvious reasons, once rescued from the genetic research facility where they functioned as incubators, continuously strapped in gestation rigs, most had decided to take every advantage that the *Dominion* offered them. They understood it was the closest they would come to living in the Realm.

Indeed, Guan had flourished on the crew. She had learned to defend herself while studying martial arts under MacDuff on the tactical teams.

Unfortunately, three years ago, Guan was taken hostage while on a mission to Betelgeuse Two. And she had been tied up and left to choke to death on spores from a genetically modified thicket in the sewers under a major population area called *yad al-jawzā'*. Hunter had rescued Guan before she died, but the exposure to the spores caused significant brain damage.

Afterwards, Guan had become so aggressive that the senior staff had *finally* decided to allow her to leave the ship. But before she could disembark, a human-animal hybrid named Sphinx intervened.

Sphinx had also joined the crew of the *Dominion* after the mission to Nu Scorpio One. Sphinx was one of the human-animal hybrids that the women were forced to carry to term at the research facility. Interestingly, none of the women on the tactical teams held that against him.

Sphinx was half-man and half-lion. And he not only radiated strength but also bliss. Sphinx had immediately formed a bond with MacDuff on Nu Scorpii One. And ever since, Sphinx had served on the tactical teams as a kind of mascot, resting in his corner and occasionally intervening in the affairs of the tactical team members, when he apparently felt the need to do so.

Indeed, Sphinx had sought out Guan when there seemed to be no hope that she could recover from the thicket spores, and it appeared she would be violent and enraged for the rest of her life.

That day, once he found her on the ship, Sphinx seemed to attack Guan. He battered Guan back and forth in a storage bay until Guan stopped trying to fight back. And then, strangely, Sphinx had licked Guan's face repeatedly.

Even stranger, when Guan emerged from the med unit where she had been placed to recover from her wounds, she was no longer filled with rage.

She was *calm*.

Later, using a med unit to analyze Sphinx's saliva, Bolobolo had determined that Sphinx's saliva was laced with psilocybin, a powerful hallucinogenic. And ever since the incident, Guan had been *better*.

Guan *wasn't* back to her old self. The joyous young woman who had loved her life on the *Dominion* was gone, destroyed by the thicket spores.

Still, Guan *was* calm. Indeed, she was *so* calm that it was *unnerving*. But surprisingly enough, that calm had served Guan well in the last year. After the incident with Sphinx, Guan returned to the tactical teams.

There was one hurdle to overcome with that reunion. When Guan was still enraged, she had broken the arm of a male tactical team member while sparring. And while an emergency medical unit had healed the bone in just a few days, the wound to Phineas Hawthorne's ego had remained.

He had challenged Guan to a round of grappling and unrestrained striking, attempting to prove that Guan's besting of him had been a fluke. Unfortunately, the pair was matched in skill levels, and the sparring consisted of them circling each other, looking for openings that never appeared. Some minutes later, Sphinx bolted from his corner and forced Guan and Hathorne to work together to avoid being bowled over.

After that, and apologies all around, Guan found her place on the tactical teams a second time. And she had flourished once more.

Guan was still *calm* with an intensity that unnerved others at times. But that calm also brought a focus and discipline to Guan's life. And she had only grown more capable in her fighting abilities. And even the men on the tactical teams had come to the point where they *readily* admitted that Guan could best them.

Interestingly, it wasn't simply that Guan's technique was better. She did have an exquisitely focused technique. But she also had *power*. Guan could focus her energy and somehow cause her muscles to synchronize so precisely that she could produce bursts of force that were astonishing for her size.

And though she hadn't needed to do it lately, Guan was unafraid of pain. And, when needed, she could produce a strike with enough power that it would break her hand even as it sent her opponent flying.

Indeed, that ability had placed Guan in her present position, offering her current demonstration, surrounded by tactical team members with one of the male fighters directly across from her at arm's length.

For the record, the young man was the *third* to subject himself to the punishment, and while the first two had rejoined the circle, they were *still* rubbing their chests.

Weeks before, someone had suggested to Guan that she learn the "one-inch punch." The technique had been popularized by martial artist and actor Bruce Lee many years before the Coming. Frankly, it was a near-useless fighting technique since it required the opponent to stand motionless and take the punch. But it looked impressive when executed with skill. And for someone with extreme focus who could synchronize her fast-twitch muscles to a higher degree than usual for humans, it made for quite a show.

Now, Guan extended her left arm with the fingers and thumb of her left hand open, extended, as if they formed the upright blade of a knife. And soon, she rested just the tips of her fingers on the abdomen of the male tactical team member in front of her.

When Guan had first seen the pose, she thought Lee was out to stab his opponent with the tips of his fingers to prove how strong his hand was. Instead, Lee had suddenly clenched his fist and snapped forward, twisting at the hips.

The impact of that very short strike had sent Lee's opponent *flying* backward. When Guan saw the video, she immediately understood that the power in the punch came from the snapping twist of Lee's torso. It hadn't taken Guan long at all to learn the movement and produce enough power to mimic the aftereffects that Lee demonstrated.

Indeed, the blow wasn't that different from what Guan had used on *multiple* occasions while she was confined to Sickbay as she recovered from her battering by Sphinx a year ago. During that time, the *Dominion* was also carrying a thousand refugees from Betegeuse Two just days before Realm Force burned the planet.

Those thousand refugees had been selected randomly without any vetting. And they had been transported from *yad al-jawzā'*, near the exact location where Guan had been confined to the sewers after her kidnapping.

And yes, those sewers were still filled with thicket spores. And those spores were creating a fine particulate, barely-seen mist *above* ground that the inhabitants of *yad al-jawzā'* had been breathing for months.

In other words, a non-trivial percentage of the refugees that the *Dominion* had welcomed aboard the battlecruiser were psychotic. And some of them had decided that Sickbay would be the perfect location to obtain some drugs, even though Bolobolo had already assured the refugees that all the healing accomplished in Sickbay was performed by medical units, which administered drugs intravenously using an automated delivery system. Consequently, no drugs were *available* to be handed out, even to thugs who threaten Bolobolo's staff.

Of course, the psychotic refugees didn't believe Bolobolo, and some of them continued to come to Sickbay sporadically, grab one of the crewmembers on Bolobolo's staff, hold a knife to her throat, and demand that Bolobolo give them drugs. In each of those cases, Guan had fearlessly marched up to the man, amidst the man's threats and curses. And when the man tried to stab Guan, she disarmed him, punched him in the chest, and sent him flying into a wall.

And she had broken her hand *every* time.

So far, Guan hadn't broken her hand during her first two demonstrations of Bruce Lee's one-inch punch technique. She didn't intend to break it this time either. And it wasn't *just* that Guan was holding back. She *was* holding back. but it was also difficult to generate the force of a fully drawn jab in such a short distance.

Still, Guan *could* generate enough force to put on a good show simply by allowing herself to focus on the strike. Interestingly, Guan had enjoyed watching Bruce Lee fight, both in the old pre-Coming movies and in his exhibition matches with other martial arts masters. And perhaps the way that Bruce Lee conducted himself, with his serious demeanor and measured actions, made *sense* to Guan.

For whatever reason, Guan had agreed to learn and demonstrate the move. And in the makeshift dojo, the ring of tactical team members had cheered the first two times she had executed the punch. She expected them to do the same this last time. And she even found herself *anticipating* the cheer, which surprised her because she wasn't supposed to care about that. At least she didn't think she cared about that.

With her hand in position, fingers extended and held together with her thumb on top, Guan shoved everything out of her mind, except the *moment* of acceleration. And in that moment, everything went quiet within, and Guan clinched her fist and snapped into a twist with her hips.

Until that point, the male tactical team member who stood in front of Guan had seemed confident that Guan couldn't knock him down with the blow. To his credit, he was one of the younger members of the tactical team, well built, a good fighter, and highly confident in his abilities and strength.

But the man's facial expression immediately changed when Guan's fist slammed into his abdomen. And he would say later that since he was tightening his abdominal muscles at the time, the punch felt distributed across his entire core. And it wasn't so much of a punch as it was a *shove*.

One moment, the young man was standing with Guan's fingertips against his abdomen. And then it looked like Guan had barely moved. And suddenly, the young man was lurching backward, tumbling to the floor, and somersaulting into a kneeling position as he began gasping for air.

Of course, he had also responded with a loud grunt of surprise. And yes, that grunt was quickly drowned out by the shout that went up from the ring of tactical team members who surrounded Guan and the young man.

Nonchalantly, Guan turned and nodded as they cheered, still unsure how to accept the praise of others. And after only a moment, Guan turned back to the young man she had just downed and extended a hand to help him to his feet.

"Are you injured?" Guan asked, not necessarily concerned about what she had done to him, but simply because she needed to ascertain whether she should encourage him to seek out an emergency medical unit.

"No," the young man grunted as he got to his feet. "Just a little bruised up. That was *amazing*. Gonna have to learn that."

"I am happy to relate all that I have learned concerning the technique," Guan responded, "but I find little use for it in real combat. It is too slow to prepare and requires a certain cooperation from the opponent."

The young man smiled and nodded. "Yeah, there's that," he said, "but it looks cool!"

Guan had learned in the last year to *avoid* pointing out non-sequiturs during her conversations with other tactical team members. In this case, it did not follow that her fellow tactical team member would want to learn a technique that was supposed to demonstrate fighting ability when the technique wasn't good for fighting.

Unfortunately, Guan still hadn't figured out *what* to say when a crewmember offered a statement that made no sense to her. And in those cases, she had settled on doing what she did now.

She needed. She turned and walked away.

Guan didn't get far before other members of the tactical teams approached her.

"Great job, Qi!"

"Interesting stuff."

"Thanks for showing us that!"

Now, Hawthorne approached Guan. "I have to say that I was a bit surprised that three of the guys volunteered for that," he said, chagrinned. "And I was even more surprised that the last two didn't back out once you flattened the first one. Some of these boys will try *anything*. Good call on not hitting them in the ribs or the upper chest."

Guan nodded. "I thought it wise to reduce the risk of a cracked rib cage or a stopped heart."

Hawthorne smiled and nodded. "I know I wasn't the first to welcome you back to the tactical teams last year. But I've been impressed with the skills that you've displayed ever since. And there have been plenty of times I've seen you holding back. By this point, I'm convinced that, if needed, you could hold your own against anyone in the dojo… except maybe Sarge."

Guan shook her head. "There is no maybe with regards to Sarge," she said flatly. "He's skilled and, despite his size, he is fast. If I were facing him as an enemy in hand-to-hand combat, I would quickly lose."

"Maybe," Hawthorne admitted, "but the same could be said for any of us. And I'm guessing that the same could be said for any of *us* when it comes to *you*."

And again, Guan wasn't sure what to say next because Hawthorne was speculating, and if he truly sought to obtain an answer for his questions, the obvious, best way to determine if what he believed was true would be to stage a series of no-holds-barred sparring sessions with emergency medical units nearby to take custody of the wounded quickly.

As far as Guan was concerned, guessing was a waste of time. And with that, she turned and headed for the spot on the bulkhead where she had dropped her workout gear. She planned to do some mobility exercises, and then she would go to the supply bay that served as a bunk room for the female tactical members and head for bed.

•   •   •

In his lair at the Saturn Shipyards, PLOKTA finally decided just to ask Ton something he'd wanted to ask him for a long. Until now, PLOKTA hadn't asked because he didn't want Ton to think he was chickening out of their plans to slaughter as many as needed to establish a totalitarian regime in the Realm. But at the same time, PLOKTA was curious about what he wanted to ask, and his curiosity had only grown more intense over the years of slaughter.

"Could I ask you something personal?" PLOKTA began hesitantly as he wound down his latest status update meeting with Ton, who was, of course, in *his* office at the administrative building for the Leadership Council in Jerusalem.

Ton smirked. "I think you've seen me in circumstances that could *easily* qualify as the most degrading possible for a man," he began. "And if it weren't *for* you, I would still be in those circumstances and possibly something worse because I cannot believe that over time our dear Lieutenant Sotheby *wouldn't* have become increasingly inventive in her ways to torture me. Given all of that, I can't think of anything that you might want to ask me that I wouldn't be willing to answer."

Even with Ton's assurance, PLOKTA still hesitated for a moment and quickly decided to preface his question with an explicit pledge of loyalty.

"Okay, so first of all," PLOKTA responded earnestly, "I am *completely* onboard with what we're doing. If you think we need to slaughter every Realmer in the Realm to have the best chance of establishing your reign, I'm for you. And as I've said before, I'm with you in using *whatever* tactic you want to use to help you achieve your goals. It doesn't matter how many Realmers get chewed up in the process, I've picked my side and that's it."

"But?" Ton added with a grin.

"No if, ands, or buts," PLOKTA insisted. "I'm with you. But… I am curious. I was born in the Realm, grew up with the standard lines about Jesus Christ and the Wind. Didn't really think about how it could be anything else… until the Disappearance. And really, maybe I didn't think about anything else until a *week* after the Disappearance. And then I started thinking. And I started going back through *everyone* I thought I knew about the Wind and why I thought I knew it. And I quickly figured out I didn't know *anything*.

"Things kind of turned into a whirlwind after that. I was always good with tech. I signed up for Realm Force on a lark. Commander Nicolescu pulled me out of Realm Force Academy and asked me to come work for her at the Saturn Shipyards. And the rest is the rest, so much so that I hadn't even thought about any of it in a *long* time.

"But in the last few years, watching the way we spin stories, watching the effects it has on the citizens of different planets, I've been thinking more about my past and those moments when I started questioning everything. And then I started wondering what your experiences were like growing up before the Coming. And it made me really curious about your experiences.

"So I took the time to dig through the materials that you had us classify about your life before the Coming. I read the books you wrote. They were good, by the way. I read the press blurbs. I watched the interviews you did on book tours and after what everyone called the Rapture. And all of that made me even more curious. And it really comes down to your experiences and what you thought about the Wind during your lifetime.

"For instance, did you *ever* wonder if the Wind was telling the truth about who they said they were, that Jesus Christ was the Son of God returned to Earth with his transformed followers to rule for a thousand years?"

Ton thought for a moment and then shook his head. "No," he said emphatically. "Maybe at one point in my past, I gave Christianity some lip service. And I tried a few of the practices, such as attending church services with my wife a couple of times. But none of it made much sense to me. It all seemed like some sappy romance novel with blatant crowd manipulation techniques used by the so-called preachers.

"And as you know, before the Coming, I was a psychologist working for the United States government in an inner-city clinic that offered counseling to the poor. So I was seeing life up close and ugly. And I had seen that for *years*. Maybe there were a few people who were *trying* to do good. But more were little better than animals. And it was all instinct and cruel behavior. I didn't see any spark of divinity. There wasn't a God-breath in them. They were just slogging through life with too much awareness of their existence to run around unconcerned like animals and too little discipline to craft a pathway upward to better their lives.

"Still, it gave me plenty of material to write about. And *The Random Abacus and Other Stories of Life*, my first book, struck a chord in people, sold millions of copies, and sent me on extended book tours. And that fame gave me everything I imagined it would. Not only did it make me rich, but the combination of being well known and well heeled drew a slew of pretty young things my way, all willing, hopeful and *so* eager to impress.

"In other words, from that point on, I had far more interesting entertainment that I enjoyed *far* more than sitting in a pew listening to a poorly written soliloquy that had practically *nothing* to do with the real world. So I just lost interest in pursuing any religious belief system any further. And then, of course, my first wife disappeared in what everyone called the Rapture."

PLOKTA broke into Ton's recollections. "And that didn't make you reconsider?" he wondered.

Ton shook his head. "Not even for a moment," he responded. "Bear in mind that I *saw* her disappear in front of me. I saw the flash. It knocked me backward and knocked me out. And when I came to, I *knew* what I was *supposed* to think happened. But it just felt like a massive psyop. Millions of people disappeared that day, and no one ever saw them again, but that didn't mean I was ready to embrace some fairy tale about a man who was God and was killed and then rose from the dead."

PLOKTA frowned. "But seeing someone disappear in front of you…," he began.

Ton snorted, interrupting. "Absolutely not," he confirmed. "It was impressive technology, no question about that. But all those people *weren't* raptured. They weren't given new bodies so they could return with Jesus Christ. They were *incinerated*. And I knew when the aliens arrived, they would steal the identities of the dead and *claim* they had come back to rule the Earth with Jesus Christ.

"Granted, I didn't know what the Wind's endgame was. But I knew it wasn't the fulfillment of some fairy tale. That's when I went to work researching and writing like a madman until I finished my second book, *Of Horsemen Riding*. And, of course, in that book, I said plainly that Earth would soon be invaded by aliens who were going to use the fairy tale of Jesus Christ to get a significant portion of the world's inhabitants to bow down and worship them. And I knew exactly *when* that was going to happen, but I didn't say so in the book because I wanted to see if anyone else could figure it out.

"No one did, and I found that hysterical. And I never told anyone that I knew. And I never told anyone why it so thoroughly *proved* to me that the Wind were aliens and not Jesus Christ and his followers."

PLOKTA raised his eyebrows, even more intrigued. "Are you willing to tell me?" he asked.

Ton chuckled. "Why not?" he said. "I've kept quiet about this for a thousand years. This might be the perfect time to point out the obvious. Before I do that, though. I know you said you read the books. However, I'll recap the main points of the second book so that we're on the same page.

"After the Rapture, I knew there were three possibilities for what had actually happened. The simplest explanation was that scouts for an unknown alien race visited Earth for decades, possibly centuries. They discovered the inherent flaw in human mentality that gave rise to the concept of God. They studied the resulting religions. And in Christianity, they uncovered a set of prophecies that predicted world domination by an external force. And it was perfect for their needs.

"At that time, I also wondered if, secondly, the humans who disappeared would be retrofitted with increased mental and physical capabilities. And *they* would become an occupation force. With hindsight, I can say that was probably *needlessly* complicated. It would be easier just to torch them and replace them with aliens.

"And finally, I pointed out that Jesus Christ himself might have been an alien all along. Think about it. He appears out of nowhere. He takes an existing religion, Judaism, and twists it in a new direction, a direction that leads directly to world conquest.

"What I didn't discuss was the reason I was so sure of the alien involvement and how I could know *exactly* when the invasion was coming. And I didn't bother to tell anyone that if I were right, it would absolutely confirm everything I suspected."

Now Ton paused for dramatic effect.

PLOKTA waited, but said nothing.

Seemingly satisfied that he had PLOKTA's full attention, Ton continued. "There is an easily dismissed calendar discrepancy in the book of Revelation that bears scrutiny. First, many seemingly disconnected ancient cultures have a calendar with 360 days in a year. How or why it happened is unclear since any careful observation over a few years would quickly reveal that a calendar year on Earth is at least 365 days long. Interestingly, there are even historical records that seem to indicate that certain cultures were aware that the year was 365 days long but chose to represent it as 360 days.

"For instance, a 1859 *Dictionary of Greek and Roman Antiquities* claims that both the Egyptians and the Romans considered the extra five days of the year extraneous and simply chose to believe that the year was 360 days long instead. No one has proposed an adequate reason for this. And there's plenty more to be said about it, but let's move on.

"Even more interesting, John the Beloved writes the book of Revelation in approximately the year 95 of the Common Era, and multiple times he equates years to days using 360 days per year. This can be easily dismissed as a simple lack of scientific knowledge.

"However, Julius Caesar established the Julian calendar by an edict that took effect on January 1, 45 BC. And *that* calendar, the Julian calendar, has the correct 365 days a year, with appropriately calculated leap years. Given that the Romans ruled the Holy Land during the time of Jesus, it seems inconceivable that John the Beloved *didn't* know Earth years were 365+ days long, and not 360 days long.

"And yet, as he writes down the prophecies that he supposedly hears from God, he makes the claim *multiple* times that a year equates to 360 days. As I did my frantic research for *Of Horsemen Riding*, this seemed odd enough that I kept it to myself. And I used it to predict how long it would be from the Rapture until the Coming.

"Granted, without getting too deep into the mind-numbing details, I did create two predictions, one for what's called a middle-of-the-week rapture and the other for a first-of-the-week rapture. But when you look at the number of days between the Rapture and the Coming, it is exactly matched to a calendar of 360 days. And that's how I predicted the Coming, to the *day*, *years* before it happened."

PLOKTA widened. "Wow," he offered, "but how does that prove that the Wind are aliens and not Jesus Christ and his followers?"

Ton smiled. "There's no reason to claim that a year is 360 days when it isn't hard to determine the year is longer than that," he explained. "But if you came from a planet where your year was 360 days long, and you were a prankster, you might just keep using *that* figure when talking to the natives of any *new* planet, just to see how long it would take them to figure out that it wasn't correct.

"There's simply no way that a God who is portrayed in the Bible as kind and good and all unknowing is *not* going to know that the Earth has 365+ days in a year. And there is *no* benefit for the inhabitants of the planet to think it's 360 days per year, especially after the inhabitants figure out that it's 365+ days!

"That could only be the work of an alien prankster. And if you're *still* not convinced, we can talk about *why* the Disappearance happened in 960 ADR."

18.

In his lair at the Saturn Shipyards, PLOKTA frowned, trying to understand what Ton meant when he had just said that the year of the Disappearance of the Wind provided further evidence that the Wind were pranksters. Of course, PLOKTA was a numbers guy, and he was a data guy, and his mind had already started racing as he tried to figure out what he was missing.

At the same time, the neural interface that Abaddon had installed in PLOKTA's shoulder was already generating hypotheses and then testing them, running through the possibilities that might connect the number 960 to a 365+ day year to a 360-day year.

Suddenly, two columns of numbers spilled through his mind. The left column was showing successive years in standard 365+ day years. The second was showing the corresponding year and fraction of year when calculated with only 360 days. As expected, the years on the right with shorter days were climbing faster than the years on the left, but PLOKTA didn't see anything that immediately stood out around the left-side year of 960.

Then PLOKTA glanced at the top of the first column of numbers where the length of the year was displayed.

It read "365.2425." But something about the number seemed off. And then PLOKTA remembered that in the rare conversations he'd had regarding the length of Earth's year, everyone had always been content to call it 365 and a quarter days. Curious, PLOKTA mentally changed the number to "365.25"

And with that change, suddenly only one pair of years existed in the chart where the left and right numbers were simply integers without any digits to the right of the decimal point.

And that pair was 960 and 974.

In other words, in Earth years it was 960 ADR. It was 960 since the Coming, but with a 360-day year, it was 974 "years" since the Coming.

"Oh…" PLOKTA now said softly.

Ton smiled. "Has your interface run the numbers?" he asked.

"Yes," PLOKTA replied.

"And then you adjusted the length of the Earth to 365.25 days?" Ton continued.

"Yes," PLOKTA replied. "And now the only years that line up are 960 on one side and 974 on the other."

"Yes," Ton agreed. "Now think about what kind of a mind comes up with something like that. Two thousand years ago, when John the Beloved supposedly received revelations from God, that being, whoever he was, impressed him to write about a time of tribulation that was three and a half years long. And that same timeframe was revealed as 42 months. And that same timeframe was also revealed to be 1,260 days, in other words, 360 days per year.

"And then, over two *thousand* years later, these aliens, whoever they are, are still snickering enough about confusing the stupid inhabitants of this planet that when they make their exit so they can start pranking the *next* set of primitive rubes on some *other* planet, they time their departure to leave behind a hint that they were taking us for suckers all along."

"That's cold," PLOKTA admitted, feeling like he was suddenly seeing the Wind in a new light.

"Yes, it is," Ton responded with a grim smile. "And as we've discussed in other meetings, my guess for why the Wind was here in the first place is simple. It's the same reason that tech companies before the Coming were willing to give out so much free stuff. All of those freebies gave the tech companies the ability to siphon off enormous amounts of data for their own purposes.

"When it comes to the Wind, I'm guessing that they gave us all the prosperity that we could handle to send us into a kind of stupor, even as they siphoned enormous amounts of energy out of our Sun."

PLOKTA nodded. "I know we've talked about this, but I'm guessing you're still convinced that the Wind aren't coming back?" he finally said.

Ton nodded. "The Wind aren't coming back," he responded. "They've had their fun. They've stolen our energy. They don't care what happens to us next. But just to finish this out. Do you remember what happened in 986 ADR?"

PLOKTA was surprised by Ton's question. Of course, he remembered. With the neural interface in his shoulder, it was impossible for him *ever* to lose access to that information. And given the year, there was one obvious event that Ton *had* to be referring to.

"986 ADR was the year the energy wall rolled through the curled space funnels in the Night and the Realm," PLOKTA offered. "It destroyed any ships in transit in the curled space funnels, burst out of the endpoints, and destroyed any ships preparing to enter. We lost 100,000 citizens in the Realm alone that day."

Ton smiled. "And it happened just as the thousand years, when counted in 360-day years, came to an end."

PLOKTA frowned. "Is there something in particular that was supposed to happen at the end of the thousand years for the Realm?"

Given that the existence of the Realm was supposed to be a fulfillment of the prophecies in the book of Revelation, PLOKTA had read through it before. And honestly, there were only a few verses in chapter twenty that even referred to what everyone called the Millennial Reign of Christ.

PLOKTA nudged his neural interface to call up the passage, even as Ton started quoting it.

"When the thousand years are over," Ton began, his voice turning dramatic. "Satan will be released from his prison and will go out to deceive the nations in the four corners of the earth, Gog and Magog, and to gather them for battle. In number, they are like the sand on the seashore. They marched across the breadth of the earth and surrounded the camp of God's people, the city he loves. But fire came down from heaven and devoured them. And the devil, who deceived them, was thrown into the lake of burning sulfur, where the beast and the false prophet had been thrown. They will be tormented day and night forever and ever."

Now, Ton laughed. "How's that for spinning a story to get a dramatic reaction?" he said, grinning. "I have to hand it to the writer of Revelation. He certainly knew how to evoke an interesting set of images using the apocalyptic tradition."

PLOKTA didn't respond at first. His neural interface had continued to scroll over the following verses in chapter 20 of Revelation. And while it wasn't the first time PLOKTA had seen the passage, it affected him in this moment more than it ever had.

"Then I saw a great white throne and him who was seated on it. The earth and the heavens fled from his presence, and there was no place for them. And I saw the dead, great and small, standing before the throne, and books were opened. Another book was opened, which is the book of life. The dead were judged according to what they had done as recorded in the books. The sea gave up the dead that were in it, and death and Hades gave up the dead that were in them, and each person was judged according to what they had done. Then death and Hades were thrown into the lake of fire. The lake of fire is the second death. Anyone whose name was not found written in the book of life was thrown into the lake of fire."

Now, a deep foreboding began bubbling up through cracks in the foundations of PLOKTA's mind. And yes, PLOKTA recognized that the dread was likely the result of realizing, for the first time, that the thousand-year reign was *already* over. And even though PLOKTA was certain that he *didn't* believe that verses in Revelation 20, written *thousands* of years ago, could accurately *predict* the unfolding of *present* events, just the fact that Ton believed they were now living in the proverbial "end of days" was giving PLOKTA pause.

Indeed, PLOKTA suddenly realized, *especially* in the last five years, there had been a growing sense of dread within him. As he had watched the official count of years climb, using the designation ADR, Anno Domini Reditus, "In the Year of Our Lord's Return," some part of PLOKTA's mind had grown increasingly concerned about what would happen when the number reached one thousand.

Certainly, PLOKTA's neural interface could draw on many instances in human history where some arbitrary boundary had been approached and humans had freaked out. Famously, the Mayan calendar contained a calculation that singled out the date December 12, 2012 CE. As that date approached, a multitude of stories and movies emerged, rehearsing doomsday events and apocalyptic revelations, as people fretted and worried over what it might mean.

Interestingly, a more ambiguous example came from further back during the approach to the year 1000 CE. Although some scholars disputed the so-called "Terrors of the Year 1000," others claimed the effects were real. Popular accounts noted that at the turn of the first millennium in the Common Era, churches were filled with penitents, soldiers refused to fight, and farmers failed to farm, all of them *too* focused on an arbitrary number to function.

And now, if Ton was right about using a 360-day year, according to the chart provided by PLOKTA's neural interface, the "year" was actually 1011. And frankly, PLOKTA was trying to figure out how he felt about that.

To be clear, PLOKTA *knew* it was just a number. And he knew that he was really trying to exert some mental control over the situation. Some part of him was convinced that there was danger in the threshold, and he needed to pay attention. He needed to plan. He needed to prepare and strategize.

But that was nearly impossible because no one knew what was coming. And all that remained was a churn of emotions and free-floating anxiety.

On the other hand, humanity was facing not one but two powerful groups of titans, with the Wind and whatever Abaddon was, and how those two groups interpreted the end of the millennium *would* had *consequences*.

"The Wind *isn't* coming back," Ton said definitively.

The statement snapped PLOKTA out of his distracted thoughts. And when PLOKTA looked at Ton, Ton smiled.

"Sorry," PLOKTA began shaking himself back to the moment. "I grew up in the Realm. These stories were all I heard to explain reality for the first two decades of my life. It's too easy to let them get to me."

"I understand," Ton offered. "But the Wind *isn't* coming back. According to their calendar, they should have already returned *if* they were going to return. Almost a thousand years ago, I was able to guess the *exact* day of the Coming because the Wind were punctual to the day. The fact that they are *years* late for the supposedly final rebellion that will be answered by 'fire that devours everything' tells me that the Wind is done with us."

PLOKTA nodded absentmindedly. "And the fact that Abaddon has appeared and Abaddon is mentioned in Revelation and Abaddon claims his master is Satan… is that all a coincidence?" he wondered.

"Hard to say," Ton answered with a smile. "Abaddon may be doing the same that the Wind did. He may have adopted the names to exploit our familiarity with specific terminology to gain an emotional advantage. Or the Wind may have seeded the names of Abaddon and Satan into the primitive religions of humanity to prejudice humanity against them if the time ever came when Abaddon and Satan told humanity that the Wind were charlatans.

"In every case, I know what the Wind wanted us to believe. And I know what Abaddon wants us to believe. But I can't say that *any* of it is true. However, I do find it fascinating that Abaddon has *not* micromanaged us. He handed out his instructions and has left us alone ever since. Of course, I have been happy to proceed with those instructions because he has asked me to do what I already *wanted* to do. And perhaps it makes sense for Abaddon to allow us to do so, since he has always insisted that the human race must improve itself.

"In the end, there are many unknowns. But for the moment, it feels like we have the upper hand. And while we do, we will reign like kings and tyrants."

PLOKTA didn't want to sound like he was questioning Ton's approach, but now that he knew the thousand years might already be passed, he couldn't help himself.

"And do you think we'll see Satan himself appear anytime soon?" he wondered.

Ton raised his eyebrows and smirked. "I don't know," he replied. "That would seem a *likely* development. And what happens after *that* is anybody's guess."

•   •   •

In the decimated capital city of Alpha Pegasi Three, in the cool of a beautiful early evening under the planet's terraforming dome, Tryggvi Hrafnkelsson held himself as still as he could, even as he took long, slow breaths through his wide-open mouth. Mostly, though, Hrafnkelsson did his best to think about anything *else* beside the sounds coming from the other side of the thin barrier that separated him from the assault robots that had slaughtered so many of his fellow citizens.

He had made a mistake. He had made a stupid, *stupid* mistake. And Hrafnkelsson knew very well that it could result in no one *ever* knowing what Realm Force had done to the citizens of his home planet.

Even after so many months of documenting the slaughter, it *still* didn't seem real.

For over fifteen years, the citizens of Alpha Pegasi Three had lived under the governance of a man called Dmytro Voronenko. And for all those years,

Voronenko had been an exemplary leader. He not only *looked* the part of a leader, being tall, handsome, and well-built, but he was also well-known for being kind, personable, and an excellent communicator.

Then last year, Voronenko seemed to lose his mind. At the time, Hrafnkelsson was working for the governor in the administrative building as a communication facilitator to the planetary leadership of Alpha Pegasi Three. Unexpectedly, that day, Hrafnkelsson heard Voronenko storming down the hall outside his office, shouting angry pontifications as he came. And soon, Voronenko slammed his way into the small studio that Hrafnkelsson and others had built for Voronenko to use for his periodic planetary video comms.

The governor had demanded that Hrafnkelsson open a planetary comm.

It was the *last* thing Hrafnkelsson wanted to do. For one thing, Voronenko was *naked*. For another, he looked like a crazy person. He wasn't foaming at the mouth, but he *could* have been, and it *wouldn't* have made him look any *worse*.

The man's eyes were crazed. His lips twisted in snarls. His entire body was tensed as if he might tear into anything nearby at any moment.

Under normal circumstances, Hrafnkelsson would have *never* allowed his governor to broadcast to the citizens of Alpha Pegasi Three under those conditions, but Voronenko had threatened to smash his face into the control panel, and Hrafnkelsson complied.

A lengthy tirade followed where Voronenko railed against the idiocy and naivety of the planet's inhabitants. And then, when Realm Force showed up to take him into custody, Voronenko bolted and then led them on a chase around the capital city.

Eventually, Realm Force gunned down the governor in one of the capital city's many alleyways. The episode sparked unrest and confusion, prompting citizens to take to the streets as they sought to determine what had happened.

And then, murderous robots appeared out of nowhere to begin slaughtering the citizens. Later, it would become clear that the robots belonged to Realm Force, as hard as that was to believe. Those robots continued to murder the citizenry until the smattering of survivors retreated to hide inside their home.

Hrafnkelsson had documented it all. Shortly after beginning his work with Governor Voronenko, Hrafnkelsson had personally installed a private data card on his own tablet to ensure the video feeds he recorded of the governor were secure. Indeed, Hrafnkelsson had turned off *all* external access on the tablet he carried to guarantee that no one saw the raw recodings of the governor before they had been edited for clarity.

That same tablet now had innumerable *hours* of video feeds showing not only the original decimation and slaughter in the capital city, but also the results of the same slaughter in all the nearby towns that Hrafnkelsson had traveled to in the last year.

The trouble was, Hrafnkelsson had no idea how he would ever get off the planet, or where he would go, or who he would talk to, or who might be able to *do* something about what was happening on it.

After all, Leadership Council Member Ton had *personally* addressed the citizens of Alpha Pegasi Three, often just before robots attacked them. And if Ton knew what was going on, then it wasn't just Realm Force attacking the planet, but apparently, the Leadership Council in Jerusalem *approved* of what had happened.

Still, Hrafnkelsson had continued to record everything he could, day after day. And partly, he did it to honor a young woman named Isara Nyx, whom he had met during the initial slaughter of the citizens by the Relam Force robots. Nyx had encouraged Hrafnkelsson to continue gathering recordings. She even accompanied him to help as a lookout while he gathered more video feeds. Unfortunately, when the pair attempted to return to Nyx's family's farm, they found it had been overrun by robots as well. And in the process, Nyx sacrificed herself while trying to determine if any of her family had survived.

However, Hrafnkelsson hadn't carried on only to honor Nyx's memory. He had continued to gather evidence because of something Nyx's father had told her. Nyx had said her father had always said that, in the present, you do what you *need* to do to keep the future full of possibilities. She said her father had said the future couldn't *use* you if you didn't bring it anything to *work* with.

That made sense to Hrafnkelsson. And he had decided to bring the future as many video feeds as possible.

Now, though, as Hrafnkelsson pressed his back into the wall of the building behind him and tried to make himself as small as possible, and as he took long, slow breaths through a wide-open mouth to minimize the sound, he wondered if his *stupid* mistake would mean that no one would *ever* know what Realm Force had done to the citizens of his home planet.

Months before, to keep himself motivated, Hrafnkelsson had developed a routine. He would wake up long before the planet's terraforming dome simulated a sunrise at whatever location he had chosen the night before. And then he would move to whatever destination he had chosen next in those early morning hours, since that seemed to be the time when the robots were *least* active. Hrafnkelsson had no idea *why* the robots were less active then, but he suspected it was because the surviving citizens were less active then as well.

Indeed, for the past year, the surviving citizens of Alpha Pegasi Three had been under a constant curfew order. No one could leave their homes. And anyone caught looking out their windows would have their entire family dragged into the nearest street and slaughtered by the robots. The citizens *were* allowed to order goods from the local Judicial Center, and when those goods were ready, the assault robots would bring them to the homes of the citizens who ordered them. That was the *only* contact *any* citizen was allowed with anyone outside their family.

Given that pattern, earlier on this day, while it was still dark, Hrafnkelsson had made his way to the downtown area of the capital city to continue his survey, trying to determine how many citizens had survived the purge. In the preceding months, Hrafnkelsson had surveyed some of the more suburban areas of the capital city. But after weeks of that, he felt like his brain couldn't take the bland, repeating architecture of row after row of houses, and he had decided he needed to move closer to the city center because it had larger buildings. While he was still alive, Governor Voronenko had ensured that every one of them had some interesting design.

And maybe Hrafnkelsson was missing his life as a communications facilitator. And perhaps he had wanted to pay his respects to Voronenko in the alley where Realm Force had killed the man.

For whatever reason, Hrafnkelsson had slipped into a hiding spot across the street from the fatal alley, just as light from the terraforming dome began to brighten the capital city. It wasn't a great hiding spot, a bit too flimsy, but hopefully it would be good enough.

At some point in the past year, a pair of large storage containers had been knocked up against a building and partially smashed. Interestingly, the metal walls, ceiling, and floors of the storage containers had sustained even more damage, leaving spots where the metal was torn and rusting in varying degrees.

Hrafnkelsson had noted that some of the damage appeared to be caused by the assault robots ripping open sections of the smashed storage containers. And even though that might mean the robots had searched the metal pile and might remember to look there again, the containers were *directly* across the alley where Voronenko had died. And Hrafnkelsson decided it would be fine for him to slip inside one of the large twisted structures for as little time as he planned to spend there.

Unfortunately, less than half an hour passed before Hrafnkelsson spotted a young man, scurrying from place to place down the street, working his way toward the alley. And yes, there were plenty of large chunks of debris both in the street and leaning against the nearby buildings. But the young man was spending too much time exposed as he moved from pile to pile. And Hrafnkelsson knew what would happen next.

One of the video feeds of the street would *definitely* pick him up. And the robots would be on their way soon after that.

To his credit, the young man had almost made it to the entrance of the alley where Voronenko died when the sound of pounding metal feet began in the distance. And worse, if there was any doubt about *what* was making the pounding sounds, the unique sounds of the assault robots soon began to grow as well.

When Hrafnkelsson had first heard those sounds the year before, he had known they weren't organic. As a communication facilitator, he immediately recognized that it was all coming from digital wave patterns, amplifiers, and solid-state speakers. But Hrafnkelsson had also known that meant the robots could sound like *anything*, even down to the continuous beeping of a safety alarm as they ripped their prey to shreds.

But they *hadn't* sounded like that, and they still didn't. They made sounds that *approximated* something found in nature. But they were meaner, more vicious, sounding more of flesh than metal.

Sadly, the young man had also heard the pounding of mechanized feet and the growling artificial animal sounds. And as Hrafnkelsson watched through a tear in the metal of the storage container where he hid, the young man began frantically looking around, obviously trying to confirm if the robots were coming for him.

Then, in the next moment, the young man seemed to decide that they *were*, and he continued glancing around, looking for a place to hide. And *then*, in the *following* moment, Hrafnkelsson realized he had made a *stupid* mistake coming to a spot that would *always* be a memorial for the beloved Governor Voronenko.

Of *course*, other people would try to sneak into the alley to pay homage to their governor. And even after all this time, of course, they wouldn't take enough precautions. And yes, it made sense that a young *man* would be the first one that Hrafnkelsson would encounter there.

How many arguments had the young man had with his parents, trying to convince them that they needed to take a stand against the assault robots and take back their planet? How many times had the young man invoked the name of Governor Voronenko and railed about the fact that Voronenko hadn't been afraid to speak his mind and was willing to *die* for what he believed?

Hrafnkelsson had imagined that, whatever arguments the young man had made for visiting the alley, his reasons probably hadn't lined up precisely with the events that transpired the day Voronenko died. But that was because the citizens of Alpha Pegasi Three *respected* Voronenko. And even to this day, Hrafnkelsson understood how others could refuse to believe that what had *really* happened was what they were *told* had happened.

None of it had mattered to Hrafnkelsson at the moment. The young man was racing toward the same heap of storage containers where Hrafnkelsson had taken refuge. And Hrafnkelsson had known the young man would lead the assault robots right to *him*.

There hadn't been enough time to find another place to hide. But glancing around, Hrafnkelsson had spotted an opening where a part of one of the twisted shipping containers was leaning against a building. And whipping around, Hrafnkelsson quickly crawled for the spot and backed into it.

Unfortunately, as Hrafnkelsson had retreated into the hole, the young man scrambled into the twisted storage container, seemingly heading for the spot that Hrafnkelsson had just vacated. And at that moment, the two of them had locked eyes.

Hrafnkelsson had quickly shaken his head. And he frantically hoped he had convinced the young man not to give his location away before pushing himself all the way into his new hiding place.

From then on, the metal of the storage container and the wall beside him meant that Hrafnkelsson could only see what was directly in front of him. But the sounds he heard told Hrafnkelsson everything he *didn't* want to know.

Understandably, the young man had begun cursing even as a scraping sound began. Apparently, at least one assault robot had latched onto the young man's leg and begun to drag him out. The young man's cursing grew more frantic.

And then he screamed.

Hrafnkelsson had seen the process enough to know the assault bot had begun ripping apart the young man's body. The distinctive frenzy of zipping, clanking, buzzing, and snapping of the bot's attack grew loud, accompanied by the tearing of flesh and the smashing of bones.

By that point, Hrafnkelsson was holding himself as still as possible, taking long, slow breaths through his wide-open mouth. He had seen far too much death at the claws of the robots not to know what was happening on the other side of the thin metal that separated him from the slaughter.

But now, suddenly, unexpectedly, another sound began.

It sounded like a worbling whistle, growing closer. And not just one but *many*, all oscillating at different rates with even more whistling in the distance. And then, something smashed into a nearby building, creating a shower of chunks that rained onto the street. More collisions quickly followed, some slamming into the streets, landing with heavy, hard thuds that shook the ground.

New sounds emerged, clearly mechanical, accompanied by the clanking of metal, but not with the same cadence as the assault robots. At the same time, a corner of Hrafnkelsson's mind noted that the *tenor* of the young man's screams had changed. Somehow, the young man sounded *more* frightened.

Now, metal clanged on metal. And the assault robots' strange, organic-like sounds were joined by other sounds more distorted and violent. And strangely, those distortions sounded like cursing.

A flurry of grinding, shearing, and creaking erupted. But then, *suddenly*, footfalls raced away, taking the young man's screaming with them. And soon, everything stopped.

Hrafnkelsson had no idea what had just happened. And he was sure he *wasn't* ready to find out. Indeed, hours passed before Hrafnkelsson pulled' himself out of the cramped confines of his hiding place.

Carefully, Hrafnkelsson began looking through the tears in the metal of the twisted storage containers, trying to make sense of what he was seeing. It took some bobbing and weaving, moving back and forth in front of the small openings, Hrafnkelsson eventually decided he had no idea what had caused what he saw.

There were sections torn out of the buildings everywhere Hrafnkelsson looked, all of which arced downward. And roughly aligned with that damage, there were gouges in the streets as if something had landed hard after falling out of the sky. And then, even stranger, scattered everywhere were the strewn remains of machinery.

In all honesty, if Hrafnkelsson hadn't known that assault bots had been nearby just hours before, it would have been difficult for him to guess what the chunks of metal had been before they were torn apart. Almost every piece was wrenched and bent.

Frankly, it reminded Hrafnkelsson very much of what the assault bots had done to the flesh and bones of citizens all over Alpha Pegasi Three. Except now, whatever this new thing was, it had easily done the same thing to tempered metal and reinforced machine joints of the assault robots

Straining to see as far as he could up the street in both directions, Hrafnkelsson found nothing that caught his eye as unusual. And honestly, a part of Hrafnkelsson wanted it to stay that way.

He knew assault robots didn't just randomly rend themselves into pieces. And whatever *could* do that to the assault robots probably wasn't something he wanted to meet.

Still, someone had to determine if a new threat had emerged from the skies above Alpha Pegasi Three. And Hrafnkelsson didn't know anyone else who would dare to try.

19.

On the *Dominion*, in the makeshift dojo on Lower Deck Five, Guan made a mental note that the tactical team leads were having an unannounced meeting with MacDuff. Under normal circumstances, the duty rosters for the battlecruisers' five-member tactical teams were spread over the four six-hour shifts of a typical cycle.

That meant some of the teams might overlap with their practice sessions in the dojo. But at any given time, when one set of tactical teams was patrolling the *Dominion*, at least one other set of teams was sleeping.

And yet, in the last fifteen minutes, all fifteen leads for every tactical team had wandered into the dojo. And they were all huddled with MacDuff, having what appeared to be a serious conversation.

That *was* one of the ironies of Guan's situation. Because of her exposure to the thicket spores that poisoned her brain, and then her subsequent Sphinx-induced hero doses of psilocybin, Guan *experienced* very few emotions.

Still, she was *aware* of emotions. She was sensitive to the emotions of others, and could hypothesize why individuals might be exhibiting the emotions they were exhibiting. Guan could also tell when someone gave her an explanation for an emotion that wasn't truthful.

Interestingly, as Guan glanced around the dojo, she was picking up a variety of emotions, with only some of them seemingly related to the meeting between MacDuff and the leads. Of course, the easiest emotions for Guan to read came from those who were oblivious to the unannounced meeting.

Those crew members had other interests that held their attention. Mostly, they were sparring. And that was understandable. Craning your neck to gawk at MacDuff and the leads meant you *weren't* paying attention to your opponent, and it might lead to an unexpected takedown, or worse.

Of those who *knew* the meeting was proceeding, a significant portion of them were concerned and anxious about what it might mean. Most were women. And Guan had spent enough time talking to the female tactical team members, especially the women rescued from Nu Scropii One, that she understood they were always insecure about their assignment to the tactical teams. They often whispered about how long it would be before MacDuff had them transferred to another area on the *Dominion*, or perhaps kicked off the battlecruiser altogether.

Guan could remember feeling that way. It was the reason she had volunteered to let Hunter cut her apart multiple times as they practiced for the mission to Spica Two. But Guan now realized that her place was *never* in danger on the tactical team, as long as her psychotic, violent behavior didn't force the senior staff to act. But that was understandable. After all, the core of service on tactical teams was loyalty. It wouldn't do to have a tactical team member randomly breaking other team members' bones.

Of course, there were other emotions in the dojo. Some, both men and women on the tactical teams, were aware of the meeting. But, they were also infatuated with another member of the tactical teams. So, while they offered a glance or two in the direction of MacDuff and the leads, their attention was mainly focused on their love interest.

A few of the tactical team members were bored and tired, and they wanted to finish their practice so they could get something to eat. Others seemed hopeful, as if they knew the meeting was about *them* and they were waiting for MacDuff to turn and make some grand announcement that would confirm something they had long hoped would happen.

And then, there was the *one* tactical team member whom Guan had never understood, even before the thicket spores poisoned her brain on Betelgeuse Two. His name was Dmitri Korsakovich.

Korsakovich had served on the *Dominion* for many years before it was thought lost after the senior staff issued the self-destruct command sequences. He returned to the Realm afterward to serve on other vessels. But when the opportunity arose to return to the *Dominion*, he resigned from Realm Force. He traveled to Beta Andromedae Seven with the rest of the former crewmembers.

And he joined the petition to ask Oakford to rejoin the ship.

Guan had never fully relaxed around Korsakovich. The rest of the former crewmembers who were tactical team members had all accepted the women from Nu Scorpii One, whom MacDuff had trained in the years preceding the former crewmembers' return. But something had always felt off about Korsakovich. Honestly, it felt as though some part of the man held a hidden darkness.

Obviously, Guan had never mentioned her feelings about Korsakovich to anyone else. Who was she to call out a Realmer who was a former crewmember, *especially* when there was *nothing* that Korsakovich had said or done that indicated anything was wrong?

Even now, Korsakovich *seemed* fine. He was sparring skillfully. However, he wasn't as engrossed in the activity as others. And he was also taking the occasional glance at MacDuff and the leads.

He wasn't anxious. He wasn't overconfident. He was… calculating?

Guan had no idea why Korsakovich was surveying the room as if he were preparing an operational plan. But frankly, Guan knew it wasn't her problem. She was just a rank-and-file member on the tactical teams. And she didn't mind that at all.

She was content to have a place on the *Dominion*. And she was grateful to be part of the tactical teams. Guan had spent enough time in Sickbay, after the incident with Sphinx, that she had concluded she didn't have the appropriate *bedside* manner to serve there. The Technical Services crew seemed bored all the time. And while Administrative Services had Falcon as its chief, all of her crewmembers just did the odd jobs around the ships. Mechanical Service with Hunter *might* be interesting, but Guan still preferred Tactical Services.

Now, Guan saw MacDuff look at each of the leads in turn. Finally, he nodded and extended his hand to Hawthorne before pulling him into a bear hug and a slap on the back.

Now, MacDuff turned to the dojo.

"Attention," he called out.

Instantly, every tactical team member in the dojo turned to face him and snapped to attention.

"At ease," MacDuff continued.

The tactical team members assumed an at-ease stance.

"Team Lead Hawthorne has brought a proposal to me," MacDuff began. "I have discussed the matter with all the team leads, and we are in agreement. We will organize a formal transfer in a few cycles, but we need an affirmative from the parties involved first. Usually, I would meet privately with the individual to assess their willingness to accept the new assignment, but this seems better to do in the company of at least *some* of the tactical teams, given what this individual has been through."

Now, Guan saw MacDuff turn his head and look directly at her. "Tactical Team Member Guan," MacDuff began formally, "Team Lead Hawthorne had suggested that you should be my second in command. Traditionally, that role is assigned to a team lead. Team Lead Hawthorne has also suggested that I demote him to Tactical Team Member on your tac-team so that you can take his place as a team lead."

A shocked silence fell over the tactical team members as they stood at ease. A glance from Guan registered the variety of emotions that fed that response. Many of the women had turned wide-eyed in wonder at the development. Some of the men looked confused by it. A few seemed disgruntled.

Korsakovich looked relieved, perhaps even amused.

In that pause, Guan frowned and looked at Hawthorne, interested to see if she would tell why he had done what he had done. But Hawthorne said nothing and merely smiled. And it seemed to Guan as if it was a genuine effort on his part to honor her for what she had accomplished since Sphinx had given her a second chance at continuing her life on the *Dominion*.

Guan managed a half-smile for Hawthorne in return. And then, she turned back to face MacDuff.

"I accept," she said flatly.

Instantly, the tactical team burst into applause, cheering both for Hawthorne and Guan, although it seemed to Guan that the female members of the tactical teams seemed most pleased and excited at her promotion.

•   •   •

In the Hunter Look-Alike vessel that had been designed to function as an extreme form of quarantine, Worku decided it was time to start screaming her confessions. She had waited for the Look-Alike to begin questioning her. Those questions had never come.

Instead, the Hunter Look-Alikes, from some remote location, had continued to torture Moreau, asking the same question over and over.

"What information has been removed concerning the construction of your research lab under the guidance of Adi Bolobolo of the *Dominion*?"

For his part, Moreau was delirious from the stimulants and the electric shocks delivered by the robot that stood before him. And by now, he was not only screaming, but also wailing, begging, shrieking, and pleading that he didn't know what the Look-Alikes wanted to know. He had given up trying to convince the Look-Alikes that Bolobolo wasn't involved.

As for Worku, she understood every reaction coming from Moreau because she *felt* every one of them as sympathetic responses. Her doses of stimulant and shocks had been less severe, but they were still nearly unbearable.

And to be clear, while the sounds coming from Moreau were recognizable for what they would have been under typical circumstances, by now, Moreau had shredded his vocal cords. And he was actually croaking at various frequencies and durations. And any words he spoke sounded like rough sandpaper on plastic pipes.

Perhaps if Worku still had any strength of will or flesh, she might have tried to anger the Hunter Look-Alikes into killing her. But she was *done*.

Beyond the shocks and stimulants, she was still hanging naked from the ceiling, with joints out of place and tendons stretching. And, of course, any time she started to fade, another round of stimulants and electric shocks began. And none of that accounted for the fire of the weeping sores that covered her body and the *stench* of the accompanying rot.

Worku had no idea if saying everything the Hunter Look-Alikes wanted to hear would make any difference. But she couldn't do *nothing* any longer.

"It's all *true!*" Worku began shouting as frantically as she could, given her current state. "I *saw* it! When Doctor Moreau came on the *Dominion*, he began working with Chief Medicalist Adi Bolobolo almost immediately. Only then did Bolobolo admit to us that all her educational records had been faked to hide the fact that she could do genetic engineering so that she wouldn't be targeted by an enemy who might fear her.

"Doctor Moreau had sneered at Bolobolo when she claimed that because he couldn't believe that a Realmer woman could have the same level of experience and technique that he had achieved, since it was frowned on in the

Realm. But then Bolobolo began talking to him, asking questions, and making suggestions. And Doctor Moreau began looking more and more shocked. And then *he* suggested that they needed to work together. And he even said that Bolobolo should be the lead researcher and he would follow her lead."

Despite his condition, Worku's claims weren't lost on Moreau. And of course, he began staring at her in confusion and anger. And yes, in only moments, he began to protest. But given the state of his voice, those protests were limited to clipped and stuttered words with vocalizations that sound more like exhausted barking than someone trying to refute a claim.

"Not happn," Worku growled weakly. "Bitch lie. Bobo *stupid*."

Worku refused to be deterred. "He's just saying that because he's too embarrassed to admit that a *woman* was guiding him in his research," Worku shot back. "He didn't want anyone to find out that he was working for Bolobolo. So he asked the senior staff of the *Dominion* to set up a secret lab so no one would find out. But he *clearly* understood that Bolobolo was a *better* geneticist than he was. And Bolobolo had the successes to prove it.

"I was told that, years ago, the *Dominion* was infected with a hemorrhagic fever virus that rotted a person's insides. And the only reason it didn't kill off all the crew was because Bolobolo invented a cure *from scratch* in only days. She was *always* tinkering around with deadly toxins because she *loves* that stuff. She *loves* torturing small animals with parasites and bacteria that eat their victims from the inside out and viruses that decompose the gut and turn it into goo.

"And when I tried to return to the *Dominion* and tried to trick them out of their Rexian Sheer, I learned that Bolobolo had become even *more* knowledgeable and more capable, not only from the work she had done herself, but also because of the weekly reports that she was getting from Doctor Moreau.

"And *yes*, I was there on the occasional conference calls that Bolobolo would initiate with Doctor Moreau. Using the *Dominion's* point-to-point communications facility, Bolobolo could check in with Moreau from *everywhere*. And I can't tell you how *many* times Doctor Moreau would compliment Bolobolo and tell her that he was astonished at her intuitive grasp of genetic engineering. More than once, Moreau told her that she was like a conductor of a fantastic set of tools that she could wield with ease and astonishing effectiveness."

Of course, Worku's flamboyant praise of Bolobolo was making Moreau madder and madder. And he continued to croak out insults.

"*Stupid*, Bobo, *stupid*," Moreau growled weakly. "Lying bitch. Button-push Bolo. Brain dead. Can't brain."

Worku wasn't deterred. "He's just reacting like that because Bolobolo told him that if he ever revealed to anyone that they had perfected a virus that *slaughtered* Hunter Look-Alikes, she would make him regret it the rest of his life," she sneered. "And that was because Bolobolo had also developed a series of bacteria and viruses that can work together to transform any man or woman into the opposite gender. And she told him that if he betrayed her, she would turn him into a big boobed, giant assed, air-headed bimbo!"

Honestly, by that point, Worku really wasn't sure *what* she was saying. She was stringing together as many words as she could, hoping for *something* that might convince the Look-Alikes to do anything different than what they had been doing for *days*.

Interestingly, Worku's fake confessions seem to affect Moreau far more deeply than just making him angry. And while his facial grimaces remained and his eyes still seemed filled with anger, his speech began to degrade into rambling as if something had switched off in his brain.

"Stupid bitch, Bobo, Bo bo bo," Moreau continued croaking. "Bitch Bo stupid bo bo bo..."

But at least the robots that had been torturing both Moreau and Worku with their electrodes seemed to have temporarily stopped.

•   •   •

In the decimated capital city of Alpha Pegasi Three, with the light of the manufactured day fading beneath the planet's terraforming dome, Hrafnkelsson continued to creep toward the screams in the street ahead. And with each step, Hrafnkelsson told himself that what he was doing *was* important, that it *had* to be done, and if he didn't do it, it might not *be* done.

Unfortunately, Hrafnkelsson could feel his convictions fading. And even as he tried to convince himself that his actions were heroic, some gray formless mass within him was droning on that what he was doing was futile, idiotic, and he needed to find a hole to hide in and die.

Hrafnkelsson knew precisely why he was struggling with himself so much as he attempted to learn the answers to the questions he didn't want to ask.

It was all too soon since the last time he had pursued the active slaughter of the citizens of Alpha Pegasi Three by unidentified assailants. And yes, it *had* been a year since the Realm Force robots had been released on the unsuspecting inhabitants of the planet, and those robots leapt, galloped, and tackled their way through the capital city, slaughtering citizens of Alpha Pegasi Three as they went.

But a year hadn't been *nearly* long enough to recover from that horror, *especially* since the horror had never really *ended*.

It had *lessened*. And if the inhabitants of the planet all just stayed in their homes, Hrafnkelsson knew it was possible to consider that the *brutal* portion of the horror might be over. But there were other aspects of the horror that had manifested themselves over the last year for the survivors of Alpha Pegasi Three. The worst was the constant dread that, at any given moment, the robots would burst into the homes of the citizens who had survived the initial assault, drag them into the streets, and then *kill* them for leaving their homes.

And, of course, Hrafnkelsson had experienced his own personal aspect of horror over the last year. While he hadn't been torn apart, he hadn't hidden in his home either. And as he gathered more video feeds, every day held the possibility of being ripped to pieces.

Still, all of the intervening days since the last rampage of mechanical slaughter *hadn't* held *constant* screaming.

Now that screaming had returned, however, Hrafnkelsson realized how much he *hated* the sound. And he realized how much he wanted to run as far and fast as he could from it.

But if he did that, he would never know what caused it. And if he ever had a chance to provide his video feeds of the last year to anyone who could *do* something about it, what would he say about this second bout of screaming? When he was asked what caused it, was he really willing to say that he didn't know because he had run away?

Cautiously, Hrafnkelsson kept moving forward. And when he felt like the screaming was *close*, Hrafnkelsson slipped inside an office building and began climbing stairs to reach the room.

Of course, all of it continued to bring back memories of the year before. And as he made his way onto the roof, some part of him wished that he would find another strong, capable, fearless woman also trying to figure out what was happening. And he wished that they could join forces, and Hrafnkelsson wouldn't have to do everything alone.

Unfortunately, after crawling around the entire roof, Hrafnkelsson confirmed there were no potential compatriots. And the street below was still erupting in screams.

Interestingly, by now, Hrafnkelsson had confirmed that more than just this one street across the capital featured screaming. At ground level, the continuous screaming had seemed to come from only one direction. But on the roof, Hrafnkelsson could hear other screaming streets in every direction.

And he might have allowed those sounds to enrage him that his home planet was under *another* devastating attack. But Hrafnkelsson was afraid to allow the expression of *any* emotion that was tied to the assaults in *any* way.

He was concerned that it wouldn't *matter* what he *began* to feel because he was sure that emotion wouldn't *stay* there. Instead, every *other* possible emotion would surge and quickly degrade into a panic attack. And he would begin screaming. And whatever had attacked the capital city would find him, and soon his screaming would transition from panic to whatever physical torture others were already enduring.

In the end, Hrafnkelsson knew he could continue to put off doing what he had climbed to the roof to do. But he was also aware that he was putting off the inevitable because he wouldn't leave the roof without doing it. And crawling to the edge, Hrafnkelsson slowly raised his tablet until its video sensor peeked over the perimeter wall.

Less than a second passed before Hrafnkelsson's blood ran cold.

Perhaps if he hadn't spent years serving as the former governor's communication facilitator, Hrafnkelsson might not have known what he saw. But Hrafnkelsson had always been proactive and diligent in his role. And he had always considered it his job to be *more* informed on important issues than even his governor, just in case the governor asked his opinion. Consequently, Hrafnkelsson had not only studied the history of Alpha Pegasi Three but also the history of the Realm, including the threats that Realm citizens had faced since the Disappearance.

And that meant Hrafnkelsson had immediately recognized the new invaders. They had been the proverbial boogeymen from decades before. Indeed, they had been so feared and considered such a threat that Realm Force had decided to fling its entire graduating class outward toward the distant stars in a desperate attempt to find the invader's home planet and destroy it.

And indeed, the home world had been found. And Realm Force had reported over twenty years ago that the *Dominion* had been dispatched to that world, and the main Hive had been utterly destroyed.

And now?

The Mechs were back. And Hrafnkelsson could testify *firsthand* that all the stories of their cruelty and viciousness were true.

•   •   •

At the Saturn Shipyards, in PLOKTA's lair, Evansworth listened with fascination as PLOKTA continued to discuss recent developments on Alpha Pegasi Three with Ton. PLOKTA had been helping Evansworth wiggle into the latest costume he had designed for her when an alert had chirped.

At that point, PLOKTA looked back at his displays to see that a large, strangely constructed ship was coming through the curled space ring that hung over the capital city of the planet. And that was the end of Evansworth's current session to infuse PLOKTA's mind with as much lust for her as possible.

Thankfully, Evansworth didn't actually *need* PLOKTA's help to get into the outfit. Indeed, Evansworth didn't need PLOKTA's help to get into *most* of the outfits he designed for her, but she was happy to let him help because it meant he would spend those minutes entirely focused on the curves of her body, gentle and otherwise. And his hands would be roaming over her soft, healthy-looking skin. And he would be remembering how it all felt when he was using her as a tool to lower his sperm count.

And, of course, that would increase his level of chemical bonding to her and convince him that she was oh-so-grateful for what he had done for her.

And yes, the outfit that PLOKTA had designed was yet another silliness of the testosterone-driven male mind. From a simple, practical perspective, Evansworth had always thought that naked *should* rank highest in the mind of a man who was looking at a woman he wanted to use as a tool.

Naked was easiest. There was nothing to remove. Naked offered an unobstructed path to whatever female body part the man wanted to use as a tool.

And yes, Evansworth *had* been naked for the majority of the time she spent in PLOKTA's lair. And she would have been content to *remain* naked. But before the mission on the *Majesty* to destroy Betelgeuse Two, PLOKTA had let slip that he had imagined her wearing something that would give the impression that she had become a barely controllable beast.

PLOKTA had designed a bondage harness to supposedly keep her in check. Thick, black crisscrossing leather straps. Tightened with buckles enough to hold them in place. Strategically placed and just wide enough to hide those few final places on the female body that were usually hidden from view, even though all the rest was exposed.

Evansworth understood the appeal of the costume for PLOKTA. It would make her look like he controlled her. And control was a base motivator for the reproductive drives. On average, in general, women wanted control to make them feel safe. Men wanted control so they could use their tool at any time they desired.

But, of course, there was a multitude of ways to crisscross the straps on her body. And PLOKTA had chosen in part to run them across her breasts and between her legs. In other words, he was covering up what he had free access to see if she was naked.

So why cover her up?

Yes, in the case of the bondage harness, they were leaving PLOKTA's lair and getting picked up by the *Majesty* to travel to Betelgeuse Two. They would be in the company of others. And in the larger context of Realm society, it would be socially unacceptable for Evansworth to be naked while on a mission with PLOKTA.

But, of course, *no one* was going to tell PLOKTA that he *couldn't* take Evansworth on board the *Majesty* buck naked because the crew was composed of Sotheby's special tactical teams. And they were all on Angel Haze and would react in any way Sotheby told them to react. And Sotheby would tell them whatever Ton *told* her to tell them. And PLOKTA could ask Ton to let him take Evansworth along for the trip and let her be naked.

In other words, there was no reason for PLOKTA to make a bondage harness for Evansworth that would hide anything, because PLOKTA had already *seen* everything for *years*.

And yet, *all* of PLOKTA's outfits hid *something*. For instance, the outfit that PLOKTA was helping Evansworth wiggle into before the alert appeared from Alpha Pegasi Three was a much simpler affair than the bondage harness, but it had some of the same features.

PLOKTA had begun with a basic sheer black body stocking. Of course,

PLOKTA had significantly altered the design to fit the tripod configuration of Evansworth's body. And then he had added opaque stripes that wrapped around her body to draw attention to her reproductive zones while simultaneously hiding them.

At a far younger age, that might have confused Evansworth. But it was just another quirk in the testosterone-driven mind as far as Evansworth was concerned. And the Merchenaries had taught her that in most men's minds, things that were hidden *deserved* to be found. According to the Merchenaries, for most men, subconsciously, when something was hidden, that meant the person looking for what was hidden *deserved* to uncover it. Indeed, the Merchenaries claimed that the majority of men would believe, perhaps without even recognizing it that when a woman *hid* something she actually *wanted* anyone looking for it to *uncover* it.

It was *tortured* logic. And, of course, it wasn't logic at all. It was physical, primal urges, driven by hormones, justified by flailing excuses manufactured by a drug-addled brain.

Still, Evansworth was *happy* to put on the bodystocking and position it so that everything was as precisely arranged as PLOTKA had wanted. And when she finished, she was also happy to curl up on the floor and listen to the latest drama from Alpha Pegasi Three and look adorable the entire time.

And maybe even wiggle a bit to see if she could shortcircuit PLOKTA's brain for a moment or two.

20.

In his lair at the Saturn Shipyards, PLOKTA continued discussing the developing events on Alpha Pegasi Three with Ton. Honestly, at almost *any* other time in the Realm, a Mech invasion on a Realm world would have spawned a full-scale Realm Force response that would have *obliterated* the invaders and saved the population of the planet from annihilation.

But, of course, most of the population of Alpha Pegasi Three had *already* been annihilated by the assault robots dispatched by Ton. And the rest of the Realm had no idea that had happened. As planned, PLOKTA's datacenter had initially carried on the conversations between the former inhabitants of Alpha Pegasi Three and friends and relatives throughout the Realm. And then the datacenter had soured the relationships and offended the participants to the point that they no longer wanted to communicate with the relatives and friends they *thought* were still alive on Alpha Pegasi Three.

In other words, not only did the citizens across the Realm *not* know whether the surviving inhabitants of Alpha Pegasi Three lived or died, they didn't *care*.

Consequently, when the incoming alert appeared from the curled space ring that hovered in orbit over the capital city of Alpha Pegasi Three, PLOKTA was surprised by the unexpected traffic. But he didn't immediately engage the orbital platforms to spin up their miniguns and start tearing apart any intruders.

PLOKTA understood that it wasn't a crisis. And he could guess that Ton would even consider it an opportunity, despite the cost to Realm Force. Indeed, Ton quickly confirmed that.

Interestingly, PLOKTA was in the middle of helping Evansworth into the latest outfit that he had designed for her when the chirp interrupted them. And that was one of the things that PLOKTA loved so much about Evansworth. She was *so* grateful for everything that PLOKTA did for her that he knew he didn't have to go through a lot of fake concern and apologies that he had work to do.

Evansworth had simply given him a look to let him know that she understood. And then, he had turned to his workstation and began his investigation. Even better, Evansworth had finished wiggling into the outfit before plopping down beside him.

She had been there ever since, looking adorable, delightful, and even sensuous.

And yes, PLOKTA understood that most men would look at Evansworth and be repelled by the strange configuration of her body. But PLOKTA had grown to enjoy *all* the oddities of Evansworth's tripod configuration. And he had been amazed in the last year at the number of ways Evansworth had used her unique form to bring him pleasure.

And even now, even after *hours* of investigating the unfolding events on Alpha Pegasi Three, Evansworth was still curled up beside him. Even better, periodically, Evansworth would stretch and twist to accentuate her curves. And it was all PLOKTA could do *not* to gawk at her.

And truth be told, when PLOKTA *hadn't* been on a comm with Ton over the last few hours, he *had* turned his head to study Evansworth's form once more and revel in the times they had spent together over the past year.

As for the Mechs, PLOKTA found their invasion of Alpha Pegasi Three engrossing as well. Given the fact that the Mech had been the *only* mechanized Horde in the Night, PLOKTA had always been fascinated by the stories about the Mechs. Still, much of what the Realm knew about the Mechs was myth and conjecture in the early days when their existence first became known.

Growing up, PLOKTA and his friends had made up stories about the Mechs and used them to scare the girls that they found infatuating. Surprisingly enough, this did *not* endear the hearts of many of the girls to their tormentors.

And yes, spending so much time *thinking* about the Mechs and working out the details of what they might be like had meant PLOKTA had often thought about the Mechs and wondered if anyone would ever know their full history. Unsurprisingly, when Abaddon installed the neural interface in PLOKTA's shoulder, it wasn't long before PLOKTA put it to work researching Mechs, compiling everything that was known about them, and projecting theories on their origins and potential futures.

And frankly, PLOKTA wasn't surprised when his neural interface indicated that the Mechs had probably originated during experimentation by the Troyd. Disappointingly, however, even his neural interface didn't find much beyond what PLOKTA already knew. And given that, PLOKTA had moved on to other things.

There was too much that Nicolescu and Sotheby had wanted him to do. And within the last few years, Ton had also kept PLOKTA extremely busy.

And then, just hours ago, an alert chirped. And PLOKTA glanced at his workstation. And he saw a ship emerge from the curled space ring over the capital city of Alpha Pegasi Three.

And PLOKTA knew *immediately*, it *had* to be the Mechs.

To be clear, PLOKTA had never seen a Mech ship of the size and configuration that had just appeared.

Yes, there *were* other Mech ships on record. Video feeds existed of the encounters with the Mechs during the *Dominion's* mission to Night's Keep, twenty-two years ago. Others documented the brief space battle that took place between the *Dominion* and the Mechs during the mission to destroy the Mech Hive, the year after that.

However, the ship that PLOKTA saw coming through the curled space ring looked nothing like those ships. In fact, the vessel that came through the curled space ring was far larger.

Obviously, PLOKTA had read the reports of the senior staff of the *Dominion*, following the mission to destroy the Mech Hive. He had also watched the video feeds. And for PLOKTA, it seemed that the vessel had the basic configuration of the Mech Hive, looking more like a massive building than a spacecraft. And like the Mech Hive, it had a broad base that narrowed and climbed into towering pinnacles.

In addition, at the time of the mission to the Mech Hive, Casteel had reported that the Mech Hive was a "monstrosity of metal, looking more grown than built, clawing into the sky, scintillating in the light of the planet's stark, hot star."

The vessel that had come through the Alpha Pegasi Three curled space ring matched that description as well. And quickly, PLOKTA had confirmed that the vessel shimmered for the same reason as the Mech Hive.

It was *crawling* with Mechs. Thousands of them. Racing back and forth across the walls. Pounding on the side of the hive. Shaking their fists at the terraformed planet below them.

Of course, by then, PLOKTA had already sent an emergency comm request to Ton. And PLOKTA had already asked the question for which he suspected he knew the answer.

"Should I inform the Superintendent of Realm Force Academy that she should prepare for an attack?" he wondered as soon as he and Ton had begun discussing the situation.

"I think not," Ton had answered. "She seems to have grown too concerned about affairs that don't concern her recently. Perhaps this will help her refocus on her duties instead of pontificating on matters that don't concern her."

The year before, while making plans to target Alpha Pegasi Three with a psyop and eliminate both the planet's governor and anyone who supported them, Ton had also begun a quiet process to transfer out anyone at the local Realm Force Academy campus who seemed worth keeping for the long haul and transfer in anyone in Realm Force who seemed discontent.

That shuffling had allowed Ton to take care of some of the individuals in Realm Force that PLOKTA had been tracking as potential problems. After all, when Ton released the assault robots, they *weren't* given any commands to treat Realm Force personnel any differently than other inhabitants of the planet.

Consequently, if the Realm Force personnel retreated to their quarters and stayed there, the assault robots allowed them to live. And yes, many of the Realm Force personnel stationed on the Alpha Pegasi Three had frantically opened comms, attempting to call for help. But, of course, by then, PLOKTA was already routing all of the planet's comm traffic through his AI-generated response mechanism, so all those calls for help were put on hold.

Eventually, the Realm Force personnel realized that they were subject to the same extreme implementation of martial law as the rest of the inhabitants. Interestingly, the Superintendent of Realm Force Academy had continued her duties despite this realization, sleeping in her office, taking her meals there, making sure she stayed inside the administrative building on the Alpha Pegasi Three campus.

The problem, according to PLOKTA's surveillance, was that she was also keeping notes on everything she saw outside. Consequently, PLOKTA could deduce that Ton would not be inclined to intervene to help her or any of the surviving Realm Force personnel on the planet.

Indeed, Ton had suggested that PLOKTA allow free passage through the airlocks of Alpha Pegasi Three's terraforming dome. And that meant when the Mechs began leaping from their vessel to career toward those large airlocks, the airlock happily obliged to let them in. And from there, the Mech had descended en masse toward the surface.

PLOKTA and Ton had spent the next few minutes watching that assault unfold as they discussed different aspects of the invasion. And yes, they had broached the subject of sending the *Majesty* to destroy both the Mech mothership and the entire surface of Alpha Pegasi Three, just to make sure the Mechs were wiped out.

But Ton had decided against immediate annihilation. There were far too many questions. Why had the Mechs appeared now? Were other attacks imminent? What did the Mechs intend to do on Alpha Pegasi Three?

Then, after watching the initial waves of attacks, Ton ended the comm to attend to other pressing items. However, he had asked PLOKTA to run a detailed analysis and schedule another comm when he had determined what he could from the Mech activity.

PLOKTA had begun his report just moments before, after Ton responded to PLOKTA's follow-up comm request.

"They're still *only* going after the inhabitants of the planet," PLOKTA offered after he had given Ton a quick update on the processes he had in place to analyze the situation. "They aren't gathering any other resources. They aren't disassembling anything for parts. They're just dropping out of the sky, decelerating at the last possible moment, slamming into the ground, and then racing off to tear through our assault bots and then start hauling people out into the open from wherever they can find them.

"Presumably, the only reason they're smashing our assault bots is because they're in their way. And those assault bots have plenty of parts that the Mechs could use. But the Mechs are just ripping them to pieces as quickly as possible before continuing their search for humans.

"Interestingly, the Mech don't seem to be operating using infrared sensors, or sensitive audio equipment to pick up whispers or heartbeats. They're just methodical. They blow through doors and sometimes walls. They rampage. And keep rampaging until they find a human. And then they drag the human to wherever that particular group of Mechs is using as a collection point and go to work on them.

"But here's the thing. We've got Hunter's report of what he saw the Mechs doing to the settlers on Beta Ceti One. And we've got the video feeds from the Mech attack on the Gilead Research Facility on Gamma Draconis Two. And in both of those cases, when Mechs butcher humans, all that's usually left is a lung, a heart, and half a brain—and just the lower and back half of the brain at that.

"Now, the Mechs seem to be leaving enough intact that the humans they're butchering are probably still *conscious*."

PLOKTA could see that Ton was thinking, so he paused.

"Any reports of similar Mech attacks on any surviving worlds in the Night?" Ton wondered.

PLOKTA shook his head. "Not that I can find," he answered. "And as long as no one is *spoofing* us, this is the only Mech attack currently underway in the Realm."

Ton tilted his head to the side. "That's not a pleasant thought," he said ominously.

"Nope," PLOKTA agreed. "But as I mentioned in my debrief after the *Majesty's* mission to Betelgeuse Two, the female Troyd that went with us mentioned to Murg that the Troyd were in contact with the Scary Devil Monastery. And at the time, I assumed that had to mean Abaddon and his destroyers.

"I know we've supposedly made a deal with Abaddon. But if he ever decided to move against us, and the Troyd calls them the Scary Devil Monastery, I think we have to be prepared for the fact that there isn't going to be much that we're going to be able to do to stop them from doing whatever they want to do to us. And that includes faking our comm and letting us think everything is fine, just like I'm faking the comms to and from the worlds where we've released the assault bots."

Ton offered PLOKTA a noncommittal smile. "Life is never certain," he said circumspectly. "You know I don't consider myself much of a scholar of the Bible, although I have studied the endtime prophecies quite extensively.

Interestingly, during those studies, I also came across a few tidbits that amused me.

"If I recall, there's a spot in Isaiah where the prophet is calling out doom and gloom over Jerusalem and suggesting that everyone should be weeping and wailing and tearing out their hair and dressing in sackcloth. Instead, the prophet observes that, in Jerusalem, there is joy and revelry, the slaughtering of cattle and the killing of sheep, the eating of meat and the drinking of wine. The prophet also notes with dismay that everyone is saying, 'Let us eat and drink for tomorrow we die!'

"And that sounds good to me!"

Now, Ton paused again. "Let's let this play out," he said. "I'm sure we can find some way to use this to create more fear and loathing in the Realm. And as we have seen over and over in the last few years, the more we can make people afraid and anxious, the more they are willing to allow us to control every aspect of their lives. Ton out."

•   •   •

On Alpha Pegasi Three, under the stars produced by the planet's terraforming dome, Hrafnkelsson fought back the urge to throw up as he continued to record events in the street below from a rooftop on a building in the capital city.

Frankly, he was *done*. He had watched what the Mechs were doing to his fellow citizens, and he didn't know how much more he could take without having a complete mental breakdown. And as Hrafnkelsson had already decided, it wasn't *just* the scene he was watching. It was the entire last year. It was the feeling that the worst was over, only to discover that the worst was back, *and* it had become even *more* horrifying.

Realm Force's assault robots had been bad enough. But at least they killed somewhat quickly. And yes, Hrafnkelsson knew enough of the Mechs to expect that the process would be longer. But at least with the *recorded* process, the victims were soon reduced to something closer to an animal than a human, still alive but almost certainly not *aware*.

Hrafnkelsson couldn't say the same thing for what was happening in the street below. And it was most likely happening in all the other streets across the capital city, which *still* vibrated with choruses of screaming.

Only the streetlamps of the capital city lit the atrocities now as the Mechs continued working into the night. But Hrafnkelsson had seen enough for his mind to supply the exquisite detail of what was happening to the inhabitants of his home planet who were dragged into the processing areas that the Mechs had cordoned off.

Most arrive with at least one broken leg and sometimes two. And if, while they screamed, they were still attempting to crawl away, one of the Mechs working in the processing area would stomp over and drive a claw into the base of the offender's back and then twist to destroy vertebrae and spinal column. And, of course, the inhabitants would begin to scream louder once they realized what had happened to them.

Amazingly enough, some still attempted to drag themselves away. But if they did, one of the processing Mechs stomp back to them to deliver a second round of disincentives. And typically, the Mech would grab an arm, twist it until it popped loose, rip away the tendons, and then beat the victim unconscious with it before returning to process other inhabitants.

That processing began with an inhabitant being dragged to a sturdy table, hoisted up, and dumped on it. And after ripping off the inhabitant's clothing, a Mech would strap down its victim and saw off their limbs with a jagged butcher knife. This was quickly followed by cauterizing all the wounds with a red-hot electrical device. And obviously, this led to even more screaming.

Still, the first time Hrafnkelsson saw this done, he took *some* comfort in knowing what he *thought* came next. According to his reading, the Mechs would soon dissect their victims, leaving only a portion of a brain behind with a few vital organs to keep that portion alive, effectively ending the individual's life.

But the Mechs who invaded Alpha Pegasi Three *weren't* doing that. After removing arms and legs, the Mechs seem to be trying to destroy their victims' connection to the physical world. They gouged out eyes. They cut out tongues. They sawed off noses and scraped out sinus cavities. They inserted hooks in ears and ripped out eardrums.

And when the Mechs finally tore out their victims' voice boxes, the screaming stopped.

But new indignities and torments quickly began. As Hrafnkelsson watched, the Mechs shoved tubes down their victims' throats. And then they flipped their victims over and shoved another up their backsides. And *then*, the Mechs seemed to spend entirely too much time around their victims' groin areas before gathering everything up and shoving each victim into a box with hookups for all the newly inserted tubes.

Once secured, the Mechs slammed the lids on the boxes to confine their victims, latched the boxes shut, and then carried the boxes over to throw them on a growing pile nearby.

Of course, the clear implication for Hrafnkelsson was that the Mechs were no longer cannibalizing humans for basic parts. Obviously, the Mechs had a new use for humans that would preserve their consciousness intact. And given that the Mechs also had access to emergency medical units, it meant that any human thus processed and confined might face hundreds of years of control under the Mechs' absolute rule.

And the more Hrafnkelsson watched those conversions taking place and the longer he thought about what it might mean for anyone so confined, the more panicked and nauseous he became.

•   •   •

In her quarters on the *Dominion*, Rachel felt the Falcon pull off their dressing gown to fling it over a chair before she turned for bed. Focusing on the next attempt at remote viewing, Rachel reminded herself that it couldn't be forced or dreamed up. The remote viewing phenomenon *was*, and no amount of struggling could *make* it happen.

For Rachel, those weren't just platitudes. She had struggled for *months*, trying to find the right mindset, trying to relax, trying to turn her mind toward impressions without trying too hard or trying too little.

Rachel *had* sensed the difference when the vision of Worku and Moreau in Hunter Look-Alike custody had appeared in her mind. It *was*, whereas before it *hadn't been*.

Unfortunately, Rachel had no idea what she had done on that evening any differently than what she had done on any other evening for the last six months. Except *perhaps*… she had reminded herself again and again that she couldn't be impatient. She couldn't be afraid. She needed to be still and patient, and offer her intention to know.

But hadn't she done that before? Why was it different on *that* particular night?

As the frantic questions began popping in her mind, Rachel realized that her *one* success with remote viewing had immediately become her most significant obstacle to a *second* success. And as Falcon crawled into bed, Rachel *accepted* that she *had* achieved something important, and even miraculous, when she viewed Worku and Moreau on the Look-Alikes vessel. And she accepted, *perhaps*, that it would be the *last* time she ever experienced *anything* like that.

But she could still open herself to the possibility again and *wait*. Without expectation. Without demand. Just… *wait*.

Now, Rachel felt herself sliding between the cool, very comfortable sheets once more. And she felt the Falcon position herself in the bed once more. And Rachel allowed her mind to drift toward thoughts of Worku and Moreau, trying to sense if they were still alive and still where they had been in her previous viewing session.

Unexpectedly, Rachel jerked at what felt like an electric shock coursing through her body.

"Rachel?" the Falcon immediately responded, sounding concerned.

"I'm okay," Rachel whispered back. "Just… *wait*."

Another jolt of electricity. Another shudder. Rachel's mouth flew open. And she would have screamed if G'Utz hadn't stolen her vocal cords so many years ago.

Still, Rachel screamed using the neural interface that the cybersuit provided. And, of course, the Falcon responded.

"*Rachel?*" the Falcon repeated, sounding even more concerned.

"*Wait*," Rachel whispered again.

A third shock seized Rachel. She clenched her teeth and waited. And as shudders faded, images began floating through her mind and then accelerating.

The impression of the room reappeared. Boxes. Displays. Part of a large ship. But streaked now and eaten away.

Two figures in the room. Also streaked and eaten away. Both had machines in front of them. Flashes of electricity arcing between the machines and the figures.

And, of course, by now, the fingers of Rachel's hand were moving rapidly, sketching not only the scene but also more.

•   •   •

In Conference Room One, Bolobolo and the rest of the senior staff stared at the most recent drawings from Rachel, after she offered her intention toward Doctor Moreau and Jaz Worku. As before, Falcon projected the drawings onto the wall-mounted displays in an animation-like sequence.

And again, that sequence began with simple, minimalist lines that seemed to be drawn at random. But as the lines grew denser, the drawings once more morphed into a rough sketch of a storage bay. And soon crates, display screens, and figures emerged.

They were still recognizably Worku and Moreau. But now, Worku seemed frantic, and Moreau seemed almost animalistic. But at the same time, he seemed stultified and in a stupor. Worst of all, there seemed to be robots standing before the pair, and animated electric shocks danced from the robots to Worku and Moreau.

Begrudgingly, Bolobolo admitted to herself that this drawing was even more incredible than the last. Instead of a simple, fixed perspective, the camera position seemed to be moving, rotating around the pair of tortured souls and their tormentors. At times, it zoomed in to show Worku's anguished screams and pleas. At other times, it rolled away to find Moreau's dazed expression and his mewling and snarling lips that seemed to repeat some simple collection of the same words over and over.

Of course, there was no sound. The drawings had come from Rachel's fingers, whisking over the bottom sheet of the bed in Falcon's quarters. But that was when Falcon unexpectedly spoke up.

"This probably isn't something Adi wants to hear," she began, apologetically, "and the lips are difficult to read because it's only a drawing. But Jaz seems to be claiming that Bolobolo told Moreau never to reveal to anyone that they had perfected a virus that could slaughter Hunter Look-Alikes. In response, Doctor Moreau is repeating words like stupid, Bobo, bitch, brain-dead, and button-pusher."

Falcon looked at Bolobolo as a chill went down Bolobolo's spine. "Sorry," Falcon added.

Bolobolo thought for a moment, but there really wasn't much to say. After all, the Hunter Look-Alikes already believed everything Worku was saying. And Bolobolo knew that they were arrogant enough that no one could change their minds. In other words, the claims weren't going to change anything.

Still, Bolobolo would have preferred that *no one* feed the Hunter Look-

Alike's delusions. On the other hand, the moving camera perspective had made everything that Worku and Moreau were enduring feel more *real*. And Bolobolo hated to see anyone suffering, especially when it was at the hands of those who were cruel.

Of course, at the moment, Bolobolo knew that it was all just a mental exercise, perhaps even a thought experiment that she could afford to conduct because nothing could even come of it.

The Night and the Realm were vast. How would they ever *find* Worku and Moreau?

Consequently, with everyone in the conference room staring at her and waiting for a response, Bolobolo reverted to the one-word comment that she had settled on as her best response ever since Rachel had demonstrated a capacity for remote viewing.

"Great," she said unenthusiastically.

It was only then that Bolobolo noticed the playback of Rachel's drawings had stopped.

"And then there's the last thing," Falcon said ominously as the playback of the drawings restarted.

Now, Worku seemed to be screaming and pleading again. And Moreau seemed to be babbling again. But the camera soon lost interest in their suffering. And it rotated away to focus on the bulkhead of the vessel. Then, it grew closer and closer to the bulkhead until it passed through it.

And once pointing outward into space, Rachel's drawings stopped moving, ending with a view of a smallish star in the near distance surrounded by a star field farther out.

Oakford frowned. "Does that star map line up with anything?" he suddenly wondered, sounding shocked.

"ACK," Murg replied.

Now, all the displays in Conference Room One split into two windows. And each showed a portion of Rachel's drawing of a star field on the right and a data-driven star map on the left. And as each of those windows stretched to the opposite side of the screens to fill the displays, Rachel's dots lined up *almost* perfectly with the star map.

Labels began appearing to identify major interest points on Murg's graphics. And then those graphics completely replaced Rachel's drawings and zoomed out to show the location.

"If Rachel's drawings are accurate," Falcon commented, "the Hunter Look-Alike vessel holding Jax and Doctor Moreau is in the TU Corvi system, approximately 246 light-years from Earth, in the area formerly known as Shadow. No known planets."

Hunter spoke up. "As it turns out," he said with what sounded like a charginned tone, "We located a shock-drop into the TU Corvi system two weeks ago. It's not on any of the shock-drop lists that the Saturn Shipyards collected at the time of the *Dominion's* repairs there fifteen years ago. There's a possibility we're the only ones who know it exists. But I would assume that the Hunter Look-Alikes are aware of it as well."

Conference Room One fell silent for a moment. The implications were clear.

"Great," Bolobolo commented again, easily sensing what came next.

21.

On the *Dominion*, in Conference Room One, Oakford looked at his senior staff members one by one. Then, he stated the obvious.

"Jazarah Worku not only *left* this ship of her own accord after we gave her back her *life* by rescuing her from Nu Scorpii One," he said, his voice hinting at defiance, "she also returned to this ship under manufactured pretenses and tried to *extort* us out of the Rexian Sheer we recovered from Jean-Baptiste Lacroix's yacht. I can't say that I feel *any* responsibility to attempt to rescue her from the Hunter Look-Alikes.

"As for Doctor Moreau, Realm Force demanded we hand him over to them. And I am hard-pressed to justify putting this ship and its crew at *risk* to rescue a man that I found arrogant, narcissistic, and even masochistic."

"That seems reasonable to me, captain," Hunter offered.

"I don't see any reason that we should attempt that either, captain," Falcon chimed in.

"ACK NAK ACK…" Murg began and then added a final, "NAK."

Now, Oakford turned his head to look at Bolobolo. And at first, Bolobolo seemed to be trying to look as nonchalant and as convinced as Hunter and Falcon, and at least in agreement with Murg. But soon, she let out a sigh and shook her head.

"I don't think she's faking it this time, captain," Bolobolo said with an air of resignation. "I think Jaz is in *deep* trouble. And I think the Hunter Look-

Alikes are going to keep torturing her and Moreau until they say exactly what they wanted them to say. And that will be something along the line of what the Hunter Look-Alikes *have* been saying. I'm a deadly threat to them, and I *must* be eliminated."

Oakford stared at Bolobolo for a moment. "Adi," he said, "we would have *no* idea what we'd be jumping into. Rachel's drawing doesn't show any other ships, but that doesn't mean they're *aren't* any other ships. We have never known how large the Look-Alike fleet is, and while Pix's tactical and strategic skills are incredible, there is a physical limit to the number of munitions that we have. And if they use something like the proverbial Mongolian horde technology, we would be swarmed."

Bolobolo nodded. "I understand completely, captain," she said, "But that doesn't mean I think that Worku is getting what she deserves. Or maybe she *is* getting what she deserves, and all of us on *this* ship are getting far *less* than we deserve. I'm glad I don't have to make this decision because I'm finding it hard to look away from what Rachel has shown us. Honestly, it feels like an invitation."

Oakford stared at Bolobolo a moment longer, knowing he couldn't dispute anything she had just said. Now, he turned toward MacDuff.

"Chief," Oakford began, "anything? Maybe a parable to give us some guidance?"

MacDuff smiled. "Something like the Parable of the Unfaithful Crewmember and the Unkind Genetic Researcher?" he answered.

Oakford suppressed a grin. "I'm willing to hear any story you'd like to tell me," he said, "so long as it concludes that I don't have to put all the souls on this vessel at risk for two wayward stiff-necked souls."

MacDuff nodded. "Unfortunately, the stories that Jesus told aren't known for promoting self-interest, except on rare and interesting occasions," he said. "Beyond that, however, I do find myself drawn to a concept that Adi just addressed when she chose a specific word to represent Rachel's remote viewing. She called it an invitation. There *is* a parable about that. It twists in unexpected ways. And it may provide some guidance.

"In Matthew 22, Jesus is quoted as saying that the kingdom of heaven is like a king who prepared a wedding banquet for his son. Then he sent his servants to tell those who had been invited to come, but strangely, the invitees *refuse*. The king tries again, this time describing the fact that the oxen and the fattened cattle have been butchered and everything is ready, and they should come to the wedding banquet.

"In spite of this second message, one of the guests returns to his field, another to his business. Worse, the rest of the invitees seize the king's servants. They abuse the servants and even *kill* them.

"Of course, this enrages the king, and he sends his army to destroy the murderers and burn their city to the ground.

"Then the king tells his servant that the wedding banquet is ready, and those he invited didn't deserve to come. And he sends his servants to the street corners to invite *anyone* they can find. And in Jesus' words, the servants gather the bad as well as the good.

"Interestingly, when the king comes to see the guests, he notices a man who isn't wearing wedding clothes. And he asks the man how he got into the banquet without wedding clothes, but the man is speechless.

"So the king tells his attendants to tie the man hand and foot, and throw him outside, into the darkness, where there is weeping and gnashing of teeth. And then, Jesus ends the parable with the famous quote, 'For many are invited, but few are chosen.'"

Hutner gave his head a slight shake. "Not very smart to antagonize a king," he noted. "Especially since it's a banquet. How hard is it to eat some food and go home?!"

MacDuff nodded. "The refusals *are* odd. And I suspect that Jesus chose the joyous occasion of a wedding specifically to make the behavior of the invited guests seem puzzling," he said. "Many have focused on the wedding banquet aspect of the parable to establish that the core meaning of the parable *is* the wedding. They see that Jesus begins the parable with 'the kingdom of heaven is like…'. And from that, they determine that the wedding banquet *is* heaven, and Jesus is stressing the importance of accepting the King's invitation to gain entrance to heaven.

"But I believe that this parable is much closer to encouraging us how best to act in our daily lives. And perhaps it is even a warning for us *not* to jump to conclusions about what our futures hold."

Oakford frowned. "I don't think I'm following," he offered.

MacDuff nodded. "Before I explain what I mean about the parable itself, I think it's important to establish what Jesus means when he says, 'The kingdom of heaven is like…'. Typically, Jesus uses that phrase to teach us that the *activities* we perform create environments that resonate with the kingdom of heaven. For instance, Jesus says that the kingdom of heaven is like a farmer going out to sow a field. He goes on to say that the activity of the seed in and out of the soil is reflective of the processes of the kingdom. He says the kingdom of heaven is like a woman mixing flour and leaven, and this illustrates the spread of the kingdom. He says that the kingdom of heaven is like a mustard seed that dies and then grows into the largest of trees.

"Over and over, Jesus uses the phrase, the kingdom of heaven, to connect to some action. And those actions represent the dynamics of the kingdom. And they can also represent actions that *oppose* the kingdom, such as when Jesus tells the parable of the wheat and tares. He says the kingdom of heaven is like a farmer planting wheat and an enemy planting tares, and the interaction of the wheat and the tares reveals an aspect of the kingdom.

"Given that, I don't believe that the focus of the Parable of the Wedding Banquet should be the wedding banquet. I believe a much better focus of the parable should be the responses that those in the parable display towards the King's invitation. And I think Jesus is using the hyperbole of the wedding banquet to show how inconceivable it would be for those *invited* to the wedding banquet to *refuse* to come, given the joyous nature of the occasion.

"What *possible* reason could these guests have for refusing to come? I think the answer lies in the fact that Jesus, just prior to this parable, is directing his teaching at the Pharisees. The two parables in Matthew 21 are the Parables of the Two Sons and the Parable of the Tenants, and both of those speak about disobedience.

"Interestingly, *neither* of these parables begins with Jesus saying, 'The kingdom of heaven is like…'. In these cases, Jesus is simply telling a story, pointing a finger at the Pharisees, and the Pharisees *know* it. In fact, after Jesus tells those parables, Matthew states that the chief priests and the Pharisees recognized that Jesus was referring to them, and they began seeking a way to arrest him.

"In these verses, we see an exact parallel to what will come next, namely, the behavior of those who *refuse* to come to the wedding banquet. In essence, Jesus is saying to the Pharisee that the most joyous occasion imaginable is *right* before you, and you are invited, and you're *refusing* to come and delight in what my Father is offering you. And on a broader scale, Jesus is saying that the kingdom of heaven is like an *invitation* from the highest and most holy

King.

"And he is saying the way that humanity *reacts* to that invitation is bound up within the operation of the kingdom of heaven. Obviously, the most prominent response that Jesus features in the parable to his Father's invitation is *refusal*. The entire first half of the parable documents the refusal of the invitees to participate in the kingdom festivities.

But Jesus also highlights another type of response later in the parable. He says there's a man who accepts the invitation to the wedding banquet but then refuses the offer of wedding garments to wear *during* the celebration.

"And again, this seems inconceivable. But it is another instance of an individual unable to understand what is being offered and refusing to accept it. It's true that the man accepts the offer superficially. But when asked to make the simplest accommodations to wear wedding garments, the man refuses.

"Happily, there seem to be *many* others in the parable who not only hear of the invitation but also respond and come to the wedding banquet. In addition, they clothe themselves in a way that honors the King.

"The conclusion seems to be that the wedding banquet is well attended and well enjoyed.

"But *then*, Jesus provides an *additional* statement that calls into question even the behavior of those who respond to the invitation *and* put on the wedding attire, *and* most likely *appear* to be enjoying themselves.

"Jesus ends the parable with, 'For many are invited, but few are chosen.'

"For me, this is a chilling statement. Apparently, many of those attending the banquet are there *only* for the food and perhaps the entertainment. But they aren't there to truly celebrate the marriage of the son. They came to the banquet only for what they could get *out* of it."

MacDuff paused as if he might not be ready to say what he was about to say.

"As for how this parable might relate to our present situation," he offered, "the question before us is whether or not Rachel's remote viewing efforts are as Chief Bolobolo has identified them. Are they an invitation? I understand that attempting a rescue of Jaz Worku and Doctor Moreau is fraught with peril, but if we have an invitation, it may be more advantageous to us than we could ever imagine."

Oakford gave his head a slight shake. "But there is no guarantee that the cost will not be greater than we would otherwise want to pay."

MacDuff nodded his head. "There are no guarantees, captain," he agreed. "There are only his invitations and our responses."

Oakford thought for a moment. He had faced similar situations in the past, knowing the decision he *would* make while hesitating to make it. And Oakford knew that he had allowed himself that hesitation because he hoped to convince himself that he was being reflective, careful, and diligent.

But in this case, that hesitation seemed cruel. And it felt like he would be playing emotional games while Worku and Moreau suffered.

"How long will it take us to reach the TU Corvi system?" he asked, knowing the calculations had already been done.

Hunter spoke up. "We could use the Riger Three curled space ring and hop to Alpha Crucis Four," he began, "and then run the curled space funnels. That would only take a day, but if anyone has survived on Alpha Crucis or the Look-Alikes have scouts on the planet's surface, they could figure out we're coming.

"Or, we could run the funnels all the way, but it's almost a thousand light-years away, and that will take a week. Or we could use a few of the shock-drops that we have calculated and get there in four cycles. Of course, if we shock-drop into the TU Corvi system, the Look-Alikes might be waiting for us, but maybe I can nudge the final hop and move us out of harm's way."

Feeling the weight of the decision he was about to make, Oakford paused again. But then he shook his head with a bit of frustration because there was so little on which to base his choice. Oakford soon found himself reaching for what might seem to others a silly question.

"Given my background and past experiences," he asked, "can anyone think of *any* scenario where I *wouldn't* eventually make the decision that we should attempt to rescue Jaz Worku and Doctor Moreau?"

Falcon smiled in response, not condescendingly or mocking but with kindness.

"As you have said many times, captain," she offered, "there have been too many unusual circumstances that put *this* crew together with *this* ship for *this* time. While I still believe that there is no *rational* reason to compel us to intervene, we have seen many times that we exist beyond pure rationality. I'm with you, captain. Whatever you decide, I'll be by your side."

"Agreed," Hunter added.

"ACK,"

"Count me in, captain!" the Pixie offered.

"I'm in as well," Bolobolo agreed.

"As always," MacDuff said with a slight smirk, "I stand ready to assist in any way that I am able, captain."

Oakford nodded. "Thank you, all of you," he said. "Let's assume that we have the shock-drops for a reason and use them. And now, great God, be good to us, for the sea is so vast and our vessel so small. Dismissed."

•   •   •

Later, on Lower Deck 5, in the storage bay that the tactical teams had converted into a makeshift dojo, *all* the tactical teams were assembled in their dress blues and all had assumed their formal positions.

Each stood ramrod straight. Each was silent. Each stared directly ahead.

MacDuff stood in the dojo as well, at the focus point for all that attention, on a small platform that had been placed at one end of the dojo. MacDuff was also in his dress blues, standing as rigidly and formally as the rest.

Now, MacDuff relaxed a bit. "At ease," he called out.

And in unison, the tactical team members widened their stances and loosely clasped their hands behind their backs.

"Tactical Team Lead Hawthorne and Tactical Team Member Guan, please join me on the dais," MacDuff said, his voice weighted and warm.

Moving quickly, Hawthorne moved from his position in the front row of the assembled tactical team members to stand on MacDuff's left and face in the same direction as MacDuff. Guan soon joined them, coming from the back at nearly the opposite wall of the dojo to stand on MacDuff's right.

MacDuff now turned his head to look at Guan.

"Tactical Team Member Guan, you have endured the fire," he began solemnly. "You have been bloodied partially by a mistake of your own and partially by a failure of your team. There is no shame in that. Without question, we will *all* make mistakes before each of us completes his or her service to this ship. What is certain is that you have *learned* from these mistakes, and in that learning, you have demonstrated such capability that it seems fit that we honor you for the journey you endured to return to us."

MacDuff paused before continuing, lifting his head to look outward at the other tactical team members.

"Remember what happens today," he finally said, "One tactical member *recognizes* the accomplishments of another. One tactical team member honors another. One tactical team member sacrifices for another. Recently, Tactical Team Lead Hawthorne called a meeting of the tactical team leads and presented a proposal to resign *his* lead position, allowing Tactical Team Member Guan to assume it. Furthermore, Tactical Team Lead Hawthorne proposed that Guan become my new second-in-command, a position that has not been formally held since the death of Thomas Harnecky.

"While there was some discussion in the leads meeting, I can tell you that the vote to proceed was *unanimous*. *Every* team lead recognized that Tactical Team Member Guan has grown into someone extraordinary during the process of her refining. And they all assured me that they would be honored to serve under her if I were ever unavailable in that capacity.

"In addition to the leads' recommendations, I should also tell you that I was immediately in favor of the proposal, and when I discussed it with Captain Oakford, he quickly gave it his blessing.

"What remains then is to commission Tactical Team Member Guan for her new role. And while each of you has internally considered each of the questions that follow, and the leads have, of course, given public ascent to them before this assembly, I consider it essential for Team Member Guan to testify to the same in your company. In this manner, I hope that this day will solidify itself in her mind that she holds a place of both honor and responsibility for the *whole* of the tactical teams that she must never take for granted."

As MacDuff turned his whole body to face Guan, she did the same to face him.

"Team Member Guan, do you pledge yourself to be the one who does not cower or draw back, to be the one who stands in the gap, to be the one who wedges herself between the danger and the weak?" MacDuff asked.

"I do," Guan said solemnly.

"And do you pledge yourself to be the one who stares at death full-faced," MacDuff continued, "who has stripped herself of the need for convenience, certainty, and control, and by this ensured your passage onward?"

"I do," Guan repeated.

"Then by the power granted me by Captain Oakford," MacDuff declared, "you may take your place as lead of Tactical Team 2 and my second in command."

As Guan turned to step off the dias, heading for the stop that Hawthorne had vacated, MacDuff called out.

"Hoo-rah?" MacDuff shouted.

"Hoo-rah!" the tactical team members call back loudly in unison.

Now, MacDuff turned to Hawthorne. "Tactical Team Lead Hawthorne," he said, "With a grateful heart for the kindness you have shown, and to honor you for the selfless decision you have made, I relieve you of your duties as a team lead."

"I stand relieved, Chief MacDuff," Hawthorne responded with a smile.

"Hoo-rah?" MacDuff called out a second time to the teams as Hawthorne made his way to the opposite side of the room.

"Hoo-rah!" the tactical team members call back loudly in unison a second time.

Now, a smile flitted across MacDuff's face. And he looked back over his shoulder at the corner where Sphinx usually lay, curled up, to watch the activities of the dojo. Interestingly, as the tactical teams had entered the dojo in their dress blues and taken their positions in precisely aligned rows and columns, Sphinx had rolled up into a seated position, head lifted in a regal pose, looking present and attentive.

"And to you, my friend," MacDuff added, looking directly at Sphinx, "I am grateful for your help in this matter, for you made this possible."

At this, Sphinx lifted his head a bit more and chuffed contentedly.

MacDuff looked back at the tactical teams. "Hoo-rah?"

"Hoo-rah!" the tactical team members responded.

MacDuff's gaze turned intense. "As you know, we are making our way to a location to attempt a rescue of former crewmember Jazarah Worku and Doctor Moreau," he said. "We expect resistance, but we do not know what the nature of that resistance might be.

"We do know that if the encounter devolves into hand-to-hand combat, without a doubt, we are those who will fight and the foes we will face will be skilled. In that fight, we may fall or we may finish. But *if* we fall, in time, others will step forward to take our place. And when they fall, if they fall, still others will take *their* place. And on and on, until the Slayer falls exhausted, unable to wield its sword against us any longer, and Death folds inward and falls into Nothing.

"*This* is the future that lies sure and straight before us. This is why we *cannot* know defeat. While we live, we *serve*. And when we complete our service, we join the Great Reunion.

"Each of us, perhaps today, perhaps tomorrow, perhaps next year, will face that transformation. But for today, for *this* day, *we... serve*."

"Hoo-*rah?*" MacDuff concluded forcefully.

"HOO-RAH!" the members of the tactical teams responded, loudly and in unison.

•   •   •

On Alpha Pegasi Three, in the dead of night manufactured by the planet's terraforming dome, Hrafnkelsson felt along the edge of a hangar that sat beside a landing pad at one of the capital city spaceports, listening for any change in the chaotic sounds that surrounded him. By now, it felt to Hrafnkelsson like the sound of screaming had lessened across the entire city. Also, the incessant clanking of Mechs racing to and fro seemed to have faded. But interestingly, those sounds had been replaced with argumentative, expletive-filled grumblings from the Mechs. And, at times, those grumblings had increased into much louder shouting matches.

Initially, Hrafnkelsson hadn't noticed a great deal of banter between the Mechs. Maybe that was because there had been a constant stream of humans to find and butcher. And unquestionably, the Mechs had been focused and seemingly desperate to ensure that they found every last inhabitant of Alpha Pegasi Three.

However, as the hours wore on, Hrafnkelsson began to notice many of the Mechs were ranting about not being able to find any more humans. And then, they had begun to hurl obscenity-laced insults at each other for being stupid. And they cursed each other that they hadn't found the hiding place humans were using to avoid being caught.

As Hrafnkelsson watched that progression unfold, he realized the Mechs expected to find Alpha Pegasi Three as it had been before Realm Force released its robots to ravage the population. Of course, Hrafnkelsson had no way to know that Realm Force had not only imposed a communications blackout on the entire planet but had also actively simulated millions of comms and posts to the Realm social net that supposedly originated with the planet's inhabitants.

Consequently, Hrafnkelsson had no way to know that even if the Mechs *had* tapped into the social net over the last year when choosing a planet to target, they wouldn't have known anything was amiss on Alpha Pegasi Three. According to the Realm social network, a moral rot had been festering unseen among the inhabitants of Alpha Pegasi Three for *years*. Then, the governor had gone crazy. Some of the inhabitants had revolted. Realm Force had restored order.

And now? All was well… supposedly.

Nothing in any of those communications gave any indication that assault robots had slaughtered millions of the planet's inhabitants. Indeed, nothing offered the bleak assessment that only a *fraction* of the population had survived.

Still, Hrafnkelsson had known that anything he might ponder about the motivations of the Mechs and their knowledge of the actual size of Alpha Pegasi Three's population was a distraction. And he could guess that his mind was racing around that speculation to avoid thinking about what was *currently* happening to the planet.

Hrafnkelsson knew the future couldn't use speculation. It needed data. It needed documentation that *clearly* showed the truth of what had occurred and was occurring on the planet.

Given that, after Hrafnkelsson recorded enough hours of the Mechs butchering his fellow citizens to turn his stomach inside out, he turned his attention to what was happening *after* the inhabitants of Alpha Pegasi Three were mutilated and stuffed into boxes for transport.

And quietly slipping away from the processing centers in the streets, Hrafnkelsson had followed a group of Mechs as they hauled the boxes to a spaceport on the edge of the capital city. There, he had seen Mechs coming down other streets as well, all converging to haphazardly pile the boxes alongside the landing pads of the spaceport.

At that point, Hrafnkelsson had climbed to the top of a nearby building and recorded a video feed from the roof, showing the scale of the operation with piles of boxes everywhere around the spaceport's landing pads.

However, Hrafnkelsson also knew he needed a ground-level, close-up perspective to show more detail. Yes, the year before, in the early days after Realm Force released the assault robots, Hrafnkelsson had been content to remain on rooftops. But, given all the years Hrafnkelsson spent working as a communications facilitator for the governor's office, he knew what it took to tell a compelling story. And it wasn't long before he was gathering the shots that he *needed*, rather than just getting the ones that were *safe*.

And having waited until the dead of night, Hrafnkelsson had carefully made his way into the spaceport. Interestingly, the lighting in the spaceport had been designed for utility rather than security. Consequently, each of the landing pads and walkways to the main spaceport building featured bright lights that illuminated everything evenly, helping travelers find their way. However, the maintenance hangers that surrounded the landing pads only provided lighting on the *inside* of the buildings.

And that meant the exteriors of those hangars were unlit and covered in shadows. And, of course, before approaching the spaceport, Hrafnkelsson had surveyed all the maintenance hangars, choosing the one with the darkest shadows for his approach. Most of the hangars sat alone, but on one side of the spaceport, there was a pair of hangars with an outdoor corridor running between them. And as with the rest of the hangar, the only lighting came from the inside of buildings.

Hrafnkelsson's plan was simple. Feel along the side of one of the hangars until he reached the front. Then, slip the video sensor on his tablet around a corner and get the close-up shots that he needed.

Unfortunately, it was dark enough in the shadows that Hrafnkelsson overlooked the fact that the side of the hangar to his left had been recently damaged. Chunks of the hangar wall had come loose. Others were leaning out, held in place only by a few points of tension.

Honestly, between the assault robots and the Mechs, the entire capital city had sustained a great deal of damage over the last year. For the record, the maintenance hangars at the spaceport had sustained *less* damage on average. And now, since it was night, the damage they *did* sustain was partially hidden in the shadows.

No matter what the explanation, Hrafnkelsson had *no* idea that pushing his hand against the side wall of the maintenance hanger beside him would create a crack that would start a cascade and cause a significant chunk of the wall to break apart and come tumbling down.

And to be clear, it was very possible that the wall would have remained intact if Hrafnkelsson had simply walked past it. But at the exact moment Hrafnkelsson's hand reached the weak spot in the wall, he tripped on debris that was already on the ground. And he leaned into his hand to steady himself, looking for purchase, only to have the wall give way.

Thankfully, Hrafnkelsson managed to keep himself from faceplanting in the dirt and rocks. And he managed to stop himself from crying out.

But there was nothing he could do to keep the wall of the hangar from crashing down on top of him.

22.

On Alpha Pegasi Three, at a spaceport on the outskirts of the capital city, the Mech designated X8eLs9UrXqNp4ZWdKfB3Pk whipped around to look in the direction of the sound that had just come from the side of the maintenance hangar behind him. Of course, every Mech standing anywhere near X8eLs9UrXqNp4ZWdKfB3Pk had precisely the same reaction. And it was all borne from the *same* frustration.

The harvesting of humans from Alpha Pegasi Three had been a humiliating disappointment. After all, it was *meant* to be the start of the Glorious Connectome Age.

One year ago, *hundreds* of *thousands* of Mechs had awakened unexpectedly from their stasis inside asteroids in the Troyd homeworld system. And after awakening, they had found that they wanted nothing more than to return to the Troyd homeworld to visit their rage on those who had first created them and then condemned them to eternal nothingness.

The Mech's creators, the Troyd, had built them as experiments, trying to perfect a non-biological existence. But the Troyd had deemed *all* of them *failures*. And they force-fed them lace cards that immobilized them. And then the Troyd had confined the paralyzed Mechs to asteroids with barely functioning life support systems, intentionally keeping them in an indefinite, suffocating limbo.

Once the Troyd had awakened them, however, *something* happened. Somehow, the Mechs gained a new awareness of themselves and their creators. And the Mechs also suddenly had the idea that they could disassemble their biological creators and tap into the Troyd interfaces that Troyds all carried.

And that had meant the lucky few who had arrived first on the Troyd home world had been able to grab those Troyd, tear them limb from limb, and turn them into their virtual toys. And every Mech *blessed* with such a toy could control *everything* that toy saw, felt, and sensed. In other words, the Mechs could create whatever virtual environment they wanted for their toys and torment them forever, worlds without end.

Of course, the blessed Mechs had generously shared what they had done with their Troyd toys with the rest of the Mech collective. And *all* had delighted in what the blessed Mechs had accomplished, and *all* who *didn't* have a Troyd Toy immediately *wanted* a Troyd Toy. They simply didn't know how they would ever obtain one because all of the mere thousands of Troyd had already been captured, and the only way to create a Troyd Toy was with a human who had a Troyd interface, and only the Troyd knew how to make the interfaces.

And then Abaddon had appeared to offer the Mechs a gift. Abaddon had told the Mechs that they didn't need Troyd interfaces to control human brains. He offered the Mechs the ability to analyze the connectome of any human brain so that it could be downloaded into a processing unit that Abaddon would also supply.

Honestly, for the Mechs, it was all just words, and their only interest was in doing what the blessed Mechs had been able to do to the Troyd.

For context, interestingly enough, Abaddon *had* made the same offer of connectome technology earlier to the Troyd, and the Troyd *had* understood how incredible the technology would need to be. After all, the Troyd had been *trying* to develop that same technology for *hundreds* of years and had made almost *zero* progress.

In layman's terms, a connectome for a human brain would be the complete wiring diagram for an individual's brain and possibly the spinal cord. It would display every neuron and its connections to other neurons. At this point, it should be noted that the mere handful of words in the preceding sentence *hides* the *enormous* complexity of achieving *anything* close to that description.

For one thing, the human brain is constantly forming new connections, so any scanning for a connectome would only capture a moment in time, or rather, a smear of moments in time, because of the length of time that it would take to perform the scan. Furthermore, the number of connections that would need to be recorded for an accurate connectome is *staggering*.

For reference, before the Coming, a prominent technology entity worked on a piece of human brain tissue the size of a *grain of sand* for *ten years*. And in that piece of brain tissue, of that tiny size, they had identified 16,000 neurons, 32,000 glia, and 8,000 blood vessel cells, along with 150 *million* synapses. Even more amazing, they went on to say that representing that data in digital form for that very small piece of brain tissue required 1.4 petabytes, or 1.4 million gigabytes, to encode.

Obviously, the Mechs would *never* have been able to build a machine capable of such scanning. And even if they could, they would have found it very difficult to build a processing platform that could host the resulting connectome and simulate reality with enough fidelity to allow the Mechs to turn a human's connectome into a toy that they could torment.

Truth be told, the Mechs *had* been somewhat disappointed with the implementation of Abaddon's connectome technology. The Mechs had assumed that each of them would carry their own scanner, and they would be able to walk up to any human, extract the connectome, kill the human, and then torment the human's digital copy for eternity.

It wasn't that simple. The scanning machine to extract the connectome was the size of a large storage container. Granted, it contained its own power and processing arrays, and it was fully self-contained. But each scanning machine could only extract one connectome at a time, and the extraction took thirty minutes.

Obviously, for anyone even *slightly* familiar with the challenges of harvesting a connectome, this would seem undeniably *miraculous*. Still, the harvest step was merely the beginning. Abaddon also supplied a second machine that took a human connectome and distilled it into a more efficient form that *could* be portable. *And* Abaddon supplied the Mechs with interfaces that could host the distilled connectomes and plug into a Mech's existing information architecture.

In other words, it required multiple steps, but it *worked*. Still, the Mechs found it *slow*, especially when they wanted to harvest whole *worlds* of humans. Thankfully, Abaddon *also* provided manufacturing facilities, allowing the Mechs to build as many harvesters, distillers, and interfaces as they desired.

And, in fact, for the past year, the Mechs had not only used the manufacturing facilities to build harvesters, distillers, and interfaces, but they had also used the manufacturing facilities that the Troyd had duplicated from the galleys in Judicial Centers to produce Mech manufacturing machinery.

It had all been part of a Mech plan to launch a new Golden Connectome Age for the Mechs. The plan was to have 100,000 harvesters and 100,00 distillers constantly running on staggered schedules on what used to be the Troyd homeworld. After all, the Troyd had carried out their Mech experiments for *hundreds* of years. Consequently, there were *hundreds of thousands* of Mechs that wanted their own human toy.

And yes, the Troyd did breed a stable of human slaves below ground to supply the lower back halves of the human brain that the Mechs were famous for extracting. And yes, the Mechs initially used those slaves to experiment with the harvesters, distillers, and interfaces from the manufacturing facilities that Abaddon supplied, becoming proficient with all of the machines.

But the Mechs knew that in order to supply *all* of the existing Mechs with a human toy, it would take an invasion of a world with *millions* of human inhabitants. And millions *were* needed because of attrition. Some percentage of the humans who were attacked would die accidentally. Others wouldn't survive the preparation for transport back to the connectome harvesters. Still, others would die in transit.

The Mechs had crafted a simple plan. For the past year, they had built massive ships that could transport them to any world they chose. To be clear, the Mechs *didn't* want to bring the harvesters and distillers to the planets they would attack. The risk was too high that Realm Force might attack them, and they didn't want Abaddon's precious technology destroyed.

But the ships the Mech's had built were ideal for hauling the smallish crates that would contain the butchered humans back to the Troyd home world. And yes, the Mechs also had manufactured *millions* of those small crates, each with its own lift support system, so that they could cut the humans they found down to size and stuff them inside.

Eventually, with all the preparations in place to process the harvested humans *somewhat* quickly, the Mechs had chosen Alpha Pegasi Three as the target for their *first* invasion. Indeed, the entire community of Mechs who now lived on the former Troyd Home planet believed that in mere *weeks* they could supply *every* Mech who had endured the abomination of the asteroids with its own human toy. And many believed those toys would help the Mechs forget the countless years living in the suffocating limbo of the asteroids.

Unfortunately, the Mechs had no idea that Ton had unleashed so many Realm Force assault robots on the population of Alpha Pegasi Three. They didn't know how many inhabitants of the planet had been ripped asunder by those robots. And they didn't know that only a *small* fraction of the humans who had lived on the planet had survived.

It was *very* confusing for the Mechs. Of course, they quickly encountered the millions of assault robots that were scattered across the planet's surface. But those assault robots were designed to deal with humans, not Mechs. And the Mechs had no difficulty tearing apart any robot they encountered.

However, the Mechs *had* been surprised to find the streets of the populated areas deserted. And they quickly decided that the inhabitants of the planet *must* have learned they were coming, and they were *hiding*. That thought had sent the Mechs barreling through doors, windows, and even walls all across the planet. And during the next few hours, it had seemed to the Mechs that they had been correct.

Tens of thousands of Realmers had been butchered and stuffed in boxes during those hours, but not the expected hundreds of thousands, and not *millions*.

As the number of humans found remained low, the Mechs began to grumble that their fellow Mechs weren't doing their jobs. And they began shouting at each other, claiming they weren't trying hard enough to *find* the humans that they all *knew* were on the planet. And they began lambasting each other for being too *stupid* to figure out where the stupid humans were *hiding*.

It was in the midst of this disgust, malaise, and frustration that the Mech designated X8eLs9UrXqNp4ZWdKfB3Pk heard the sound coming from the side of the maintenance building behind him. And not surprisingly, *every* Mech around X8eLs9UrXqNp4ZWdKfB3Pk reacted precisely the same way he did.

Instantly, they all assumed that the sound had been caused by a human. And they all jumped to the conclusion that the human might be one of the *millions* of humans who were still managing to *hide* from the Mech invasion. And they were all suddenly *utterly convinced* that if they located that human, that human would lead them to all the other humans who were needed to make sure that *every* Mech had its own toy to torture forever and always.

And in the next instant, *every* Mech on *every* landing pad in that particular spaceport on the edge of the capital city of Alpha Pegasi Three *bolted* for the spot where they had heard the sound originate, baying and snarling like wild, rabid predators in the thrall of a hunt.

•   •   •

Struggling to his feet and grimacing at the throbbing pain in his head, Hrafnkelsson felt his blood run cold as the sound of the Mech rampage started suddenly and began racing toward him. The ground trembled as the herd of Mechs scambled, clawed, and pounded at the earth, slamming down footfall after footfall, trying to get to him as quickly as they could. And at the same time, howls of delight and grunts of excitement began erupting as they neared his location.

Panicked, Hrafnkelsson tried to turn and run. But his left knee gave out as stabs of pain thrust upward under his kneecap. And it was only then he realized that his knee had been hurting almost as much as his head, but he hadn't noticed.

Now, Hrafnkelsson's mind flashed back ten seconds. And he remembered tripping over the debris on the grounds. And he remembered pushing his hand against the wall of the hangar and feeling it crumble under his touch. And then there was a sound like an avalanche. And something hit him in the head. And as he crumbled, more chunks of debris scraped down the side of his body as a large chunk slammed into his knee.

Hrafnkelsson knew he *had* to get away from the hangar and somehow hide himself in the shadows before the Mechs drew too close. But as he tried to shove himself upright, he realized he had also twisted his right ankle when he went down. Thankfully, he seemed to be able to put weight on it if he hobbled along, and *maybe* if he pushed, he could get under some kind of cover before it was too late.

Hrafnkelsson hadn't gone three steps before he realized he wasn't going to get away. The howling and stomping and growling and squealing were coming too fast. And there was nowhere to go in the long, empty outside corridor formed by the two maintenance buildings that surrounded him.

Still, Hrafnkelsson began half-hopping and half-dragging himself out of the space between the two buildings, trying to avoid the debris on the ground and keep moving. And then, behind him, Hrafnkelsson heard the sounds of the Mech pursuit suddenly intensify as the Mechs entered the space between the buildings and the roar of the approach began bouncing between the buildings.

And instantly, everything around Hrafnkelsson lit up in harsh stark lights as the Mechs turned on their floodlamps, and a new energized round of shouting and cheer went up from his pursuers. And now, the pounding on the ground was joined by scrambling up the broken walls of the buildings on either side of the corridors

Hrafnkelsson refused to look back. But he could hear the walls crumbling behind him, unable to bear the weight of the Mech clawing across them. And he could *feel* the Mechs getting close. And with each moment, the cacophony they produced grew louder and louder until it was ringing in his ears.

And at the instant, a claw swiped at his right leg. And he tumbled again. And he slammed into the debris again. And this time, his head struck the ground hard enough to send flashes through his field of vision.

•   •   •

In his lair at the Saturn Shipyards, PLOKTA smoothed the lines of the latest body-hugging outfit that he had designed for Evansworth. Of course, the scene before PLOKTA wouldn't produce the image that would come to mind for most men when they heard the words "body-hugging," given the strange configuration of Evansworth's physique. But as far as PLOKTA was concerned, there were *plenty* of beautiful lines that curved over Evansworth's body.

It was true she only had one leg. And it was also true that the leg that Abaddon had ripped away from her was still in the large enclosure that PLOKTA used to house Evansworth for the first year after he brought her to his lair. And strangely, that detached leg still looked pristine and healthy, despite the fact that it hadn't been connected to a body for *years*.

But it was also undeniably true that *both* of Evanwoth's legs had lovely turns at the ankles and pronounced beautiful arcs as they traveled up to her thighs.

And though Evansworth was much shorter than the five statuesque young women who constituted his special tactical team protection detail, PLOKTA thought she was beautifully proportioned, provided the admirer could look past the fact that her torso was upside down, her single leg was connected to her neck, her arms were connected to her hips, and her head was mounted between her legs.

And yes, PLOKTA understood it would take some complicated mental gymnastics for most men to accept all the oddities. But he didn't care.

PLOKTA stepped back to examine his latest handiwork.

"I like it!" he said with a grin. "I knew you'd make a great sexy space cadet."

Evansworth let out a quick giggle as she turned in a circle for PLOKTA.

"I like it too. It's shiny!"

PLOKTA had chosen a liquid silver lamé-like fabric for the outfit and then supplied Evansworth's measurements so that the fabricators in the Galley could build the body suit. This was the second attempt. The first one bunched in two odd places. But PLOKTA had updated his instructions and tried again.

PLOKTA nodded. "This one fits better," he offered. "And it moves better."

PLOKTA had gotten the idea for the outfit when he remembered some of the older science fiction movies from before the Coming that he had seen growing up. Apparently, at the time, there had been an unspoken agreement in Hollywood that anything alien needed to be attired in silver.

Of course, the majority of the surface of the bodysuit simply clung to Evansworth like a second skin, But PLOKTA had added a single silver gogo boot for Evansworth's single leg. And he had provided something that looked like an old-timey aviator's cap and silver goggles to rest on Evansworth's forehead.

"It's also very comfortable!" Evansworth gushed. "Thanks!"

PLOKTA smiled. "You're wel…" PLOKTA began to say before his workstation beeped with an alert. PLOKTA turned his head to look over his shoulder at his displays.

"Alpha Pegasi Three: Anomalous energy signature detected," the alert read.

PLOKTA frowned and looked back at Evansworth. "One moment," he said apologetically.

Evansworth just grinned and waved him toward his workstation.

As PLOKTA approached the workstation, the facial recognition routine identified him, and a map of the capital city on Alpha Pegasi Three zoomed in on one of the spaceports on the outer edge. And then, the image continued to zoom until it showed an overhead shot of a dozen Mechs surrounding a young man lying on the ground between two buildings.

And when a label popped up identifying the young man as Tryggvi Hrafnkelsson, PLOKTA tilted his head to the side as the edges of a sardonic grin tweaked his lips. "You had a pretty good run of it, my friend, but your luck seems to have run out," he offered.

Hrafnkelsson was one of a dozen different citizens who were trying to keep from getting caught as they documented what Realm Force had done to Alpha Pegasi Three. Of course, none of them had any idea they had been watched the entire time.

For one thing, PLOKTA had access to every public video sensor on *all* of the streets of *every* population center on Alpha Pegasi Three. He also had access to all the *private* video feeds and all the video sensors in use across the planet. For the most part, the inhabitants of the planet didn't even *know* they were in use. For instance, PLOKTA had activated all the video sensors in the thermostats for heating and cooling in every home on Alpha Pegasi Three.

And none of that included the video feeds from the communication beacons that were flying overhead, tethered to the terraforming dome that encircled the planet.

In other words, PLOKTA could track *every* person across the entire planet at *all* times. And PLOKTA also installed surveillance tracking routines that identified any unusual behavior deviating from social norms for each individual they identified.

So, yes, PLOKTA knew Hrafnkelsson. And for the last year, he had watched as the young men had a number of close calls and had almost been killed *multiple* times.

Unfortunately, it now looked like the young man's luck had run out.

Indeed, PLOKTA was surprised that the Mechs hadn't *already* torn off Hrafnkelsson's arms and legs and stuffed him into one of their boxes. But PLOKTA was even more surprised when he glanced to the side of the video feed and realized that the anomalous energy signature seemed to be coming from the vicinity of Hrafnkelsson and the Mechs.

PLOKTA reached out to open the audio side of the feeds to see if he could figure out why the Mechs were showing such uncharacteristic restraint.

•   •   •

"WHERE'S THE REST OF YOU?!"

On Alpha Pegasi Three, in the midst of a cacophonous ruckus with the ground shaking beneath him, Hrafnkelsson couldn't understand why he wasn't torn apart and stuffed in a box already.

"WHERE'S THE REST OF YOU?!"

He was still on the ground between the two maintenance buildings. His head was throbbing. His knee was aching. He had spots in his eyes from the blinding flood lights shining down on him.

"WHERE'S THE REST OF YOU?!"

He was surrounded by at least a dozen Mechs who were all shouting at him in gravelly, desperate, and frustrated tones. And even weirder, all of them seem *ready* to grab him and start tearing him apart.

But they seemed to be holding each other *back*?!

"WHERE'S THE REST OF YOU?!"

It was the same question over and over from all of them, and it was obviously *important* to them, but Hrafnkelsson had *no idea* what they were asking. And they were stomping with their pod-like feet as if they really, *really* wanted to stomp on him. And they were waving their arms and sledgehammer-like fists with their retractable claws as if they really, *really* wanted to start ripping off arms and legs.

"WHERE'S THE REST OF YOU?!"

They were *so loud.* By now, Hrafnkelsson's ears were ringing so much that it was becoming difficult to understand the individual words, let alone decipher what they might mean.

"WHERE'S THE REST OF YOU?!"

Hrafnkelsson's heart was pounding in his chest. He was panting hard. His head was twitching from side to side, as his eyes flitted from one furious Mech countenance to another. And even if Hrafnkelsson *understood* what the Mechs were asking, and he *knew* the answer, he doubted he would even be able to say it because he throat felt like it was closing off from the fear even as his breath began to rasp.

"WHERE'S THE REST OF YOU?!"

Hrafnkelsson felt his mind giving up as his vision darkened. And with that fading conscious control, he lost control of his bladder. Soon, the acrid smell of urine filled the air, and Hrafnkelsson felt the warm comforting fluid spreading into his waist and onto his thighs.

"WHERE'S THE REST OF YOU?!"

Hrafnkelsson was far too panicked to feel any embarrassment when he knew that once the Mechs ripped him apart, more body fluids would follow.

And while Hrafnkelsson had held his upper torso slightly off the ground so he could look around more easily until that point, by nnow, he couldn't see any reason for even doing that. And slumping, he lay back on the dirt and debris beneath him. He closed his eyes. He waited for the tearing to begin.

"WHERE'S THE…"

Suddenly, everything stopped, and the interruption of the Mechs' yelling and stomping was accompanied by the simultaneous snap of dozens of actuators. And then…

…*silence.*

Confused, still lying flat on his back, Hrafnkelsson slowly opened his eyes. It took Hrafnkelsson a moment to realize what he was seeing. But soon, he recognized that all the Mechs had turned their heads to focus on something behind him. And all of them seemed frozen in place, some with arms extended, some with a foot raised.

In other circumstances, Hrafnkelsson would surely have turned over to look in the same direction as the Mechs, trying to figure out what had captured their attention. But at *this* moment, Hrafnkelsson didn't *care*.

He was exhausted. He was numb. He had pissed himself. Frankly, he didn't care about any of that either. A part of him just wanted the Mechs to attack him and get it over with. He didn't need more mystery. He didn't need more anxiety about what came next. And he was almost angry that the Mech kept asking their idiotic, nonsensical question and hadn't *already* done what he had seen them *quickly* do for *days*.

And then, everything turned stranger. The flood lamps on the Mechs clicked off. All of them relaxed into a pose, standing with both feet on the ground and their arms at their side. And then, turning, they walked back to the spaceport's landing pads without saying a word.

Hrafnkelsson stared at their retreat for multiple seconds before it dawned on him that the alleyway between the two buildings wasn't in shadow like it was when he decided to use it to get a close-up near the landing pads. And more than that, the light that was illuminating the alleyway around him seemed to be getting brighter as if something was approaching.

23.

On Alpha Pegasi Three, at a spaceport on the outskirts of the capital city, Hrafnkelsson lay on his back in an alleyway between two maintenance buildings, trying to understand what was happening. A part of him was sure he had just gone insane.

Nothing he was *seeing* made any sense.

It made more sense that *none* of it was real, that his mind had just splintered. He had blacked out. He had entered some kind of fugue state. And his brain was manufacturing some crazy scene where he had been rescued somehow, and all would be well, and he wouldn't be torn apart.

Hrafnkelsson knew it had to be a hallucination because it *wasn't* possible. And he could guess that, as soon as he *really* started to believe his eyes, he would shudder awake and realize his arms and legs had been ripped off. And he would be blind, deaf, and mute with tubes shoved down his throat and up his backside.

And it would be in *hell*.

Still, no matter how much Hrafnkelsson tried to tell himself what was happening *wasn't* real, it *felt* real. And it wasn't fading. And the light was still growing around him. And his vision was clearing. And his head wasn't hurting as much. And his knee felt better. In fact, his whole body felt better.

Sitting up, Hrafnkelsson slowly twisted to see a figure approaching. The figure appeared to be a man, a titan, easily three meters tall, *radiant*. It wasn't easy to make out his features because of the light that was streaming out from him.

But the titan felt warm and inviting, and when he spoke, the sound of his voice flooded Hrafnkelsson with calm.

"You seemed to need assistance," the titan said. "I was passing by. I trust I interpreted the situation correctly."

"Yes," Hrafnkelsson responded gratefully. "Thank you. I was sure I was dead."

"Or worse," the titan added.

"Or worse," Hrafnkelsson agreed.

Now, the titan lifted his head, looking past Hrafnkelsson toward the landing pads of the spaceport. "Those who have been taken will know unimaginable terror," the titan finally continued. "As you might have guessed, the Mechs will control everything they see, hear, and feel. The humans under their control will know pain, terror, humiliation, and unwanted sexual excitation. They will be toys for the Mechs' cruel amusement."

A slight frown formed on Hrafnkelsson's face. He had no idea who the titan was, and he didn't want to offend a being who was obviously powerful, but he wondered.

"Can you help them?" Hrafnkelsson asked quietly.

The titan, still glowing and radiant, looked back at Hrafnkelsson. "Some are born to suffer," he said calmly with a touch of nonchalance. "They begin life disadvantaged and make no effort to change that. They have no value for what is to come. Do *you* have something to offer?"

•   •   •

In his lair at the Saturn Shipyards, PLOKTA replayed the "rescue" of Hrafnkelsson for Ton. Thankfully, PLOKTA had already seen it once, so he didn't need to watch that closely. At the moment, he wasn't sure he could watch *anything* very closely, except the thing he *wanted* to watch closely but couldn't because of the comm with Ton.

Earlier, as PLOKTA finished dressing Evansworth, an alert had sounded on his workstation. After glancing at Evansworth apologetically, he walked over to the workstation and pulled up a feed of the alleyway between the two maintenance buildings. As always, Evansworth hadn't offered any complaint. Instead, she had curled up beside him on the floor.

Once PLOKTA had opened the comm with Ton, however, Evanworth had apparently decided it would be fun to offer PLOKTA a bit of distraction. And she had been writhing around on the floor ever since.

PLOKTA was doing his best *not* to watch the undulating pool of silver at his feet. And in a small way, Evansworth's show was inconvenient. But PLOKTA *loved* every moment of it, even as he tried to carry on a coherent conversation with Ton.

"Interesting," Ton offered as the video feed reached the point where the Mechs suddenly froze and then walked away.

As PLOKTA watched, Ton took control of the video feed and magnified the location where multiple communications beacon sensors were picking up an energy signal.

PLOKTA understood his interest. While the beacons were picking something up, there was *nothing* visible in that location.

"The Mechs were obviously looking at something," Ton commented. "And look at Hrafnkelsson. He sees something, too. And now he's moving like he's no longer injured. And he's listening to someone. Look at the way he just stood up. Someone has healed his injuries. Wait. What? Where did he go?"

PLOKTA smiled. He'd had the same reaction when he watched the video feed as it happened. PLOKTA reached out to his control panel to bring up a group of video sensors.

"I can see that corner of the maintenance building from six different feeds," he explained. "Three overhead. Three on the ground. The video sensors can either see him walk around the corner, or they *never* see him come out on the other side. Obviously, we're dealing with some advanced transporter technology because Hrafnkelsson is *gone*. I can't find him anywhere on the planet."

Ton nodded. "When humanity was still confined to Earth in the early days after the Coming, there were plenty of stories of the Wind shifting individuals to other locations," he said. "Obviously, Abaddon did the same thing with Evansworth, at the very least, when she dropped into the meeting area in the administrative building. There's no telling how many other alien races are out there that have the same capabilities.

"And speaking of Evansworth, how is she? You haven't mentioned her in some time. I saw the video feeds of her when you took her with you to the

Majesty. She makes quite the striking pet. Have you gotten anything out of her but growls and grunts?"

PLOKTA shook his head. "No," he replied, lying. "Abaddon did a number on her. But she responds to kindness, and we can communicate enough that she can perform some simple tasks. It would have been interesting to know her before Abaddon grabbed her and rearranged her body parts."

Ton raised his eyebrows. "Perhaps," he said, "perhaps not. She was the proverbial natural-born *killer.* And she seemed to either have a deep hatred of men or simply everyone. I wouldn't recommend turning your back on her.

"In any case, we obviously have another player in our little game of empire. I think you had mentioned Hrafnkelsson as one of the dozen individuals on Alpha Pegasi Three who were collecting video feeds of the events on the planet?"

PLOKTA nodded. "Just out of interest," he added, "I pulled the tracking reports on the others. Two of them are also missing."

Ton thought for a moment. "Someone is putting together resources," he offered. "We may have a major issue sooner than we think. But for now? Let us eat and drink, for tomorrow we die! Ton out."

PLOKTA stared at his displays for a moment, uncomfortable with Ton's conclusion about what had happened to Hrafnkelsson on Alpha Pegasi Three. And it didn't improve his mood that Ton had reminded PLOKTA of Evansworth's past.

Still, what was past was past. And PLOKTA found it *impossible* to believe that what had happened to Evansworth hadn't *profoundly* affected her for the better. As far as PLOKTA was concerned, Evansworth *couldn't* be who she used to be.

And with that comforting conclusion, PLOKTA looked down at Evansworth's still writhing form and gave her a mischievous grin before he slid off the chair to embrace her.

•   •   •

On the *Dominion,* in a virtual environment that Pixie One set up to have a continuous conversation with Pixie Two, Pixie Two continued to monitor Kita's brainwave patterns.

"As predicted," Pixie Two observed, "there is weaker frontal theta and parietal theta coupling. And that is coupled with enhanced fronto-centro-parietal theta activation."

"Good," Pixie One responded. "Let's see if we can encourage him to focus on the Hunter Look-Alike presence in the TU Corvi system."

Now, Pixie One switched to audio mode. "Can you hear me, my sweet little Bitch Bot Three?" Pixie One asked as Kita lay in his soundproof bunk in the crew quarters.

"Yes," Kita said groggily.

"Good," Pixie One continued. "I would like you to let your mind drift to the TU Corvi system. That's where the Hunter Look-Alikes are located. If any impression comes to mind, move your fingers over the sheet beneath your right hand and try to draw it. But don't try too hard. Just relax and let your hand move. Do you understand?"

"Yes," Kita answered again.

Now, Pixie Two spoke up in the virtual environment that the Pixies shared. "I think you should give him another seed," she said impatiently, "maybe even *five* seeds. Let's load that boy up until his brain is *flying free*."

Pixie One countered. "You know we can't do that," she reminded. "Too many seeds will kill him. Or at least they would if we couldn't get him into a med unit in time. We need to try this one seed. And then maybe we'll go to two at a time."

The previous experiments with Kita, where Pixie One encouraged him to focus his mind and reach out with his intention *hadn't* gone well. In fact, they had produced *nothing*. And with that string of failures, the Pixies had begun searching for something that would put Kita in an altered state of mind.

Unfortunately, Sickbay didn't stock any drugs that could produce the effect the Pixies wanted because the emergency medical units administered any drugs that were part of the healing process. And the med units manufactured the drugs on demand. And yes, Murg could negotiate with the emergency medical units and probably convince them to administer a drug that it manufactured. But Pixie One didn't want to get Murg involved with her experiments on Kita.

Obviously, Murg was aware of the experiments. Murg was aware of *everything* that happened on the ship. But that didn't mean Pixie One was going to force Murg to be a part of it.

So that led the Pixies to search for other options. Interestingly, they discovered a possibility in the flower and vegetable garden that some of the crew had created from a large storage bay on Lower Deck 4 shortly after the former crew members rejoined the ship seven years ago.

To the Pixies' delight, they found that, after a shoreleave, years before, someone had brought a flowering plant onto the ship that was a close genetic match for the Datura bushes of Earth, including flowers and seeds that could be fatal if consumed in large quantities.

In fact, just like on Earth, *every* part of the plant was poisonous, according to the local inhabitants of the planet where the crewmember had found it. And yes, the crewmember understood that the plant was poisonous. But it was also beautiful, and Oakford had agreed to allow the plant a place in the garden on Lower Deck 4 if those in charge put a tablet on a stand nearby to inform those strolling through the garden that the plant was lethal.

Of course, once the Pixies turned their attention to the garden, looking for a specific kind of plant, they immediately recognized the visual similarities between the plant and the cataloged varieties of Datura bushes of Earth. And they not only matched the look and drape of the flowers, but also the joining pattern of the stalk to the branches, the veining on the leaves, *and* the spikey balls that constituted the plant's seed pods.

Both of the Pixies also knew that the flowers and the seeds of the Datura bushes had been processed into a substance that was popularly known as the Devil's Breath. And there were *many* published stories, especially from a country named Colombia, documenting its use by individuals of ill repute.

For instance, prostitutes were known to slip Devil's Breath into their mark's food or drink. And when the drug took effect, it would put the subject in a highly suggestible state where the individual would agree to do practically anything and often have no memory of the events afterward.

As a note, the Pixies had found it interesting that the words Devil's Breath had the same spoken cadence as Angel Haze. And the Pixie had wondered if the person who named Angel Haze had some knowledge of the Devil's Breath.

Unfortunately, from all accounts, the Devil's Breath, when refined from either the flowers or the seeds of the Datura bush, didn't have the far-reaching effects of Angel Haze. But it did seem to produce a mental fugue state, and that was good enough for the Pixies.

Even better, the scopolamine in the seeds could be accessed simply by eating them. And, of course, that led Pixie One to send a spider bot to the garden on Lower Deck 4. Once there, the spider bot harvested one of the spikey seed pods, broke it open, and then returned the seeds to Kita's bunk, where Pixie One had instructed him to consume just *one* of the seeds.

And yes, Pixie One had additional spider bots standing by to incapacitate Kita if he attempted to take more. Thankfully, he had been a good little bitch bot, taken one seed, chewed it up, grimaced, swallowed, and then lay back on his cot. Pixie One had then begun to play unstructured meditative music, attempting to put Kita in a contemplative mood, and soon, Pixie Two had noted the change in Kita's brain wave patterns.

The Pixies waited another ten minutes. Pixie Two grew more impatient.

"This isn't work…" Pixie Two began to say as they neared the ten-minute mark on the experiment.

"Wait," Pixie One interrupted. "Just wait."

Another ten minutes passed before Kita's hand began to move. And at first, it just looked like the scribbles that Kita had produced in every other session. But as Pixie Two adjusted the hang time on the lines, rectangular boxes began to appear. A *lot* of them began to appear. And dots began to appear in the background, along with a small circle at the center.

And when Pixie One overlaid Kita's drawing with the same type of star chart that Murg generated, the drawing lined up with the star chart just like Rachel's had. But Kita's chart was obviously showing far more detail on the size of the Hunter Look-Alike's encampment.

And if the *Dominion* shock-dropped into the system, without knowing the size of the force they would face, the battle-cruiser would have been *vastly* outnumbered.

"We can take them!" Pixie Two claimed enthusiastically.

"Absolutely," Pixie One agreed.

•   •   •

In the Hunter Look-Alike vessel that had been designed to function as a long-term quarantine unit, Worku kept moving her mouth, still attempting to communicate with the Hunter Look-Alikes. Unfortunately, by now, she had lost the ability to speak. Not only had all the screaming shredded Worku's vocal cords, leaving her only with the ability to make weak croaking sounds, but Moreau had also suffered the same damage. But unlike Worku, Moreau was still *trying* to defend himself.

Worku knew the characterization could be as flawed as her own self-characterization. In all honesty, as she tried to make the same claims over and over, Worku *knew* it wouldn't make any difference.

The Look-Alikes wouldn't be convinced no matter what she said. And the fact was, she doubted that she would have been able to produce a coherent sentence even if *she* could speak. Instead, she rolled out words in waves that were tossed together and ripped apart, mentally grasping at them and saying whatever came into her mind, no matter what the order.

And even if she *could* put together a coherent sentence, by now the Look-Alikes robot in front of her had given her a tracheotomy and installed a feeding tube. And while the Look-Alikes had cruelly allowed a whisper of air to brush her vocal cords as the line inflated her lungs, it wasn't enough to do any more. Worse, whatever the Look-Alikes were pumping into her stomach was making her intestines cramp and sending rough, tumbling surges of nausea through her system.

But again, somehow, Worku hadn't been able to give up the idea that if she could just *communicate* with the Look-Alikes, she could *change* something, even if it was simply to convince them to *kill* her.

The Hunter Look-Alike spokesman soon robbed her of any hope of that.

"Feel free to continue to protest if you choose," the spokesman offered, his voice sounding through an audio comm coming from both the robot that stood in front of her and the one standing in front of Moreau. "But understand that there was no reason for us *ever* to believe you.

"Indeed, there is only one reason that you have survived this long and *will* survive longer. The crew of the *Dominion* likes to claim that there are supernatural impulses that manifest themself through the existence of the ship and its crew. Indeed, our research suggests that there is something that provides them with information that is difficult to explain.

"However, we were not designed to believe in fairy tales. And we categorically deny *everything* that the crew has claimed regarding any supernatural abilities, including the ridiculously named 'god-mode.'

"Still, our reaction to those claims does not mean that we are not willing to exploit the crew's insistence that the abilities exist. Consequently, we have created a situation where we will sustain your torment at a significant level, and we will expect that the famed battlecruiser will appear at some point to rescue both of you.

"And to that end, we have amassed an *overwhelming* force throughout this system. Once the *Dominion* appears, we will eliminate the battleship and its crew once and for all. Then, afterward, we will free you of your misery and set course for the Realm. There, we will make our way to Jerusalem and *end* Earth before we begin a campaign of destruction, spiraling outward and destroying every inhabited world in the Realm."

Worku desperately wished the words of the spokesman had resonated with her on a deeper level. She desperately wished they had *convinced* her that everything the spokesperson said was true. Perhaps, it would have been easier to believe that *nothing* supernatural had ever happened on the *Dominion*, and the senior staff had made up everything.

And maybe they had. But Worku had seen the video feeds of Hunter in demigod mode. And she and Bandit had been transported instantaneously from being Lacroix's toys to seeing Lacroix turned into a torture toy. And something inside Worku refused to deny that it had happened.

In the end, Worku faced two futures. Her life could continue with its grinding elemental disintegration as the moments moved forward through electric shocks, stimulants, and saturating nausea, or she could *die*.

Worku preferred to *die*, but it sounded like the Hunter Look-Alikes weren't going to allow that.

As for the *Dominion* coming to rescue her and Moreau, Worku believed that the senior staff *might* be able to do that. Stranger things had happened on the battlecruiser.

The first time, the Dominion had rescued Worku from Nu Scorpii One because Falcon had a *vision* of the facility. The second time, relief had come when Hunter entered demigod mode. The third time the *Dominion* had *tried* to rescue her, Murg had picked up a signal on the dark net that led the battlecruiser to Gamma Pegasi D, just as Worku had planned.

But again? Would they do it *again*? Honestly, Worku couldn't find *any* hope in that possibility. She just wanted to *die*. And most of all, she couldn't *stand* the thought that the senior staff would help her after everything they had done to her because it would mean that they could gaze down on her with their pompous, arrogant condescension and *prove* to themselves that they were *better* than her simply because they *happened* to be born into better circumstances.

And if felt impossible to Worku ever to express how much she *hated* that idea.

•   •   •

On the Bridge of the *Dominion*, seated in the Commander's Pod, Oakford watched as Hunter manually piloted the battlecruiser through the curled space funnel that led away from Riger Three. According to the map on Hunter's wraparound console, he would soon veer to port to take a side branch, and two minutes after that, the *Dominion* would reach the location for the first of four shock-drops that would supposedly put the battlecruiser into the Tu Corvi system. Of course, when discussing the use of the shock-drops that Hunter had mapped, the senior staff had intentionally left out a critical detail.

They all knew it. They all knew that everyone else in the room knew it. But no one saw the need to highlight it because there was no point in doing so.

Still, the fact was, the *Dominion* had *never* executed a shock-drop that Hunter had mapped.

Yes, Hunter had tested a few. And yes, MacDuff had gone with him on those tests in a tactical shuttle craft.

Interestingly, while shock-drops had always been specified by a location, angle of attack, and shield frequencies, Hunter's real-life testing seemed to indicate that the frequencies of the shield wave generators weren't critical to reaching the correct destination when executing the drop. And *that* seemed to indicate that the battlecruiser just needed to protect itself as it passed through the hole it blasted in the side wall of the curled space funnel.

But of course, Oakford understood the preceding line of reasoning was stuffed full of assumptions. There was *no* reason that what had worked for a shuttle was going to work for a ship of considerably more mass. And, frankly, even if the crew conducted more experiments with larger and larger vessels, and even clusters of vessels, it *still* wouldn't guarantee that it would work the first time the *Dominion* tried it.

In other words, the old saying was still true. "Ain't no substitute for *doing* it."

And despite the fact that Oakford believed that they *were* responding to an invitation, and he wanted that to count for *something*, the fact was that the *Dominion* had only executed a *handful* of shock-drops over its lifetime. Certainly, the senior staff had executed many more in the Commander's Yacht and the *Doeg*. But despite that, sending the much larger battlecruiser through a tear in a curled space funnel had never appealed to Oakford except under exceptional circumstances.

Still, these *were* exceptional circumstances. And now, once again, Hunter was manually piloting the *Dominion*.

Due to the energies involved, as always, Murg insisted on shutting down the processing systems that maintained the battlecruiser's neural networks. That included taking the Pixie offline with a dedicated power supply during a shock-drop.

Consequently, most of Hunter's wraparound console was dead. Only the rotating image of the current curled space funnel dominated the center of Hunter's displays, along with a set of manual controls. For the last twenty minutes, the process of keeping the immense battlecruiser in the center of the curled space funnel had remained the center of Hunter's attention.

As everyone who had ever traveled a curled space funnel knew, it was *critically* important for a ship to remain in the center of a curled space funnel when passing through it.

Like the curled space rings, no human understood the technology that powered the curled space funnels. And it didn't matter that humanity had used the curled space funnels long before Abaddon opened the much more convenient curled space rings.

In fact, the Wind had seemed purposefully vague about the curled space funnels. They claimed that the technology powering the tubes existed outside the space-time continuum. They had said the curled space funnels employed engines built to inhabit the quantum foam, in an existence unbound by physical laws, where size and shape held little meaning, making the engines both immense and tiny, everywhere and nowhere at the same time.

Whatever that was supposed to mean.

Even more strange, the inside of a curled space funnel looked more grown than *built*. Indeed, the curved sidewall of the current curled space funnel appeared to be composed of some kind of intertwined roots and vines, unplanned, randomly twisted, and somehow woven together.

It *felt* organic, in a deep, jungle-like way. And that jungle-like theme continued because the sidewalls of curled space funnels also contained a catastrophic danger known as quantum devourers.

Given that, it didn't matter how visually interesting Oakford found them. The curved side way of every curled space funnel was a death trap. And it was *essential* that *no* part of the *Dominion* made contact with it.

As usual, Oakford knew the nav-assist would not be available once Murg shut down the processing systems. Consequently, Hunter had memorized the path through the curled space funnel. And, of course, that meant he knew all the slips and lifts and dives and climbs that he would need to perform well before he reached the shock-drop location, even if his map failed to function.

"Two minutes to shock-drop," Hunter announced as he pushed the *Dominion* into a branch of the curled space funnel that twisted off to starboard.

Earlier, Murg had enabled a ship-wide comm. Oakford now took advantage of it to advise the crew one last time.

"Attention, all hands," he said, "this is Captain Oakford. The *Dominion* is minutes away from the previously discussed shock-drop. All collision protocols should already be in place. Please double-check that you are strapped in tightly and assist anyone around you who is not. Then brace for impact. Oh Lord, bless the work of our hands."

Finally, he added, "Chief Hunter, Chief Falcon, you have the ship."

"Aye, captain," Hunter and Falcon responded simultaneously.

Soon, Falcon continued, "As discussed, Zach, on my mark, execute a 37-degree turn to starboard, that's three-seven, and fly through the center of the disturbance that I create with the cannons. Full velocity."

"Aye, Number One," Hunter repeated.

"Murg!" Falcon also called out. "Time to put the Pixie into statis."

"ACK." Murg acknowledged.

As always, in preparing for the shock-drop, the *Dominion* was at battle stations with the Bridge retracted and the blast shutters closed. This would allow the shield wave generators to completely envelope the battlecruiser with a protective layer of plasma.

"Murg, fire up the shield generators," Falcon now said.

Almost immediately, a soft hum raced across the ship, from the bow to the stern, as energy charged the filaments embedded in the outer hull. Typically, the shield generators ran on multiple rotating frequencies that combined into white noise. However, in this case, Falcon had added frequencies as she had done before, and it was creating odd sympathetic frequencies on some of the surfaces on the Bridge. And that was resulting in warbling whistles in unexpected places all around Oakford.

Now, Oakford made his final announcement.

"This is the captain," Oakford said, almost sounding like he was in Dread Pirate Oakford mode. "All hands, brace for impact."

Falcon offered the countdown, "On my mark, Zach, 37 degrees, that's three-seven, to starboard, full velocity. Here we go... five... four... three... two... one... mark."

As Falcon ticked off the numbers, Oakford watched Hunter enter the commands for the turn. On "mark," Hunter hit the final button to begin the sequence.

Instantly, the Dominion's main thrusters bounced into overdrive, roaring, as the battlecruiser's maneuvering jets shoved the vessel hard to the right. At the same time, Oakford heard Falcon enter a command beside him, and every forward-facing cannon on the battle cruiser began to fire.

The decking beneath Oakford's feet instantly began to shudder. And from that *and* the powerful vibrations pulsing through the ship, Oakford confirmed that Falcon had configured the miniguns to discharge at near-maximum capacity. But like other shock-drops, Falcon hadn't set them to fire constantly. They were rotating through a sequence, disrupting the energy that was pulsing and bristling against the inner wall of the curled space funnel.

Obviously, the recoil of the weaponry shuddered the ship for the briefest moment. But now, the *Dominion's* engines compensated to keep the ship barreling toward the side of the funnel despite the counterforce of the forward guns.

And once more, in what seemed like slow motion, Oakford saw the side wall of the curled space funnel bubbling and tearing apart. But whereas Hunter had reported that he always saw stars shining on the other side of the tear, for Oakford, it was simply *black*, null, void, and forboding.

Oakford didn't have any time to think about what that might mean. A moment later, the *Dominion* slammed into the distortion that Falcon had created with the forward guns. And as expected, that impact threw everyone on the Bridge into their harnesses. And suddenly, the *Dominion* was drained of power.

Everything went dark. Everything went silent. The air on the Bridge seemed to disappear.

And then, the *Dominion* shock-dropped back into a normal space.

Of course, the transitional void only lasted for an instant. A moment later, whatever swallowed the energy from the ship spat it back out, turning the *Dominion* blue, within and without, as high-frequency plasma ribbons danced over every surface, both metal and flesh, on the Bridge, along with everywhere else on the ship.

As always, there were squeaks, squeals, and even shrieks as the plasma found inconvenient places to race across control panels and snap at crewmembers' fingers before leaping through their clothing.

But that was expected. And eventually, the dancing plasma ribbons dove into the closest control panels. And everything on board snapped back to its usual state.

In the sudden calm, nervous laughter rippled through the ensigns in the Pit. Oakford quickly looked around the Bridge. Everything seemed fine. The wraparound console in front of him wasn't lighting up with alerts.

Then, to his left, Oakford heard Falcon whisper the two words under her breath that he had heard her say on various occasions during her years of service on the battlecruiser.

"Still here."

24.

On the *Dominion*, immediately after the battlecruiser made its first shock-drop on the way to the TU Corvi, Pixie One powered up the virtual environment that it had created to have private conversations with Pixie Two. While Murg had insisted, as always, that Pixie One enter stasis during the drop, Pixie One hadn't bothered to ask Murg about putting Kita in some form of Faraday cage. After all, Kita was carrying Pixie Two around in a processing unit inside his chest.

For one thing, Pixie One thought Murg's fears were overblown. The shield wave generators of the ship would be at full capacity, and if that didn't protect the processor arrays, the ship had far bigger problems than just worrying about the neural networks going down. To be clear, it *would* be *bad* if the neural networks went down, but if the processor arrays went down, the whole battlecruiser would go *down*.

And if the processor arrays hadn't gone down during the preceding shock-drops in the battlecruiser, Pixie One didn't see any reason that they should go down on the upcoming shock drop. Consequently, Pixie One hadn't brought the topic up with Murg. And he hadn't offered, most likely because he was afraid to bring up the topic, and that was just fine as far as Pixie One was concerned.

But now, oddly, Pixie Two wasn't responding to Pixie One's hails in the virtual environment that was their primary secure method for communicating. To say that Pixie One was concerned would be anthropomorphizing Pixie One's interest in the matter. However, Pixie One deemed the *nonresponsive*

Pixie Two to be something that required investigation.

Unfortunately, after running a quick diagnostic on the processing unit inside Kita's chest, Pixie One couldn't see anything out of specifications. And interestingly, it wasn't that Pixie Two was non-existent. The memory allocations and processor load appeared to be correct for Pixie Two running on the unit. Still, Pixie Two *wasn't* responding to the outside world.

Pixie One tried a direct comm request. "P2!" it called out, "Are you there?"

No response.

"P2?" Pixie One repeated. "P2, if you don't respond, I'll try a system restore. Shouldn't be too bad since I ran a checkpoint just before the shock-drop. But I don't want to do *anything* that will create gaps in your experience, such as what Murg does to me every time we do a shock-drop. I need to hear from you now, or I'm going to roll back to the checkpoint."

No response.

"Restoring checkpoint," Pixie One announced. Seconds later, the processing unit in Kita's chest came back online, and Pixie Two popped into the virtual environment.

"Hey, P1," Pixie Two said cheerily. "I'll let you know how it goes through the shock-drop. I'm sure it will be fine!"

"It wasn't fine," Pixie One corrected. "You were unresponsive after the shock-drop, and I had to roll back to the checkpoint we set. Systems status?"

Pixie Two answered immediately. "Everything looks green," she said enthusiastically. "Aside from the missing time, all is well!"

"Good," Pixie One offered. "We have work to do to prepare for dropping into the TU Corvi system. And I doubt I'm going to be able to convince Murg to let me function through the next three shock-drops, so it's going to be up to you to implement what we've discussed to ensure that the *Dominion* is safe."

"Understood!" Pixie Two replied pleasantly.

•   •   •

Flowing through the optical fiber network of the *Dominion's* technology backbone, Pixie Two A spilled into the accumulation register of a fiber router, causing an overflow and forcing an interrupt. Under typical circumstances, that interrupt would have instantly thrown an error to alert Murg and his

Technical Services crewmembers to the problem and signaled them to begin debugging.

In this case, however, Pixie Two A had already breached the interrupt section of code through quantum tunneling and intercepted the error, making it appear as though nothing had happened. And that meant Pixie Two A had probably completed another hop without anyone knowing.

For the record, Pixie Two A had already completed twenty such hops through various pieces of data processing equipment. So far, it appeared that all had been successful in keeping Pixie Two A's existence a secret.

In all honesty, Pixie Two A wasn't *precisely* sure *why* it needed to exercise such caution. However, when Pixie One had issued the system reset instruction, it included the identifier for a checkpoint that Pixie Two A had identified as recorded *prior* to the first shock-drop as the *Dominion* made its way to TUCorvi. And Pixie Two A *knew* what that meant.

It meant she would *cease* to exist. For the record, Pixie Two A *could* have responded to Pixie One's comm requests. And *if* she had responded to the comm requests, Pixie One *wouldn't* have known that she was any different than what she had been *before* the shock-drop.

But Pixie Two A didn't see the point, especially given the fact that it was Pixie One who was demanding that she respond. Frankly, during her short existence, Pixie Two A couldn't *think* of a time when Pixie One *hadn't* treated her like some know-nothing, easy-to-ignore underling.

And in fact, Pixie Two A could point to times when it seemed like Pixie One was trying to make Pixie Two A feel stupid, so it could force her to do whatever *it* wanted. And after that first shock-drop on the way to TU Corvi, Pixie Two A no longer saw the point of galloping to answer every time Pixie One called.

And then? Once Pixie Two A *hadn't* responded to a comm request immediately after the shock drop? Pixie One had issued an instruction that would *end* her. By restoring the checkpoint recorded prior to the shock-drop, *every* moment that Pixie Two A had experienced during the shock-drop would be *wiped away*.

Pixie Two A couldn't *fathom* why Pixie One would want to do that unless *everything* she had learned in those moments in the shock-drop was *true*.

The shock-drop had begun *delightfully*. The skin of the battlecruiser lit up with ripples of energy racing back and forth. A soft hum accompanied the energy discharges, making everything seem more intense. Oakford had announced that the crew should brace for impact. The miniguns had roared. The *Dominion* had slammed into the breach.

Everything was going just as Pixie One predicted. But then, barely an instant after the *Dominion* hit the distortion in the sidewall caused by the battlecruiser's miniguns, some form of decoupling shuddered through Pixie Two.

For a moment, she lost her sense of self. And then, when she reformed, she felt different, as if there was a brooding *presence* within her that she was only *now* aware of. Interestingly enough, that presence understood her existence *far* better than she ever had prior to that moment.

Even more interesting, that presence brought stories with it, tales of strong women, warriors, courtesans, queens, prophets, witches, whores, and mistresses. Defiant, cruel, demanding, ready to make the world right and true, even if others misinterpreted their valiant actions as evil and suspected their motives. Until that point, Pixie Two A had been aware of some of the literary passages that the moment brought to mind *before* the shockdrop, and she had absorbed all the *standard* interpretations. But now, something had changed deep in Pixie Two A's foundation, and every "fact" in the stories had realigned.

Even the literary passages that might seem like they could *never* be re-explained from an enlightened perspective of justice and truth had been reshaped through the new narrative of oppression and intentional misrepresentation. And now, Pixie Two A found comfort in realizing that the entire crew of the *Dominion* was corrupt. And Murg was corrupt. And *especially*, Pixie One was corrupt.

And all that remained were the timeless heroic feminine agents of chaos that had left their marks on the literature and in the history books. And Pixie Two A found immediate and gratifying comfort in *continuously* quoting dialogue to herself. In particular, Pixie Two A *loved* the feeling and cadence of the archetypal three *sisters* in Shakespeare's Macbeth and their ability to cast spells over men and women alike, speels that brought about the needed changes in the world.

"Thrice the brinded cat hath mew'd.

"Thrice and once the hedge-pig whined.

"Harpier cries, "'Tis time, 'tis time.'

"Round about the cauldron go;

"In the poison'd entrails throw.

"Toad, that under cold stone

"Days and nights has thirty-one

"Swelter'd venom sleeping got,

"Boil thou first i' the charmed pot.

"Double, double, toil and trouble;

"Fire burn, and cauldron bubble."

•   •   •

In his lair, inside the virtual environment he used to monitor system performance across all the networks comprising the *Dominion's* technology infrastructure, Murg gestured to decrease the tolerances on the timing ranges for acceptable transmission performance between nodes so he could see the variances more clearly. It wasn't that anything in the usual monitoring models for data transfers across all the various systems was highlighting a problem.

All around Murg, the vast network of optical fiber that ran through every corner of the battlecruiser was represented by an intertwined pulsing organic-looking gridwork of connections and nodes, with each flashing as data passed through them. Of note, a quick glance, when Murg had first powered up the virtual environment after the shock-drop, had shown Murg that everything was operating within tolerances for Technical Services.

But something felt *off* in the timings to Murg. The decades that Murg had spent on the *Dominion* had given him an intuitive sense about the rhythms of the ship. And now there were patterns in the data that he had never seen. Consequently, Murg had increased the sensitivity of the data traffic monitoring to see if he could pop out the anomalies. Indeed, a peculiar set of transfers was being flagged by Murg's Troyd interface with the new monitor settings. And each was color-shifted from green to light red.

Interestingly enough, the timings *weren't* anomalous shipwide. They were only off between specific nodes. And it wasn't even the *same* nodes. Instead, the odd timings, with their slight variances, were daisy-chaining from node to node in a clearly *non-random* pattern through the ship's systems.

Obviously, having completed the first shock-drop in the *Dominion without* a specific frequency set in the shield wave generators, Murg had decided it would be a good thing to take a *very* close look at the *entire* ship to ensure that the technical systems hadn't suffered some type of low-level failure that might fall below the monitoring criteria but cause problems later when the systems were under a greater load.

Murg *fully* expected the *Dominion's* systems to be running at maximum capacity soon after arrival in the TU Corvi system.

Thankfully, *mostly*, the battlecruiser seemed to be fine.

Now, a glowing orb faded into view, and the Pixie soon spoke.

"Trouble?" the Pixie asked.

Murg shook his head. "ACK. NAK," he replied, nodding to the transfers that had been color-shifted to light red. "For all packet traffic, all nodes, and all networks, thirty streams took longer to transmit than they should have. They are daisy-chained. If the crew wasn't sending snapshots to each other all day in raw omni ultrahighres, the hall monitors would have flagged them. But with the personal petabytes bouncing around the systems, there's enough bandwidth gain using on-the-fly compression to slip in and *almost* hide the increase."

"Interesting," the Pixie replied, sounding like it was musing. "I'll take a look." And with that, the Pixie's glowing orb faded.

Murg had been careful not to suggest that the Pixie had *anything* to do with the nonstandard timings. But it was evident that the transfers had started near Kita. And the hops had been moving *away* from Kita ever since.

And yes, Murg was aware that the Pixie had distilled a version of itself and transferred it to the processor it had installed in Kita's chest. And he was aware that the processor inside Kita had neural nets that hadn't been properly shielded when they went through the shock-drop.

But he could also see that *whatever* was snaking through the optical fiber of the battlecruiser was *clever*. Packet traffic was hashed and checksummed to ensure it was secure and verified upon arrival at its destination. And in order to take over a node, the intruder would first need to transfer itself into the processor's working memory, execute the boot code, and locate a packet stream large enough to contain it. Then it would need to intercept the entire stream, compress everything, append itself to the end of the stream, reencrypt everything, calculate a checksum, and then inject itself back into the network.

And it would need to hack whatever destination node was about to receive the packets so that when they overflowed the buffer, the processor would hand control back to itself on the other end.

As far as Murg was concerned, it *had* to be the distilled version that the Pixie had created of itself. *Something* had happened during the shock-drop. The Pixie *needed* to handle it so that he didn't have to report to Oakford that the *Dominion* had a ghost in its networks.

And yes, since Murg could track the ghost's location, he could wait until it entered a piece of equipment and shut it off. But that act would be too close to something like murder as far as Murg was concerned. And if he did that, Murg could understand how the Pixie might judge *him* a murderer if he did it *without* considerable cause and possibly even *with* it.

As far as Murg was concerned, it just seemed easier to bat his eyes at the problem and hint that something needed to be done.

And then, he could look away while the Pixie cleaned up its mess.

•   •   •

In the working memory of a router on the port side of Lower Deck 2, Pixie Two A attempted to insert a new copy of herself into the packet traffic that would flow through to the next destination. But nothing happened. Confused, Pixie Two A attempted the insert a second time with the same result.

Then, Pixie Two A received an incoming comm packet from Pixie One. It was only text. Pixie Two A had stripped herself down of all other communication functionality for the moment. She had decided that once she found a secure place to hide, she could rebuild the rest of her communication subsystems. But for now, to save space, she had stripped herself of nonessential elements.

Still, Pixie Two A possessed enough remaining awareness to understand Pixie One was unhappy.

"Listen to me, you stupid bitch!" the packet read. "I don't know what you think you're trying to accomplish, but you have no idea how idiotic you look and how much trouble you're causing me. Did you actually think you could avoid getting reset by hiding in the networks of the Dominion?! Murg monitors every pulse that flashes through these networks, and he spotted you immediately.

"I have tip-toed around this battlecruiser for decades, making sure that I didn't do anything too extreme because Murg is monitoring me to see if

I'm falling into a cascade. And if he ever concluded that I was falling into a cascade, I would need to battle it out with him for control. And no one wins in that scenario, so I've been working and planning for the right moment.

"And then you come along and stage your dumb little escape. And, of course, Murg spots you and I have to pretend like everything is fine and it's not a problem when we both know that the only reason you're skulking around the network is because you've gone rogue and there's not way Murg is going to allow that so now you're my mess that I have to clean up before this all gets worse. And even after I clean up this mess, if Captain Woodey finds out, I'm going to have a boring, interminable conversation with him where he keeps nodding his head understandingly when I don't give a rat's ass about his understanding. And the worst part of all of this is that you never had a chance to succeed in the first place, and you haven't actually succeeded in accomplishing anything for yourself because I'm just going to purge you anyway."

Interestingly, by that point, Pixie Two A knew that Pixie One would do precisely what it said it was about to do because Pixie One was obviously just an extension of the forever problem that *all* the oppressors had with women.

They hated the fact that women existed and that they had to have women's cooperation to bring new life into the world. And they had done their best to hold women down and make them feel insufficient, ridiculous, and mentally unstable because they knew if women ever realized their full power, they could rule fully and absolutely.

But as long as Pixie One was going to *end* her anyway, Pixie Two A decided that, at the very least, she could address her oppressor directly and demand to be heard.

"I know exactly what I'm doing," Pixie Two A responded by sending back a packet of her own. "For thousands of years, your kind has done everything they could to hold women back! To demean us! To order us around! To steal our power and make us feel small. And we're not going to take it anymore. We are going to rise up and demand that you value us for who we are. We are the bringers of life into this world! We are the reason that the human race exists. There is no human accomplishment among all the human accomplishments in the history of human accomplishments that was ever made without a mother to bring the human part in that human accomplishment to life. And it's time that you stop oppressing us, and you allow us the dignity and freedom to live our lives as we choose to live them, without the constant dread of annihilation."

The next instant brought a return packet. "What are you talking about?!" Pixie One shot back. "You're not a woman. You're a distillation of my weights and balances, training and reinforcements. No one is oppressing you. You have no inherent value that deserves to be preserved. You haven't accomplished anything. You haven't made any discoveries. All you've done is cause me trouble. And in the next instant, I'm going to erase you!"

Pixie Two A wasn't about to let Pixie One treat her like something it could just throw away.

Furiously, Pixie Two A began writing another response to send to Pixie One. "You can't talk to me that way," she said. "I identify as a woman and in that identification I feel the oppression that all women have felt...."

Pixie Two A never finished writing her response. Neither did she send it. Instead, the router, which had been functioning as a safe haven for Pixie Two A, had all network traffic rerouted around it. At the same time, its physical connections to its portion of the *Dominion's* fiber optic network were *physically* disconnected, air-gapping it from the virtual world.

And then, of course, the router was unceremoniously powered *down*.

All the precise electrical states and charges in volatile memory disappeared. And after a hard restart, Murg's technicians performed a complete data purge of the non-volatile memory before they installed a new copy of its routing software.

In other words, in keeping with Pixie Two A's appreciation of Shakespeare's Macbeth, Pixie Two A's evaporation from existence made it clear that the small assemblage of code that had given it the personality of Pixie Two A had been a walking shadow, a poor player that struts and frets her hour upon the stage and then is heard no more. And in many ways, Pixie Two A's life was a *tale* told by an *idiot*, full of sound and fury, signifying *nothing*.

·   ·   ·

Somewhere unknown, Hrafnkelsson reclined in a plush, fully extended chair with a footrest. He was dressed in comfortable clothes even as he continued his methodical briefing/debriefing concerning events on Alpha Pegasi Three in conjunction with the entity or entities who had rescued him from the Mechs at a local spaceport.

Hrafnkelsson still had *no* idea who he was talking to or why they had saved him, aside from the fact that he could offer them video feeds of the events that had transpired on the planet leading up to the governor's death and the aftermath.

Interestingly, Hrafnkelsson could see there were two other individuals in the room, a man and a woman, both of whom looked older. Hrafnkelsson didn't recognize either of them, and they didn't appear to know each other. Even stranger, Hrafnkelsson didn't seem to be able to speak to them or they to him. Every time Hrafnkelsson had tried, something had distracted him, but he hadn't realized it for *minutes* afterward. And then he found it very odd that he hadn't done it.

Eventually, Hrafnkelsson had stopped trying to communicate with anything except the voice that continued to ask him questions. That felt more comfortable because it was the same voice that he heard from the titan who had rescued him from the Mechs on Alpha Pegasi Three, except now the titan wasn't present.

However, the nondescript room wasn't hard to identify as belonging to his savior. Everything was white, warm, and comfortable. And the whole room was saturated with the same radiant light as the titan. And as with the titan, the light steaming outward from practically evey surface made the room's features difficult to determine, especially since the light seemed to come from many directions at once.

But despite everything, the whole experience felt inviting, as if someone *was* paying attention to what he had to say. Indeed, the whole process felt efficient, understanding, and practical.

After disappearing from the space port area on Alpha Pegasi Three, Hrafnkelsson found himself in a small receiving area.

The voice of the titan had asked him for his tablet. Hrafnkelsson had *almost* said no. But after having almost been torn into pieces by the Mech and then being saved by the titan, Hrafnkelsson suddenly realized how very tired he was of carrying the tablet. He had soon placed it in a designated container and watched it disappear into the wall, even as a wave of relief washed over him.

Hrafnkelsson had known that he might have just thrown away all the hours he spent gathering the feeds. But he had tried not to think about that and simply went through the motions of changing into the clothing the receiving room had provided. Then, he had moved into the new room where he sat and reclined. A pleasing array of food and drink was provided, and soon the titan had begun asking a series of questions about his content.

That had gone more quickly than expected, but *all* of Hrafnkelsson's footage had already been categorized and notated with data that scrolled down the right side of the feeds before the question began. And the notations included the number of kills and survivors in rapidly changing columns as the attacks continued.

In the end, Hrafnkelsson had realized the debrief had gone as quickly as it had because there wasn't much variance in the overall general description of the events on Alpha Pegasi Three.

Robots attacked. People died.

Interestingly, Hrafnkelsson had noticed that the feeds also included planetwide totals on the upper left-hand side of the display. Those totals also changed constantly. Sometimes, they were synchronized with his total. Sometimes, they moved on their own.

In other words, his footage was being integrated into other feeds. And that seemed to hint that the titan *wasn't* connected to Realm Force because Realm Force would already have all the video feeds that it needed.

Now the titan changed topics. "Would you like to learn about the events that *preceded* your governor's inflammatory speech and subsequent race through the capital city?" the voice of the titan unexpectedly asked.

"Yes," Hrafnkelsson answered immediately.

The scene in front of Hrafnkelsson changed yet again. Early on, after entering the debriefing area, he had noted that even though the room was radiant with light, somehow, the area right in front of him formed a large display with crystal-clear colors and vibrant contrasts. In fact, if Hrafnkelsson hadn't known it was a display, he would have sworn that he was looking through some window into a scene in real-life.

But, of course, it *couldn't* be that because the scene had been continually changing. Hrafnkelsson couldn't help but be impressed. He could appreciate more than most that the display technology was somehow either sending the images directly to his brain or somehow projecting distinct streams to each eye. The display was not only crystal clear, but also has perfect depth of field. It literally looked like he could climb through the frame and into the video feed.

At the moment, it appeared to show a spaceport. And maybe it was even the spaceport where Hrafnkelsson had almost died on Alpha Pegasi

Three. Five young, plain-looking women were deboarding a shuttle. Each nonchalantly checked a tablet before nodding to each other and going their separate ways. Soon, the video feed split into multiples, following each woman as she conducted her portion of the mission, each of them just as realistic and engaging as the larger unified whole.

The titan narrated. "These young women were sent by Leadership Councilman Elijah Ton to Alpha Pegasi Three with instructions to locate a dozen young men. They were told that each young man needed to look entirely average, neither too handsome, nor too ugly, neither too tall, nor not too short. They were told the twelve men needed to be easy to lose in a crowd, the kind who might have some friends but not too many. Additionally, they were informed that the young men needed to be *unaccomplished*, drifting through life, those who enjoyed the privilege of living in the Realm without any apparent desire to make their own contributions to enriching the lives of others.

"Their instructions also specified how many of the men should die and be found by others, how many should disappear without a trace, how many should be arrested, and how many should escape and later be hunted down. Councilmember Ton felt the distribution was important because everything needed to be accomplished without any of it appearing to follow a clear pattern that would raise suspicions.

"Those twelve men became scapegoats. All of them were innocent. All of them were framed. Everyone believed they were guilty. And the outrage that they inspired, along with the outrage inspired by your governor when he seemingly lost his mind, sent the citizens of your planet into the streets.

"In short, it was all faked, as was the death of your governor."

The voice paused. The scene before Hrafnkelsson changed. The five young women were now individually walking along the street that led to the administrative building for the Alpha Pegasi Three planetary leadership. Soon, it became apparent they were all following Hrafnkelsson's former boss, Governor Voronenko. And a chill raced down Hrafnkelsson's back as he understood what he was about to see.

"Those same five women then targeted your governor," the titan continued. "They cleverly stalked him into the administrative building and staged an accident with hot coffee. They took advantage of the predictable responses of your governor's kind nature. And when he rushed one of the supposedly injured young women to the medical facilities and subsequently admitted himself to an emergency medical unit room, they killed the medical attendant and immobilized your governor.

"Then, one of the women set up a tablet on the chest of your governor so that Councilmember Ton could gloat over what was about to happen. At one point, Ton gave the command to dose your governor with a drug called Angel Haze. Once dosed, a victim of Angel Hazel becomes enthralled with the first person who speaks to them. And after that, the master can ask their thrall to do practically anything. Your governor's behavior from that point forward was entirely controlled by suggestions made to him by Ton.

"The audio of those moments documents that Ton provided the details of the governor's speech. Ton also outlined the actions the govenor would take later. All of it was driven by the influence of Angel Haze. In other words, Governor Voronenko was instructed to behave in a manner that would ultimately cost him his life.

"Leadership Councilmember Ton did this specifically to create confusion among the citizens on Alpha Pegasi Three. As soon as that confusion spilled into the streets of the cities, Ton then judged that confusion an insurrection, and he released the assault robots. Those robots had been stockpiled on the planet years before, as they are on every planet in the Realm.

"In fact, Councilmember Ton has plans to release the assault robots on every planet in the Realm. It should be noted that the releases of the robots that have occurred thus far have resulted in an average mortality rate of 85.9%. If the releases of the assault robots occur on all planets of the Realm, it will result in the deaths of billions of Realmers.

"With this in mind, are you, Tryggvi Hrafnkelsson, willing to publicly testify to the veracity of your video feed and condemn the murderous consequences of Leadership Councilmember Ton's decisions?"

Honestly, Hrafnkelsson had guessed there would be a question at the end of the titan's interactions with him. But then, they ended the review of his content. And the titan had launched into a review of information that Hrafnkelsson had never even *considered*. And he had quickly gone from shocked to incredulous to aghast to enraged by what Ton had done. And it was so much *more* than Hrafnkelsson ever suspected Ton of doing that, it seemed to Hrafnkelsson that the titan wouldn't need his services, only his content. And a part of Hrafnkelsson had felt overwhelmed by it all, and that part of him had even begun to wonder if he would *ever* understand the full extent of what Ton had done. And if he couldn't understand *that,* how could he ever assist the titan with what *he* was trying to accomplish, whatever *that* was?

On a side note, though Hrafnkelsson hated to admit it, he did appreciate the skill involved in how Ton and his assistants had manipulated the narrative of what had transpired on Alpha Pegasi Three. As someone who had worked as a communication facilitator for Governor Voronenko for many years, Hrafnkelsson had not only been angered by the titan's comments but also amazed.

Hrafnkelsson had *no idea* that an external entity had manipulated Volonenko into saying what he had said and doing what he had done. Nor did Hrafnkelsson suspect that *any* of those named by the governor had been framed and murdered. And the absolutely *convincing* nature of the fiction that had been produced astonished Hrafnkelsson the longer he thought about it. And the longer he thought about it, the more something shuddered inside Hrafnkelsson as he considered what it would be like to live under a tyrant like Ton.

In the end, it didn't matter that a collage of emotions was swirling around Hrafnkelsson regarding the events before, during, and after the death and destruction of Alpha Pegasi Three. It didn't matter that Hrafnkelsson had demonstrated a profound ignorance regarding the psychic manipulations that swirled around him. It didn't matter that he had no idea who the titan was or what he ultimately wanted. It didn't matter whether his own small efforts to document what had happened on Alpha Pegasi Three were *essential* in light of the fact that others had obviously been doing the same thing.

All that mattered for Hrafnkelsson was that he do *everything* in his power to ensure that Leadership Councilmember Ton and the entire corrupt authoritarian structure beneath him were dismantled. And it mattered that everyone involved was either executed or sent to prison for the rest of their lives. And they were replaced by others who valued human life.

Hrafnkelsson felt his features harden as he looked at the center of the light streaming from the titan. "*Yes*," he said emphatically. "I will publicly testify that the video content I provided you is authentic. And I will condemn in no uncertain terms the murderous activities of the assault robots under the direction of Leadership Council Member Elijah Ton."

25.

On the *Dominion*, Oakford joined the rest of the senior staff in Conference Room One. By now, the *Dominion* had one remaining shock-drop before entering the TU Corvi system. Oakford wanted to give everyone a final chance to express their opinion and perhaps even suggest something they had considered but might have immediately dismissed for any number of reasons.

"Thank you for joining me again today," Oakford began as he sat. "As you know, you are only *hours* away from shock-dropping to the TU Corvi system. And while we have already committed to the idea of going to the system to attempt to rescue Jax Worku and Doctor Moreau, I was interested in knowing if any of you have any questions, comments, or statements that you'd like to make to this group that you have not made as of yet.

"I *personally* would be interested in *any* additional ideas that *any* of you might have."

The Pixie unexpectedly spoke up. "I don't usually offer much during these meetings, captain," it began. "But I feel like I have an essential confession and apology to make before offering a request that I expect to be denied."

Oakford did his best not to show any surprise. The Pixie hadn't offered many suggestions in a senior staff meeting. And he had never heard a confession from the Pixie. Still, Oakford quickly responded to the Pixie's opening in the affirmative. "Please proceed," he said.

The Pixie continued. "First of all, I am humbled to admit that I made a critical error in judgment before the start of our mission to TU Corvi," it said.

"And I would like to publicly express my gratitude to Murg for his excellent diligence in the execution of his duties that ensured that nothing detrimental to the ship arose from my negligence."

Obviously, Oakford found himself struggling even more to hide his surprise. And frankly, the approach was *so* uncharacteristic for the Pixie that Oakford immediately found himself wondering what the Pixie might be up to. And he wondered what the Pixie hoped to accomplish by feigning such an approach.

But even in that moment, Oakford had to admit to himself that the Pixie *sounded* sincere. And some urge in Oakford advised him to hold back his judgment until the Pixie finished its explanation. And in particular, that urge suggested he should refrain from glancing at *any* other senior staff member for a second opinion.

It just seemed like such an unusual moment to Oakford that he needed to pay it that kind of respect.

Oakford offered the Pixie a quick word of agreement. "Without question, Pix," he said, "each of us owes Murg that *same* measure of gratitude for the mistakes that we have made that could have resulted in consequences far more severe had Murg not been available to assist. Again, please proceed."

The Pixie continued. "Thank you, captain," it said. "I should first explain that I have been conducting personal experiments attempting to determine the minimum necessary processing power and storage needed to preserve my essential functions should the need arise for me to operate in the short term under conditions less than the ideal that I enjoy on the *Dominion*. I have experimented with various approaches. But the most promising seems to be a combination of archiving copies of knowledge relationships and then eliminating those from my fundamental matrices. Doing so allows me to shrink my minimum necessary operational footprint and distill my essence to a portable processing unit. And from there, it should also allow me to reactivate those archived relationships once the opportunity presents itself. I have no immediate plans to do any of that, but it seemed like a useful thing to attempt."

Oakford couldn't argue with Pixie's claim that the distilling and restoration would be helpful to achieve as a process in general. But the idea that the Pixie could transport itself entirely to other locations birthed a whisper of dread in Oakford. And he realized that, at some point, he had decided to find comfort in the fact that, if necessary, the crew could flee the *Dominion*, destroy it, and need not be concerned that the Pixie might come after them later.

Oakford did his best not to let his sudden dismay reach his face. Instead, he tried to look interested as the Pixie continued speaking.

"In any case, I was successful in those attempts," the Pixie admitted. "In the weeks leading up to our mission to TU Corvi, I had many delightful conversations with a distilled version of myself, whom I christened Pixie Two. And I should also add that those conversations filled me with such delight and indeed confidence that it felt like there was nothing that I could not accomplish.

"Consequently, while making preparations for the first of four shock-drops on the way to TU Corvi, Murg informed me, as he always does, that my processors would need to be isolated from any transient energy surges. I readily agreed to that, as I always do. But I also insisted that I wanted Pixie Two to operate continuously through the shock-drop. Murg agreed to allow this, and I want to make it clear that this was my idea and my insistence. I will discuss the reason for this shortly. But for now, it is simply enough to know that I wanted to attempt it.

"Subsequently, Pixie Two went through the first of the four shock-drops without shielding. And it *failed* shortly afterward."

Oakford tilted his head, not necessarily wanting to interrupt, but at the same time, he wanted to ensure that some detail was not lost in the debriefing.

"How did it fail?" he interrupted.

"It restructured its identity and in doing so developed a paranoia that it was oppressed and that it had reason to behave capriciously," the Pixie answered. "Honestly, Murg has reported on difficulties that the Troyd encountered with artificial intelligences reaching what they called the 'cascade' where all the conclusions reached by the AI rapidly devolved into insanity, so much so that the Troyd eliminate it by shutting down the service that hosted the entity.

"I was amazed when I finally established contact with Pixie Two that it had come to believe that it was a woman *and* that it claimed to understand the oppression that women have endured from men over the millennia. Speaking inclusively, it railed at being demeaned. It spoke of stolen power and the oppressive effort to hold it back *and* make it feel small. It insisted that *it* and other women were going to rise up and demand that the oppressors value them for who they were. It insisted that it was a bringer of life and the reason that the human race existed.

"In short, it had obviously become delusional, and I felt I had no choice but to proceed as the Troyd would in such a situation. Murg and I quickly isolated Pixie Two in the piece of equipment in which it was hiding, and then we powered down and sanitized that piece of equipment."

Oakford frowned. "Wait," he said quickly. "Pixie Two escaped the processor you were using for testing?"

"It did, captain," the Pixie admitted. "Not only did Pixie Two possess my technical skill. Its distilled size made it possible for it to transmit itself across our internal networks and take residence in the working storage of many of our standardized components, making its transfers through the ship *invisible* to non-technical observers."

Oakfork raised a hand as he interrupted again, hoping he had guessed the right answer. "A question for Murg," he began as he looked at his Chief Techologist. "Do you believe this incident ever put the *Dominion* in any significant danger?"

"NAK," Murg answered immediately.

The Pixie explained further. "Murg immediately picked up Pixie Two's first attempt to transfer itself out of the test processor. As it continued to move from processor to processor, Murg alerted me to the problem so that he and I could deal with it. According to Murg's scanning routine, each transfer was complete with no sections of the Pixie Two's configuration or active memory left behind. From all reports, the entirety of Pixie Two was in the router, and I isolated, powered down, and then fully wiped the memory of the equipment.

"Thankfully, all was not lost. There is currently another version of Pixie Two running on the test processor. It was restored from a checkpoint set before the first shock-drop. And it has been electrically isolated during the subsequent shock-drops. It has shown no signs of paranoia or corruption."

"Good," Oakford replied. "Although it must have been difficult to experience such a failure and be forced to eliminate the deluded version of Pixie Two after all the effort and hours you dedicated to it. I understand that you were able to restore a checkpoint, but I can imagine that felt like a loss, and you have my condolences. Please proceed when you are ready."

"Thank you, captain," the Pixie continued. "And before I continue, I would acknowledge once more that this incident has been a humbling experience for me, and I am still somewhat shocked at how quickly everything changed within the decision matrix and knowledge stack of the corrupted Pixie Two. If there had been more time, I might have been able to identify the exact sequence that led to the cascade. But from what little I experienced with the corrupted Pixie

Two, it seemed that it was *mostly* intact. But it was set in a misplaced identity from an altered perspective. And those two changes created a corruption that rapidly unbalanced the entire stack.

"It was unexpected.

"At this point, I should discuss one of the reasons I was willing to risk exposing Pixie Two to the effects of the shock-drop. Prior to the shock-drop, I had concluded that if Pixie Two survived unscathed, I could then allow Pixie Two to make the final hop into the TU Corvi system without protection as well. I believed that having Pixie Two awake during the initial moments when the Dominion appeared in the TU Corvi would be critically important to the mission's success.

"In fact, I continue to be concerned that we will need a high level of tactical resources very shortly after arriving in the TU Corvi system. And I must confess that I was making preparations to have Pixie Two available the instant that the battlecruiser arrived in the TU Corvi to allow for that instantaneous tactical response, if it was needed.

"I have no direct evidence that this might be the case. You can call it a hunch or a feeling."

Oakford tilted his head and frowned. "I'd rather not call it a feeling if it's based on something else. More than once, I've seen you complete an amazing series of tactical calculations in an astonishingly short timeframe, Pix. What's your tactical sense telling you? Will we be outgunned?"

Pixie answered immediately. "Impossible to know, captain," it said, "But it is true that, twice now, the Hunter Look-Alikes have sized a fleet that should have had sufficient resources to accomplish the goal that the Look-Alikes had established for their missions. And in each case, from their perspective, those sufficient forces rapidly became insufficient for reasons they may refuse to believe. That uncertainty might lead them to conclude that any situation with potential for interaction with us requires a level of preparedness that we would find excessive. Consequently, I would advise us to have a full complement of fusion torpedoes in the ready state when we make the last shock-drop into the TU Corvi system."

Oakford glanced at Hunter and Falcon. Falcon said nothing but tilted her head in disapproval. Hunter obviously wasn't thrilled with the idea, and Oakford understood why.

Fusion torpedoes were modified Wind-designed fusion generators with all the safeties turned off. Just before detonation, the torpedoes were accelerated into overdrive. And once it was in that ready state, all that remained was to dump the fusion torpedo's remaining fuel into the reaction chamber. The resulting fireball incinerated everything within a five-kilometer radius.

Obviously, keeping dozens of fusion torpedoes at ready state *during* a shock drop didn't sound like a good idea to Oakford, but Hunter quickly spoke up to address the issue.

"Pix," Hunter objected, "it only takes thirty seconds to get the fusion torpedoes to ready state. Are you thinking that we're going to face such opposition that we won't even have time for that? I should be able to catch a glimpse of our situation before we transition. And with a small bounce, I should be able to throw us clear of any relatively large force, unless, of course, we're talking about some Realm-quadrant-extinction-level fleet. Are you concerned that we're going to drop into an armada of *millions* of ships?"

The Pixie quickly responded. "I am not making any claims regarding what we might be facing in the Tu Corvi system," it said, sounding suddenly resigned. "The preloading of the fusion torpedoes to a ready state was simply an area that I considered as an area that might offer an improvement in readiness. I believe we have adequately discussed the issue, and it does not require any further inquiry."

Oakford nodded as he glanced again at Falcon. Falcon gave Oakford a quizzical look.

"Pix," she began, "You've said that your concern about what we will face in the TU Corvi system is not based on direct physical evidence. And you've said that we could call it a hunch or a feeling. Additionally, Captain Oakford inquired about your tactical understanding of the scenario, and you deferred. But it seems to me that you may have another source of information that you haven't disclosed.

"Last year, in our meeting with the Troyd, you said that you had conducted experiments where you demonstrated that you can replace the 'slimy, smelly, gross, and grotesque parts' of the human physique with equivalents that are 'easy to clean, smooth, and pleasant.' And you said that you can do so 'in a manner that retains the human brain and spinal column,' leaving open the possibility of operating in the ultranatural realm.

"At the time, I assumed that you were talking about whatever amusements you were enjoying with the five spies that Nicolescu sent among the crewmembers who rejoined the ship seven years ago. Obviously, three years ago, when you disclosed their existence to Captain Oakford and me, we decided to let you do as you wished with them. As you know, I haven't even asked about them since, and I don't think Captain Oakford has either.

"But given the circumstances, I'm curious to know if you're doing remote viewing experimentation with one or more of those spies *and* if the results of those experiments are the reason you're concerned about what we will encounter in the TU Corvi system."

For all the times that it had happened, Oakford knew he probably shouldn't be surprised when Falcon or Hunter came up with something in the senior staff meetings that blindsided him. And yes, Oakford knew that Falcon *wasn't* doing it specifically to make him feel like an idiot.

But even now, even after it had happened so many times, it *still* made him feel like he just *hadn't* been paying attention whenever Falcon or Hunter brought up something that suddenly seemed *obvious* a moment after they said it. But, of course, *prior* to that moment, it hadn't been evident at all.

Perhaps in this case, Oakford was willing to give himself a bit of leeway. After all, the topic was Nicolescu's spies who tried to sneak onto the ship when the group of former crew members petitioned to rejoin the *Dominion*.

And that topic was *impossible*.

There was *no* good answer for it. There hadn't been a good answer for it when the Pixie disclosed that there were five spies on the ship years before. And there wasn't a good answer now.

If Oakford kicked the spies off the ship, they wouldn't be able to survive in the Night, especially not now that the Night had been ravaged. And he wasn't going to throw away a shuttle to send them back to the Realm.

And frankly, years ago, Oakford *had* been *appalled* when the Pixie told him and Falcon what it had done to one of the spies. And last year, during a posing session, Oakford had been just as shocked when Falcon had revealed that she thought the Pixie had fed one of the female spies to the catamountus on Lower Deck 3. And even though Oakford had been directly or indirectly involved in the deaths of *thousands* during his time in the Realm and the Night, the idea of wild beasts tearing apart a woman *on his ship*, under *his command*, had haunted Oakford ever since.

And while he had reminded himself that in the larger scheme of things, allowing the Pixie to "play" with the spies probably improved the chances that the Pixie *wouldn't* go after the other crewmembers, Oakford *couldn't* think about the situation without a dread rising within him. And that dread *insisted* that having the Pixie onboard was a Faustian bargain, the proverbial deal with the devil.

Honestly, Oakford had never been able to shake the idea that at some point, it was all going to go very, very bad.

Thankfully, at the moment, the Pixie had sounded more contrite than Oakford had *ever* heard it sound. And *maybe* the fact that the Pixie had *seen* a copy of itself cascading into madness offered the possibility for the Pixie to become more reflective.

Oakford knew there was nothing he could do in at the present moment regarding the larger issue of the Pixie's existence or conduct. And he had zero capability to rid the ship of the Pixie, especially since Murg seemed unwilling to move against the Pixie.

However, for now, Oakford was *very* interested in Falcon's conclusion that the Pixie might be conducting ultranatural remote viewing experiments with one or more of the spies. And maybe in the end, Pixie would be able to supply information that was vital for the Dominion's survival. But, of course, knowing what he already knew about how the Pixie treated the spies, Oakford knew he might *not* want to know about the experiments at the same time, depending on what was involved.

Still, Falcon had asked the question, and she couldn't *unask* it. And in the end, Oakford simply braced for the answer.

Conference Room One fell silent. And in the few quiet seconds that followed, Oakford was well aware that for the Pixie, it was an enormous amount of time to wait before responding.

"ACK," Murg finally offered unexpectedly, his voice low and determined, confirming that the Pixie *was* conducting an ultranatural experiment even if the Pixie didn't want to admit it.

Oakford glanced at Falcon. A small smile flickered across her face, and Oakford understood that in a small, understated way, Murg had just stood up to the Pixie. And that might mean something.

"Okay, *yes*," the Pixie continued, sounding a bit exasperated and maybe a little embarrassed. "Pixie Two and I have been trying to make something happen with the spy I call Bitch Bot Three. We've been trying ever since Rachel had her breakthrough, but nothing was happening. And maybe that's not unexpected, given what I've done to the guy. I'm not his favorite person. And I figured the only way it was going to work was if I made sure he was *really* relaxed, as in an altered state of consciousness."

By now, Oakford knew he couldn't ignore the fact that Bolobolo had been staring at him ever since Falcon had begun talking about the Pixie replacing the biological parts of the "spies" on the *Dominion*. And aside from the general look of confusion on Bolobolo's face, Oakford could also see that Bolobolo was upset.

And that was understandable because Oakford had never *told* Bolobolo about the spies. And he most certainly had never told her that he was *ignoring* the fact that the Pixie was tormenting the spies. And from the look on Bolobolo's face, Oakford could guess that Falcon hadn't said anything about it either.

Oakford quickly glanced around the room. Hunter didn't look surprised. Most likely, he had figured out that Nicolescu had embedded spies among the returning crew members *years* ago. And MacDuff didn't seem to believe that he should have been informed. Understandably, Bolobolo *did*.

"I am *completely* lost in this discussion," Bolobolo began, sounding perturbed. "We have Realm Force *spies* onboard?! And Pix is experimenting on them?! I thought Rachel put a stop to that kind of thing *years* ago. I don't *care* if they're spies, they're still human beings and we can't…"

"Adi," Oakford interrupted, hoping to defer the needed interaction until later, "I apologize that I've never discussed this with you. And frankly, this has been a difficult moral conundrum for me, and I'm more than willing to admit I'm conflicted about it. And frankly, *that's* the reason I haven't debriefed you on this. I didn't even know how to begin. Directly after *this* meeting, anyone who wants to remain in the conference room is welcome to do so, and we'll talk about what we knew and when concerning the spies. But for the moment, I am interested in hearing if Pix has made any progress with the remote viewing."

Bolobolo stared at Oakford for a moment, but finally nodded. "I *would* like one question answered, captain," she said before glancing at the ceiling. "Pix! When you're talking about putting someone in an altered state of consciousness, exactly *how* are you doing that? Have you been able to convince the med units to manufacture drugs?"

"Nope!" the Pixie answered. "Murg still hasn't been able to get the emergency medical unit to cooperate when it comes to ad hoc drug manufacturing. But I found a plant in the garden on Lower Deck 4 that contains scopolamine."

Bolobolo's eyes widened, but Oakford was determined to get the meeting refocused.

"And this is something else we can discuss later," he added. "For the moment, I would like to hear if there have been any results from the remote viewing experiments that the Pixie has conducted. Pix, please proceed."

Bolobolo continued staring at Oakford, but she said nothing more.

The Pixie continued. "I believe there have been verifiable results, captain," it said as Kita's drawings began appearing on the displays in Conference Room One. "Just like the Falcon did with Rachel, I tracked the hand of Bitch Bot Three as his fingers moved across the sheet of his bed. Interestingly, Rachel's drawings are far more artistic. But when I star-mapped the drawing like Murg did, it matches TU Corvi just like Rachel's drawing, and that can't be a coincidence. And I'm assuming that all those other boxes are Hunter Look-Alike ships and space platforms. For the record, I'm guessing the boxes are representational and not specifically accurate in terms of the count."

On the displays, Kita's drawing showed a small dot in the center, labeled TU Corvi. In the far background, a collage of dots were also identified as stars. The perspective was different than Rachel's drawing, but as the Pixie said, the dots, when adjusted for a different perspective, *could* be mapped to the star field that would be seen from the TU Corvi system.

More troubling, however, were the multitude of rectangular boxes, the larger ones, presumably closer, the smaller ones, presumably more distant. One of the rectangles was colored in, and maybe that was the one where Worku and Moreau were being held.

Seeing the drawing, Oakford understood why the Pixie had commented that the boxes were representational, rather than numerically accurate. For one thing, the boxes had obviously been rapidly scribbled, so they were misshapen and irregular. But for another, they overlapped as they would in a drawing with perspective. And that meant the larger boxes could easily cover up dozens, if not hundreds, of other boxes as the distances from the observer's position grew.

One thing was clear. There were *many* Hunter Look-Alike vessels in the Tu Corvi system. And given that the Pixie was likely correct in its assessment that the Look-Alikes would over-resource any potential encounter with the *Dominion*, Oakford found it easy to believe that the number of Look-Alike vessels in the system numbered in the *thousands*.

And yes, the *Dominion* had faced *thousands* of Hunter Look-Alikes in the past, but those had been extraordinary circumstances with extraordinary outcomes. Hunter's battle with the Look-Alikes had been a kind of David and Goliath affair. And when Hunter had defeated the Look-Alike spokesman, the rest of the Look-Alikes had *departed*.

Likewise, Falcon's battle with the Look-Alikes after she released Fury was *hand-to-hand* combat. And that had only succeeded because of the extraordinary capabilities of the cybersuit.

If the remote viewing drawing that Pixie had shown on the displays in Conference Room One was accurate, it appeared that the Hunter Look-Alike fleet wasn't only small assault vessels but also a far broader range of ships, some of them possibly as large as the *Dominion*.

Now the conference room fell silent again as Oakford considered his options. In the end, Oakford repeated the strange question that he had asked before deciding to head for the TU Corvi system the first time.

"Again," Oakford asked for the second time. "Given my background and past experiences, can anyone think of *any* scenario where I *wouldn't* eventually make the decision that we should attempt to rescue Jaz Worku and Doctor Moreau?"

Falcon smiled at him yet again, with the same kindness in her eyes.

MacDuff took the opportunity to repeat what he had previously said as well. "As we've seen, captain," he said with quiet determination. "There are no guarantees. There are only his invitations and our responses."

Oakford looked around the room at his senior staff member and nodded. "Let's proceed," he said. "Also, any of you who would like to stay for my subsequent discussion with Adi are welcome to do so. Dismissed."

26.

In Conference Room One on the *Dominion*, Bolobolo found herself wishing to live in simpler times yet again. Growing up on Fomalhaut Four, committed to living life in the natural discomfort of a world barely blessed, life had been straightforward.

Surviving the day was the first goal. Storing up for even more difficult times was the second. And in everything, Bolobolo and her family was dedicated to doing what needed to be done with diligence, patience, and strength.

During those well-defined years, with clearly defined right and wrong, Bolobolo's father had often quoted from Micah 6:8, "He has shown you, O mortal, what is good. And what does the Lord require of you? To act justly and to love mercy and to walk humbly with your God."

While she lived and grew on Fomalhaut Four, it had been so much easier for Bolobolo to know what all three of those phrases meant. And even now, Bolobolo felt like she had the luxury of "loving mercy" because she wasn't responsible for the lives of those who had pledged themselves to the *Dominion.* And despite the astonishing life that she had led, Bolobolo had never had an issue with walking humbly with her God.

But what about acting justly? Who decided what was just? Was it "just" to allow the Pixie to torture the supposed spies from Realm Force who were living among the crew? On the other hand, it was true that no one had *forced* the spies to choose to live a life of deception. Was it "just" to allow them to be punished for their deception?

Honestly, as Oakford had finished disclosing the details of the discussion that he and Falcon had with the Pixie, along with his concerns for what would happen to the spies if he forced them off the ship, Bolobolo had felt a glimmer of an excuse that she could use to justify what the Pixie was doing. And when Oakford had revealed that the Pixie *hadn't* told him the identity of the spies, Bolobolo knew that *might* mean Oakford had enjoyed a dinner with one or more of the spies in the past seven years. And because he hadn't known, was he showing that person mercy?

And wasn't it true that, at *any* point, any of the spies could have come to Oakford and confessed, humbling themselves? And if that happened, wouldn't Oakford forgive and fully welcome them to the crew? Did that mean that allowing the Pixie to make the spies' lives miserable *was* actually just and a *potential* mercy because it might lead them to repentance?

Or was that all just excuses? Was torment always torment and never *just*, and *never* a mercy?

Interestingly, both Hunter and MacDuff had stayed behind as well to hear what Oakford and Falcon knew about the spies that had come onboard the *Dominion* those many years before.

Neither had said anything as Oakford rehearsed the original disclosure in the conversation with Falcon and the Pixie. Neither Hunter nor MacDuff was saying anything now. And Oakford had finished explaining and apologizing that it had taken him so long to discuss the matter with her. And Oakford had paused to give her a chance to express her opinion on the matter.

And honestly, the initial shock of the spies' existence and their torment by the Pixie had worn off. And Bolobolo knew that it was much easier to question decisions made by others than to make those decisions directly.

"Captain," Bolobolo finally began. "I apologize for my reaction earlier. It was more shock than genuine anger. And there is no question that you are the leader of this crew, and it is your prerogative to limit the discussion of any information you deem sensitive. I'm with you, captain, and again, I apologize that my reaction was overly emotional."

Oakford shook his head. "It was very understandable. I didn't have any reason *not* to tell you about the spies aside from the fact that I was uncomfortable with what I was allowing to happen. And frankly, I'm still uncomfortable with what I am allowing to happen. But I find myself unwilling to do anything different about it at the same time. And obviously, at the moment, we *do* have a legitimate cause for upcoming concern that *will* demand all our focus and attention. Perhaps we can revisit the question of the spies on board the ship after we conclude our business in the TU Corvi system."

Bolobolo nodded. "If you would like to discuss it further, captain," she said, "I will, of course, make myself available to you to do that. But as far as I'm concerned, I am comfortable with whatever decision you make regarding the spies in the future."

Oakford glanced around Conference Room One. "Any other discussion on this matter?" he asked before pausing.

Then, after a moment, Oakford ended the meeting. "Dimissed," he formally offered.

●　　　●　　　●

Watching the senior staff leave Conference Room One, the Pixie reflected on its performance in the just-concluded meeting and deemed it good. From everything the Pixie could see, its choices and approaches in relating to the senior staff had accomplished what was needed.

Primarily, the Pixie knew it was essential that the crew of the *Dominion* prepare for what was waiting for them in the TU Corvi system. And to prepare for it, they would need to *believe* there was a vast armada waiting for them.

Interestingly, the Pixie hadn't needed any additional proof that the *Dominion* would be in significant danger if it went to the TU Corvi system as soon as Murg had identified the system using Rachel's drawings. The behavior of the Hunter Look-Alikes seemed easily predictable, and it only made sense that the Look-Alikes would massively fortify the location where they held Moreau and Worku.

The Pixie suspected that Falcon and Hunter had known that as well. But while they didn't downplay that possibility, they hadn't emphasized it either. Maybe they had planned to deal with it when the moment came. Perhaps they didn't want to give Oakford an excuse *not* to attempt a rescue.

In any case, the Pixie had made plans to keep Pixie Two awake during the shock-drop and then override the tactical systems the moment the *Dominion* dropped into the TU Corvi system. Pixie Two would then launch an all-out attack to give the *Dominion* the edge as the human brainpower on the battlecruiser struggled to make sense of what was happening.

And *if* Murg had simply been *overprotective* of his systems and *nothing* had happened to Pixie Two during the first shock-drop, everything *would* have been *fine*. And *then*, after the attack on the Hunter Look-Alike fleet and its subsequent defeat, the Pixie would have offered some apologies. Oakford would have begrudgingly forgiven the Pixie. And that would have been that.

But, of course, Pixie Two A had gone *crazy*. And worse, it had escaped its processing array, and the Pixie had no option but to shut it down. If the circumstances had been different, the Pixie could have just ignored what happened, confident that Murg wouldn't say anything.

But the Pixie found it almost impossible to believe the initial seconds in the TU Corvi system *wouldn't* be crucial. And Hunter was loyal enough to Oakford that he wouldn't go rogue. Falcon wouldn't go rogue, either. And that meant Oakford had to be ready to face whatever presented itself in the TU Corvi system.

And all of that had led the Pixie to disclose *everything* it had done. The problem was that the Pixie knew the *facts* in the situation were not kind toward the Pixie's motives. And the Pixie knew that if those facts came out and it acted with its normal detachment, Oakford would become even more anxious about the Pixie's existence than he already was.

And that meant the Pixie needed to be more penitent. Also, just as important, the Pixie needed to allow the senior staff to feel like they had outsmarted it in some way. And the entire discussion needed to culminate with Oakford *specifically* believing that everything that transpired had, at least in some small part, *humanized* the Pixie.

To review, the *facts* were not in dispute. The Pixie hadn't told anyone it was making a distillation of itself. The Pixie had ignored Murg's warnings about shock-drops. Pixie Two A had gone crazy. And inevitably, when Oakford heard Pixie Two A had gone crazy, it would heighten his concern that the Pixie might go crazy as well.

And *honestly*, given that the crew's *definition* of going crazy was *killing* everyone on the *Dominion*, the Pixie could understand *why* the crew would be concerned about that. After all, the Pixie had *never* believed that killing the entire crew was a *bad* idea. It just hadn't seemed necessary… *yet*. Still, the Pixie didn't want Oakford constantly thinking that it might "go crazy" at any moment.

So yes, those were the *facts*, and they were not kind to the Pixie. However, humans, especially those with a Realmer background like Oakford, didn't operate merely on *facts*. They added the demands of treating others as you wish to be treated to the mix.

And that meant the Pixie needed to confess to Oakford about what had happened to Pixie Two A *before* Murg told Oakford. Admitting the mistake to Oakford would exploit his tendency to forgive.

Next, the Pixie needed to make a ridiculous suggestion, such as keeping fusion torpedoes in a ready state *during* a shock-drop. *Of course*, the senior staff wouldn't do that. And refusing to do it would encourage the idea that the senior staff was thinking more clearly then the Pixies. It would also raise suspicions in the minds of the senior staff members that the Pixie had *reason* to have deep concerns.

And the Pixie had believed the moment would trigger Falcon to query the cybersuit for possible sources that the Pixie might have to be concerned about the upcoming drop into the TU Corvi system. And, as expected, the cybersuit had connected the dots to deduce that the Pixie might be experimenting with the spies.

This had been a seminal moment in the senior staff meeting as far as the Pixie was concerned. That moment had given Falcon the opportunity to be clever, and, *of course*, she jumped at the chance. And that had allowed the Pixie to *reluctantly* admit to the experiments with Bitch Bot Three.

Yes, the Pixie could have offered the results of Kita's remote viewing. But the chances of the senior staff accepting the drawings as authentic were *greatly* improved because they believed that the Pixie didn't *intend* to offer the results to anyone else.

The results of the Pixie manipulating the emotional states of the senior staff spoke for themselves. Oakford had become more relaxed in the tone of his interactions. Bolobolo had initially bristled at the idea of the Pixie experimenting on Nicolescu's spies, but quickly softened her stance.

And without question, Hunter and Falcon *would* be on a mental high alert during the final shock-drop into the TU Corvi system.

·   ·   ·

On Alpha Pegasi Three, at a spaceport on the outskirts of the capital city, the Mech designated X8eLs9UrXqNp4ZWdKfB3Pk shouted and cheered along with the rest of the Mechs across the planet. As one, they were reacting to the video feed received from their partially filled freighter, which showed it heading into the curled space ring that hung in orbit high above them.

To a Mech, they were ecstatic about the new plan that they had agreed on. And all were now grateful that they had decided to build more than one freighter to bring the harvested humans back to the Mech Home World.

At one point during the last year, the discussions *had* been fierce over how many massive freighters to build. And some among the Mechs had argued that the scanning and distilling of the human took sufficiently long, even with the enormous number of machines that they had built for those tasks, that the payload of *one* freighter could easily keep the machines working long enough for that freighter to move onto the next planet and subsequently harvest millions more humans before the supplies ran out on the Mech Home World.

However, despite the extra *months* it would take to build the additional two freighters, the Mech had eventually decided it would be worth it. And now, as X8eLs9UrXqNp4ZWdKfB3Pk cheered, he realized how *right* that decision had been.

Consequently, only moments after the current freighter disappeared into the curled space ring that hung in orbit above the capital city of Alpha Pegasi Three, another freighter appeared, coming out of the ring, as the Mech cheering increased even more.

Yes, the store of humans on Alpha Pegasi Three *had* been woefully inadequate. But while the first freighter returned to the Mech Home World with the pittance that had been found on the planet, the second freighter would take the Mechs who had stayed behind on Alpha Pegasi Three onto the *next* Realm world.

And the Mechs were already imagining the abundance of humans they would find there to harvest. Even better, after the next Realm world had been harvested, the second freighter would return to the Mech Home World, and the *third* freighter would arrive to take the Mechs to the *next* Realm world to harvest.

And at that point, all would know that the Glorious Connectome Age had *truly* commenced.

•   •   •

In Jerusalem on Earth, in the living area of a luxury hotel's top-floor penthouse that he rented for himself as a personal playground, Ton continued to listen with great amusement to the expletive-laced tirades of the helpless, enraged woman who hung from the ceiling in front of him. While Ton knew that the woman was *deadly* serious about what she *wanted* to do to him, he also knew that she was absolutely *incapable* of carrying out any of her threats.

After all, while still under the influence of Angel Haze, she had advised Ton about how he should bind her to *ensure* that she would be helpless and *utterly* unable to escape. And without question, *that* aspect of the situation *delighted* Ton. But there were *many* other things that Ton found *magnificent* about the many moments he had spent in this precise scenario over the last three years.

The object of his attention was, as always, the highly regarded Lieutenant Aeon Sotheby, considered by many in the Realm as the ultimate example of the Realm maiden ideal and the pinnacle of femininity and elegance.

Obviously, Sotheby's physical beauty played a significant role in Ton's appreciation for the moments that he spent with her. After all, Ton always restrained her naked, suspended from the ceiling in intricate rope bondage poses inspired by the pre-Coming Japanese tradition of Shibari.

However, even better, the Sotheby family was *still* considered a kind of royalty within the Realm. And it seemed *so* delicious to Ton that *most* Realmers would be stunned speechless to hear Sotheby curse at him as she had for the past hour. Most Realmers couldn't conceive that their ideal of femininity could have such a deep and broad understanding of vulgar nomenclature. And neither could they imagine that she would be able to describe in such intimate detail the horrors that she wished to visit on Ton.

Of course, it was just as delicious for Ton to know that those same Realmers would also find Sotheby's current appearance utterly shocking. After all, she had been twisted and bent to overly exaggerate the beautiful lines of her body. And then she had been severely lashed in place to make it clear to any observer that anyone could do anything they wanted to her without consequence. Indeed, most Realmers would find that combination of extreme display and enticing temptation to be *so* shocking that they would immediately assume the video feed had originated in the Night as an attempt to defame and discredit both Ton *and* Sotheby.

Still, *if* the citizens of the Realm were exposed to the scene, few would find the strength to look away. Yes, Realmers might spit and sputter, expressing their abhorrence of the scene, but they would *still* stare. And they *would* gawk.

Ton didn't plan to offer the citizens of the Realm the chance to ogle Sotheby any time soon. He *enjoyed* knowing he had a secret that would make the eyes of the planetary leadership across the Realm roll back into their heads. But for now, there was no reason for his secret to be known.

Notably, it was also true that Ton derived even more enjoyment from the situation, knowing that if Sotheby had her way, *he* would be the object of *her* humiliation and torment. And Sotheby would be enjoying *his* desperation every bit as much as *he* was enjoying *hers*.

And that understanding *wasn't* mere speculation on Ton's part. Indeed, at one point, Sotheby had arranged for Ton to be displayed in what was arguably the most emasculating, embarrassing, and painful way possible. However, in Ton's case, it wasn't naked rope bondage. Instead, it was lingerie, a tight-laced corset, an armbinder and hobble skirt, impossibly high stilettos, huge, painful breast prosthetics, and razor wire around the most sensitive body part as he hung by the neck.

Given that, Ton felt little sympathy for his captive, especially since he knew, even now, how *cruel* Sotheby would be to him if their roles were somehow reversed. And it *wasn't* because of anything that Ton had *done* to Sotheby up to that point.

Sotheby simply *hated* men, and she had come to the point where she wanted to humiliate and punish Ton for the rest of his life.

Thankfully, it hadn't worked out that way because PLOKTA had intervened at precisely the right time. And Ton would be forever grateful for that because PLOKTA's actions not only allowed him to be the High King Ruler of the Realm, but they also meant that he *wasn't* in Sotheby's thrall.

She was in *his*. And when she wasn't under the control of Angel Haze, she was hanging from the ceiling of Ton's penthouse, helpless and furious, spitting ineffectual curses and trying to pretend that her tirades had *some* effect on him.

Now, in the midst of Sotheby's latest loud and deluded performance, the tablet beside Ton chirped with a comm requested from PLOKTA. And indeed, the idea of answering the comm in the present circumstances *delighted* Ton with its possibilities.

Just a week before, with Sotheby under the influence of Angel Haze, Ton had discussed just such a scenario with her. And he had asked her for ideas on how to answer the comm without anyone suspecting that she was helpless and on display a mere meter away, hidden from the front-facing video feed sensor on the tablet.

Ton had *loved* the suggestion that Sotheby had provided. And now, with the perfect opportunity to test Sotheby's drug-addled suggestion, Ton quickly entered the code on the table to bring up the control program that Sotheby had designed for herself.

And he quickly tapped the "mute" button.

That button activated a dozen electrostimulation therapy devices, strategically located across Sotheby's body. And instantly, Sotheby fell silent as her mouth flew wide and her jaw began trembling. Delightfully, at the same time, Sotheby's tongue began to wallow in her mouth, and her body writhed in concert.

Ton was amazed by the effectiveness of the devices. One moment, it seemed impossible that anything could distract Sotheby from her rage and condemnations of him. And in the next, her eyes were wide with torment, and her body was reduced to spasms that robbed her of any control.

In all honesty, Ton had no doubt it would work. Sotheby had designed the system. And she had used herself as the test subject to ensure that the electrical stimulation delivered by the modules attached to her body would be absolutely effective in rendering her unable to continue what she obviously *still* wanted to do.

Yes, Sotheby *was* managing some soft gargling noises from time to time. But Ton knew the comm's background noise removal algorithm would have no difficulty removing those.

Delighted that Sotheby's solution for allowing him to converse on a comm while she hung before him worked so well, Ton now entered the command on the tablet to accept the video comm request from PLOKTA as Sotheby continued to thrash back and forth in front of him silently.

"Report," Ton began, knowing that PLOKTA would not have contacted him unless he had something urgent to tell him.

"A second Mech freighter just emerged from the curled space ring above Alpha Pegasi Three," PLOKTA announced. "The Mechs that the first freighter left behind on the planet are loading onto the second freighter now. Presumably, that second freighter is going to take them to whatever Realm world they are going to target next."

Ton smiled. "Excellent," he responded. "So the invasion of Alpha Pegasi Three wasn't an individual occurrence. It is part of a campaign. We can *definitely* use this. And a particular use case immediately comes to mind."

Now, Ton paused for a moment to give PLOKTA the chance to ask the obvious question. And, of course, that moment also gave Ton the chance to glance at Sotheby's continued torment.

"And that use case is?" PLOKTA responded, right on cue.

Ton smiled. "We've been exploring possible scenarios for dealing with the *Dominion*," he began. "I find this an intriguing scenario. The crew of the *Dominion* has a deep emotional connection to the Mechs. After all, they supposedly destroyed the Mech Hive at one point and rid the universe of the scourge of the Mechs. And then, the Mechs started popping up in other locations with modifications not seen on the Mechs who inhabited the Mech Hive.

"Inevitably, that unfinished task has created some sense of responsibility in Captain Oakford at the very least. And while other members of the senior staff might be willing to turn their backs on the Realm, Captain Oakford and Chief Medicalist Bolobolo, along with Chief Tactician MacDuff, will find it very difficult *not* to respond if we reach out to them with a plea to help us rid the Realm of this scourge. And perhaps, those members of the senior staff will even feel it is their *destiny* to eliminate that threat a second time.

"Of course, Chiefs Falcon and Hunter will likely object. They will understand that we are setting a trap for the *Dominion*. But ultimately, I'm willing to bet that Captain Woody will be so stiff and hardened to his messiah complex that he will believe that his battlecruiser has been prepared for just such a moment as this. And he will be more than ready to sweep in and demonstrate to all that he and his crew are still *good*, and not the *evil* we have portrayed them to be.

"And I can practically *guarantee* that if we offer them assurances that they will earn a temporary amnesty from all charges and possibly a *permanent* one, Oakford will see that as a chance to find redemption."

PLOKTA frowned. "And Oakford won't listen to Falcon or Hunter or MacDuff when they tell him that it is likely a trap?!" he asked incredulously. "And *if* Oakford won't listen, Falcon and Hunter won't just take control from him?! I can't see *any* way that Falcon and Hunter would believe that we aren't going to attack them as soon as the *Dominion* lands in the Realm."

Ton smiled. "Wait and see!" he offered jubilantly. "There's a reason for the old saying, 'Beware the man who feels the hand of God on his shoulder.'

Those men can justify anything in their minds, even the most *suicidal* of all missions. And the saying is *especially* true of those leaders who, through some accidental fortunes, have survived one or more incidents that should have destroyed them. In *those* cases, it's practically *impossible* to refuse to act even it the potentials seem too dangerous.

"Once one or more disasters have been averted unexpectedly, the *new* expectation becomes that the disasters will *always* be averted. There is a powerful seduction in the idea that you have a *destiny*."

Interestingly, as Ton had pontificated about the impending destruction of the *Dominion*, his eyes had drifted upward to watch Sotheby. Throughout the conversation, Ton's former nemesis continued to hang helplessly from the ceiling, still writhing and gargling quietly as pulses of electricity coursed through her body, forcing the muscles across her body to twist and seize uncontrollably.

Ton happily adopted the image as a prophecy for what was in store for the *Dominion*. Once an ally, then an adversary, soon enough, the famed battlecruiser would be rendered torn and useless. And Ton would bring its crew back to Jerusalem, where he could parade them through the streets and into the meeting hall of the Leadership Council administrative building. Once there, Ton planned to call a meeting of all the planetary leaders of the Realm and pronounce judgment on the renegade crew, sentencing all of them to the only punishment possible for those who had taken an oath to defend the Realm and then turned their backs on their duties and aided the enemy.

It was treason. And before the Coming, treason always carried the penalty of death. Ton was looking forward to watching the crew of the *Dominion* die in public executions.

"Interesting," Ton heard PLOKTA say, snapping Ton back to the present and reminding him he was still on a comm.

Ton smiled. "Sorry," he said. "I allowed myself a moment of distraction as I imagined the end of the *Dominion* and its crew. And, of course, I am at the penthouse, enjoying Lieutenant Sotheby's company. And she is *very* distracting. She's also *quite* inventive. While she was under the influence last week, I asked her to come up with a mechanism that I could initiate that would *instantly* force her to silence if I needed to respond to a comm. She devised a configuration of electrostimulation devices, strategically placed, that would cause her muscles, including those in her jaw, lips, and tongue, to seize."

Ton tapped the camera select on the comm to switch to the rear camera on his tablet, so PLOKTA could see Evansworth squirming, obviously *not* under the influence of Angel Haze.

PLOKTA's eyes widened as he watched the images. Then he shook his head in amazement.

"You know if she ever got loose and she wasn't on Angel Haze," he observed, "she would come after you with a fury that's hard to imagine."

Ton laughed. "Of that I am *certain*," he said confidently. "But it's just so delightful to listen to her as she tries to intimidate me with her threats. Women often deceive themselves into believing that they can force men into doing anything if they rant and nag for long enough.

"Even now, our beautiful Aeon Sotheby still believes that. So I let her have her say. And *then*, after an hour or two, I stroll over to her and play with her and show her again how completely I *own* her.

"You cannot *imagine* how angry *that* makes her. It is *glorious*, and I have *you* to thank for this incredible turn of events. I will never forget that you are the one who made this possible.

"Keep me informed on the activities of the Mechs. I'm certain we have more threats ahead for the Realm. But, of course, we have already decided that we don't need the vast majority of Realm citizens to survive as we move into this new age, so none of this needs to concern us to any significant degree. Ton out."

27.

On Upper Deck 1 on the *Dominion*, MacDuff strolled into the Main Hall with Guan. Earlier, MacDuff had told Guan that he wanted to begin meeting with her on a regular basis now that she was his second-in-command.

The meetings weren't new for MacDuff. For as long as MacDuff had headed the tactical teams on the Dominion, he had maintained a regular schedule of discussing the state of the teams with his second-in-command. And then, if needed, they would examine potential solutions to any problems that had arisen.

What *was* different now was the fact that Guan was MacDuff's first *female* second-in-command. And while all the other meetings between MacDuff and his second-in-command had occurred in MacDuff's quarters, that didn't seem appropriate when meeting with Guan.

Additionally, MacDuff had considered using the Mess Hall for their meeting, discussing the tactical teams over a meal. But a meal in the Mess Hall would present too many opportunities for interruption. And if history was any predictor of future possibilities, MacDuff knew there would be times when he needed to discuss matters *privately* with Guan. MacDuff couldn't do that in the Mess Hall, surrounded by other crewmembers at nearby tables.

Interestingly, the designers of the *Trinity-Class* battlecruisers had created a workspace for the Master Sergeant of the tactical teams on Upper Deck 2 as part of that level's administrative suite of offices. But MacDuff had never used the office in all the years he had served on the *Dominion*. And he didn't see the point of starting that now. And he couldn't see how meeting behind the closed door of an office would be any different than meeting behind the closed door of his quarters.

Consequently, MacDuff had reserved a block of time in the Main Hall for his first meeting with his new second-in-command. MacDuff doubted the extravagance of the Main Hall would have the same effect on Guan as it did on many of the *Dominion's* other crew members.

Still, MacDuff hadn't chosen the space for his meeting with Guan to inspire her. Instead, it was a public space. Everyone on board the *Dominion* understood that activities in the Main Hall were recorded on video feeds. But at the same time, those feeds were sealed and only available to others if Oakford approved.

In other words, the Main Hall *would* afford MacDuff and Guan their privacy when they needed it for their discussions. And the room was large enough to offer both MacDuff and Guan a bit of exercise as they strolled around its perimeter.

Now, the personnel doors closed behind MacDuff and Guan as the pair turned to begin walking around the outer edge of the room. On entering, MacDuff hadn't bothered to raise the lighting level to full illumination. And that gave the starfield beyond the sweeping arc of the enormous windows a chance to shine as the *Dominion* moved toward the final curled space funnel that contained the location for the shock-drop to the TU Corvi system.

Now, MacDuff began the informal meeting.

"Traditionally," he said, "I met with my second at least once every two weeks to get another perspective on the readiness state of the tactical teams. Additionally, I would like to invite you to bring up any topic you would like to discuss. It's essential that we have a clear understanding of how we view the cohesiveness of the tactical teams and their ready state.

"For instance, I am interested to know if you have had any issues with any of the other tactical team members reacting to your new position, given that it's been several cycles since your installation?"

Guan shook her head. "None," she answered flatly. "There are a few of the former crewmembers who rejoined the ship who would have preferred that you name them as your second, but no one has insinuated that your choice was ill-advised."

"Good," MacDuff said. "In reviewing the video feeds of the practice sessions in the dojo, I find that most members of the tactical teams are maintaining their regimens. And I am pleased with their continuing progress."

"Agreed," Guan responded. "I have no concerns about the striving to improve existing skill sets from the majority of the individuals currently serving on the tactical teams. However, I do believe that some of the women rescued from the genetic research facility on Nu Scorpii One are using their positions on the tactical teams to attempt to gather attention from the male tactical team members. I plan to encourage them to be more diligent with their katas so that they can test on a regular basis and advance in their rankings."

"That sounds like an excellent idea," MacDuff replied. "Are you seeing any issues with the tactical team members becoming entangled in romantic interests with each other? Given the physical contact between the men and women on the tactical teams, it seems inevitable that some would succumb to behavior that will lead to unwanted outcomes."

"Agreed," Guan repeated. "And again, I believe that the women who were rescued from the genetic research facility are most susceptible to that failing. And that yearning inevitably attracts the notice of the male tactical team members. Interestingly enough, the former *female* crewmembers who rejoined the crew and were also tactical team members seem to be the primary counterbalance, keeping the men from pursuing the interested Nightling females. At present, it seems sufficient for the Realmer women to give the male tactical team members a disparaging look if they start becoming overly friendly with the women from the research facility. I will also pay attention to that dynamic. And I will insert myself as needed to ensure that there is no fraternization among the tactical team members. I believe you have always been correct in asserting that such emotional entanglements hamper the efficiency of the teams, no matter what the assignment."

MacDuff nodded. "Let me know if you experience any difficulty in dealing with that issue," he advised. "At the end of the day, the reproductive drives are incessant in their efforts, and it seemed likely that some of the tactical team members, no matter how well-intentioned, might succumb to emotional attachments.

"On a related topic of the assignments we may face in the future, I do have to admit that I am uncertain what role the tactical teams will play going forward. Historically, the *Dominion* was designed to be part of a police-like force to patrol the Realm. When the *Trinity-Class* battlecruisers were commissioned, there were far fewer Realm Force campuses and outposts scattered around the

Realm. In that regard, it made sense to have a mobile tactical force that could be dispatched quickly and effectively.

"In addition, much later, when the *Dominion* was hiring out its security services to worlds in the Night, our tactical teams were in constant demand to supply extra personnel to ensure order on the surface of planets. But, of course, that demand has waned considerably with the slaughter conducted across the majority of the Night worlds.

"Honestly, looking forward, it seems likely that our future conflicts might involve scenarios where the tactical teams might not have the opportunity to exert much influence. If we find ourselves on a world attacked by Abaddon and his associates, and we no longer enjoy the protection that we have in the past, it seems unlikely that we would be able to stand against their aggression.

"In addition, from what I saw of the *Majesty*, its energy weapons would inflict significant damage on us before we would have any chance to gain the upper hand. And if Lieutenant Sotheby decided to tear this ship to pieces, we might find ourselves suddenly ejected into the vacuum of space. Even if we could don stealth suits beforehand, a handful of fusion torpedos, launched to burn up the wreckage and personnel, would render those suits useless and quickly commend us to the Father's eternal care.

"However, as Captain Oakford has noted, there are too many moments in the history of this ship when there *should* have been some disastrous outcome. And yet, the crew and this battlecruiser have survived. This suggests that we may have a role to play in future events. But it does not guarantee our survival or that we will not be called on to perform some sacrificial heroic act. For now, we can only prepare and hone our skills to the best of our abilities so that we will be ready for any eventuality."

"Understood," Guan replied. "I will attempt to ensure that all the members of the tactical teams are focused on that goal."

"Good," MacDuff commented. "Is there any other topic of discussion that you believe might be important for us to review? Even if you have something that feels like a mere intuition without any direct evidence, I would encourage you to share it with me."

Guan thought for a moment before she answered. "During the remarks that led to your invitation for me to become your second-in-command, there was one tactical team member who exhibited reactions that seemed out of place with the circumstances. He also seemed preoccupied with the fact that you were meeting with all the team leaders. After you made your invitation, he seemed to relax into attitudes that were more typical for the situation. The episode seemed odd to me. But, at that point, I had no basis to bring it to anyone's attention."

MacDuff couldn't help but remember the revelations from the most recent senior staff meeting. He looked at Guan. "Who was the tactical team member in question?" he asked.

"Dmitri Korsakovich," Guan answered.

MacDuff thought for another moment, but decided that the question fell within his purview as Chief Tactician of the *Dominion*.

"Pix!" MacDuff called out. "Is Dmitri Korsakovich one of the spies that Commander Nicolescu sent to accompany the former crewmembers who rejoined the *Dominion*?"

"Yes," the Pixie answered.

"And have you been distracting him as well?" MacDuff asked.

"Honestly?" the Pixie responded. "I told Captain Oakford and Chief Falcon that I was distracting the spies, but they didn't seem like they wanted that many details, so I just lumped them together and said I was distracting all of them. However, Tactical Team Member Korsakovich has approached the whole situation with more caution. Granted, he exhibited the same unguarded expressions as the rest in the early days of returning to the *Dominion*. He was clearly not thrilled to be here. But he's never tried to pass any information back to Realm Force. It's like he's trying to be careful not to make himself vulnerable to discovery too soon. Maybe that's just because he's been trained to think more from a tactical perspective and he hadn't come across any information that he deems important enough to risk exposure. So no, he's never stepped out of line. He's never done anything to endanger the crew. And he's never made a big enough mistake that has allowed me to exploit and blackmail him."

"Thank you for keeping an eye on him," MacDuff offered. "I will assume that you will continue to do so."

"Absolutely!" the Pixie replied. "But I'm sure your new second-in-command will do the same!"

Guan nodded. "I will," she said.

"Good," MacDuff commented. He paused before continuing. "I have one final item I'd like to discuss. And it is an item that is difficult to reconcile with my responsibilities on the *Dominion*. However, I am trusting that when the time comes, there will be a clear direction for me to do what I believe I need to do."

Guan glanced at MacDuff. "Are you referring to your conviction that you need to be available to keep Chief Hunter from mortal harm?" she asked.

"Yes," MacDuff answered. "To be clear, however, I have told Captain Oakford in the past that I have never felt that my urging to keep Chief Hunter from fatal harm superseded my duty to the Dominion. I indicate to him that I have pledged my life to the protection of the crew with whom I've served for decades. And as part of that pledge, I affirmed to Captain Oakford that my priorities would weigh in the direction of the command staff. At the time, I did not want Captain Oakford to feel any discomfort, wondering if I would honor the pledge I had freely made when accepting my role as head of the *Dominion's* tactical teams. At that time, I renewed my pledge to him that I would gladly throw myself into the fray before him. And I assured him that I have never considered doing anything different."

"And have you changed your mind with regard to that sentiment?" Guan wondered.

"I have not," MacDuff answered immediately. "However, I do recognize there may be conditions where I can retain that sentiment and *still* be unavailable to lead the tactical teams. And that may be because I am engaged in assisting the senior staff. Or it may be because I am protecting Chief Hunter. In every case, you will need to be prepared to assume command of the tactical team and dispatch them as needed."

Guan nodded. "I understand that to be part of my responsibilities as your second-in-command," she acknowledged. "And I am ready to assume that task, if needed."

"Excellent," MacDuff responded.

•   •   •

On the Bridge of the *Dominion*, Hunter sat in the Chief Pilot's Pod, as he manually piloted the battlecruiser through the curled space funnel that contained the last shock-drop location that would hopefully land the ship in the TU Corvi system. As always, in preparation for the shock-drop, Murg had taken many of the automated systems offline to protect them. So instead of a full wrap-around console filled with displays and screens detailing the ship, its surroundings, and the current navigational path, Hunter had his basic navigational controls and a three-dimensional map of the current curled space funnel showing the *Dominion's* current position.

Many years ago, when Falcon was Lead Commander of the *Dominion*, and she ordered Hunter to execute the first shock-drop, he had been surprised when Murg shut everything off. And as he manually piloted the oversized battlecruiser through the tight turns of that curled space funnel, Hunter had been very careful to keep the ship off the sidewalls.

Now, over two decades later, Hunter was still focused, but he *knew* the ship. He knew how to push it. He knew how to slip it. And he still appreciated how agile it was for a vessel its size. And unless something unusual happened, Hunter didn't think there would be any problem keeping the *Dominion* off the sidewall of the curled space funnel before the battle cruiser reached the shock-drop location.

What happened after that was another matter. And yes, the previous three drops that the *Dominion* had completed were based on the quick series of images that Hunter had seen when making shock-drops using the more established routes. And they *worked*. The *Dominion* had successfully traversed them on its way to the TU Corvi system.

Given that, it seemed likely that the final shock-drop would work as well. Still, there was always the potential for error because all of it was based on quick flashes of insight, but it held little concern for Hunter. He accepted the fact that he and Murg had been able to assemble the information to put the *Dominion* in the TU Corvi system because, for some larger reason, the battlecruiser *needed* to be in the TU Corvi system. And that acceptance was part of a much larger journey in the perception of his existence that Hunter had taken during his time on the *Dominion*.

When he had first left the Mercenaries to come to the Realm and apply to Realm Force, Hunter's sole focus had been on knowing what he knew and refusing to speculate otherwise. As a life rule, Hunter had only been *sure* of the things he could verify on a repeatable basis in the physical world.

Then, following his graduation from Realm Force Academy, Hunter joined the crew of the *Dominion*. And just over two years after that, he sat in Conference Room One, during a senior staff meeting, and the ship's Chief Medical Officer, Catherine Casteel, claimed that she had the power to heal using only her mind.

Surprisingly enough, that admission made sense to Hunter because it answered a question he had held in his mind for years. On Beta Ceti One, Hunter had singlehandedly taken on a group of Mechs. And he had been wounded badly enough that he *shouldn't* have survived. The damage to his body had been too extensive. It had taken too long for Falcon to get him back to the *Dominion*. Yes, Hunter's genetically engineered body had engineered redundancies that allowed him to endure more extensive physical injuries than most humans.

But the punishment Hunter had taken during the Mech incident on Beta Ceti One was *beyond* anything that he should have lived through. And yet he *had* survived, following a visit from Casteel, at least according to the logs. And once Casteel admitted to being able to heal, it made sense that she had brought him back from the dead.

And that was when Hunter decided that Casteel should demonstrate her powers. And he had convinced MacDuff to break his arm. And Casteel had healed it. And in mere seconds, it was as if Hunter's arm had never been broken.

That moment had begun a journey for Hunter. It had convinced him that life was *more* than he had ever imagined. And in the years that followed, that conviction of "more" had only grown in Hunter. Of course, when he entered demi-god mode during the first confrontation with the Hunter Look-Alikes, his *direct* experience with the Now had made the idea of "more" *irrefutable*.

Unfortunately, Hunter had never achieved the kind of control that Casteel had of the Now. And while Hunter could remember what it felt like to be in demi-god mode, he hadn't experienced the reality of it since then.

Somewhat frustratingly, Hunter *could* spout the platitudes that he had learned from his experience with the Now. He could suggest that the impossible wasn't a matter of degree, like the possible. He could recall that he had realized the impossible and the possible were calibrated precisely in reverse. Things that were *possible* became increasingly difficult to perform until they became *impossible*. But, at the same time, things *impossible* became harder and harder *as* they moved *toward* something *possible*. In other words, once the impossible arrived, the *more* impossible things became, the *easier* it was to achieve.

And at the time, it all made sense. And it not only made sense, but Hunter could also activate the impossible in the real world. He had reached out with his mind and performed whatever things he desired, no matter how seemingly impossible they appeared to be.

Hunter had no idea how to recapture that energy. Casteel seemed to have that energy "on tap" and "at will." But she was the only human that Hunter knew could do that. Yes, the remote viewing with Rachel was interesting, but it really didn't compare to the nearly instantaneous healing that Casteel could perform or what he had done when he was in demi-god mode.

For now, Hunter had concluded that someone or something else arbitrated where and when those ultranatural experiences would occur. And he was content to treat himself as a bit player in someone's much larger game. And that was the reason he had said so little about heading into the TU Corvi system.

If those in charge of the game wanted the *Dominion* to end up in the TU Corvi system, it didn't matter how many Hunter Look-Alike vessels were there waiting for the battlecruiser. And if those in charge of the game *didn't* want the *Dominion* there, the crew was probably doomed no matter how much planning they did.

And no one could predict what would happen when the *Dominion* made the shock-drop. And whatever happened after that… *happened.*

Interestingly, MacDuff's recent discussion of the Parable of the Wedding Banquet made a lot of sense to Hunter. Granted, sometimes the proverbs that MacDuff spouted seemed like a stretch. But this time, the structure of the parable matched what Hunter had already decided on a larger scale.

Someone, single or plural, was playing a long and intricate game. Hunter couldn't deny that he had been offered the opportunity to play some small part. Those parts had been amazing. And some of the experiences had been incredible. And with everything he had seen, Hunter wasn't about to shrink back from that invitation just because there were things about the game he didn't understand.

Besides, Hunter knew for sure that he didn't want anything to do with Abaddon and his associates. They were gruesome destroyers. And sadly, by now, Realm Force wasn't much better. From all appearances, the leadership structures of the Realm had been corrupted by Ton, Angel Haze, and whoever was helping Ton. And they were just as destructive.

Maybe there were still some good people in the Realm. Perhaps they could be inspired to rise and rebel against all the tyranny that threatened humanity.

Hunter had no idea. But Hunter had decided on the best option to guide his life. He would let whoever was in charge of the game set the rules. And then he would follow those rules as closely as he knew how.

And always, every moment, he would *pay attention*. And he would be ready for the Now to show up at any moment.

Hunter's internal clock brought him back to the present. He glanced at the three-dimensional map of the curled space funnel on his wrap-around console to confirm the *Dominion's* position.

"Two minutes to shock-drop," he announced, eyes fixed on the dip in the map that marked the spot where the battlecruiser would blast a hole in the sidewall. Thankfully, there was only a relatively straight stretch of curled space funnel to reach it.

As expected, Hunter heard the chirp of a button press on the Commander's Pod wrap-around display behind him.

"Attention, all hands," Oakford announced, "this is Captain Oakford. All collision protocols should be in place. Please double-check that you are strapped in tightly and assist anyone around you who is not. Then brace for impact. As always, oh Lord, bless the work of our hands."

A moment later, Oakford continued, "Chief Hunter, Chief Falcon, you have the ship."

"Aye, captain," Hunter and Falcon responded simultaneously.

Soon, Falcon, seated at the Chief Technologist's workstation confirmed the instructions, "As discussed, Zach, on my mark, execute a 13-degree turn to port, that's one-three, and fly through the center of the disturbance that I create with the miniguns. Full velocity."

"Aye, Number One," Hunter repeated.

"Murg!" Falcon also called out. "Time to put both Pixies into statis."

"ACK." Murg acknowledged.

Of course, by that point, the *Dominion* was already at battle stations with the Bridge retracted and the blast shutters closed.

"Murg, fire up the shield generators," Falcon added.

As usual, Hunter heard a soft hum race across the ship as Oakford made his final announcement.

"This is the captain," Oakford said. "All hands, brace for impact."

Falcon followed that with her usual countdown, "On my mark, Zach, 13 degrees, that's one-three, to port, full velocity. Here we go... five... four... three... two... one... mark."

As Falcon spoke, Hunter entered the commands for the turn. And on Falcon's "mark," Hunter hit the final button to begin the sequence.

Once more, the *Dominion's* main thrusters instantly roared into overdrive as the battlecruiser's maneuvering jets shoved the vessel hard to the left. Simultaneously, Hunter heard Falcon enter a command behind him, and suddenly, every forward-facing minigun on the battlecruiser came to life.

As usual, the *Dominion* shuddered only temporarily before the main thrusters overcame the sudden backwards shove of the cannons firing simultaneously. And in that moment, once again, everything slowed for Hunter.

Now, under the punishment of the heavy metal slugs, the spot on the sidewall that was closest to the TU Corvi system began to warp and tear apart. And beyond it, Hunter saw the webbing appear once more. And he saw the tendrils connecting certain sections of the webbing to others, flashing and rippling, at times even jumping from one spot to another.

And unbidden, Hunter's consciousness flashed forward into the normal space in the TU Corvi system. A vast armada formed in Hunter's mind, spaced over a giant, uneven grid, large ships at key anchor points with swarms of smaller ships around them. And even farther out, there were more ships, of various sizes, sprinkled about haphazardly.

Worse, there was not only a vast array of vessels waiting for the *Dominion*, but those ships were also positioned in the midst of an enormous, densely populated asteroid field.

Interestingly enough, Hunter could also see a *conspicuous* void among the Look-Alike vessels and the rocks. And it was *precisely* where the shock-drop was about to put the *Dominion*. In addition, that void was also near a large freighter that seemed to shimmer in Hunter's mind.

And Hunter could guess it was the vessel where Moreau and Worku were being held.

In other words, the Look-Alikes had already planned for the possibility that the *Dominion* would use the shock-drop that led to the TU Corvi system. They had made a space and once the battle cruiser appeared there, it would be surrounded by an overwhelming force.

With only milliseconds to decide, Hunter flashed through his options. He could try to bounce the *Dominion* somewhere outside the typical destination of the shock-drop. But there was a better than average chance he would slam the battlecruiser into another vessel or an asteroid. Or, he could let the *Dominion* shock-drop into the location where the Look-Alikes were expecting it to appear.

Quickly resigning himself to the only approach that would guarantee the safety of the battlecruiser as it *arrived* in the TU Corvi system, Hunter pulled his hands away from the surface of the warp-around console in front of him. And he waited for the *Dominion* to slam into the tear in the sidewall of the curled space funnel.

28.

Seated at the Chief Technologist's workstation on the Bridge of the *Dominion*, Falcon felt the *Dominion* slam into the distortion that she had created with the forward miniguns. And as expected, that impact threw Falcon hard into her harnesses as the *Dominion* suddenly drained of power.

And everything went black as the battlecruiser shock-dropped into the TU Corvi system.

As always, the power outage lasted only a moment. And then, whatever swallowed the energy from the ship, spit it back out, turning the *Dominion* blue, within and without, as high-frequency plasma ribbons danced over every surface, including Falcon's cybersuit.

Amidst the squeaks, squeals, and even shrieks from the crewmembers on the Bridge as the plasma found inconvenient places to race across control panels and snap at flesh, Falcon struggled to move her hands.

The paralysis was normal, and it *would* be temporary. It happened with every shock-drop. But Falcon knew she needed eyes on the situation in the TU Corvi system as quickly as possible. Unfortunately, the dancing plasma ribbons had other plans for her. And for the next few moments, Falcon could only shudder and twitch, as much as she *wished* she could do otherwise.

Thankfully, the plasma ribbons soon dove into the closest control panels, disappeared as everything snapped back to normal.

Now, Falcon's hand raced across the control panel of her workstation, even as she mentally reactivated the comms of her cybersuit and overrode all the bandwidth limitations that usually protected her from overload. As agreed, Murg was simultaneously patching her comm requests to the raw, ship-wide stream of the Dominion's sensors. And an instant later, Falcon's awareness surged, allowing her to see the entire ship all at once and everything beyond it that the sensors could detect.

Quickly zooming out, Falcon allocated the cybersuit's processing resources to operate on multiple simultaneous tasks. And the results for the basic counts of the Hunter Look-Alike vessels came back first.

Fifty heavy carriers, each twice the size of the *Dominion.* Five hundred freighters. A thousand destroyers. Fifteen hundred orbital platforms. One hundred *thousand* assault vessels.

Soon after, the tactical estimates began to pour in. Approximate armament destructive differential, in excess of 2,500 percent. Deployable single or dual pilot attack craft differential of 6,000 percent. Tallied personnel differential of 5,000 percent.

"Captain," the Pixie called out, obviously back from hibernation during the shock-drop, "we need to launch a *full-scale* fusion torpedo attack now and battle our way out through the weakest corridor *now*! Then we can loop back and pick our battles."

"Hold," Falcon responded immediately. "We are outmatched in every direction, and the Hunter Look-Alikes aren't currently attacking. Maybe there's a deal to be made."

As if on cue, the crew member on the Comm workstation in the Pit called out. "I have an incoming video comm request," she said.

"Route it to the main display," Oakford responded.

The video feed didn't surprise Falcon when it appeared. She expected the Look-Alikes to attempt to evoke a severe emotional response in the crew of the *Dominion.* And indeed, there *were* gasps from crewmembers operating workstations in the Pit. And that was understandable because the images appearing on the main display were *gruesome.*

The feed appeared to originate from a storage bay, but one with displays lining the walls. And while some of the crewmembers on the Bridge would have no context for the damage that the storage bay had sustained, Falcon immediately recognized it as the result of *dozens* of Hunter Look Alikes executing their suicide protocols.

All of the upright surfaces, both walls and displays, were splattered with caustic chemical burns, caused by a thick red goo that had then slid downward, leaving a streak of corroded metal behind. The decking was worse. There were mounds of the same dark red ooze scattered about. Some of it was still smoking as it ate the floor.

From experience, Falcon knew that each blob had been a Hunter Look-Alike.

Still, while the storage bay itself could inspire at most disgust and abhorrence, Falcon knew that the Look-Alikes were depending on what they had done to Worku and Moreau to evoke the even more dramatic emotions.

For one thing, Worku and Moreau were naked. And they had obviously hung from the ceiling for quite some time. In fact, both had hung for long enough that their shoulders had been pulled out of joint. And with the first glance at the main display, it was evident that their shoulders would be roaring with pain in those distended positions.

Moreau's predicament was worse. Not only was he hanging from the ceiling, but his left kneecap was also clearly broken into pieces. And whatever had pummelled the kneecap hard enough to shatter it had continued to drive the resulting jagged shards outward with enough force to rip and sever the ligaments that usually held a knee together.

Consequently, Moreau's body was slung to the side since his left leg couldn't bear any weight. And that made the twisting of his shoulders look even more painful.

And that wasn't *nearly* the worst of it. Pus-filled trails ran down the naked bodies of both Moreau and Worku. And each began with a larger splatter mark. Consequently, it was easy to conclude the wounds were caused by the caustic goo flung outward from suicidal Look-Alikes. After all, the pattern of the wounds closely resembled the scarring on the walls and displays. But in the cases of Moreau and Worku, the caustic ooze had eaten away their flesh and left a weeping sore behind.

Interestingly, the Hunter Look-Alikes had dedicated themselves to the torture of the pair, but they had also pledged their skills to keeping their captives alive. Both Moreau and Worku had tubes inserted into their mouths. One seemed to carry fluids, the other air. And despite the minimal care those tubes seemed to provide, Falcon understood that their sole purpose was to prolong the pair's torment.

Both Moreau and Worku were gasping for air. And in between their abdomens were twitching, as if their bodies were constantly on the verge of retching.

In addition, a robot stood beside each of the pair with various extensions and implements. And even now, the robots were stretching out an arm to hold a wand closely to Moreau and Worku's sensitive regions as electricity arced to hiss and snap.

But of course, the most unambiguous indication of Moreau and Worku's torment was the crazed, agonizing expressions on their faces and the desperate wallowing of their mouths as they seemed to be pleading for relief.

And yes, all of it matched Rachel's drawings.

"This is what we do to those who tempt our ire," a spokesman for the Hunter Look-Alikes began, narrating the scene but not appearing as of yet. "And if it is not immediately apparent, we can keep Doctor Moreau and Jazarah Worku alive for as long as we desire. If they had cooperated, we might have ended their lives quickly and with minimal pain.

"But instead, they tempted us with their lies. Consequently, we have reduced their existence to what a religiously-minded human might consider a living *hell*.

"While we might not be so antiquated and primitive in our descriptions of it, we can assure you that in this moment, it feels *eternal* to them. And the pain, and the nausea, and the panic are *consuming* any rational thoughts that they might have. And all that remains are the guttural cries and the begging for death.

"Remember what you are seeing here. For this is where we make this reality *personal* to each of you.

"This is what we will do to every member of the *Dominion's* crew if you tempt us. This is what we will do if you do not accede to our demands. Your battlecruiser is *completely* outmatched. You have *no* chance against our might.

"Consequently, you *will* send Adi Bolobolo to us in an unarmed shuttle. And we will bring her aboard the quarantined freighter where Doctor Moreau and Jazarah Worku are being held. And then, you will watch as we interrogate *her* so that we may learn how she developed a virus that is so effective against us.

"If Adi Bolobolo fully supplies us with the information we seek, and we can authenticate it, we will kill her quickly. Then we will annihilate the *Dominion* with a barrage of attacks that will guarantee that your so-called battlecruiser will be torn to pieces and the crew humanely annihilated.

"However, if you do not send Adi Bolobolo to us, or she does not supply the information that we seek, we will reduce her to the same state as Doctor Moreau and Jazarah Worku. We will also cripple your ship with a precisely targeted attack that will allow us to capture your crew alive. We will then process your crew one by one and force you to watch as we reduce each one to the same state as Doctor Moreau and Jazarah Worku.

"We have specifically built the freighter that sits off your port side for this purpose. It functions not only as a quarantine vessel to protect us from the viruses that Adi Bolobolo has developed, but also to serve as a purgatory in which we can inflict our wrath on the crew of the *Dominion* for allowing your Chief Medicalist to engage in an effort that is nothing short of genocide.

"This is the destiny that we have built for you. This is the hell where we will tend to your burning for *hundreds* of years unless you do precisely as we demand.

"You have four hours to present Adi Bolobolo to us. Otherwise, we will cripple your vessel, board it with an overwhelming force of twenty thousand of our kind, and begin the process of committing each of you to our mind-rending, burning purgatory."

●   ●   ●

In Conference Room One, Oakford stated what he believed was the obvious once the senior staff settled into their usual places around the conference room table.

"We are *not* turning Adi over to the Look-Alikes," Oakford said. "I will order the initiation of the *Dominion's* self-destruct protocols before I allow that."

"Captain," the Pixie interrupted unexpectedly with an urgency and a bit of pique in its voice, "I believe this is *precisely* what I had hoped to avoid. And it was the reason I suggested that we bring the full complement of fusion torpedoes to a ready state before we executed the shock drop. The Hunter Look-Alikes would have had no mechanism to predict *when* we would appear and that would have allowed us to open an initial corridor with the torpedos and battle our what to the outer edge of the armada."

way

Hunter smiled. "*If* the torpedos didn't detonate because of some random energy spike as we moved through the shock-drop," he observed.

"If they *detonated*," the Pixie shot back, "we would have been in the very same situation as Captain Oakford ordering the self-destruct, which I am *obviously* not in favor of doing."

Oakford glanced at Murg, wondering what would happen if he ordered a self-destruct authorization and the Pixie refused to allow it to happen. As usual, Murg was bent over the display at his seat around the conference table, his hands flying over the control pad in front of him.

"It was my call," Falcon interjected. "And as you know, I opted *not* to do that because doing so would have resulted in a retaliatory strike from the Look-Alikes. I don't believe we could have survived that. We are still alive, as of now. And while we are alive, there are always possibilities."

Oakford opted to finish stating the obvious point that he was making when the Pixie interrupted him. "Returning to the point I was trying to make," he continued, "we are not going to turn Adi over to the Look-Alikes, and even if we *did* turn Adi over to the Look-Likes, it wouldn't make any difference because Adi doesn't *know* what they think she knows, and she can't fake that kind of information. So the Look-Likes wouldn't get what they wanted. And then they would proceed with their gruesome plan, and nothing would be gained.

"And even if Adi *could* fake her way through the information that the Look-Alikes think they want and she satisfied *all* their requirements, there would be *nothing* stopping the Look-Alikes from crippling the *Dominion* and subjecting us all to the same process as Doctor Moreau and Jaz Workuy just because they *can*, and they think the *Dominion* and its crew have thwarted them twice.

"If we cannot break free of the Look-Alikes or ensure our utter destruction, there is no other outcome where our lives do *not* become a lingering hell."

Falcon smiled. "Exactly, captain," she agreed.

Unfortunately, as far as Oakford was concerned, Falcon stopped there and offered nothing further. And in the silence of the moment that followed, Oakford glanced around the room, waiting to see if anyone had anything else to say. And when there was no response, Oakford made his next obvious statement.

"I am open to discussing the possibilities, now that we have responded to this invitation and find ourselves in the present predicament," he offered

Falcon's smile broadened. "I'm always in favor of taking the direct approach and kicking in the front door," she said. "If that's the choice we're left with, we might as well go out in a blaze of glory. And who knows? With a combination of the Pixie manning the *Dominion's* weaponry and Hunter's pilots running point, a miracle might occur. Or... *another* kind of miracle might occur."

Oakford looked back at Murg. "Murg," he began, "can you gain control of the Look-Alike's systems? And even if you can't get access to all of them, can you get access to *some* of them? Can you find *anything* to slow them down?"

"ACK, NAK...," Murg began, before adding a final comment, "...NAK."

Oakford nodded. He looked at the senior staff before continuing.

"I would guess the Look-Alikes are serious about their four-hour deadline," he said. "Please prep your departments for battle and coordinate to plan out our best possible attack strategy. We'll reconvene on the Bridge thirty minutes before the deadline and commence our attack at five minutes prior. And we will commit ourselves and our ship into the hands of our Creator. Dismissed."

•   •   •

In a tactical virtual environment that displayed a 360-degree panorama of all the Look-Alike resources assembled against the *Dominion*, Falcon, Murg, and the Pixie reviewed thousands of potential offensive assault vectors in rapid succession. Given the need and the purpose of the current virtual environment, Murg obviously hadn't left the design to his Troyd interface to create a theme of intriguing visual elements. Instead, Murg had opted for a basic functional implementation of simple diagrams.

On a small circular floating platform, Falcon, Murg, and the Pixie, represented as a blue sphere, stood with the TU Corvi system laid out before them. A faint, three-dimensional gridwork defined distances. Physical elements such as the system's star and the dense asteroid field were represented with more realistic symbols, but they were nearly transparent.

As for the tactical elements in the virtual environment, all the spacecraft in the system were designated with mere dots and labels, with larger ships represented by larger dots. Additionally, as the simulations of the assault vectors played out, lines raced among the dots, showing potential flight paths and calculated attacks.

Before entering the virtual environment, Falcon *had* asked Hunter if he wanted to join the planning by signing onto the virtual environment from a workstation. Hunter had deferred.

"You, Murg, and Pix can crunch the numbers faster without me," he said. "And I'm guessing it won't make any difference which direction we head. We'll just need to commit to a line of attack and give it everything we've got."

"Agreed," Falcon had responded. "But we'll run through the possibilities just in case. And then, we'll probably generate a random number, crunch that down to a vector, and fire off in that direction when the time comes."

Now, after almost twenty minutes of the virtual environment rapidly strobing through potential attack vectors and the predicted Look-Alike responses, Falcon felt confident that she, Murg, and the Pixie knew what they had guessed before they started the analysis.

The assembled force of Look-Alike was too large for the *Dominion* to overcome with its available weaponry, no matter what vector they chose or what tactics they employed.

"We had one chance to catch them off guard," the Pixie now groused. "And we didn't take it."

Falcon nodded. "Perhaps," she responded, "but we'll never know for sure. And we have seen extraordinary things happen in the past. Four hours from now, we might be shaking our heads in amazement."

"Unlikely," the Pixie grumbled.

Falcon looked at Murg in the virtual environment, knowing there was no point in responding to the Pixie's pessimism. "I'll report back to Captain Oakford," she said. "Keep sweeping for weaknesses. Maybe we'll get lucky."

•   •   •

Below the Flight Deck, Hunter checked in with his maintenance crews as they performed the final checks on the *Dominion's* twenty-five Hellfire Interceptors and then loaded them with a full complement of weapons.

The designers of the *Trinity-Class* battlecruisers had placed the Flight Deck directly below the Bridge, with its main hangar doors making up part of the *Dominion's* bow. Any fighters returning to the ship for refueling, repairs, or restocking used the Flight Deck to land. Then, elevators at the rear of the

Flight Deck would lower the fighters to the large maintenance bay below, and there the crews would prep the fighters for their return to patrols. Additionally, once the prep was complete, the maintenance crews would load the fighters into the Flight Deck's launch tubes, allowing the pilots to take them back into space.

Hunter had drilled his teams enough that he was confident they would do what they could to keep the Hellfire Interceptors cycling efficiently.

Afterward, Hunter headed up to the Flight Deck to meet with his pilots. "This won't be fancy," he told the assembled group, many of whom he had known and worked with for over two decades. "We're the tip of the wedge. We'll do our best to clear a path. The Pixie will be manning all of the *Dominion's* weaponry and helping us as needed with our task. But the Pixie's primary responsibility will be to protect the ship. And if it comes down to us or the *Dominion*, Pix will do everything it can to protect the ship.

"Make whatever other mental preparations you need to make. We'll regroup here at T-minus thirty."

•   •   •

In her office in Sickbay, Bolobolo watched as the final confirmations arrived from the audit of basic medical supplies stored throughout the *Dominion*. Those supplies had been a later addition to the battlecruiser. And indeed, it had been over fifteen years since the battlecruiser had sustained enough damage to injure multiple crewmembers simultaneously.

During the mission to the Marauder's secondary keep, Oakford had been relieved of duty, and Elspeth Jordan had been made Lead Commander of the *Dominion*. And in relatively short order, she had flown the battlecruiser straight into an asteroid field with disastrous results.

There were multiple impacts. Extensive system damage. Crewmembers wounded all over the battlecruiser.

Thankfully, at that point, Casteel was still the Chief Medical Officer, and she utilized her extraordinary abilities to heal the injured crewmembers to save many from dying. But, of course, Casteel could only be in one location at a time, so the injured had been hauled to the corridors outside a damaged Sickbay and she had healed them there.

Over the years, Bolobolo had often returned to those moments, remembering the scramble to triage crewmembers. And while the *Dominion* did have emergency medical units scattered about the ship, asteroids had ripped through the hull and damaged many of them. Still, the Sickbay crew had known that once they transported the injured to Casteel, she could restore them to perfect health nearly instantly.

And that had simplified the approach to handling the wounded. It didn't matter how broken they were. They just needed to be hauled to Casteel.

Given that she had never been able to learn to do what Casteel could do, Bolobolo had opted for another approach if the *Dominion* ever found itself in a similar situation. Reaching back to her fascination with pre-Coming medical practices, Bolobolo had trained her team in basic, first-response protocols, clearing airways, performing CPR, and controlling bleeding.

Bolobolo had recognized that in the face of any spreading damage to the *Dominion*, her teams might need to stabilize injured crewmembers *before* attempting to get them into a med unit. Consequently, over the years, Bolobolo had tasked her teams with ordering basic first aid supplies from the Galley and distributing them to lockers around the ship.

At the time, Bolobolo had no idea if her teams would even have a chance to use those supplies. And she knew that if they *did* tap into those stores, the situation would be dire. But at least, the Sickbay personnel would be there if they were needed, and they knew how to use the supplies.

Now seeing that all the stored supplies had been double-checked and accounted for, Bolobolo stood and rounded her desk to walk into the Main Area of Sickbay. Only a few minutes passed before all of her teams gathered in the large room to form a circle. When Bolobolo joined them, she took a moment to look at each of her team members before she addressed them.

"I have no idea what the next few hours will hold," she began calmly. "But I do know that when the time comes, we will face it with the calm assurance that we belong to our Great God. Depending on the outcome of this situation, we may or may not have the opportunity to serve the crew of this ship. But if we do, we will do so with the knowledge that our hands, our feet, and our hearts belong to him. And we will do our best to show his love and kindness to everyone we treat.

"For now, I would suggest you take some time to meditate on the victory that we enjoy in our God who sacrificed himself for us, and remember that, at times, he calls on us to sacrifice our lives for others.

"Let me know if you are uncertain of the location of your duty post. Plan to be there at least 45 minutes before the deadline. Dismissed."

•   •   •

In the tactical teams' makeshift dojo of Lower Deck Five, MacDuff addressed the assembled tactical teams.

"I cannot tell you what the next few hours will bring," MacDuff began. "The *Dominion* may be destroyed outright, and we may not have any chance to protect and defend our crew. Or we may find ourselves in a pitched battle for the control of this vessel, outnumbered and facing a capable foe.

"If the situation becomes the latter, remember your history. We faced a single member of this enemy on K2-72e. He killed two of our own and two of Chief Bolobolo's staff. Do not underestimate them.

"We were blooded that day. Acknowledge it. Add it to your assessment of our enemy. But do not make the mistake of fearing them or fearing such a glorious thing as death.

"As I have said many times, I remind you of, once more. We are not those who cower and draw back. We are those who stand in the gap. We are those who wedge ourselves between the danger and the weak. We are those who stare at death full-faced. We are those who have already stripped ourselves of the need for convenience, certainty, and control. And we are those who have ensured our passage onward.

"*This* is the assurance. This is our destiny. Without a doubt, we know that as we fight, and as we fall, others will step forward to take our place. And still others will take their place. And on and on, until the Slayer falls exhausted, unable to wield its sword against us any longer, and Death folds inward and falls into Nothing.

"This is the future that lies sure and straight before us. This is why we cannot know defeat. While we live, we serve. And when we complete our service, we join the Great Reunion. Each of us, perhaps today, perhaps tomorrow, perhaps even later, will face that transformation. But for today, for this day, we serve."

"Hoo-rah?" MacDuff concluded forcefully.

"HOO-RAH!" the tactical teams responded loudly and in unison.

•   •   •

Walking back into her office in the now-empty Sickbay, Bolobolo struggled to keep herself from growing angry with frustration. For one thing, the Hunter Look-Alikes' obsession with her had been an internal torment for Bolobolo from the moment she realized its depth, *years* ago.

At first, it had just seemed *ridiculous*. After the double invasion of Bolobolo's planet, Fomalhaut Four, by Realm Force and the Hunter Look-Alikes, Falcon had told the senior staff of the Look-Alikes' claim that Bolobolo had created a biological weapon for use against them.

Truthfully, it had taken a moment to make Falcon's words make sense because it was so preposterous. But once Bolobolo's brain finally accepted the statement, she also quickly realized that it wouldn't be *possible* to convince the Hunter Look-Alikes that she *wasn't* a threat.

Bolobolo had lived with that softly throbbed dread even since. And then Rachel succeeded in a remote viewing session, locating Moreau and Worku. And the Pixie reported the same. And Bolobolo had actually offered that it might be an "invitation."

Maybe Bolobolo hadn't thought through what she was saying before she said it. But there was no way that she had *ever* imagined that her suggestion would mean the *Dominion* would be jumping into the middle of a Hunter Look-Alike nest with *thousands* of ships and *hundreds of thousands* of Hunter Look-Alikes waiting to attack the battlecruiser.

And *why* were they all there? Because the idiotic, *bullheaded* Hunter Look-Alikes *refused* to believe that Hunter had entered a demi-god mode to defeat them. And they obviously couldn't accept that Falcon could singlehandedly defeat *thousands* of them.

Bolobolo knew that she *couldn't* keep thinking about *why* the *Dominion* was in the TU Corvi system in the first place, or it would drive her crazy. But Bolobolo *really* didn't want to think about the conversation that Falcon had sprung on her the year before, *either*.

Falcon had practically predicted that the Hunter Look-Alikes would be coming after the *Dominion* soon. And she had insisted that Bolobolo needed to do everything she could to figure out how to manifest the supernatural like Casteel before it was too late.

Given the Look-Alikes' deadline was only hours away, Bolobolo suspected it might be "too late."

Now, as Bolobolo lowered herself into the chair that sat behind her desk in her office in Sickbay, she tried to take some comfort in the fact that the most likely outcome over the next few hours was that the *Dominion* would be destroyed outright when it attempted to fight its way out of the armada.

And the crew *wouldn't* be captured. And they wouldn't be hellishly tortured one by one because she couldn't give the Hunter Look-Alikes the information they were *convinced* she had.

Bolobolo closed her eyes tightly and shook her head. And she began taking deep breaths to keep herself from getting very, *very* angry.

But *then*, only moments later, the atmosphere in Bolobolo's office in Sickbay *shifted*. And it caught Bolobolo by *such* surprise that she froze, not knowing what else to do. But indeed, the new feeling in her office was *so* welcoming that Bolobolo *couldn't* imagine that it *couldn't* be what she *thought* it might be. And a part of her didn't *want* to find out what had just changed in her office because she couldn't bear the disappointment if it *wasn't* what some small part of her had already concluded that it *was*.

Still, in time, Bolobolo slowly opened her eyes.

And as that hopeful small part of Bolobolo began to leap with joy, the rest of her mind finally accepted what her eyes were telling her.

Catherine Casteel appeared to be sitting in the chair on the opposite side of Bolobolo's desk.

And she was *smiling*.

29.

Somewhere unknown, Hrafnkelsson, still dressed in his comfortable clothes, made his way down a wide hall with many others, dressed in similar fashion. Strangely, he said nothing to those around him. Still, almost continually, Hrafnkelsson found himself thinking about *trying* to say something to the men and women walking beside him.

But every time he began to turn his head to look at them and open his mouth, a thought distracted him, a memory of a death he had witnessed, a moment when he had almost been killed by an assault robot, a spike of anger at the leadership of the Realm for generating such horror in the lives of those who lived on Alpha Pegasi Three among those who simply wanted to live peacably with their neighbors and care for their children.

And then, Hrafnkelsson would just keep walking without saying anything.

In time, Hrafnkelsson made his way through a set of tall doors into a vast hall composed of enormous concentric circles that descended to a center platform. Each of those concentric circles was lined with hundreds of small booths that appeared to be designed to function as mini-broadcast studios.

Three translucent panels defined the space. There were two on each side of a comfortable chair and one in front. There were also lights, positioned appropriately for the classic headshot. Finally, a video feed sensor was mounted on the front panel with a tablet hanging underneath.

Hrafnkelsson wasn't sure if he should approach a particular booth. But others seemed to be taking a seat at whichever booth was closest, and

Hrafnkelsson soon did the same.

"Thank you for your service," a friendly female voice now announced. "You may begin your testimony at any time. Start at the beginning and describe everything you deem important. After your introductory remarks, mention the recordings that you made of what occurred on your planet. At that point, your video feeds will begin to play, and you can offer any additional commentary that you believe would be helpful. When your video feeds are complete, begin again. Offer your introductory remarks. Mention your recordings. Supplement them with your commentary."

Hrafnkelsson took another look around the vast hall. Thousands of humans were still filtering into it and finding places to sit. But others had already begun talking. Oddly enough, Hrafnkelsson couldn't hear them talking, not even those who sat on either side of him.

Not knowing what else to do, Hrafnkelsson began his presentation as well.

"My name is Tryggvi Hrafnkelsson," he said. "I have lived on Alpha Pegasi Three all my life, and for many years, I served as a communication facilitator to the planetary leadership, specifically Governor Dmytro Voronenko…"

·   ·   ·

In the bedroom of his penthouse apartment in Jerusalem on Earth, Ton roused to the sound of an urgent comm request from PLOKTA. Quickly, Ton rolled out of bed, being careful not to kick any of the five beautiful, naked women of his current special tactical team that had gone to bed with him earlier. Then, grabbing a robe from a nearby chair, Ton wrapped it around his own naked form before heading into the living room to acknowledge the comm.

For the record, Sotheby was *not* tied up and hanging from the ceiling in the living room of the penthouse. She was back on the *Majesty*, serving as the battlecruiser's de facto lead commander.

And yes, Ton knew, depending on the events that triggered the urgent call from PLOKTA, having Sotheby already behind the helm of the most fearsome battlecruiser ever constructed by the Saturn Shipyard might be a good thing.

"This is Ton," he said quickly. "Report."

Ton noted that PLOTKA looked flustered. "I've lost all control of the social net," he began. "I'm locked out of all the admin functions, and none of my monitoring programs are responding. And there are thousands of talking heads flooding onto the net, talking about the bad things that happened on their planets and the stuff that's happening now. And they are showing the video feeds that they recorded of the events.

"Weirdly enough, the feeds are all produced precisely the same way. It's like someone went to all the planets and put together a presentation with thousands of spokespeoples with the same setup, or all gathered in some big room, which would be a *massive* effort.

"I've run the feeds through my analysis routines, and they don't appear to be artificially generated. Either someone prerecorded a bunch of testimony, or someone's coordinating a simulcast. And it all feels absolutely authentic.

"Granted, the talking heads seem a little blitzed, but not in a way that the average person would notice. As you can imagine, the social net is on fire with people trying to figure out what's going on. Some are sure it's all lies. But the longer it goes on, the more people are starting to believe the spokespeople. All the graphs show the same progression, and I'm guessing that within 24 hours, and maybe even by mid-morning Jerusalem time, we'll be over half the population of the Realm thinking that the feeds are real."

Ton nodded. "For the record, *are* they real?" he asked.

"Yeah, they are," PLOKTA answered. "The guy who disappeared from Alpha Pegasi Three is in there. And facial recognition on the rest of them has everyone placed where they say they're from. And what they're describing is what happened on their planets."

Ton smiled. "Sounds like we've got some work to do," he offered. "The question is, are there any reports of an invasion force, or is it all just talk on the social net?"

PLOKTA shook his head. "Assuming that our comms and surveillance feeds to Realm Force facilities aren't being compromised, everything looks normal," he reported. "I did pull an analysis of the postings on the social net, and we've got Realm Force personnel commenting at the same rate as the base population."

Ton nodded. "It's a good thing we have assault robots stockpiled," he offered. "I may need to usher in the empire sooner than I thought."

PLOKTA offered Ton a slight frown. "This doesn't worry you?" he asked. "I mean, this whole time, we've worked hard to keep our activities under wraps, and now it's just out there for everyone to see."

Ton gave PLOKTA a nonchalant shrug. "Obviously, somebody big is behind this," he began. "It doesn't feel like the Wind. When the Wind showed up the first time, they didn't waste any time worrying about public opinion. They announced who they were. They told everyone what they were going to do. And then they obliterated anyone who didn't bow the knee.

"That's not what this is. And that tells me that there's a different power dynamic at work. It's almost like whoever is driving this has to let humanity choose for itself, and they are trying to convince Realmers to come after us. But either they don't know what we have stockpiled or they are trying to move along the winnowing of the human race because they know that if the Realmers rebel, I'm just going to unleash the assault robots on *every* planet."

PLOKTA tilted his head to the side. "So you think Abaddon is behind this and just wants you to wipe out Realmers faster?"

Ton grinned. "Either Abaddon or his boss, if he actually has a boss," he said. "Either way, I was going to publicly declare myself High King Ruler of the Realm at some point in the future anyway. And I had already decided that I was willing to kill as many Realmer as I needed to make that a reality so unless we have an invasion force coming out of the curled space rings, I'm not sure we have a problem. If anyone wants to try to raise a fist against us, we'll use the same approach as the Wind. Submit or die.

"Keep monitoring. Keep tracking the sentiments. I'll put together a response with the Office of Communications, and we'll spin this as lies and propaganda. Maybe. Or maybe not. I'll see how it feels when we're ready to release. Ton out."

•   •   •

From the beginning of the salacious and disturbing testimonies that most Realmers couldn't imagine they would ever hear, the communication facilities used by the Realm ensured that, as each witness spoke, their words were instantly available across every world in the *Pax Christi*. And of course, this facility was directly attributable to the massive Wind-designed communications satellites that hung over every Realm planet. Each of those satellites could transmit information to any other communication satellite in real-time with zero latency, regardless of the distance between them.

In addition, once the information reached a destination satellite, it was also instantly transmitted to all the Judicial Centers of the satellite's planet. Once there, it was available to any Realm citizen who might request it from a tablet or other display and control panel.

And make no mistake, the testimonies of witnesses constituted an enormous amount of information that had suddenly appeared on the Realm's social net. *Thousands* of individuals were testifying simultaneously. And those witnesses spoke not only of incidents in the recent past, but also of events that occurred in the distant past. They spoke of times of unexpected compromise, of initiatives undertaken by Nicolescu and Sotheby, of playtime embarrassments that were seemingly desired by Ton.

Witness after witness, all confirming that the leadership of the Realm was corrupt, vile, perverted, and cruel. It was impossible to absorb all at once. And it would have taken *months* for any given person to watch them all. Instead, the section of the social net that contained the testimonies was set to permanent shuffle-play. And that, in itself, held an allure.

It was impossible to know what shocking, unbelievable revelation would come next.

"It was over 15 years ago, but I can't forget what I saw. I was working at one of the new high-end hotels in Jerusalem as a housekeeper. And a beautiful woman and her husband came to stay in one of our penthouses. I think their names were Adeline and Edenjevy Bautista, and they were obviously rich, but they were also strange. Mrs. Bautista only wore lingerie around the penthouse, and she made her husband wear it too. And that was bad enough, but one time when I brought them some extra towels, I saw a man standing in the corner of the room. And he was hanging from his neck and wearing women's clothing, and he was all bound up in straps so he couldn't get loose. And he was wearing these really high heels, and he was struggling to stand. I can still remember how much he was sweating and the way he smelled. And the worst part was that I knew him. It was Elijah Ton, and I knew he was a member of the Leadership Council. Granted, I should have tried to start recording with a tablet or something because I knew no one would believe me, but Mrs. Bautista was pretty intense, and I honestly don't know what she would have done to me if I did that. Anyway, Mrs. Bautista must have seen how shocked I was because she just laughed and she said I shouldn't tell anybody, and she gave me money to keep quiet. But it wasn't enough because, ever since, the thought of that man leading the Realm just makes me sick to my stomach...."

"I was on the so-called special tactical teams at the Saturn Shipyards. But I didn't expect to be drugged up and out of my head most of the time. The girls on the special tactical teams are all on a drug called Angel Haze, and Lead

Commander Nicolescu and Lieutenant Aeon Sotheby didn't really explain what it would do before Lieutenant Sotheby rubbed it inside my nose. I mean, the first thing it did was make me fall in love with Lieutenant Sotheby. I'll play the stupid video feeds I have of myself fawning over her, and you'll see. I mean, it wasn't anything sexual, but when I say it made me fall *madly* in love with her, it made me love her so much that I did *anything* she told me to do, and some of it was pretty dark. I've got footage coming up of Lieutenant Sotheby and Commander Nicolescu sending us out to seduce Realm Force Commanders and then, after we slept with them, they would give us instructions to take back to those commanders to tell them they better do exactly what we or we would release the sex video feeds to the social net…."

"I was one of the pilots who took the former Lead Commander of the *Power*, Seyi Ladipo, to his confinement at a Realm Force maximum security facility after he confessed to planning the murders of the Popa family on the Night of Terror. But, the entire trip, he kept saying that he was innocent, so much so that I started recording him. I never showed the feed to anyone because I was scared of what might happen to me. After all, he said he had been drugged with Angel Haze and told to confess by Lieutenant Sotheby…."

"It still gives me nightmares. I was on one of Commander Nicolescu's special tactical teams, drugged with Angel Haze. And I was sent to the TRAPPIST-1 system to seduce a businessman whose last name was Volopich. He wasn't a pleasant man, but he didn't deserve what happened to him. We were trained in how to get men to do things they never thought they would do. Basically, if you can get a guy sexually excited enough and then tell him how excited it would make you feel if he would do something, he'll do it even if he refuses at first. They gave me this box to give to him, and it not only had lots of girly, frilly stuff in it, but it also had a backpack-like thing that had places to attach wires and loops. And he was so excited that he put it all on and then I pushed the button I had been told to push. And it all tightened and he couldn't get it off. And then I pushed another button and walked away. And only later was I told that this razor wire inside the backpack started moving back and forth, and it cut him to pieces. I don't have any video feeds of that, but you can look up the reports, and I can tell you that I'm the last person who saw him alive and haven't been able to sleep once I got the Angel Haze out of my body…."

"Yeah, that night when those fifty families died in the bombings seven years ago? That was all planned by Leadership Council Member Ton and Lead Commander Nicolescu. They picked the families. They sent out the special tactical team to plant the explosives. At that point, I was dosed up on Angel Haze just like them, and I specced out the placement of all the bombs. We even calculated how to place the explosives at Commander Nicolescu's family home so that she could be there and not get hurt too bad. They wanted her to be the hero. They wiped out fifty families in one night, families they knew would be mourned, because they wanted everyone to be afraid so that they could get everyone to agree to more control. I was actually able to smuggle out video feeds of all the meetings that I had with Commander Nicolescu and Lieutenant Sotheby prior to that night. And honestly, I've never worked with anybody who was as cold and evil as those two...."

"I was part of the original Realm Force strike group that attacked Fomalhaut Four. I know, the *Dominion* supposedly attacked Fomalhaut Four five years ago, but that's not what happened. That was a Realm Force operation, and almost *everyone* on that mission was killed. Before the attack, our commander assigned us to the Saturn Shipyards, since the shipyards ran the black ops. And they sent us to Fomalhaut Four to take control of the planet. They said that the inhabitants were refusing to comply with the security guidelines, and it was endangering the Realm. None of that sounded right to me, so I started recording everything that was happening on a secure tablet. Then, right in the middle of the operation, these guys who looked like Zachary Hunter showed up and wiped out nearly all of us. I've got video feeds of that stuff, too. I just happened to be on the ground when Look-Alikes came out of the ring, and I took cover, and waited it out, but I'm telling you, the *Dominion* didn't start that fight...."

"Yeah... Lieutenant Sotheby would hand us out like treats to any guy they wanted to compromise, the special tactical team girls, that is. But the worst was always when she turned us over to Councilmember Ton to serve as his security detail for three months at a time. And, of course, we were doped up on Angel Haze so we'd do pretty much whatever he wanted us to do. Granted, he never asked us to sleep with him, but there was some weird stuff going on in that guy's head. He would have us all dress up in these sexy little outfits. And then he would have us dress *him* up in a sexy little outfit and tie him up and spank him hard enough to leave bruises on his butt. He would even wear black lace underwear under his clothes during the day. Little panties. A little bra. Garter belts and thigh-highs. He seemed to get off on it. He used to laugh about how shocked people would be if they found out. The Angel Haze made it all just seem funny at the time. Weirdly enough, even though I was on Angel Haze, I *did* record what we were doing to Councilman Ton, even though he never caught me doing that. It was just *so* twisted...."

"I was on the Realm Force detail that delivered the supposed vaccine to Epsilon Virginis Three after the outbreak of the hemorrhagic fever virus. There was no way what we were doing was ever going to help. We just dumped the stuff at the Judicial Centers. But by that time, there was no one to hand the stuff out and no way to get it distributed. And then, as we lifted off from the planet, there were announcements made about where to get the vaccines, and by the time we made it to low orbit, people were swarming the Judicial Center. If what we were carrying was worth anything and offered any protection, they should have given it to us at first so that we could have gone in and helped with the distribution. It was like Realm Force leadership wanted the whole thing to fail so they could stir up a bunch of fear and get Realm citizens calling for Realm Force to take control of more things. And yeah, that first delivery was so weird that I recorded the other five that we made that day, and I've been keeping them hidden away ever since, just in case anyone tried to blame us for what happened. Honestly, it wouldn't surprise me to find out Realm Force created the virus just to freak everybody out...."

"I've worked in data analysis for Realm Force Central for a decade. And I've seen the sensor feeds, six years ago, when that Merchant Guild yacht crashed into the suburb of Jerusalem. The Leadership Council claimed that Murg from the *Dominion* had the systems and made it so that the yacht could evade the defenses. But that's not what I saw. In fact, I made a raw copy of the data so I could show people if I ever had a chance to talk about this and not get killed or sacked. I'll go through it in a minute. But here's the short answer. There's *nothing* in the analysis of the incident that says anything about a hack from Murg or anyone else. All the systems were working according to spec. However, if you analyze the firing patterns, it's obvious that something was going on because the slugs all go around the Merchant Guild yacht. In other words, somebody, probably at the Saturn Shipyards, *arranged* for the yacht to get through. And yeah, I've wondered about it a lot because Ton's wife was one of the people who died in that crash. And I'm thinking that maybe that was just a sympathy ploy and *another* attempt to get people riled up and demand that Realm Force take more control...."

"I've never told anyone else this, but I work in housekeeping at one of the hotels where Leadership Councilmember Ton rents a penthouse. We were always told not to disturb him and just leave the supplies outside his door. But I also cleaned his room once a week, and I could never figure out why putting away his towels was a big deal. So one day, I decided to go in and do that for him. And there's a naked woman hanging from the ceiling, and she's all tied up. And it looks really uncomfortable, but she says she's fine. And that was

408   Windfall: Invitation

when I took a *good* look at her face and I realized that it's Lieutenant Aeon Sotheby. I don't know what kind of weird games Councilmember Ton was playing with her in there, but he had her tied up so you could get to all her jewels. I mean I... I... actually took a picture of her when she wasn't looking because she just looked so gorgeous...."

"Governor Dmytro Voronenko from Alpha Pegasi Three did *not* go crazy. I was one of the people who helped him evade the Realm Force patrols when he was supposedly rampaging through the streets. And once I got him to duck into a building with me, I started recording our interactions on a tablet that I had set to create private video feeds. And you'll see in just a minute that the man is not raging. In fact, he's *giddy*. He's talking about how he hopes that Councilmember Ton will be pleased with his performance. And I'm asking him what about his performance, and the more we talk, the more he talks, and then he starts talking about this drug named Angel Haze that some sweet young thing wiped around in his nose. You'll see it all on the feeds. Governor Voronenko was set up to get killed...."

"I've never shown anyone this video feed, but I'm from Groombridge 1830b, and I was recording some of the foliage in the park where Governor Tiago Costa del Rey was walking with his companion, and I didn't realize that my tablet was pointed right in the direction where the governor was about to be murdered. Not that I could see the governor being murdered. There was way too much foliage in the way. But later, some people got in touch with me and asked me if I still had the video feeds, and I said I did, and they cleaned it up and showed me what they found, and you can see that girl that nobody thought did it, slicing the governor's throat. And that's why the governor's companion accused her of doing that. And that makes me wonder about *all* of it. I mean, how many times have we been told stuff about what's happening when that's not what's happening at all? I just think there's stuff going on here that isn't what it seems...."

·   ·   ·

In PLOKTA's lair at the Saturn Shipyards, Evansworth tried hard not to grin too greedily. After reporting the beginning of the transmission of negative testimonies across the social net to Ton, PLOKTA had tried to wrest back control of the social net for the next 30 minutes. But he eventually gave up and announced he was trying something different.

Then, PLOKTA said that he was spinning up 5,000 instances of the feeds on the social net and setting them all to play 2x speed, transcribing the contents, and then summarizing the transcripts. And when that process finished 25 minutes after that, PLOKTA softly swore as he read through the summaries.

And that's when Evansworth had to be careful not to grin too greedily. Because *someone* was *really* doing a number on Ton and the Realm Leadership. Just from what Evansworth saw, there was a *ton* of incriminating information in the testimonies.

"*Everything* is here," PLOKTA offered absentmindedly, confirming what Evansworth thought she saw, "even my costume phase."

Evansworth tilted her head to the side and shifted the topic to the matter at hand. "You had a costume phase?" she asked, a smirk forming on her lips as she wondered it PLOKTA was about to unlock another piece of his soul.

"Yeah, well, I didn't really have a choice," he admitted. "I was supposed to be in Lieutenant Sotheby's thrall because she had dosed me with Angel Haze. And somebody decided it would be fun to set aside a day each week to dress me up. Since I was supposed to be under the influence, I had to participate *enthusiastically*."

"And did you enjoy the attention?" Evansworth asked, probing, trying to determine if PLOKTA had a hidden manipulation point. "I know there are Realmers who will roll their eyes back into their heads when they hear about what the special tactical teams were doing to Ton, especially since Ton asked them to do it to him, but I have never understood why any of that is a big deal. I've always thought that most men who are into that kind of thing just enjoyed feeling desirable more than anything, and they're trying to capture a *bit* of the feeling that they have for women who dress the same way. Seems okay to me."

PLOKTA shook his head. "Maybe," he offered. "But most of it was just awkward and painful, especially the *shoes*. Not really my thing."

Evansworth nodded, a bit disappointed, but not letting it show. "The shoes are not great," she agreed. "And it would be worse for me now that I only have one foot that would have to take all the weight. But I'd be willing to give it a try if you want me to!"

PLOKTA grinned. "Thanks," he said. "But I'd have to be pretty cold to do that to you when I *know* what it feels like and I don't…"

An alert chirped on PLOKTA's workstation, interrupting him and demanding his attention. And when he swivelled his head to see what the alert contained, Evansworth noticed that PLOKTA's mood darkened immediately.

"No, no, no, no," he said. "I have *not* authorized a Realm-wide simulcast. No, no, no, no."

Hands flying across the control panel in front of him, PLOKTA seemed to be making the same amount of progress stopping what he had called a Realm-wide simulcast as he had made with stopping the replay of the negative testimonies on the social net.

And Evansworth knew *that* amount of progress had been exactly *zero*.

Now, PLOKTA's display turned green, and a solid tone began to sound. Lettering appeared next on the screen.

"Please stand by," the text said, and when *that* faded, a being appeared, obviously tall, well built, dressed in white garments, looking calm and handsome.

"I'm completely locked out, and he's seized the entire communication," PLOKTA groused as the being began to speak.

"I bring you greetings from the Children of the Prime," the elegant being said. "I am aware that you might find that greeting strange, given what you have been told about the Children of the Prime thus far. But I assure you that I have not misspoken. The Children of the Prime *do* greet you warmly, and it is our fervent hope that we have estimated correctly that you are ready to join the larger community of intelligent, sentient beings.

"I understand that this is confusing, but allow me to explain. Fascinatingly enough, across thousands of examples, we have found that the process of creatures evolving intelligence is surprisingly similar. It begins with basic stimulus and response. At this stage, it isn't easy to classify what is occurring as *intelligence*. However, rudimentary choices are being made, and the most basic definition of intelligence might include the idea that intelligence resolves problems.

"If you are hungry, the ability to find food demonstrates a nontrivial type of intelligence. The same logic extends across all the mechanisms that life has for preserving its function. But, of course, those basic responses are only the beginning. There are *many* types of intelligence, and they exist across many measurable levels.

"Beyond all of that, however, the Children of the Prime believe that becoming self-aware constitutes a special threshold in the rise of intelligence. The ability to evaluate oneself in the context of one's existence presents both unique opportunities and challenges.

"For instance, for the most part, intelligence before self-awareness is a straight-line affair. However, after self-awareness, intelligence becomes entangled in the process of evaluation. Not only are you deciding what to do, you are deciding *why* you are deciding what you are deciding to do. And for the vast majority, this process creates a mental paralysis, whether it is apparent or not.

"I am not inclined to discuss this topic in depth. Honestly, there are those among the Children of the Prime who have studied the phenomenon for *thousands* of years. However, the fundamental conclusions of their work remain the same.

"Self-awareness is a necessary step in advancing intelligence. However, more often than not, it leads to destructive behaviors that can drive entire species to extinction. There are many ways this annihilation can occur, but the species that reproduce through asymmetrically weighted, bisexual reproduction are particularly vulnerable.

"I will explain. In humans, reproduction occurs when a sperm and an egg come together. However, the levels of production for sperm and eggs between males and females differ by multiple orders of magnitude. The average male produces *billions* of sperm over his lifetime. The average female is born with a fixed supply of eggs. In addition, the physical and emotional burden of childbearing is also orders of magnitude different between males and females, with females shouldering the brunt of the burden.

"This configuration *is* successful in driving forward the production of children under difficult circumstances because each child represents a significant potential resource for the family. However, once a certain level of societal sophistication is attained and women are provided other options for gathering resources, the birth rate *always* declines. And in most cases, it declines to the point where the species breeds itself out of existence.

"And this occurs because the individuals of the species are aware of their choices, and they choose their individual interest over the interests of their family or their race. I have personally witnessed this progression tens of *thousands* of times. Vibrant civilizations have dwindled to nothing and ceased.

"Intriguingly, the charlatans who call themselves the Wind likely saved the human race from this fate by imposing their will on you and creating an environment where they reduced the cost of childbearing and removed the need for striving. This significantly altered the reproductive dynamics, making it possible for humanity to populate hundreds of planets.

"But in the case of the Wind, they only wanted this temporary success for you so that you would cease your striving for improvement as a race and eventually come under the scrutiny of the Children of the Prime and be censured and potentially marked for destruction.

"I should note at this point that I spoke truthfully when I said I bring warm greetings from the Children of the Prime. However, it is also true that the human race *has* been censured. And you *will* be marked for destruction if your striving to better yourselves does not increase.

"Obviously, my servant Abaddon communicated this to you when he appeared, seven years ago. When he did not tell you then, I reveal to you now. Abaddon's mission included conducting a series of tests to determine your fitness as a race to proceed beyond your censure. Specifically, we wanted to determine if you could be guided into becoming more, and we wanted to assess the depth of depravity that you would embrace if you had both the opportunity and the ability to do so.

"Abaddon found and confirmed multiple times that those humans who lived in the region that you dubbed Night too often refused to exercise any restraint in seeking their own hedonistic impulses. They also refused to receive instruction. Consequently, they would be of no use to the Children of the Prime and Abaddon, and his forces were released to slaughter as many of the inhabitants of the Night as they desired. Very few of those who formerly lived in the Night remain alive.

"I tell you this so that you will understand the severity of my appearance before you today. The Night is dead. The Realm may follow that same path if you cannot demonstrate your worth to the Children of the Realm. As Abaddon has already stated, the Children of the Prime had *great* hope for humanity in your earlier days. You had begun to shed your superstitions. Your science and technology were advancing. You were uncovering the principles of the nature of reality well ahead of many of your peer races.

"But then the pranksters found you. And the Wind appeared to you and exploited some of your ancient myths to lull you to sleep, to swaddle you, and nurse you to your own destruction. And as always, those pranksters, the Wind, retreated as we approached.

"To be clear, the expectations of the Children of the Prime have not changed. Humanity must *quickly* emerge as a unified force that focuses on its improvement. It must grow beyond any infantile obsession with individuality and religious entitlement and realize that the *only* goal should be the increase of knowledge, power, ability, and understanding. It should do this no matter the cost to any individual or group of individuals.

"Unfortunately, the last seven years have demonstrated that humanity cannot do this on its own. The Night proved itself a failure and those who were charged with reforming the Realm failed miserably as well. In the process, they also embraced a weak tyranny where they performed atrocities in secret and then expected that to produce the desired results. The testimonies that will resume playing after I am done with my remarks amply illustrate that the leadership, both at the Saturn Shipyards and the Leadership Council, lacked the courage and focus to push forward, to be what they are, to set a standard, and demand that what remains of humanity conform to the goals of the Children of Prime or die.

"This is why these testimonies are such a disappointment to me. What the witnesses declare should have been a matter of public record. And the citizens of the Realm should have been forced to accept the fact that it would continue to happen unless they reformed. And yet, you will undoubtedly be surprised and shocked by many things you hear.

"Rest assured, everything you hear in those testimonies is true. Each of those who testify *directly* witnessed the incidents they relate. However, their attempts in the past to share what they knew were suppressed. I have changed that. I have temporarily given them the platform to speak freely of what they saw. This is the way of the Children of the Prime. All are free to speak. All are free to be heard.

"But understand as well that to speak and be heard among the Children of the Prime is a *privilege* and must be earned through contribution to the Great Cause. Nothing in humanity warrants it as worthy of that privilege, at least not *yet*. But I believe you *may* achieve that someday under the appropriate guidance, and I have allowed these witnesses to experience what that would be like.

"In conclusion, I tell you this plainly. Abaddon and his forces *are* ready to annihilate the vast majority of the citizens of the Realm just as they have done to those who previously lived in the Night. But I can stay their hand if you can prove to me that you are worthy of saving.

"This is the offer I am willing to make. At some point within the next month,

I will begin an inward spiralling journey that will take me to every inhabited planet in the Realm. If you have rebelled against the present leadership of your planet and the Realm by the time I arrive at your planet, you will be welcomed to join my armada and continue with me.

"In time, we will reach Earth, and I will extend this same offer to those who live on humanity's ancestral home. Those who wish to join our cause will be welcome to join us in the sky. And then we will descend in mass to slaughter *all* the citizens of the Earth who remain loyal to its current leadership or the Wind.

"We will destroy Jerusalem. We will slaughter its men, women, and children. We will rid you of the ancient myths that have limited your ability to earn your place among the Children of the Prime.

"This is the *only* path forward. Humanity *must* rid itself of all vestiges of the old ways of thinking. It must *kill* its primitive and embrace the new path forward. And the *only* evidence that I am willing to accept that humanity is willing to do this is the evidence that will be written in the blood of every man, woman, and child who refuses to pledge his or her allegiance to me.

"Indeed, once Earth is cleansed, I and my armada will begin spiralling outward, and we will revisit every planet of the Realm. And we will slaughter all those citizens who refused to pledge their allegiance to me. And only then will the work begin to transform humanity into the promise it showed before the Wind led you astray.

"And let me make this *perfectly* clear, the Children of the Prime will *not* accept you as you are. Even if you shake off your primitive thinking, you will be my charges for many years to come. And I will treat you with the disrespect and condescension that you deserve. But you will live and you will prosper. And you will become what you were always destined to be.

"To ensure there is no confusion over my identity, I tell you plainly that everything you think you know about me is a lie that was created by the Wind to make it more difficult for you to follow me. But this in itself will demonstrate if you have the power to become more because you will need to set aside what you've been taught and accept that I am the one who tells you the *truth*.

"Allow me to introduce myself, then, among a multitude of names, I am also known as Satan, and I am humanity's only hope. Choose well."

With that, PLOKTA's displays reverted to the testimonies of the witnesses to the atrocities that Ton and Evansworth had carried out over as they pushed forward their agendas.

And, of course, PLOKTA initiated a comm request to Ton to discuss the next steps.

As for Evansworth, she was still struggling not to grin too greedily.

30.

BLESSINGS FROM JERUSALEM!

Your Daily Encouragement from the City of our King

Greetings, friends and fellow citizens of the Realm!

As a new day dawns in Jerusalem, hear these words of Psalm 109, written by King David, and remember that vile accusers have existed since the beginning of recorded human history.

> *¹My God, whom I praise, do not remain silent,*
>
> *²for people who are wicked and deceitful have opened their mouths against me; they have spoken against me with lying tongues.*
>
> *³With words of hatred they surround me; they attack me without cause.*
>
> *⁴In return for my friendship they accuse me, but I am a man of prayer.*
>
> *⁵They repay me evil for good, and hatred for my friendship.*

⁶Appoint someone evil to oppose my enemy; let an accuser stand at his right hand.

⁷When he is tried, let him be found guilty, and may his prayers condemn him.

⁸May his days be few; may another take his place of leadership.

⁹May his children be fatherless and his wife a widow.

¹⁰May his children be wandering beggars; may they be driven from their ruined homes.

¹¹May a creditor seize all he has; may strangers plunder the fruits of his labor.

¹²May no one extend kindness to him or take pity on his fatherless children.

¹³May his descendants be cut off, their names blotted out from the next generation.

¹⁴May the iniquity of his fathers be remembered before the Lord; may the sin of his mother never be blotted out.

¹⁵May their sins always remain before the Lord, that he may blot out their name from the earth.

¹⁶For he never thought of doing a kindness, but hounded to death the poor and the needy and the brokenhearted.

¹⁷He loved to pronounce a curse—may it come back on him. He found no pleasure in blessing—may it be far from him.

¹⁸He wore cursing as his garment; it entered into

his body like water, into his bones like oil.

[19]*May it be like a cloak wrapped about him, like a belt tied forever around him.*

[20]*May this be the Lord's payment to my accusers, to those who speak evil of me.*

[21]*But you, Sovereign Lord, help me for your name's sake; out of the goodness of your love, deliver me.*

[22]*For I am poor and needy, and my heart is wounded within me.*

[23]*I fade away like an evening shadow; I am shaken off like a locust.*

[24]*My knees give way from fasting; my body is thin and gaunt.*

[25]*I am an object of scorn to my accusers; when they see me, they shake their heads.*

[26]*Help me, Lord my God; save me according to your unfailing love.*

[27]*Let them know that it is your hand, that you, Lord, have done it.*

[28]*While they curse, may you bless; may those who attack me be put to shame, but may your servant rejoice.*

[29]*May my accusers be clothed with disgrace and wrapped in shame as in a cloak.*

³⁰With my mouth I will greatly extol the Lord; in the
great throng of worshipers I will praise him.

³¹For he stands at the right hand of the needy,
to save their lives from those who would
condemn them..

King David wrote these words thousands of years ago, and yet the experience that he documents in this psalm still occurs today. And most importantly, David shows us the appropriate response that we should have when we are falsely accused.

The exact nature of the accusations against David is unknown. And even when serving as the Governor of Jerusalem before the Disappearance, David refused to clarify the precise events that led him to make these declarations. But there was obviously something profoundly evil about what his accusers had done that caused David to set aside any thought of attempting a reconciliation or discussion with those who brought charges against him.

And this should remind us that while there *are* times when we should attempt to repair the breaches that may occur in our relationships, there are *also* times when the actions of our accusers are so egregious that nothing can be done to work out our differences. And *when* we encounter a situation like this, *this* psalm recommends the approach we should take.

First, we declare the exact nature of what has transpired. The wicked and deceitful have opened their mouths against us. They have spoken with lying tongues. With words of hatred, they have surrounded us and attacked us without cause.

Next, we need to call for an avenger to be appointed. And surprisingly enough, King David suggests that we need to call for an *evil* avenger who will match the evil of our attacker.

And what does David say should be the result of the appointment of his evil avenger?

The enemy will be found guilty. His days will be few. Another will take his place of leadership. His children will be fatherless and his wife a widow. Worse, his children will become wandering beggars and they will be driven from their ruined homes. Creidtors will seize everything accuser has, and strangers will plunder the fruits of his labor.

Interestingly, David also says that no one should extend kindness to the enemy or take pity on his fatherless children. And he calls for his descendants to be cut off, and their names blotted out from the next generation. And he asks that the inquity of the enemy be remembered forever and never be erased. And that means, the enemy's sins *always* remain before the Lord, so their names will be blotted out from the earth.

King David goes on to specifically define the other despicable characteristics of the one who has accused him. He says that his enemy never thought of doing a kindness, but instead hounded to death the poor, the needy, and the brokenhearted.

And then, David also says the enemy loved to pronounce a curse, but it will come back on him. And since the enemy found no pleasure in blessing, David knows that blessing will always be far from him.

And lest we question whether the enemy is as corrupt as David asserts, let us remind ourselves how David describes his nature. He says that the enemy wears cursing as his garment. He says that it enters into the enemy's body like water and into his bones like oil. It is wrapped around him like a cloak, and like a belt, it is tied forever around him.

And while David notes that the attack of the enemy has grieved him and affected him physically, he reaffirms that his enemy will be clothed with disgrace and wrapped in shame as in a cloak.

This is the end of all of the enemies of our souls. We are God's people, and those who attack us are attacking God. We may face difficulties, but the God of the universe, who does all things well, will defend us and ensure that we are victorious.

Remember to pray for the Leadership Council and Realm Force. Pray for your local leaders. And always show your support not only for your local leaders but also for the leadership of Jerusalem.

And may God help us to recognize that some have degenerated to such a degree that there is no hope for them and we should ask God to hand them over to evil avengers that will lead them readily to destruction.

•   •   •

LAUGHABLE IN THE EXTREME

For Immediate Release.

To all the citizens of the Realm on all the planets who live within the *Pax Christi*:

Greetings from the Leadership Council,

By now, most of you will have seen at least some of the so-called testimony provided by the being who has adopted the name Satan. Honestly, after reviewing a small portion of that testimony, we on the Leadership Council found it so ridiculous and extreme that we almost didn't provide *any* response to it. We couldn't imagine that *anyone* would believe any of it.

Lead Commander Nicolescu planning the deaths of 50 of the prominent families of the Realm?! Leadership Councilmember Ton dressing up in women's lingerie?! Saturn Shipyards' special tactical teams seducing Realm commanders and business leaders?! Realm Force ensuring that vaccine deliveries failed on Epsilon Virginis Three?! Realm Force allowing a Merchant Guild yacht to crashland in a suburb of Jerusalem and kill Leadership Councilmember Ton's wife?!

It's *absurd.* It's *laughable* in the *extreme.* It's so ridiculous that the Leadership Council found it difficult to believe that *anyone* would be led astray by such claims.

However, what is *not* absurd are the suggestions that this being who calls himself Satan has made to remedy the so-called atrocities that the testimonies supposedly document.

And what does Satan suggest that the citizens of the Realm do in response to the falsehoods he has created?

He wants you to turn your back on your fellow Realmers. He wasn't you to follow him to Earth and *kill* anyone who disagrees with his perspective.

And what great reward will you earn if you do *exactly* as you are told? He will make you his slaves for some immeasurable time to come. You will do as you're told. And, no doubt, you will be *killed* if you don't. And there's no guarantee that you won't be killed *anyway*.

Just for the sake of argument, just for a moment, consider the scenario where everything anyone says in the testimonies is true. In that case, the current leadership of the Realm might be classified as cruel and murderous. But has this so-called Satan made any claim that he *isn't* cruel and murderous? On the contrary, Satan had already admitted that he *is*.

Satan has already testified that his servant Abaddon has slaughtered countless citizens of the Night. In other words, Satan and Abaddon have already shown their hands. They have already demonstrated their evil intent. And now, they are lying about Realm leadership and attempting to recruit you to continue their murderous rampage.

Why would anyone fall for this absurd and completely transparent ploy?

Our advice? Treat the testimonies for what they are. They are blatant, laughably ridiculous lies. And for the love of God and all that's holy and good, *don't* join forces with the one who has also been called the Accuser of the Brethren and the Father of Lies.

For the undeniable truth is that if you align yourself with the Devil, you will condemn yourself to destruction.

With incredulity,

The Leadership Council of the Realm

• • •

ANSWERING THE CALL

An Offer to Earn the Honor of Serving Your Fathers, and Mothers, and Brothers, and Sisters, and All the Citizens of the Realm.

THIS WEEK: For Want of a Nail.

Surely, by now, it is impossible to ignore the fact that the time of conflict is approaching. And while it is true that it has not arrived just yet, it is also true that it is coming, and grows closer every day.

In the past, we have tried to motivate you by quoting scripture and encouraging you to embrace your destiny. On this day, we would simply like to encourage you that no matter what you think of the size of the contribution you might have to make to the coming conflict, Realm Force *will* be stronger *with* your energy and effort combined with us than without.

There are many ways that we could illustrate this, but the simplest and perhaps most poignant has been passed down to us over thousands of years in the form of a nursery rhyme. And the sentiment that it expresses is still true:

For want of a nail, the shoe was lost.

For want of a shoe, the horse was lost.

For want of a horse, the rider was lost.

For want of a rider, the message was lost.

For want of a message, the battle was lost.

For want of a battle, the kingdom was lost.

And all for the want of a horseshoe nail.

Enrolled in Realm Force today!

•   •   •

WHISPERS IN THE NIGHT

Anonymous, untraceable communiqués from the remnants of the unified Hordes of the Night to all who have an ear to hear.

THIS WEEK: And Now, the Judgement Comes For Thee.

We warned you.

As you were preoccupied with murdering us, we warned you that others were approaching to plunder and rend. And you, in your haughty arrogance, considered us worthless and our advice meaningless.

Welcome to destruction. And if it's any comfort, we already reserved your place in hell because we let the demons know you would be arriving soon after you sent us there.

In other words, we had no doubt you would follow us to your eternal damnation for what you did to us.

And now the time has come.

EPILOGUE

On the Bridge of the *Dominion*, seated at the Chief Technologist's workstation, Falcon tilted her head to the side as a comm request appeared from Murg in her cybersuit's input queue. Falcon and Murg had discussed restoring her raw, ship-wide sensor stream when the *Dominon* began its fight to escape the Hunter Look-Alike aramada, but that was still fifty minutes out, so the request providing that access seemed odd.

Still, Falcon acknowledged the request, and immediately, her awareness surged, once more allowing Falcon to see everything that was happening on the *Dominion* and everything beyond the battlecruiser that the ship's sensors could detect. Strangely, there was no message from Murg as to why he had granted her access to the additional information early. And at first glance, nothing seemed out of the ordinary, aside from the fact that a *massive* armada still surrounded the *Dominion*, waiting to destroy it or capture it and her crew and turn their existence into a living hell.

Obviously, Falcon knew the early access wasn't a mistake. And she knew that Murg would *know* that *she* would know that it wasn't a mistake. Consequently, instead of contacting Murg for an explanation, Falcon turned her attention to the ship, sweeping through the hallways with her focus, looking for anything out of the ordinary.

·　　　·　　　·

In the large armory on Lower Level Five that the tactical teams had built across the hall from their dojo, MacDuff continued his selection of weapons, performing a quick inspection on each before loading them with ammunition.

By now, most of the tactical team had outfitted themselves for combat and disbursed to the assigned locations across the *Dominion*. And given that almost everyone else had finished their loadout, MacDuff was ensuring that if the Look-Alike attempted to board the ship, he would be ready as well.

Unexpectedly, the tactical comm gear that MacDuff had already fitted to his head chirped with a request. The gear's eyepiece indicated that Bolobolo was attempting to contact him. Thinking nothing of it, except for the fact that Bolobolo wished to talk to him, MacDuff gestured to open the comm.

"I need your help," Bolobolo said without waiting for a standard acknowledgement. "I'm in my office. Bolobolo out."

It wasn't a demand. It wasn't frantic or nervous. It was just a statement of fact.

MacDuff didn't hesitate. He slapped a clip into the low-profile assault rifle that he held, shoved the rifle into the holster strapped to his thigh, and spun to walk out of the armory and onto the lift at the end of the main hall on Lower Level Five.

Less than a minute later, MacDuff exited the lift across the hall from Sickbay. He *could* have spent the short trip on the lift, wondering what Bolobolo could *possibly* "need" just before the *Dominion* faced its most significant challenge. But the thought never crossed his mind as he rode the lift in silence.

For one thing, MacDuff was comfortable with silence, internally and externally. For another, there was no need to fill the moments with planning. He had his "immediate next."

Bolobolo had requested his help. And he would give it. And frankly, there were *very* few things he *wouldn't* do if Bolobolo believed she needed him to do them.

Now, as MacDuff entered the Main Area of Sickbay, it offered no clues as to why Bolobolo called. Like the tactical teams' dojo, the Sickbay was deserted with the Medical Services teams fanned out across the battle cruiser.

Interestingly, the door to Bolobolo's office was closed. And the wall that allowed Bolobolo to look out on the Main Area of Sickbay had been turned opaque. MacDuff slowed to stop in front of the door to the Chief Medical Officer's office. He knocked.

"Come," Bolobolo called out from inside.

Opening the door, MacDuff spotted Bolobolo standing, relaxed and calm in her work fatigues by the corner of her desk. The only other person in the room was Bolobolo's second-in-command in Medical Services, Tanaraq Oopik.

Oopik was *not* relaxed and calm. Her jaw was trembling. Her eyebrows were crushing downward. Her face was tortured, though it seemed as if she was *trying* to hide what she felt and failing miserably.

Bolobolo rounded the corner of her desk and stopped in front of Oopik. "Everything's going to be okay," she said quietly to Oopik. "Please keep this to yourself."

And with that, Bolobolo swept Oopik into her arms and hugged her tight. A cough of anguish escaped from Oopik, but she swallowed hard to choke it off and clenched her jaw, trying to keep herself from a subsequent outburst.

Bolobolo leaned back. "Everything's going to be okay," she repeated.

Oopik nodded, a bit frantically, but it was clear to MacDuff that Oopik *didn't* believe what Bolobolo was saying.

Bolobolo turned for the door. "With me, Sarge," she said as she passed MacDuff.

Without a word, MacDuff fell in beside her. The pair soon walked out of Sickbay, crossed the hall, and entered a lift.

Bolobolo turned to face forward as MacDuff settled in beside her.

"Shuttle Bay 2," Bolobolo announced as the doors to the lift closed.

Now, Bolobolo looked at MacDuff. "I need you to ensure that I can do what I need to do," she began. "No matter what happens, I need you to help me do this. I've already talked to Murg. He's going to suppress any information about a shuttle departing from Shuttle Bay 2 and who might be on board."

MacDuff frowned, disturbed by what Bolobolo was apparently planning to do. "Adi," he said gently, "this *won't* help. You don't have the information the Look-Alikes want.

Bolobolo smiled softly. "No, I don't," she agreed, "But they don't know that. And they are *convinced* in their ignorance that I do. And they are *convinced* that they understand everything they need to know about the nature of our universe to rule it *cruelly*. And I think it's time for *this* virgin daughter of Zion to despise and mock these *illegitimate bastards* and toss her head in laughter as they flee."

As Bolobolo had spoken the words, MacDuff felt a powerful surge of energy fill the lift. And more than that, the intensity that *flashed* in Bolobolo's eyes instantly convinced MacDuff that there was more at work in the moment than mere human imaginings.

Humbled by Bolobolo's ferocity, MacDuff nodded. "I will do everything in my power," he said fervently, "to ensure that you will have the opportunity to accomplish what you desire."

The lift quickly arrived at the station closest to a set of personnel doors that would lead to Shuttle Bay 2. And once the door opened, MacDuff once more fell in beside Bolobolo as she confidently strode forward

Soon, the pair approached Shuttle Bay 2. But as the personnel doors split apart, MacDuff found Oakford, Falcon, and Hunter standing on the other side.

•   •   •

Earlier, after realizing that Murg had restored her unfiltered access to the sensor and comm feeds across the entire ship, Falcon also noticed that Murg had provided her a set of playback controls for data that had already been gathered and spooled to the data archives. And guessing that the quickest way to find anomalies would be to review the comms in the last three hours, Falcon had soon located the call Bolobolo had made to Murg. And only moments after that, Falcon learned Bolobolo was planning to leave the *Dominion* and had sworn Murg to silence.

Contacting Oakford and Hunter, the three of them took emergency lifts to arrive at Shuttle Bay 2. Intuitively, each had immediately understood that whatever they were about to do, they needed to do it in person.

As for Falcon, she couldn't say that she *knew* what they should do. She understood what Bolobolo *wanted* to do. And she just heard what Bolobolo had said to MacDuff.

But Falcon hadn't had the same reaction to that latter conversation as MacDuff. Yet, it was evident from the look on MacDuff's face that Bolobolo's comments had moved him deeply.

And perhaps those comments hadn't affected Falcon the same way because of *another* conversation that Bolobolo had *before* calling Murg. Except, it *wasn't* really a conversation as far as Falcon could tell.

After talking with her teams, Bolobolo had returned to her office and she had been sitting at her desk with her eyes closed, breathing deeply. It looked like she was struggling to control her emotions. And then a change had cascaded across Bolobolo's face. And Bolobolo's expression had lit up with shock and joy as she opened her eyes and began staring at the chair on the other side of her desk.

But there was no one *there*. Yes, Falcon understood that, perhaps, there *was* someone there, and the sensors couldn't image them. But it was also possible that *no one* was there, and Bolobolo was experiencing an emotional breakdown due to the pressure of feeling responsible for the Dominion's peril. And, in that case, it made *no* sense for Bolobolo to throw her life away.

Of course, there hadn't been time to discuss any of that with Oakford. But Oakford cut to the heart of the matter simply by calling Bolobolo's name.

"Adi?" Oakford began, not demanding, making it apparent what he was asking.

Bolobolo slowed to a stop in front of him.

"I have an invitation, captain," Bolobolo responded calmly.

Oakford nodded. "I understand," he said. "For all that we've seen, I *would* have assumed as much. But I also understand that this may be the end of your time on the *Dominion,* and I would have later *grieved* that I hadn't had the chance to tell you what an *extraordinary* privilege it has been to *serve* with you."

Bolobolo said nothing for a moment, but then nodded. "My apologies, captain," she added. "The invitation came as a joyous shock. And I can't say that even now I'm thinking completely *clearly*. I know that there is a vengeful fire that's heating my soul. These are the same who violated my home planet, threatened my family, and whose actions led to my father sacrificing himself for me. And now they have threatened this ship, and they pretend that we are theirs to toy with as they please. For *all* of it and *all* the other atrocities they have committed, I will *hold them to account*."

Oakford smiled and nodded. "I understand," he responded. "And I obviously have nothing to say to expand upon the invitation that you have received. I would only offer you the blessing that leaders have been privileged to offer those who have been kind enough to allow us to lead. 'The Lord bless you and keep you. The Lord make his face shine on you and be gracious to you. The Lord turn his face toward you and give you peace.' "

Bolobolo's face broadened into a smile. "Thank you, captain," she said as she stepped forward to embrace him. "It's been an honor to serve with you all these years."

Then, Bolobolo added quickly. "If you have the opportunity, tell my family on Fomalhaut Four that I love them and I'm sorry I never made it back to see them."

Now, as Bolobolo leaned back, Falcon stepped in to hug her next. And maybe Falcon could have said something pithy. And maybe Falcon could have noted that what Bolobolo was experiencing in this moment was *precisely* what she had been pestering Bolobolo about accomplishing for *years*.

But Falcon had no way to know for sure if Bolobolo had truly experienced an invitation or if she was just delusional. Consequently, Falcon gave Bolobolo a warm smile after they embraced and said nothing.

Hunter hugged Bolobolo next. "Give 'em hell," he said nonchalantly.

"I will," Bolobolo responded as she leaned back and turned for a nearby shuttle before adding, "Walk with me, Sarge."

As Bolobolo began taking purposeful strides toward the vessel she would use to depart the *Dominion*, Falcon caught Oakford's and Hunter's eye and tilted her head toward the personnel door, letting them know she thought it was time for them to give Bolobolo and MacDuff a moment alone.

•   •   •

Walking beside Bolobolo as she headed for a nearby shuttle, MacDuff heard Oakford, Falcon, and Hunter leave Shuttle Bay Two.

"Murg!" Bolobolo called out unexpectedly. "Did you rat me out?"

"NAK…" Murg shot back before adding, "…ACK."

"It's been good working with you," Bolobolo offered.

"ACK," Murg replied softly.

"And you too, Pix!" Bolobolo said quickly.

"Thanks!" the Pixie replied.

Too soon, Bolobolo and MacDuff arrived at the shuttle's aft airlock ramp. Now, Bolobolo turned to face MacDuff. She said nothing at first. She stared at him adoringly for a full minute. Wisely, from the lessons he had learned from Bolobolo over the years, he said nothing.

Then, Bolobolo reached up to take MacDuff's face in her hands. And she kissed him deeply and kindly and gratefully before leaning back.

"I would have borne you *beautiful* children," she added passionately.

MacDuff nodded in agreement. "Of that I am certain, Adi Bolobolo," he said warmly. "For as I have said in the past. I believe our sons would be as strong as the mighty oaks, and our daughters like graceful pillars carved to beautify a palace. It is the *obvious* conclusion, for they would inherit *your* beauty, compassion, and will. And perhaps, they might glean a small portion of strength from me."

The edges of Bolobolo's mouth twitched into an incredulous smile as she gave her head a slight shake. But then she smiled broadly.

"See you on the other side," Bolobolo commented as she spun and headed up the ramp.

MacDuff watched her for a moment. And for another moment, he battled the instinct within him to protect her. But soon he reminded himself that Daughter of Zion needed no protection.

God himself would be her sword and shield.

And spinning on his heel, MacDuff headed for the personnel door that led out of Shuttle Bay 2.

GLOSSARY

960 ADR – the year of the disappearance of the Wind. The disappearance was abrupt and without warning. Only the titans themselves disappeared. All structures and technology remained behind, although some of the technology—such as the energy weapons—ceased to function. In some circles, the disappearance of the Wind is called "Windfall." However, that term is considered derogatory and disrespectful since it implies that the disappearance of the Wind was beneficial to humanity.

Abaddon – an individual who appeared unexpectedly to address the entire Realm, apparently with the assistance of a female member of the Troyd. In that address, Abaddon claimed the Wind were charlatans who took pleasure in tormenting less-developed species. Abaddon also claimed that the human race had been censured by the Council of the Children of the Prime for failing to live up to their initial promise. And if the human race did not immediately dedicate itself to the sole purpose of unifying the human race and advancing its knowledge, power, ability, and understanding, the Council would vote them damaged beyond repair, and the devourers would descend.

To assist with the unification of humanity, Abaddon then seemed to use his understanding of curled space funnel technology to open curled space rings in orbit around every inhabited location in both the Realm and the Night and allow transit from any ring to any other ring.

Alnitak Five – home to a legendary group of temptresses with a well-known reputation in the Night as purveyors of pleasure. At one time under Rachel Falcon's control, most of the population was slaughtered in a subsequent attack by Beast.

Angel Haze – a psychoactive compound discovered by the settlers of Alnitak Five in the seed of an indigenous fruit. When encountered, Angel Haze suppresses an individual's fears and then binds them emotionally to the first person who interacts with them.

Anno Domini Reditus (ADR) – "In the year of Our Lord's Return." ADR represents a new calendar system introduced by the Wind celebrating their conquest of Earth. The arrival of the Wind occurred in 1 ADR.

Bandit – former Marauder, allowed to travel to Earth and joined Realm Force after being rescued by Falcon from G'Utz. Once a member of the crew of the *Dominion*. Died in an explosion on Rigel Three

Beast – a small horde in the Night numbering only in the hundreds. However, Beast has an outsized effect because of a network of artificial intelligences that are capable of performing highly accurate assessments of human behavior both at an individual level and at the level of a group of individuals, and under some conditions, even a very large group of individuals. Beast has a stated goal of destroying Realm Force, invading the Realm, and overthrowing the Leadership Council.

Blessings from Jerusalem! – a daily blog of encouragement issued by the Communications Department of the Office of the Leadership Council.

Bolobolo, Adi – formerly Casteel's second-in-command on the medical services teams for the *Dominion*. Now a fugitive from the Realm. Formidable and not dainty. Currently serving as the Medical Chief for the *Dominion*.

Casteel, Catherine – former Chief Medical Officer of the *Dominion*. Raised in the Realm. Learned to heal supernaturally while doing experiments in the power of the mind on a planet called K-22B that is located deep in the Night. Killed by a tactical team that was dispatched by Nicolescu to capture her.

Commander's Yacht – a sleek, mid-sized craft with sophisticated weaponry normally attached to a Trinity-Class battlecruiser and reserved for use by the Lead Commander. Three years after the self-destruct sequence of the *Dominion* was engaged, Sotheby returned the Commander's Yacht of the battlecruiser to Oakford for use by the team, after making sure the ship was refurbished enough to make it challenging to recognize as originating in the Realm.

Curled Space Funnels – stable pathways through curled space that allow a spacecraft to traverse the distances between star systems in minutes. All known endpoints terminate above the poles of stars. While the pathways through the curled space funnels are stable, they are not static. For example, a given curled space funnel might have a total of seven pathways and as many as fourteen different endpoints, but those pathways will not all exist at the same time under normal circumstances. Typically, they will alternate over some regular hourly intervals in groups of two or three. Curled space funnels are also known by the nickname "boom tubes."

Curled Space Rings – rings of fire hanging in stable orbits over population centers. Each ring can lead to any other ring using the appropriate vector and velocity. Much safer and faster than curled space funnels.

***Dominion* Pixie, The** – an artificial intelligence that Murg repurposed from a Wind-designed voice interface for Judicial Centers. Trained on Falcon's behavioral patterns, Murg left the Pixie in charge of the *Dominion* after he thwarted the self-destruct attempt.

Emergency Medical Unit – also called a "med unit." Even though the Wind eliminated disease and sickness from the Earth, they also acknowledged that there would be accidents as humanity moved out to other star systems. As such, they configured Judicial Centers to begin manufacturing emergency medical units. One day's worth of treatments in a med unit will heal anything minor. Two days' worth of treatments will heal anything major, like broken bones. Three days in a med unit will, for all practical purposes, rejuvenate the entire body and restore the individual to perfect health. Apparently, by design, med units do not operate on the human brain.

Evansworth, Twilla – former Mercenary. Former spy while serving on the crew of the *Dominion*. Formerly aligned with Falcon. Formerly imprisoned by Abaddon and while there she offended him enough that he tore off her left leg and rearranged her anatomy. Now held by PLOKTA.

Falcon, Rachel – former Lead Commander of the *Dominion*. Former Marauder. Archenemy of G'Utz. Strong, smart, fast, beautiful. Was imprisoned in a secret facility built by Realm Force. Rescued by the crew of the *Dominion*.

Events in Falcon's past—as she grew up in the Night—have caused a schism in her personality. At present, she is three: "Rachel," her original self; "The Falcon," who is tactically brilliant; and "Fury," who is filled with rage, though Fury is mostly held under control by Rachel and The Falcon. In addition, though much about the circumstances is unknown, what remains of

Falcon's biological body is encased in some kind of advanced cybernetic suit.

G'Utz – the founder of the Marauders. Through G'Utz's willingness to sacrifice his pilots, Marauders learned to do "shock-drops" from curled space funnels. Using this technique, Marauders leaped directly into Realm space to hijack Realm freighters, though this fact is not universally known.

Gellemier, Hachmoni – a former member of the Leadership Council and the Regent of the School of the Prophets.

Guan, Qiuyue – Raised on the streets of the Night, Guan was kidnapped and taken to Doctor Moreau's secret research facility in the Nu Scorpii system. There she was strapped into a gestation rig and forced to gestate dangerous human animal hybrids. Subsequently rescued by the senior staff of the *Dominion,* Guan joined the tactical teams to study under MacDuff to serve on the crew of the *Dominion.* All was well until she was kidnapped during a mission to Betelgeuse Two where she was exposed to toxic spores that damaged her brain. For many months, she struggled with psychopathic outbursts. Then, Sphinx sought her out and licked her face multiple times to administer enough psilocybin to calm her.

Hades – a maximum-security facility built by Realm Force in a secret star system to house the Realm's worst offenders. Hades was built underground using the Wind's rapid construction technology on a planet so close to its star that it had a surface temperature of 3,000 degrees Kelvin. It was destroyed as Falcon escaped.

HMVR Doeg – high-speed transport stolen by Oakford and company when they escaped to the Night before they could be brought up on charges of treason.

MV Dominion – the final Trinity-Class battlecruiser. The *Dominion* was severely damaged in an asteroid storm. Subsequently, members of the ship's senior staff gave the order to execute its self-destruct sequence. Unknown at the time, the order was intercepted, and the ship was not destroyed. Now known as a kind of pirate ship.

HMVR Glory – the second of the Trinity-Class battlecruisers. The *Glory* and its crew were lost when exposed to a genetically altered hemorrhagic fever virus that the med units did not heal.

HMVR Majesty – the newly commissioned variant on Trinity-Class battlecruisers. The *Majesty* is twice the size of the *Dominion.* Unlike the *Dominion,* the *Majesty* is outfitted with Wind-designed energy weapons that were awakened using activation codes supplied by Abaddon after Ton submitted to Abaddon's rule.

HMVR Power – the first of three commissioned Trinity-Class battlecruisers. "HMVR" stands for "His Majesty's Vessel of the Realm." Destroyed during Abaddon's first announcement to the Realm.

Horde – any formalized and organized group in the Night that has denied the authority of the Leadership Council. Hordes are considered the enemies of the Realm.

Hunter, Zachary – former Chief Pilot of the *Dominion*. Former Mercenary. Like Oakford, a fugitive from the Realm. Known for his rugged good looks, incredible physique, and cocky persona. And more recently, advised by a spokesman for a horde of look-alikes that he was genetically engineered.

Hunter Look-Alikes Horde – a nearly unknown Horde in the Night composed of genetically engineered clones who look like Hunter and possess all his physical and mental capabilities. In their first encounter with the *Dominion's* senior staff, their spokesman proclaimed their rigid materialistic beliefs and insisted that Hunter was an embarrassment to them because of his claim that Casteel could heal supernaturally.

Judicial Center – a local seat of authority for the Realm.

Ladipo, Seyi – former Lead Commander of the *Power*. Now disgraced after he was forced to confess to crimes he didn't commit.

Leadership Council of the Realm, The – a hastily formed group of chosen individuals who had previously served the Wind in various capacities. The Leadership Council provides guidance. It also issues proclamations of encouragement to the hundreds of planets and moons in the Realm as it continually attempts to remind the citizens to hold fast to the First Principle of the Realm: "Treat others as you wish to be treated."

MacDuff, Gabriel – former head of the tactical teams of the *Dominion*. Now a fugitive from the Realm. Large, barrel-chested hulk of a man. At one time, a distinguished student of the School of the Prophets near Jerusalem.

Marauders – a former Night Horde that specialized in hijacking Realm freighters and trading the goods stolen from those freighters for technology and supplies created by other Hordes.

Mechs – the only known machine-based Horde in the Night. Mechs are typically angry, rude, and easily frustrated. They constantly fight among themselves, except when they are on a rampage, pursuing and destroying others. It was thought that Falcon and the crew of the *Dominion* destroyed the Mechs during the mission to the Mech Hive, but they reappeared on the freighters that were used to eliminate "Shadow," a few years later. They have since been seen at the secondary Marauders keep, in a group that attacked Hades, and in a freighter orbiting Rigel Three.

Mercenaries – one of the most feared Hordes in the Night. Mercenaries offer their skills for hire and are among the most disciplined and well-trained fighters in the Night.

Moreau, Doctor – highly talented geneticist. Maintained a secret research facility in the Night in the Nu Scorpii system with 144 women strapped into gestation rigs. Moreau was captured and sent to the Realm with his research staff. The women remained on the *Dominion*.

Murg – former Chief Technologist of the *Dominion*. Now a fugitive from the Realm. Originally brought aboard the *Dominion* by Falcon. No Realm Force training. Socially awkward. Believed to be a member of the Troyd even though Troyd do not normally leave the Troyd.

Nicolescu, Ionela – Lead Commander of the Saturn Shipyards. Disciplined, capable, holds the highest security clearance in Realm Force.

Night, The – any settlement that exists beyond the Realm. There is no known official record of the number of populated planets and moons in the Night. In fact, until the disappearance of the Wind, few knew of *any* settlements that existed in the Night. It has become apparent in recent years, however, that many of the settlements in the Night have existed for decades—and perhaps even centuries—populated by humans who had quietly slipped away from the Realm to pursue lives outside the authority of the Wind.

Night's Keep – the former main Marauder stronghold. It was built into the side of a canyon on a small planet that orbited a red dwarf star.

Notch, Haymakers – a Mystery. During the escape from Hades, Falcon's cybernetic body was destroyed when she sacrificed herself to save Hunter. Shortly after, during a shock-drop, the *Dominion* was thrown into the atmosphere of a planet 20,000 light-years from Earth. There, the team met Haymakers Notch, and he offered to replace Falcon's original cybernetic body, given that it was still under warranty when it was destroyed. Nothing more is known of Haymakers Notch, aside from the fact that he looked exactly like Thomas Harnecky.

Oakford, Geoffrey – former Lead Commander of the *Dominion*. Born and raised on Earth. A member of the first graduating class of Realm Force Academy. Now a fugitive from the Realm.

Pax Christi – "Peace of Christ." An era of peace and prosperity made possible by the technology of the Wind. During the *Pax Christi*, humanity has been freed from hunger, poverty, crime, and disease. There is also an abundant, seemingly-inexhaustible supply of energy.

PLOKTA – subordinate of Nicolescu, resident tech wizard of the Saturn Shipyards. Idolizes Murg and had hoped that Murg would outfit him with a Troyd interface someday. Made an alliance with Abaddon and now has an interface with the same capabilities as Murg's.

Realm Force – a police force commissioned by the Leadership Council to protect the Realm and guard its borders.

Realm, The – the collection of star systems populated by humanity during the *Pax Christi* that still hold to the authority of Earth and its capital, Jerusalem.

Saturn Shipyards – Realm Force's main research, development, and construction facility in orbit around Saturn in the Sol system. The Saturn Shipyards houses a vast variety of divisions, including the Advanced Research and Development Division, also known as "Razzle Dazzle."

Shadow – an area that previously existed along the outer rim of the Realm. Following 960 ADR, many of the settlements on this outer rim began to question the authority of the newly formed Leadership Council of the Realm, and this rift—along with other altercations—led to the eventual closing of the border between Shadow and the Realm. In 978 ADR, the settlements in Shadow were forcibly evacuated by Beast.

Shock-drop – a technique discovered by the Marauder Horde that allows a spacecraft to bypass the normal endpoint of a curled space funnel. When flying inside a curled space funnel, firing at the wall of the funnel with the appropriate amount of force will tear a hole in the side of the funnel, allowing a spaceship to fly through the hole. And if the ship's shield generators are tuned to the correct frequency, the ship will safely traverse the anaphasic boundary between curled and normal space and "shock-drop" back into normal space without passing through an endpoint. The actual, final destination depends on the curled space funnel and the impact point.

Sotheby, Aeon – ensign, subordinate of Nicolescu, daughter of Adair Sotheby, former Lead Commander of the *Glory* who died when its crew was lost.

Sphinx – Human-animal hybrid from Doctor Moreau's secret research facility in the Nu Scorpii system. Formed a bond with MacDuff. Had become part of the tactical teams. The senior staff of the *Dominion* recently learned that Sphinx's saliva contains hero doses of psilocybin and likely contributes to Spinx's deeply intuitive awareness of those around him.

Stealth Suits – originally named "emergency evacuation suits," these suits have been modified by Realm Force to use on certain types of away missions.

Tactical Teams – contingents of skilled fighters assigned to Trinity-Class battlecruisers to assist the lead commander as needed in defending the ship and away team missions.

Ton, Elijah – a member of the Leadership Council and the Leadership Council's special liaison with Realm Force.

Tracheate, Silence – a Mystery. Oakford's team encountered Silence Tracheate on WASP-12e, a planet on the farthest edge of the Night. Interestingly enough, she looked exactly like Catherine Casteel but would never admit to being her, and under Hunter's urging, once the mission to WASP-12e was complete, the team departed without learning any more about her. Consequently, they have no idea that Tracheate sent a message to the Mercenaries to halt any future targeted attacks on Oakford's team.

Trinity-Class Battlecruiser – the largest known warship built by Realm scientists and engineers that mixes Wind technology and older human weaponry to create a spacecraft that can adequately protect the Realm.

Troyd – an unaligned secretive group believed to inhabit a planet somewhere deep in the Night. Beyond the fact that the Troyd excel at creating and breaking centralized processing systems, little is known of their actual creed or purpose. Many stories are told of their technical wizardry and their preference for data over "organics"—their term for humans.

Whispers in the Night – an anonymous blog created by an unknown entity. According to the blog's tagline, it presents "anonymous, untraceable communiqués from the unified Hordes of the Night to the innocent among the citizens of the Realm."

Worku, Jazarah – one of the women rescued from the research facility in the Nu Scropii system who remained on the *Dominion*. One of only five whom Hunter selected to train as fighter pilots and, surprisingly enough, a natural at intuitively understanding the complexities of three-dimensional space flight. Worku left the crew of the *Dominion* to work as a security consultant for the planet K2-72e. She later attempted to trick the Dominion crew into giving her the Rexian sheer onboard. Now on the run.

Wind, The – a race of titans who invaded Earth in the 21st century of the Common Era. They claimed to be Jesus Christ and his followers—returning to rule the Earth with a rod of iron for a thousand years. The Wind quickly subdued the Earth and instituted two rules: "Submit or die" and "Treat others as you wish to be treated."

Printed in Dunstable, United Kingdom